AND MOTHER
MAKES THREE

AND MOTHER MAKES THREE

BY

LIZ FIELDING

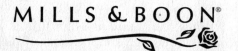

MILLS & BOON and
MILLS & BOON with the Rose Device
are registered trademarks of the publisher.

First published in Great Britain 1999
Large Print edition 2000
Harlequin Mills & Boon Limited,
Eton House, 18-24 Paradise Road,
Richmond, Surrey TW9 1SR

ISBN 0 263 16351 2

Set in Times Roman 16½ on 18 pt.
16-0002-51232

Printed and bound in Great Britain
by Antony Rowe Ltd, Chippenham, Wiltshire

CHAPTER ONE

'FITZ, thank you for stopping by. I know how busy you are.'

James Fitzpatrick took the small, perfectly manicured hand extended to him. 'Any time, Claire. I'm never too busy for anything that concerns Lucy, you know that.' But Claire Graham's response to his smile was the closest she ever came to a frown. More trouble, then. 'Has she broken another window?'

'Nothing so simple.'

'A window and a washbasin?' Lucy, tall for her age, with arms and legs that seemed to have a life of their own, had been causing chaos since she had first discovered that she could climb out of her cot. She didn't mean to break things, it was just that anything within a three foot range of her was likely to spontaneously disintegrate.

'Not even the drinking fountain. It's been a peaceful term.'

5

'It's not over yet.'

'Please, do sit down, Fitz.' Beneath her slightly prim and spinsterish exterior, Claire Graham was as soft as butter and could usually be teased to a smile; after a school governors' meeting with a glass of sherry inside her she could even be teased to a blush, but not today it seemed.

'So. What's she done?' Fitz enquired, lowering himself gingerly onto the elegant chair fronting her desk. He'd come with his chequebook in his back pocket, prepared for a catalogue of Lucy's latest string of accidents; Claire Graham's reassurance about school property, far from easing his mind, suggested that this summons boded something far worse. 'Her last report suggested that she was doing well enough,' he said, 'so I don't imagine this is about her schoolwork.'

'Lucy is a bright child. She has a particularly vivid imagination, as I am sure you know.' Claire's confirmation of something he already knew only increased his uneasiness. 'You've done a good job, Fitz.' Then she paused, as if searching for the right words.

'I've never asked you this before, but under the circumstances I think I have to now. Is there any contact at all between you and Lucy's mother?'

The apprehension took form and, despite the summer heat that was drying up the playing fields beyond the window, balled like ice in the pit of his stomach. 'None.'

'Could you contact her? If you had to?'

'I can think of no reason that would make any contact between us likely.'

'Not even for Lucy's sake?'

'She has no interest in Lucy, Claire. If it had been left to—' He stopped himself from even thinking the name. 'If it had been left to her mother, Lucy would have been adopted.'

'Then this is going to be very difficult.' She regarded him with steady grey eyes. 'I have to tell you, Fitz, that Lucy has begun fantasising about her mother.'

'Fantasising?'

'She's been making up stories about her, pretending that she's someone famous.'

The ice ball swelled like a snowball rolling down a hill but he couldn't let his concern now. He attempted a smile. 'You did say that she has a vivid imagination.'

'Yes, I did, but this isn't like her usual flights of fancy. She's very intense about it. You haven't noticed anything?' He shook his head and Claire Graham regarded him sympathetically. 'Under the circumstances I'd have to say that this is a fairly normal response. It's something that most adopted children will go through—'

'But Lucy is *not* adopted.' Did he sound as desperate as he felt?

'I realise that, but in the total absence of the birth mother, the situation becomes somewhat similar.' Fitz was too busy searching his mind, trying to think how his daughter could possibly have discovered what he had taken such trouble to hide, to respond to the sympathy in the woman's voice. 'It's the same longing,' she continued, 'the need to believe that the unknown mother is someone special, that only some great drama or tragedy could have caused her to give up her precious child. Where there is no information children will fill the vacuum with fantasy, creating a situation where the mother is someone exciting, someone admired—'

'I see,' he said, stopping her before she could continue.

'Do you?' Claire Graham looked doubtful. 'You mustn't be angry with her, Fitz. Her curiosity, her longing, is quite natural.'

He finally gave her his full attention as an escape route was dangled tantalisingly before him. 'If it's normal,' he asked, 'what's the problem?'

Claire Graham sat back, lifted her hands in a small gesture that invited his understanding. 'The other girls are the problem. They think she's putting on airs, trying to make herself special. I've spoken to Lucy, suggested that she would be wise to keep her stories to herself, but perhaps if you could try and talk to her about her mother, show her a photograph if you have one so that she would have an image to fix her feelings on. Maybe even try and arrange a meeting, if that's at all possible. I'd be happy to help in any way I can. As a neutral party I might make a suitable go-between—'

Fitz stood up, putting an end to the discussion, needing to get out of the hot, stuffy little office so that he could think. 'Thank you for letting me know what's happening, Claire. I'll deal with it.'

'You can cut off contact, Fitz, you can destroy every physical memory, but you can't stop a little girl wanting to know about her mother. There is a need, an unbreakable bond.'

'You think so?'

'I know so. She may not have wanted Lucy, but her mother too must be wondering what she's like, how she's grown up. Maybe she would welcome the chance to know her. It would be quite natural.' Except that Lucy's mother had been anything but natural. Claire walked with him to the door. 'School breaks up soon—are you going away for the summer?'

He wanted to tell her to mind her own business, the way he'd been telling the world ever since he'd brought Lucy home and had been confronted with the massed ranks of health visitors, social workers, caring citizens who all wanted to know who would be looking after this little girl, convinced that a mere man was incapable of such a thing. But Claire Graham's expression was kind, she was doing what she thought right, so he was polite. 'Yes. We're spending the summer in France.'

'Then that might be a good time to talk to her. Let her ask questions, and try to be fair. A child needs to love both her parents even if they don't love one another.' But what if the mother didn't love the child? Didn't want to know? 'For Lucy's sake it's something you are going to have to face, Fitz, no matter how painful it is for you.'

But not yet. Lucy was eight years old, far too young to have her precious dream-world shattered… 'I'll talk to her. Soon.'

Claire never frowned, but her forehead creased in something very close. 'It would be better if she got it out of her system before school begins next autumn,' she warned as they reached the main doors. Then, having said her piece and recognising a brick wall when she was faced with it, she changed the subject. 'Will we see you at sports day, Fitz?'

'Sports day?'

'It's on Friday. Didn't you get the letter? I'm surprised Lucy isn't full of it. She's doing the high jump and the fifty metres. She'll certainly win the high jump—if she doesn't demolish the jump first. It would be a pity if you weren't there.'

'I will be.'

'Good.' She held onto his hand for a long moment, her head slightly on one side. 'You haven't asked who she picked out for her mother, Fitz. Aren't you in the least bit curious?'

Claire Graham, Fitz realised, like Lucy's friends, had made the mistake of believing that she was lying. Perhaps, under the circumstances, that was just as well. 'I'd rather pick out my own fantasies, thanks all the same, Claire. I'll see you on Friday.'

'Such a shame that Brooke couldn't make it home in time for the funeral. We don't see much of her these days.'

'I haven't been able to speak to her, let her know about Mother,' Bron said, for what seemed like the hundredth time that afternoon.

Had anyone come to the funeral simply to pay their respects to her mother? Or was this huge turnout simply in hope that her famous sister would put in an appearance? She dredged up her hundredth smile. 'She's filming in Brazil. In the rainforest. A thousand miles from the nearest telephone.' Although surely not from the nearest satellite uplink? She'd have got the message, she was just too busy doing her earth-mother bit to get in touch.

'That is so sad.' Bron was dragged back to the present. 'You've taken on the burden of caring for your dear mother all these years and now you have to go through this alone, too.'

'It can't be helped.'

'No, I suppose not. And she's doing so much to help save the earth that we just have to excuse her.' The woman smiled. 'She's made me think twice these days before I use the car and I'm recycling all my newspaper and glass now and when we needed a new door I wouldn't let Reggie buy mahogany, although how she copes with the snakes and the spiders... I practically faint at the sight of one in the bath—'

'Oh, Brooke is just the same,' Bron, close to screaming herself, interrupted. 'Yells blue murder at the sight of one. I have to put them out of the window for her. And earwigs give her nightmares.'

'*Really?*' Bron immediately felt guilty. She shouldn't tease this kindly woman who had no way of knowing what Brooke was really like. 'There's hope for us all, then. Would you like me to stay and help you clear up, dear?' There was a touch of anxiety in the woman's voice as she surveyed the fine china and crystal glasses scattered about the living room.

Bron raised a wry smile. Her inability to wash a cup without the handle falling off was legendary. 'Mrs Marsh has kindly offered to clear up for me.' Even as she spoke that lady began to load a tray with a speed and deftness of touch that left Bron awestruck with admiration.

'But you will call me if I can do anything, if there's anything you want?'

Bron made up for her earlier lapse from grace with a generous smile. 'I'd be glad of someone to help me sort through Mother's things one day next week. I'm sure you'd know what would be the best way to deal with them,' she said. 'That would be such a help.'

'Of course, just give me a call,' She looked around. 'What will you do now? Sell the house, I imagine. I know your mother would never have wanted to leave, but you'd be much more comfortable in a nice little flat.'

A nice little flat with no room to swing a cat and no garden. She'd loathe it. 'I don't know. I'll have to talk to Brooke about that when she gets home.'

'Well, there's no rush. Take a holiday before you decide anything—you've had a rough time of it these last few weeks.'

Weeks. Months. Years.

An hour later, Bron finally shut the front door on Mrs Marsh, leaned against it, eyes closed, and the silence swept back like a wave bringing with it a feeling of utter loneliness, the realisation that there was no more cushion against the darkness. Her mother was gone and now it was just the two of them: she and Brooke.

And deep down she knew that she was glad that Brooke hadn't come racing home. Her appearance would inevitably have turned the whole thing into a media circus. It wasn't as if her sister were the kind of woman to put her arms around her and offer the comfort she needed. She'd simply have pointed out that their mother was no longer suffering. Brooke had always been able to see things in black and white. They were so alike on the outside it seemed impossible that they could be so different in every other way.

It took an enormous effort to push herself away from the door. She felt utterly drained. Empty. Maybe everyone was right, maybe she should go away for a few days, get right away and decide what she was going to do with the rest of her life.

Rest of it? That was a joke. Twenty-seven years old and she had never had a life. Maybe she wouldn't have noticed the lack quite so painfully if she hadn't had her sister to measure herself against.

It shouldn't have been like that. She and Brooke had been different in character, different in every way except for their looks and their brains. She had been all set to pack her bags and follow her sister to university when their mother had been diagnosed with the illness that had finally killed her.

So she had stopped making lists of the things she would need. Called the university and told them that she wouldn't be coming after all. What else could she have done? There had been no one else to look after her mother. One of them had had to stay at home and Brooke had already started her degree course. The assumption had always been that once she had graduated she would come home and then it would be Bron's turn.

But with the ink scarcely dry on her degree Brooke had been offered the kind of job that only came along once in a lifetime.

'You do see, Bron?' she'd said, with that winning smile. 'I just can't let this go.' Well, of course she'd seen. It would have been unreasonable… 'And you're so good with Mother. I couldn't do what you do for her. She's comfortable with you.'

But she loves *you* best. She hadn't said it out loud, but she'd thought it, known it to be true. It was so much easier to love someone who was beautiful, successful. Loving the daughter who saw you day in, day out, struggling with pain, at your most vulnerable, was not so easy.

So, she had never had a life—or, at least, nothing that her sister would have called a life. No career, no holidays, no adult relationshp with a man. If it hadn't been for a surfeit of champagne on her eighteenth birthday, coupled with a determination not to be the last girl in the sixth form to taste the forbidden delights of the flesh, she would probably have been that saddest of things: a twenty-seven-year-old virgin.

Probably? Who was she kidding? Who was interested in a woman whose life was devoted to nursing an invalid mother? A five-foot-eleven-inch woman, all feet and elbows, whose life was devoted to nursing an invalid mother?

And as her peer group had left town, gone to university, married, moved away, what little social life she'd been able to maintain in the early years had gradually dwindled away to visits from her mother's friends, women who ran the WI and the Mother's Union and did good works and were kind. But there was precious little fun. No one her own age.

Short of dragging the milkman in from the street and having her wicked way with him, she didn't stand a chance.

Her reflection in the hall mirror suggested that even the milkman would have thought twice. Her hair, which she'd hacked off when she was ten years old and sick to death of everyone saying she looked so like her pretty sister *but...* hadn't been near a hairdresser in the last terrible six months. She'd stuck it up in a bun for the funeral and it made her look nearer forty, and with an impatient little tug she pulled out the pins and let it fall to curl untidily around her shoulders.

Her skin, which until a week ago had had the pallid complexion of someone who spent too little time outdoors, was now suffering from the effects of too much sudden exposure to sunlight. She had told herself that the lawn had to be perfect, the borders weeded and neat

for the funeral. Her mother had loved her garden, would have hated anyone to see it so neglected. At least that was what she'd told herself. In truth, without her mother to care for,
she had simply felt useless, unneeded...

She pulled a face at herself. 'Feeling sorry
for yourself, Bronte Lawrence?' Then she
laughed. 'Talking to yourself, too? That desperate, hmm?'

She glanced at the mail where she had
dumped it on the hall table that morning. Con-
dolence cards mostly. She picked them up,
sorting through them as she walked through to
the kitchen. Then she stopped. Tucked in
amongst the cards was a letter carefully addressed in a round childish hand. Miss B
Lawrence, The Lodge, Bath Road, Maybridge.
She eased open the flap, glanced through the
letter and then, a frown creasing her forehead,
sat on one of the wooden kitchen chairs and
read it again, more slowly.

Dear Miss Lawrence,
    It is my school sports day on Friday, June

18th and I am writing to ask if you could possibly come.

So formal. Bron frowned. So polite.

When I told my friend Josie that you were my mother she didn't believe me and now all the girls in my class are saying I made it up...

At this point the careful formality lapsed, the neat handwriting wavered and there was a smudge that looked as if a tear had dropped on the page and been quickly dashed away. Bron's hand flew to her throat as she continued reading.

...made it up about having a famous mother and everyone is making fun of me. Even Miss Graham, my head teacher, doesn't believe me and that's not fair because although I break things, I never tell lies so will you please come...

The please had been heavily underscored.

...so they'll know I'm telling the truth? I know you're really busy saving the rainforest and the poor animals and I don't want to be a nuisance and if you would just do this I wouldn't ask anything ever again, I promise

And it was signed:

Your loving daughter, Lucy Fitzpatrick

Then:

PS You won't have to see Daddy because I put the letter about sports day in the bin so he doesn't know about it.

Then:

PPS I don't suppose you know that my school is Bramhill House Lower School in Farthing Lane, Bramhill Parva.

And then:

PPPS 2 o'clock.

Bron turned over the envelope, for a moment wondering if she'd misread the name, opened a letter addressed to someone else.

No. The handwriting might be that of a child but it was clear enough. Miss B Lawrence. Bronte Lawrence. So what on earth...? Then the penny dropped. '...a famous mother... saving the rainforest...' The letter wasn't meant for her, but for her sister. It was an easy enough mistake to make. It had happened fairly frequently in the days when they had both lived at home but it was a long time since anyone had written to her sister at this address.

But she still didn't understand.

Brooke had never had a baby. This must be from some poor child who had no mother, who had seen Brooke on the television and had fallen under her spell. Well, didn't everyone?

She read the letter again. 'Dear Miss Lawrence.' If it hadn't been so desperately sad it would have made her smile—as if anyone would write to their mother in such a way. And the idea of her sister as a mother, now that *was* funny!

She read it again. For heaven's sake, how could Brooke have had a child without any of them knowing? How could she have kept the

fact hidden all these years, because it must
have been years—the careful lettering had to
have been the work of a child of eight or nine
years old.

Yet even as she was discounting the possibility, her busy brain was doing the mental ar-
ithmetic, working out where her sister had
been eight or nine years before. She would
have been twenty, or twenty-one—and at university.

Bron read the address at the top of the letter.
The Old Rectory, Bramhill Bay. Bramhill was
on the south coast, just a few miles from her
sister's university. Then she shook her head.
The whole idea was ridiculous. Impossible.

She went upstairs, changed out of her black
dress and into a pair of shorts and a T-shirt,
tied her hair back with an elastic band. Then
she picked up the letter from the dressing table,
where she had dropped it.

During her third year Brooke hadn't come
home after Easter even though their mother
had been going through a crisis, had been asking for her. And Easter hadn't been much fun
for any of them. Brooke hadn't been feeling

well, had moped about complaining about feeling cold all the time, wrapped up in a huge baggy sweater, eating practically nothing.

Bron sat on the bed, her skin prickling with foreboding. Easter. After that she'd stayed away, pleaded fieldwork that she hadn't been able to put off. Then after her finals she'd been offered a chance to take part in some project in Spain. Not that they'd had any postcards from her. She'd be too busy, Mother had said.

And she hadn't been exactly tanned when she'd come back on a flying visit, high on her first-class honours and the offer of a dream job with a television company famous for its natural history programmes. She'd spent the next two months on some Pacific island and, naturally photogenic, had been an instant hit with viewers. After that the visits had been few and far between.

Hand to her mouth, she read the letter through again. It was polite, formal even, for a little girl at a primary school—formal, but just a little desperate too, Bron thought as the questions flooded through her head. Could

Brooke have had a baby and put her up for adoption?

But then how would this little girl have found out who her real mother was? Surely you had to be eighteen before you could even begin to search the records?

But no, that couldn't be right. It was there in the letter. '...You won't have to see Daddy...' Oh, God bless the child, it was enough to break your heart.

She stuffed the letter in her pocket and went downstairs, picked up the kettle, filled it and switched it on, then took out the letter again.

No, really. It had to be a mistake. It was impossible. Brooke wasn't the kind of girl to get pregnant, after all. She was too focussed, too smart, too selfish. She'd known what she wanted and had set out to achieve it with a single-mindedness that had taken her to the top. She had known their mother was dying when she had left for Brazil, chasing the latest in a long line of television awards for her *Endangered Earth* series.

If she hadn't wanted her precious car tucked up safely in the garage while she was away it was entirely possible that she would have made some excuse not to find the time to come home and say goodbye.

Yet if it was impossible why was it so difficult to simply brush away the idea?

She read the letter again, felt the tug at her heartstrings. Lucy. The child could be her niece…

No. She refused to believe it. Or was she afraid to believe it? Afraid to believe that her sister could be that heartless? No. It had to be some little girl in a world of hurt latching onto a woman who had made caring for the planet her personal crusade. A little girl hoping that a woman with so much compassion would have some love left over to spare for her.

Fitz turned from the cooker. Lucy was drawing a picture, working at the kitchen table, her arm curled protectively about the paper. 'Will you be long, sweetheart? Tea's nearly ready.'

She tucked her pencils and the picture carefully away in her school bag then looked up, her bright blue eyes unusually shadowed, like someone with a secret.

And she did have a secret. How long had she known? When had she found her birth certificate, the photograph of Brooke Lawrence, all the things he had kept locked away at the back of his desk, at the back of his life?

He had been going to tell her. One day. He had fooled himself into believing that he would know when it was the right moment to sit her down and explain about her mother, tell her what had happened. But what time was ever right to tell a child that her mother hadn't wanted her?

'I'm done,' she said with a quick smile. 'Shall I lay the table?'

God, when she smiled she looked so like Brooke. He hadn't anticipated that. The chestnut hair and blue eyes had fooled him into thinking that there was nothing of Brooke to see in the child. But that enchanting smile...

'Please,' he said quickly and looked away, making a performance of stirring the sauce. Why did it still get to him? Brooke Lawrence might have had a smile like an angel but that was as far as it went. Somewhere, deep inside him he'd always known that, even when he'd been pursuing her with a single-mindedness that had been nine parts testosterone to one part common sense.

How on earth was he to tell this child, this little girl that he loved so much that he sometimes thought his heart might break just looking at her, how was he to tell her that her mother had never wanted her, had handed her over to him and walked away without a backward glance the day after she was born?

He had never believed she would do it. He had always believed that once her baby was lying in her arms she would love her.

No. He could never tell Lucy how it had been. But Claire Graham was right—he would have to tell her something, as much of the truth as she could manage. When she was old enough she could confront Brooke herself, ask her why. Ask her how she could do that. Maybe she would be able to tell him, because he had never understood.

He should tell her now, before she fabricated a dozen fantasies about how it might be. He stared into the saucepan as if the contents might provide him with inspiration. Nothing. 'Lucy—'

'What are we having?' She hooked a long, thin arm about his waist as he stood at the cooking range and, standing on tiptoe, peered into the saucepan.

'Spaghetti carbonara.'

'Oh, yummy. Can I have a Coke with it?'

He glanced down at her and his courage failed him. 'If I can have a beer.'

'Yeuch. Beer's disgusting.'

'Oh? And how do you know what beer tastes like?' She giggled and his heart did its usual somersault. 'Go on, then, get the drinks while I dish up.'

Later, he tried again. 'Lucy, Miss Graham asked me to visit her today.'

A brief startled glanced then a casual, 'Oh?' Then, 'Can I turn on the television?' She was avoiding asking him why her head teacher had wanted to see him.

'Leave it a minute.'

'It's something I want to see,' she protested, unusually sulky. This was worse, far worse than he had ever imagined. Or maybe he had just refused to imagine this moment.

'She told me...' he began, then cleared his throat. 'She told me...' He stared at the top of her head as she suddenly became totally engrossed in her trainers. 'She told me about sports day,' he said, finally. 'Did you forget, or didn't you want me to come?'

She flung her head up. 'No! You mustn't! You mustn't come!'

'Why?' Her reaction startled him but he tried not to show it, tried to hide his concern beneath a grin. 'Are you going to come last in everything?'

For a moment he saw her struggle with a lie, with the temptation to tell him that she was going to be terrible. But maybe she realised he didn't give a hoot where she came in the fifty metres, or whether she fell over her feet in the high jump, that he would come because he loved to see her having fun. 'No. But if you come it will spoil—' She stopped.

'Spoil what, sweetheart?'

'I...I...' She reddened, swallowed. 'I've done something that's going to make you really angry, Daddy.'

He was almost afraid to ask, but he had to know, so he pulled her towards him, picked her up and settled her against his chest. 'Let me decide about that. I don't suppose it's as bad as you think.'

The words were a long time coming and when they did come they were mumbled into his chest. 'I—wrote—to—my...' His heart seemed to stop beating during an endless pause.

'Who did you write to, sweetheart?' he prompted, when he could no longer bear it.

'My mother. I wrote to my mother and asked her to come to sports day.' And then the words tumbled out, unstoppable. 'I asked her to come because they said I was lying, they wouldn't believe me, but it's true, isn't it?' She sat back and looked up at him, every cell in her body appealing to him to tell her it was so. 'Brooke Lawrence *is* my mother.'

His throat was tight, a lump the size of a tennis ball blocking the words. But he had to say them. 'Yes, Lucy. Your mother is Brooke Lawrence.'

If he'd expected anything, it would have been reproach that he hadn't told her before. Her triumphant, 'Yes!' was like a knife to his heart. 'And she'll come to sports day and everyone will know—' She slid from his lap and twirled giddily across the living room floor.

'Look out!' His warning came too late as she swept a small china spaniel from the top of the television. It hit the carpet and bounced and would have been safe but before she could stop herself Lucy trod on it and there was an ominous crunching noise.

Fitz caught her by the arms as she catapulted back towards him, holding her still, his arms about her in a protective vice, a safe place he had made for her, a place where nothing could hurt her...or so he had thought.

He eased away and bent to pick up the china dog. 'Just a little chip here,' he said, rubbing his thumb over the dog's nose. Then, 'And we can stick his ear back on.' He picked up the ear and it crumbled in his fingers. It was a sensation that was rapidly becoming familiar.

When he finally looked up, dared to face her, Lucy was standing exactly where he had left her. He had never seen her so still.

'I took the key to your desk from your dressing table,' she said. 'We were doing a project about family history and Josie brought in her birth certificate. It had her mother's name on it and I realised…' She stopped. 'I'm sorry, Daddy.'

Oh, no. He was the one who was sorry. She should never have been reduced to taking keys, hunting in drawers to find out what she should always have known. 'You saw the photographs, the custody papers?' She frowned, not understanding the word, but of course she had found them. How else would she have known where to write?

'She will come, won't she, Daddy?' She looked so desperate, so needy. How long had she been feeling this way? Why hadn't he noticed? 'I told her you wouldn't be there, that she wouldn't have to meet you.'

'Did you?' He almost smiled at her blunt-ness. Almost. 'In that case I'm sure she will. If she can. But she might be abroad, making one of her films.' *Please, God…* 'Had you thought of that?'

Lucy's face fell momentarily, then imme-diately brightened. 'No, she can't be. I saw her on television last week.'

Yes. He'd seen her too, trailing a new series that was starting next month. But they were clips from the series and meant nothing. Ex-cept of course that a new series meant a book tie-in, the endless round of the chat shows, breakfast television, the whole publicity cir-cuit.

He would have to find out, because Fitz, de-spite a cast-iron certainty that Brooke wouldn't want to come within a country mile of her daughter, found himself making a silent prom-ise to the child that if it was humanly possible, even if he had to hog-tie the woman and bring her in the boot of his Range Rover, she would put in an appearance at sports day.

CHAPTER TWO

SHE couldn't put it off any longer. Bron bit into her toast, putting it off. She would have to call Lucy's father and tell him about the letter.

The idea was sufficient to dull her appetite and she abandoned the toast. If only she hadn't opened the letter. If only she could forget she'd ever seen it. It hadn't been *meant* for her, after all. If it hadn't been for the coincidence of their initials, if her mother's first gift to her father hadn't been a hand tooled leather bound edition of the complete works of Rupert Brooke and if he hadn't responded with an equally beautiful copy of *Wuthering Heights*, she would never have opened it...

She'd drink her coffee first. She reached for her mug, sent the jar of marmalade flying, flinched as it hit the quarry-tiled floor and smashed. She spent the next few minutes carefully picking out the glass, cleaning up the sticky mess. It had to be done, she told herself, but she knew she was simply prevaricating. Putting off the moment.

The important thing was that she *had* opened the letter; whatever the truth, Lucy Fitzpatrick was a child who needed help and maybe she was the only person in the world who knew that.

She'd spent the long wakeful hours of the night—still unable to get used to the silence, the fact that no one needed her—telling herself that getting involved in other people's domestic problems was simply asking for trouble. Telling herself was one thing, however, convincing herself something else.

At first light she'd given up the struggle for sleep and taken herself into the cool, early-morning garden and tried to forget about Lucy in a furious blitz on the weeds that seemed to leap out of the ground in full flower at this time of year. She had her own problems. Like what was she going to do with the rest of her life?

She had no job skills: all she knew was caring for her mother. The thought had led her back to Lucy, to wonder who was caring for her. A housekeeper or nanny, perhaps? Or did she go home to an empty house after school while her father worked?

Eventually hunger had kicked in, reminding her that she had had no breakfast and she straightened, easing her back, dead-heading the roses as she walked slowly back towards the empty house, she finally acknowledged that nothing was going to drive Lucy from her mind. The need to do something was at war with common sense and common sense didn't stand a chance. She could not possibly ignore the letter.

But that decided, what was she going to do about it?

She had taken the envelope from her pocket, smearing it with green that had adhered to her fingers from her weeding. She had wiped her hands on her shorts before she'd taken out the letter. Lucy hadn't put a telephone number. Well, she wouldn't. From the comment about not having to meet her father, Bron guessed that Lucy was hoping to keep the whole thing a secret from him.

She had unhooked the telephone, dialled 192. 'Directory Enquiries. What name please?'

'Fitzpatrick. I don't have an initial. Bramhill Bay, in Sussex.'

'One moment, please.' Then, 'Would that be Fitzpatrick Studios?'

Fitzpatrick Studios? What kind of studios? *Film* studios? 'That could be it,' she said, her heart sinking. That could very well be it. She'd all but managed to convince herself that Lucy had chosen Brooke because she was well known, admired. Saving the rain-forest was such a big issue these days, but if her father was a filmmaker the coincidence was just too much… She stopped herself.

What kind of film studios would be in some tiny village in Sussex? A place called The Old Rectory was far more likely to be an artist's studio, or a pottery, or both. She could just imagine a picturesque tithe barn housing some artists colony… 'The address is The Old Rectory,' she said quickly.

There was a click and then she heard the recording, 'The number that you require is…' Bronte wrote it down, double-checked it and then hung up. She stared at the number. Well, it seemed to say, you've got me, now what are you going to do with me?

The child's father needed to know what was going on, she rationalised as she made coffee, dumped the bread in the toaster. She couldn't just ignore it. If Lucy was so desperate for love that she needed Brooke as a fantasy mother… And if she *wasn't* fantasising?

It made no difference. She would have to ring. But after breakfast. No one could be expected to deal with something like this on an empty stomach.

Bronte stared at her empty mug, the abandoned toast. Now. Do it now. Delaying was not going to make it any easier. And it might be all right. Lucy might do this once a week, or whenever her mother refused to be blackmailed into more sweets, later TV, a day off school, and she'd get a resigned apology from an embarrassed parent. Maybe. Why didn't she believe that?

Whatever she believed, she could no longer put off making the call. She picked up the telephone, dialled the number. It rang once. It rang twice. Three times. There was no one there. Relief surged through her and she had the receiver halfway back to the cradle when she heard it being picked up. She couldn't just hang up...she just hated it when people did that...

'James Fitzpatrick.' James Fitzpatrick had a voice like melted chocolate. Dark, expensive chocolate. It rippled through her midriff like a warm wave of pleasure and left her gasping. 'I can't come to the telephone right now but if you leave a message I'll get back to you.' There was a click and the long bleep of an answering machine. She was still holding the receiver when there was a long, insistent ring on the doorbell.

Fitz had found it impossible to talk to Lucy about her mother. The other way round would not be so difficult, he assured himself, yet when he pulled up outside the steeply gabled house with a large garden overgrown with blowsy midsummer roses, he still wasn't certain that he was doing the right thing.

It might be wiser to let sleeping dogs lie. Brooke knew where to find him but in nearly nine years had never once bothered to call him, enquire after her daughter, show the slightest interest in her health or happiness.

Well, that was the deal he'd agreed to.

Until the moment when he'd finally realised that Brooke had meant it when she'd said she would have her baby adopted, Fitz had never given much thought to what that would involve. He had never thought of himself as a man wanting a child of his own, but the unseen, unknown life that had been so carelessly created had, with the threat of rejection, become so real to him, so precious that he had been overtaken with the longing to protect her. And with her lying, hours old, in his arms, he'd known he could never bear to let her go.

He would have promised Brooke anything at that moment and he had never once doubted that he'd had the better of the deal. He'd supported her through her pregnancy, looked after her, certain that once the baby was in her arms she would love her. Then after Lucy was born, when Brooke had calmly announced that she was going to give her baby away, she'd seen his reaction and she'd made her bargain with him.

What had been so galling, so unforgivable, had been her amusement...her callous assurance that within weeks he would see it her way and hand the child over to some anonymous couple and be glad to do it. The truth was she really hadn't cared what he'd done with her baby as long as she hadn't been the one kept awake at night, hadn't been the one changing nappies. She hadn't had time for such mundane nonsense, she'd been going to make something of her life and in return for her baby he'd been going to help her do that. Well, he had to admit that she hadn't wasted her opportunity.

Maybe somewhere, hidden in the untrodden byways of his mind, he had nursed a secret hope that one day she would realise what she was missing, would come back. Eight years should have been long enough for him to come to terms with the truth, but perhaps Lucy was not the only one with a penchant for fantasy.

Maybe that was why he had found it so hard to tell Lucy the truth; maybe he hadn't wanted to believe that any mother could be so callous. Well, he could no longer fool himself. Lucy had taken the matter out of his hands, chosen the moment.

But now he was here, parked outside a house which until this moment had simply been an address on the document which gave him sole custody of Lucy, it occurred to Fitz that he was almost certainly on a wild-goose chase.

This had been Brooke's family home. It was highly unlikely that she had lived here since university, but it was the only address he had. She'd long since left the television natural history unit where he'd got her that first job, easily finding a backer to start her own film company, but no one there would give him an address, advising him to write in and his letter would be passed on. There wasn't time for that. And his contacts in the business who could have told him what he needed to know would have been just too damned interested.

He watched the postman making his way down the street, dropping letters through the boxes. The man reached The Lodge, turned in at the gate, but he had more than letters—he had something that needed signing for, or wouldn't fit the box, because he rang the bell. Who would answer? Her mother, a middle-aged version of Brooke? Her father...

'Brooke...' Her name escaped him on a breath. It was the last thing on earth he had expected. But she was there, she had opened the door, was talking with the postman, giving the man one of those blazing smiles as she pushed back her hair in an achingly familiar gesture before taking the pen he offered and signing for a letter. Before he knew what he was doing he was out of the Range Rover and across the street. The postman saw him coming, held the gate for him, but halfway up the path he stopped.

Suppose she refused to speak to him, this spectre coming back from the past to haunt her, determined to remind her of something she had chosen to forget? Suppose she shut the door on him? Refused even to discuss Lucy?

She had every right to. He had promised he would never contact her, never betray her secret. But then he had never expected to have to keep that promise. And Lucy's happiness was more important than any promise.

He stepped off the path, followed the lawn around to the back of the house.

Bron put the registered letter from her mother's insurance company on the kitchen table unopened. Her mother was dead and nothing would change that, but Lucy was alive and needing help now. She picked up the telephone again, pressed redial. She would leave a message, ask James Fitzpatrick to call her. It rang once, twice. A shadow passed the kitchen window, someone coming round to the back of the house, no doubt Mrs Marsh checking up on her, making sure she was coping…

'Come along,' she muttered impatiently. And then the voice again. Except it wasn't the answering machine.

'Brooke…' he said and as she spun around, saw the shadowed figure in the doorway, she knew exactly who he was.

'James Fitzpatrick,' she said. And as if to confirm it his voice repeated the name in her ear.

For a moment he didn't move, stayed in the open doorway with the sun streaming in around him. 'That's a little formal under the circumstances, Brooke. I still answer to Fitz.'

'Fitz,' she repeated dully, while the cogs in her brain freewheeled, trying to catch up with what was happening. Apparently taking this as an invitation, he stepped into the room, into the light. Oh, God, the voice was perfect, the man was perfect. More than perfect, he was beautiful. Tall, broad-shouldered, lean as a whippet beneath a white linen shirt that draped loosely about his torso, beneath old faded denims that stretched tight across narrow masculine hips, clinging to his thighs as though moulded to them. His hair was black, a dishevelled mass of thick dark curls that flowed over his shirt collar, his mouth was sinfully sensuous, his eyes the colour of ripe blueberries. No man had the right to be that good-looking, that sexy, that... 'I—I was just trying to call you,' she said.

'Then that answers my question. You did get Lucy's letter.'

Bron tore her gaze away from this apparition of manly perfection long enough to glance at the crumpled, slightly grubby envelope lying on the kitchen table. Unfortunately she tried to replace the telephone receiver at the same time. She missed. It swung down and hit the wall, jerking the telephone from its bracket. The whole lot landed on the floor with a crash.

James Fitzpatrick crossed the room, bent to retrieve the instrument. 'It's cracked,' he said, straightening beside her.

'It was already cracked.' A bit like her voice.

'I see.' He checked the dialling tone, re-placed it on the wall before turning to her, his forehead creased in a thoughtful frown. 'I've often wondered where Lucy gets that from.'

Lucy was clumsy? 'You made me jump,' she said defensively. 'Why did you come to the back door?'

'I thought it might be a good idea to take you by surprise—' he'd certainly done that '—before you had time to put the chain up.'

Close up to him, Bron was finding it diffi
cult to breathe. This was Lucy's father?
Brooke had walked away from this man to film
monkeys and spiders and frogs and any number of unspeakable creatures in mosquito in-
fested swamps? If anyone had ever doubted
her dedication... His words suddenly got
through to her. 'Why would I do that?'

'I made a promise. The fact that I'm here
must tell you that I'm about to break it.'

What promise? His right hand was against
the wall, trapping her in the corner, but it made
no difference, her legs weren't planning on
taking her anywhere. She swallowed. 'Because
of Lucy? How is she—?'

'You've had nearly nine years to ask that
question,' he said, cutting off her concern, re-
fusing to acknowledge it.

'I didn't mean—' She hadn't meant it in that
meaningless, 'How are you?', kind of way.
She meant, What kind of child is she? What
are her dreams? Is she happy? But his left
hand, the fingers loosely curled, was rubbing
mesmerisingly against her cheek, stealing her
wits. 'You don't have to pretend you care,

Brooke, not for me. Save that for your daughter.'

Brooke?

Brooke was looking at him as if she had
been knocked sideways and it gave him a
small charge of satisfaction to know that he
wasn't the only one struggling for breath. But
surely she must have expected him? If she had
reached the point where she was going to call
she must have realised that he was going to
come looking for her. No doubt she had been
trying to stop him. As if anything could.

It was odd—he'd seen her on television dozens of times during the years and he'd felt
nothing. He'd been so certain that she was incapable of doing this to him again yet it was
as if the years had never happened, as if Lucy
had never happened and she was still twenty
years old and looking up at him from a bench
on her university campus.

Her skin was still peachy soft beneath his
fingers, a little pink from the recent heatwave
but surprisingly unlined by the months, years
spent in tropical sunlight. He had expected her
harder, tougher, despite the girlish sweetness

with which she managed to charm her audience, had long ago charmed him. She was older and yet disconcertingly still the same; looking at him with the same misty, melting grey eyes, still with that look of surprised innocence that she had done so well, that had so captivated him. She still smiled with that made-for-pleasure mouth that had never needed lipstick and, heaven help him, his blood was still hot for her and the heat was straining against the tightness of his jeans.

She had been like a madness in his head when he had first met her. It was apparently a recurring madness and he was having to make a conscious effort to remember his reason for seeking her out.

'If you've got her letter,' he said, 'you know why I'm here. Lucy desperately needs you to come to her school sports day, Brooke.'

'No,' she began. 'Not me—'

'Yes, you.' His voice was harsher than he had meant as he refused to listen to her excuses. If that was what it took, he could be as hard as she was beneath all that phoney sweetness. 'You'll be there at two o'clock dressed in that Queen of the Amazon chic you do so well…' As she tried to interrupt him he covered her mouth with his hand. 'I'm not taking no for an answer. This isn't for me, this is for Lucy.' As the warmth of her lips heated his fingers and the heat flickered through him like fire through matchwood, he snatched them back.

'Please, just listen to me—'

'No, I've done listening. This time you'll do it my way. You'll do it or I'll let all your precious fans know just how you bargained away your baby.' Fitz was horrified at what he had said. He hadn't meant it…didn't know where the threat had come from. But as he surveyed her shocked expression he realised that his instincts had been right—her image meant more to her than her child ever would. 'I'll give the story to the tabloids, Brooke. Do you think they'll still love you then?'

Her watered-silk grey eyes widened, he could almost have sworn in pain. 'You can't do that!'

Not pain. Fear. Well, that was good. He could use that, she'd taught him how. 'Try me,' he said and the threat arced between them like a lightning fork hitting the ground with explosive force, pure electricity that he could almost taste and because he was human, because despite everything she could still switch him on like a hundred-and-fifty-watt light bulb, he carried her back against the wall and he pinned her there with his mouth, with his tongue, with his body, wanting her, hating her, hating her for wanting her so much.

Bron, pinned against her kitchen wall by the hard body of a man who thought she was her sister, trapped between his hands, pinned by his body, by his mouth, went rigid with shock. Then because she had to tell him, explain, she began to struggle. She grabbed his muscle-packed shoulders in an effort to push him away but her fingers, her short nails, made no impression; the only impression being made in that room was upon her, by James Fitzpatrick's mouth.

It was hard and angry and demanding, punishing her for what her sister had done. But beneath the anger was a hungry, sensuous longing and everything in her that was feminine, everything that had been stifled during the long barren years when her youth had slipped away, responded to that longing with a reckless disregard for what was right, what was proper, what was the truth. Her breasts tingled, her thighs melted and savage instinct, old as time, took over as her fingers stopped pushing him away and instead slid behind his head, tangling in the thick curls at his nape, her mouth parting beneath his onslaught, her tongue meeting his as her own hunger, her own long-suppressed need kicked in...

Fitz had wanted to punish her, wanted her to feel what he had felt, all the anger, the pain, the resentment, yet after the first moment of shocked resistance, as she softened against him, melted into his arms, he knew that he was only punishing himself. As her lips parted to him, as her hands stopped pushing him away and instead drew him closer, as her body moulded itself to his, he could no more stop himself than fly.

Her scent, the pure woman scent of her was overlaid with the freshness of wind-dried clothes, of grass and roses, and he could have drowned in it, drowned in her… And suddenly he was the one struggling for control, struggling to resist the clamour of his body's need as he dragged himself back from the brink of self-destruction.

For a moment he remained where he was, hands flat against the wall, his mouth inches from hers, looking down into the face of the one woman in the world it seemed who had it in her power to drive him over the edge, to make him behave in a manner that he despised. Her lips were parted softly, her mouth gentler than he remembered, her lashes darker as she raised them over eyes that looked just a little dazed, eyes in which the pupils were dilated, black with desire. And she was smiling… laughing at him… again…

'Friday,' he said hoarsely as he reeled back, putting urgently needed space between them. 'Two o'clock. Be there, or expect to read about yourself in the Sunday papers.' And he turned, walking swiftly from the bright sunny kitchen, trying very hard to erase from his head the look on Brooke's face, the bee-stung lips parted for him, breasts peaked hard against her

T-shirt, her eyes a sultry invitation to stay. Dear God, how did she do it? Why did he let her when he knew it was nothing but play-acting? Next time he would be on his guard, keep his distance.

And he found himself smiling too, but grimly. He should be safe enough at a primary school sports day. Brooke would be kept too busy by teachers, parents and children alike clamouring for a moment with her. Lucy would enjoy that. He considered calling Claire Graham and warning her. Then, as sanity returned and he dropped his forehead against his hands on the steering wheel, he decided against it.

How on earth could he have handled that so badly? He had come intending to ask Brooke to do this one thing for Lucy and he had been prepared to offer her anything that it was within his power to give her. Instead he had behaved like an ape on an overdose of testosterone. Then he grimaced. Brooke would almost certainly say that he was being unkind to apes. He undoubtedly was. And how she had enjoyed it. One look and she had switched him on like the Christmas illuminations. He had thought himself totally immune to her charm, but maybe it was one of those viruses that needed regular booster jabs.

And maybe knowing that she still had him on a string would be enough.

It would have to be, because someone as bright as Brooke, someone who knew him as well as she did, would realise soon enough that he would never expose her the way he had threatened to. Not to protect her, but to protect Lucy. He would never expose his little girl to the glare of the tabloid press, the nightmare of reporters camped out on the doorstep, at the school gates. That being so, if she decided to ignore her daughter's plea and his stupid threat it would be better if no one was expecting her. Claire would have to cope with her surprise celebrity as best she could.

Bronte remained perfectly still for what seemed an age after James Fitzpatrick—Fitz— left. One moment she had been quite inno-cently using the telephone, planning to leave a message asking someone she had never met to call her back, the next she'd been kissed as if the end of the world were nigh by that very same man. How on earth had that happened? How on earth had she let it happen? The moment his hand had touched her cheek she had known...

She touched her lips with the tip of her tongue. They were hot, swollen, throbbing with heat. But it wasn't just her lips, her whole body felt like that and she finally understood how her sister, her careful, life-under-control sister, had made the age-old mistake of getting pregnant. She touched her cartwheeling waist.

If she were young and foolish, she might have thought that being kissed by James Fitzpatrick would be all it took.

She finally moved, stumbled to the kitchen chair and sank down on it. Then she laughed, a touch hysterically, as she reached for Lucy's letter. She'd tried to tell him that she wasn't Brooke, but he hadn't been listening. Well, he'd only had one thing on his mind.

She couldn't believe that he hadn't seen the difference straight away. Brooke was so stylish, so confident, so beautiful.

It was true that they were superficially alike with matching bones and skin, the same bean-pole height, the same streaky blonde hair, but there the similarity ended. Even at school Brooke had always been the elegant, the poised, the perfectly groomed one, while she had been the one with a torn skirt, inky fingers and bruised shins from constantly falling over the furniture. She looked down at her grass stained knees, her hands which bore the scars of her tussle with the garden.

Then she shrugged. If it had been eight years since they met, if he had only seen her on the television battling against the elements, sweaty, her hair sticking to her forehead, no make-up, if he didn't know that Brooke had a sister, well, maybe the mistake was not so difficult to understand.

Eight years was a long time—long enough to blunt the details. Not long enough to dull the passion though. She shivered despite the sun spilling through the window, the open doorway, and rubbed at the gooseflesh on her arms. She had tried to tell him...

She should have tried harder.

She glanced at the telephone. She would have to call him, explain. Later. It would take him a couple of hours to get home. Then she swallowed, hard. How on earth could she call a man and tell him that he'd made a mistake like that?

On an answering machine, that was how. Right now. She would just leave a message explaining about the mistake, explaining that Brooke was abroad. That would avoid what could only be an embarrassing conversation for both of them. She would do it now and then she could put it out of her mind.

She dialled the number, waited for the tone. 'Mr Fitzpatrick,' she began firmly. 'Fitz—' She stopped. Suppose someone else listened to the message? Suppose Lucy came in from school and switched it on? She had assumed he would be going straight back, but he might not. She hung up, unwilling to risk it. She would have to do it face to face. Or rather ear to ear. She was twenty-seven years old, a grown woman. She could handle it. In the meantime she went in search of her secateurs. Cutting back the spring-flowering shrubs would help to take her mind off Mr James Fitzpatrick's hot mouth. Maybe.

The day dragged interminably, the clock seemed on a go-slow. The last thing in the world she wanted to do was to call James Fitzpatrick and make him listen while she explained that he had kissed her by mistake. Yet in some secret part of her she knew that she was just like a child counting down the endless hours of Christmas Eve, waiting to hear his voice…

Seven o'clock came. Lucy's bathtime? Time for homework? What had she and Brooke done at seven o'clock when their father was alive? Played, talked, laughed. Laughed a lot. Did Lucy and Fitz laugh together?

Eight o'clock. Eight o'clock had been bedtime for them. Indisputable. They'd been able to read, they'd been able to listen to the radio for half an hour, but they'd had to be in bed by eight. Old-fashioned rules. Nine o'clock, she decided. She would be safe at nine o'clock.

At a quarter to nine o'clock she could wait no longer. She picked up the telephone and dialled the number. Mr Fitzpatrick? she'd rehearsed the casual tone. My name is Bronte Lawrence. We met this morning when you mistook me for my sister… A little gentle laughter. No, no need to apologise, I quite understand… She hadn't got beyond that part. At that point she was hoping he would be too busy grovelling to recall how eagerly she had kissed him back.

'Bramhill six five three seven four nine.' A child's careful voice enunciated the numbers perfectly. 'Lucy Fitzpatrick speaking.'

'Lucy…' Bron's hand flew to her throat as the word escaped her lips. She sounded so grown up…

'Mummy?' The word was an essay in uncertainty, hope, longing. 'Mummy? It is you, isn't it?' Mummy. The word seemed to echo over and over in her head so that she didn't know if it was Lucy shouting it or just in her imagination, but as Lucy's careful telephone answering voice disintegrated into childish excitement Bron froze, unable to answer. In her uncontrollable eagerness to speak to James Fitzpatrick, she had done precisely what she had wanted to avoid. 'Daddy said you wouldn't get my letter, that you must have moved but I prayed...'

'Who is it, Lucy?' James Fitzpatrick's voice reached her, distantly.

'It's my mummy. My *mummy*! Daddy, she's rung, she's going to come. I *told* you she would—'

Then the mouthpiece was covered so that there was only a distant murmur. Then his voice in her ear. 'Brooke?' She didn't answer. She couldn't. This was all her fault. She should have made him listen this morning. She should have rung straight away, left a number for him to call back. Suddenly all the things she should have done seemed so obvious, so simple. Why hadn't she seen? Because she hadn't wanted to? 'Brooke, is that you?' His voice was sharper. How could she have raised the child's hopes like that when she could only dash them...? 'Brooke!'

She came to with a start. 'Fitz, I'm sorry, I didn't mean—'

He wasn't interested in apologies. 'What the devil do you think you're doing, ringing here when Lucy might answer the phone?' He practically hissed the words into the phone.

'She should have been in bed,' she hissed back.

'Motherly advice? From you?'

'No… I'm sorry… Look, I had to ring. I had to tell you—'

'What? Tell me what? After what you've just done, the only thing I'm prepared to hear right now is that you'll be here on Friday.'

Oh, Brooke! How could you get me into a situation like this? What on earth am I going to do? And as clearly as if her sister were speaking in her ear she heard Brooke laughing at her dilemma, saying, Do, darling? Why, do whatever you want. If you're so concerned about Lucy, why don't you go and play happy families for an afternoon? They already think you're me and you always were so much better at the caring stuff…

'Well?' he demanded. 'What am I to tell Lucy?'

They already think you're me. 'Yes.' She heard her voice as if at a great distance. 'Tell her I'll be there. I—um—I need directions.'

'I'll fetch you.'

'No.' Her brain was back-pedalling as fast as it would go. 'No, don't do that.' An afternoon pretending to be her sister just to make a little girl happy would be difficult enough; a couple of hours in a car with James Fitzpatrick would be impossible.

'It's no trouble.'

Then she realised why he was offering, more than offering—insisting. 'You don't have to worry that I'll let Lucy down.'

'Don't I?' The words sounded as if they had been wrenched from him. She didn't answer because her brain was yelling in her ear: Tell him! Tell him, now! Before it's too late. But it was already too late. Lucy had heard her, thought she was Brooke. No explanation, a thousand times 'I'm sorry for raising your hopes' could ever make up for that disappointment. 'Have you got a pen there?'

'What?'

'A pen. For the directions.'

'Oh, yes... No, wait,' she said as she grabbed for a pen and it skittered from her grasp, slid across the floor. 'I've dropped it.'

He waited patiently while she retrieved it and then, assuming she knew where Bramhill Parva was, explained how to find the school.

'Have you got that?' Got it? She looked at the notepad with its incoherent scribble, but she didn't ask him to explain it again, certain if she did he would insist on fetching her, wouldn't take no for an answer. She'd already had a firsthand example of his inability to listen.

'Yes, yes. I'll find it.'

Then, as if talking to her was putting too great a strain on his good nature to be sustained, he said, 'I'll fetch Lucy to say goodnight.'

'Mummy? Are you really coming on Friday? Can I tell Miss Graham? Can I tell Josie?'

Still stunned by the sudden turn of events, Bron took in a deep breath. 'I'll be there, Lucy, you can tell who you like. Goodnight, darling, sleep tight.'

The nightly ritual of her own childhood. Goodnight. Sleep tight. Watch the bugs don't bite. Oh, dear God. What on earth had she promised? More to the point, how on earth was she going to carry it through?

CHAPTER THREE

QUEEN of the Amazon chic. Easier said than done, Bron thought the following morning as she regarded the arid desert of her wardrobe. It didn't need a critic to tell Bron that her wardrobe was short on any kind of chic. Her whole life was short of the kind of glamour that came as second nature to Brooke.

Her hair, for instance. She fluffed it up, more in hope than expectation. It flopped right down again. Brooke might get away with that when she was chatting up orang-utangs in the steam of a Borneo forest, but when in London she visited her Knightsbridge hairdresser as often as necessary to keep the image diamond-bright.

Bron turned from the mirror to the framed photograph of her sister at an awards ceremony, picked it up to looked more closely at the fashionable jaw-length bob her sister had adopted—a bob with attitude was the way one

67

magazine had described it. Actually, she looked more like a little girl who had forgotten to comb her hair, a cheeky, flirty little girl, an impression that was enhanced by the backless Ribeiro dress she was wearing. Nearly wearing. A dress that showed her tanned skin off to perfection, a dress that stopped a foot shy of her knees and showed her legs to perfection too. Not much cloth to show for so much money…but what there was certainly did the trick.

Their mother had tutted when she'd seen it—tutted, but smiled indulgently. Well maybe it was her time for a little self-indulgence, time to find out exactly what it was like to be her sister.

Hair first, then. And nails. She called the Knightsbridge hairdresser to enquire if they could fit Miss Lawrence in during the morning. They fell over themselves to help and when she arrived she was treated with the kind of deference that would have amused her if she could have relaxed sufficiently to enjoy it. She didn't tell them that she was Brooke, they just assumed. Did she really look so like her sister?

They tutted over the condition of her hair, muttered about too much sun, cut it and cosseted it. Her nails were gentled into gleaming plum-dark ovals. Her skin was cleansed and toned and made up. Before her eyes she was transformed into her sister. But the likeness must have been there all along, it was just that people saw them differently.

The beauty salon expected Brooke and never considered the possibility that she might be someone else. Fitz had expected Brooke and that was who he had seen. It suddenly occurred to her that no one would question her. That if she kept her nerve getting away with it would be easy. All she needed now were some of her sister's clothes.

She left the salon and hailed a taxi, directing the driver to her sister's flat.

'Could I have your autograph for my little girl, Miss Lawrence?' he asked as he handed her a receipt for the fare without being asked. 'She's a real fan of yours. Says she wants to save the world when she grows up, just like you. Gives me hell, begging your pardon, when I spray the greenfly. Says I should leave them for the ladybirds.'

'Really?' Bron swallowed as she remembered the enthusiasm with which she had wiped out her own particular greenfly invasion the day before. Somehow she didn't think that the slogan 'Save the Greenfly' would produce quite the same enthusiasm in a nation of gardeners as 'Save the Whale.' 'She's right, of course,' she said, taking the pen and paper he offered. 'But it's hard to remember that when your roses are being sucked dry.' And she smiled. 'What's her name?'

'Katie.'

Bron quickly wrote, 'Save a greenfly, make a ladybird happy. Love to Katie, Brooke Lawrence.' Was that fraud? Not if she wasn't doing it for money, and the huge grin on the taxi driver's face went a long way to easing her conscience.

Ten minutes later, as she flipped through the racks of gorgeous clothes hanging in her sister's vast walk-in wardrobe, Bron's conscience had been put on permanent hold. For a woman who spent half the year filming in areas where clothes were rarely more than a strip of cloth and a few beads, Brooke did not stint herself. And she bought the best. Expensive labels, beautiful fabrics: Kenzo, Versace, Armani, Ghost...

Some of the clothes she recognised from Brooke's appearances on television, the many photographs in magazines and newspapers that she had cut out and pasted into a scrapbook for her mother. And recognisable clothes would help, she thought.

Despite the ease with which the hairdresser and taxi driver had been taken in by her appearance, her own confidence when she confronted her reflection in the mirror, it would only take one person to point a finger at her and cry 'fake' and she knew she would lose her nerve.

That just couldn't happen. For Lucy's sake she wouldn't allow it to happen. She'd made her decision and she would see it through, no matter how difficult. The one good thing she could do, was determined upon, would be to tell Lucy that she had an aunt and that her aunt would be there for her even when she couldn't be. Then she would write to her as Aunt Bronte and in a few months, with a change of hairstyle and in her own very ordinary clothes, she would go back as herself.

'Good grief, this is ridiculous,' she said, blinking furiously as she searched the crammed racks for a trouser suit Brooke had been wearing the last time she'd gone seen her on some breakfast programme, just before she went away. If she remembered it, maybe other people would too and it would lend credence to her deception. 'How many clothes can one woman wear?'

The suit was exactly what James Fitzpatrick had ordered. A safari suit in a pale, carefully faded khaki, the jacket all baggy pockets, the trousers combat-style. On Brooke, with a silk scarf knotted at her neck, a pair of soft desert boots, it had looked unbelievably elegant, unbelievably sexy. But then that was Brooke. She lent elegance to clothes rather than the other way around…

Bron finally found it and held it against her, regarding it doubtfully; on the hanger it looked decidedly shapeless, anything but chic and, de-

spite the similarity in their height, their figures,
Bron had the feeling that was exactly the way
it would look on her. She put it to one side,
chose a couple more possible outfits and then
carefully packed them in one of Brooke's
Vuitton suitcases along with the desert boots
and a pair of Jimmy Choo sandals.

As an afterthought she helped herself to
some of her sister's trade-mark accessories—
the stainless steel Gucci watch, the strands of
amber beads that she wore so often about her
throat and wrist and, as a last, devil or nothing
gesture, a bottle of her sister's wickedly expensive scent.

Fitz had sworn Lucy to secrecy about her
mother's visit, absolutely forbidding her to tell
even Josie, explaining that Brooke would be
very cross if the newspapers found out that she
would be at sports day. He had hated to do
that, but anticipation of the effect her unexpected arrival would have had done the trick.
Even so, by Friday her excitement was threat-
ening to boil over and it was almost a relief to
drop her at the school gate.

Claire Graham was, as always, waiting to see her charges safely inside the school gates and she crossed to speak to him. 'Fitz.' Her smile was back in place.

'Claire.' He nodded towards his daughter disappearing at speed towards school. 'How's she been?'

'Back to her usual bouncing self.'

'Oh, dear.'

'Don't worry, there's been no serious damage. I'm just glad to see her happy. The stories seem to have stopped, too. You've talked to her?'

'We've talked to each other,' he hedged.

She nodded. 'Good. You are coming this afternoon? It'll be fun.'

'And you'd like me to bring a video camera to record it all for posterity?'

'Would you?'

As if she hadn't been relying on him. 'Don't worry, I'll be there.' He reached behind him for a bag. 'I thought you might like this for the raffle. There is going to be a raffle?' He might not have seen the letter, but he didn't have to be a genius to guess at its contents.

Claire peered into the bag. 'A bottle of Scotch? Bless you. And what's this?' She took out a small, brightly coloured stuffed toy.

'A Moggle.' Claire Graham's brow rose. 'It's going to be on the want list of every child under the age of eight next Christmas. At least, that's the idea. That one's not for the raffle, by the way—he's a prototype and he's yours.'

'This is your latest character? I've heard the children talking about them, of course—'

'Characters. Plural. There's a whole family of them. Striped ones, spotted ones, and McMoggle—'

'Is tartan?'

'You catch on fast.'

'I'll have to check them out.' She leaned forward and kissed his cheek. 'You're a lovely man, Fitz—' She spun round as she spotted a child doing something it shouldn't. 'Catherine Merry stop that this minute—'

'Lovely, am I?' Fitz murmured as he slipped the Range Rover into gear and pulled away. 'Tell me that again at four o'clock this afternoon…'

*   *   *

On Friday morning Bron rose early and, hoping for inspiration, tried on each of her sister's outfits in turn. She'd done it the day before, of course, had definitely decided on the pale mint-green dress with the fabulous sandals. Almost.

Then she'd spent the entire night plagued with nightmares involving vast quantities of coffee, mayonnaise and ketchup. Not that she planned to eat anything—she would be too nervous for that. But even so, she knew that, no matter how careful she was, something awful was bound to happen and the fabric didn't look as if it would take kindly to a wash and spin—not even on the gentlest of programs. And the slender five-inch heels hadn't been made for crossing fields. One of them would break. Or she'd trip and break her ankle and have to be rushed off to hospital and then everyone would find out that she wasn't Brooke…

Definitely not the mint green dress.

The trousers and soft silk sweater looked good—it was what she would have worn herself, but that was the problem: they were beautiful, but the sort of clothes anyone might wear, if they could afford them. The look was more her than Brooke and, since she planned to go back as herself as soon as she dared, today she had better look as much like Brooke as she could manage. It would have to be the combat trousers and the jacket which, despite the expensive label, suggested an imminent safari to some steamy tropical forest.

She left the jacket open to reveal a gold silk vest-top, added the Gucci watch with the numberless black face, and instead of the scarf she wore Brooke's amber beads. A safari, but a very dressy safari. Casual but classy, and the added touch of her sister's scent was a whole lot more appealing than mosquito repellant.

There was a ring at the bell and she checked her watch. Brooke's watch. Bron could never quite see the point of a watch without numbers, particularly a square watch without numbers, since any attempt to tell the time with any accuracy was doomed to failure. She'd ordered the taxi for ten past the hour. Guesswork suggested that she had plenty of time to give her reflection one last glance, tuck a wayward trand of hair behind her ear, then flick it out gain as she resisted with difficulty the urge to ive it a good brushing, remind herself that her air was *supposed* to look like that. Then she lung a roomy leather bag over her shoulder nd headed for the door.

It wasn't her taxi. It was James Fitzpatrick. James Fitzpatrick looking impossibly more stunning than she remembered in an open-necked navy blue shirt with fine white stripes and a pair of faded denims that looked as if they had been moulded on him. He was stand-ing sideways to the door, thumbs hooked into belt loops, and he was half-way to the gate, as if uncertain whether he really wanted to be ringing her doorbell. Then he turned his head to look at her and something, something as in-substantial as the shimmer of heat from the road on a hot summer's day, seemed to leap the space between them. He looked at her, Bron thought, and it felt like being touched, stroked with a silk scarf. All over.

Then she realised why he was standing there and anger blew away the drugging sensuality that for a moment had sent her wits walkabout.

'What the hell are you doing here?' she demanded.

'Just passing.'

'In a pig's ear,' she retorted. It was an expression that she'd heard Brooke use but had never before found a use for.

'Eye.' Fitz must have seen her confusion, because he repeated the word. 'Eye. The expression is "In a pig's eye."'

Trust her to get it wrong. 'I don't care what part of a pig's anatomy is involved, you know what I meant.'

He was trying not to laugh, and that made her even madder. 'I've a fairly good idea.'

'You thought I'd let Lucy down,' she said. 'You thought I wouldn't turn up.'

Her reminder of his purpose in being there seemed to contain any danger of him laughing out loud, she noted with considerable satisfaction. Then he said, 'Let's say I decided to make quite sure you did.'

Why did that hurt so much? He thought she was Brooke, for heaven's sake, and, if everything he had said the last time he'd called was true, he had every right to be cautious. 'I promised her. I wouldn't break a promise to a child.'

'No?' She would have sworn it was impossible to invest two letters, one little word, with such depths of meaning. He might as well have called her a liar to her face. 'Are you ready?'

'I'm ready for my taxi.'

'You don't need a taxi. I'm here.'

'I'd rather take the train.'

His smile was something else. Slow, cynical, it said more with the rearrangement of a few muscles than words ever could. 'Even you couldn't have changed that much, Brooke.'

He'd never believe how much. 'Watch me,' she said as the taxi drew up at the gate. She turned to shut the door behind her but by the time she turned back he had paid the man off and the cab was pulling away from the kerb. 'Stop! Come back!' She watched the bright yellow taxi sign as it disappeared in the direction of town. Then she turned back to Fitz, who was holding the gate open for her, a look of smug satisfaction on his annoyingly handsome face. Stopping him would probably be about as easy as stopping a runaway train, she decided. 'You're not listening to me, Fitz.' How easily his name came to her lips. 'I said I didn't need a lift.'

'There's no need to fight about this, Brooke. I'm here now.' Still she didn't move. 'Any time you're ready.'

She didn't appear to have a choice. Again. She had been wondering why Brooke had walked out on a man so eminently desirable, but all of a sudden it wasn't so hard to figure. Two people that used to getting their own way in one relationship could only mean one thing. Trouble.

Behind her, the door knocker fell with a crash to the step. It was a welcome distraction.

Fitz stared in fascination as Brooke picked it up and tucked it out of sight in a tub of blue pansies standing on the step. It was exactly what Lucy would have done. But it was odd, he didn't remember Brooke being the kind of girl who had things come apart in her hands. Only him.

'Does that happen often?' he asked.

She glared at him. 'I'll fix it later.'

Fix it? Was she kidding him? 'As in fix it with a screwdriver?'

Her eyes flashed. 'No, with my nail-file.'

He grinned, couldn't help himself. The quick temper hadn't changed. 'Just asking.' He was still holding the gate for her. 'Shall we go?'

She made him wait while she walked slowly, very slowly, down the path towards him, counting inside her head as she put one foot carefully in front of the other...one, two, three... This was not the moment to fall flat on her face. And as she walked she tried to work out exactly what had got into her. She never lost her temper. That was Brooke... He opened the door of the Range Rover parked at the kerb. It was big and black. A bully of a vehicle. It suited him.

'You certainly look the part,' he said as she swept past him. '"She who must be obeyed" to the life. Lucy's friends will be impressed.'

Patronising oaf, Bron thought as she climbed aboard. Trouble with a capital T. Yet the word niggled at her. Brooke had always preferred men she could control, twist around her little finger. He might have changed in eight years, but something about him sug-gested that Fitz had been the one in control ever since the first besotted woman had bent over his crib and said, 'Ahhh…'

And after all the trouble she had taken to meet his criteria he might have tried a little harder for a compliment. But then he thought this was the way she usually looked, that she was simply putting the gloss back on after a long trip in some steamy jungle. Only she knew just how much effort had gone into get-ting the image perfect. For a girl who rarely used any kind of make-up beyond a quick pass with a lipstick, it had been a real eye-opener.

Now, conscious of being watched as she fas-tened her seat belt, something that even she could normally do without any great difficulty, Bron lost control of her fingers. And that stoked a flash of anger that was as fierce as it was unexpected.

She'd had to learn patience. She had learned to control arms that were capable of cutting swathes through china, causing mayhem in a supermarket, feet that could trip over a penny, fingers that had refined destruction to an art form. She pretty much had it worked out, had learned to think before she acted, and so long as she took her time everything was fine. Today was clearly going to put that hard-won control to the test.

'I seem to be all nerves,' she said as Fitz took the clip from her and pushed it home.

'Then we should be in for an exciting afternoon.'

'Oh?'

'If Lucy gets through the morning without some kind of disaster I shall be surprised.' And that was it for the next twenty minutes as Fitz was kept busy negotiating the suburbs of Maybridge and the busy industrial sprawl to the south of the town. Once on the dual carriageway to the coast, however, Fitz found his voice.

'I didn't come to fetch you because I thought you'd let Lucy down,' he said. 'Not after you spoke to her. Even you wouldn't be that cruel.'

'Thanks.' He acknowledged her sarcasm with a tilt of his head. 'So why did you come?'

Not for the pleasure of her company. Brooke's company.

'I just thought this might be a good opportunity to lay down a few ground rules about today,' he said.

Ground rules? Ye, gods and little acorns. Macho-man in full flight. This should be interesting. 'Oh?'

'I don't want you waltzing into Lucy's life and messing it up any more than you want to be there, so it should be simple enough.'

Oh, no. There was nothing about today that was simple. But that was for her to know and him to find out. But not yet. 'I'm all ears.' She heard the sweet sarcasm in her voice. Good grief, she was even beginning to sound like Brooke. She glanced down at her sister's clothes and wondered if Brooke-ness was catching.

'Lucy has convinced herself that all she wants is this one visit, that all she wants is to show you off to her friends, prove that she hasn't been lying.'

That was what the letter had said, certainly. 'You're not so sure?' Actually she wasn't ei-

ther, but then she had an ace up her sleeve.
Brooke might not be into motherhood—even
if she had been, she was away more than she
was at home—but Lucy had an aunt who
couldn't wait to get to know this unexpected
niece. An aunt who would love and cherish her
and do everything she could to soften the disappointment.

Fitz glanced at her. 'That's what she thinks
she wants, but once she's found you she's not
going to want to let go. You're going to have
to be firm. You've come today because she's
asked you to, but the reasons you left her with
me are still valid. You've got a serious job of
work to do—you're hardly ever home—you
know she's better off staying with me.' He
ticked them off as if he'd been rehearsing
them. He probably had.

Bron heard the firm voice laying down the
law. But she heard something else too. She
heard fear. James Fitzpatrick was desperately
afraid that he was about to lose the child he
loved, the child he had nurtured, cared for,
cherished, to a woman who had become the
idol of the caring generation. He might be big,

he was undoubtedly strong, but beneath that I'm-in-control exterior he knew just how easy it would be for Lucy to be bewitched by this glamorous mother who had none of the baggage that came with child-rearing.

Lucy's mother might never have been there to hold her when she'd been hurting, never there to read a story, never there to chase the night-time terrors from beneath the bed, but she'd never been there to tell her to tidy her room, either. Never there to insist she eat her greens, brush her teeth...none of those naggy things that were the daily currency of parenthood.

Brooke was good at that kind of long-distance relationship. She'd been that kind of daughter too. All glamour and gifts...never staying around long enough to become irritable or short-tempered or worn out when the wanting seemed endless.

Bron glanced at Fitz. His undiluted sex appeal might have knocked her sideways, his lack of trust had certainly made her angry, but this unlooked-for vulnerability was in danger of touching her heart.

But Bron knew her sister; Brooke would make him squirm a bit before she let him off the hook. She enjoyed that kind of power too much to stop herself. And for today, just for today, she had to be Brooke.

'Scared, Fitz?'

The suggestion of a challenge in her voice brought him round sharply for a moment, before he fixed his gaze upon the road ahead. 'Don't play games, Brooke. Not with Lucy. She isn't a toy you can just pick up when it suits you, something to be played with and then abandoned when the novelty has worn off. You made your choice a long time ago. We both did. If you've regrets, you'll have to live with them.'

Did Brooke have regrets? Did she ever think of the child she had given up and wonder what had become of her? How could she not think of her? 'Maybe Lucy will have other ideas.'

'I'm sure she will. I'm sure you're every little girl's dream mother.' He threw a fierce glance at her as they slowed for a roundabout. 'Or do I mean nightmare?' Bron flinched at that. Why was he being so cruel? 'I'm relying on you to explain that you're just too busy for more than a flying visit. I'm sure there are at least a dozen endangered creatures lined up in your sights right now and, believe me, they need you far more than Lucy does.'

'Is that right?' The only thing lined up in her sights was Fitz and if she'd had a weapon she'd be sorely tempted to use it. 'Am I allowed to send her a card at Christmas?' Bron snapped.

'Why would you want to? You haven't remembered her birthday, or Christmas in eight years. Don't start anything you don't intend to continue.' *Remembered?* She had no idea when Lucy's birthday was and she could hardly ask. It wasn't the kind of thing even the most absent-minded mother was likely to forget. 'I can't have you popping up every five minutes unsettling her, Brooke. Playing at motherhood.'

'If that's the case, Fitz, why did you come looking? Wouldn't it have been simpler all round to have left well alone?'

'It was too late for that. She found her birth certificate, found the photographs…'

'That was careless of you.'

'Very. And this is my punishment.'

Punishment? To think that a minute ago the man had been twanging her heartstrings. 'You don't pull your punches, do you, Fitz?'

Punishment. Brooke had paled at the word and maybe it had been a touch melodramatic, but Fitz wasn't about to rescind it. Sitting beside her, near enough to touch her, remembering what she had put him through, the word came close enough. 'Going for the throat was something I learned from you.' He was sure she never kept any photographs. She wasn't a woman who allowed emotional baggage to tie her down. 'Today you'll make *my* daughter a very happy little girl and then at four o'clock I'll drive you to the station and put you on the train home.'

His daughter. Bron couldn't believe the way he had emphasised that, excluding her— Brooke. Anyone would think he'd done it all by himself. 'You mean I'm not even invited to tea?'

'You're invited. You're just too busy to accept.' Fitz felt his hands tightening on the wheel, saw the betraying whiteness of his knuckles and made a conscious effort to relax his grip. She hadn't risen to the challenge he had thrown down. Maybe she was just toying with him, winding him up a little, and it was going to be all right. 'An important woman like you must have a dozen more interesting things to do. Contracts to sign, deals to make, interviews to give.' Just so long as she was well away from Lucy, away from him.

'Won't Lucy be disappointed?'

Disappointed? His insides curled up at the thought of the way Lucy would feel. Not that she would cry, or make a fuss. But he would feel her pain as if it were his own and this time he wouldn't be able to kiss it better because somewhere, inside where she wouldn't let it show, she'd blame him.

'Of course she'll be disappointed.'

'I see.'

'I hope you do, Brooke, because I don't want you being too nice to her, too motherly.' On reflection, he didn't know why he was worrying. Once all those eager mothers…and fathers…began paying court to the woman who had made it her personal crusade to save the endangered earth, she wouldn't be able to help herself.

'Excuse me?'

'Just stick to your role as earth mother, Brooke. It's what you do best, after all. You can dazzle and smile and steal every heart in sight—in fact, the more hearts you steal, the better I'll like it. That way Lucy will know that you're public property first, her mother a long way second.'

'You want me to treat her like just one more fan, is that it?' She looked shaken and for a moment he wondered if, after all, he had misjudged her.

He stopped the thought cold, taking the slip-road off the dual carriageway and slowing as they came to a roundabout. Only then did he turn to her. 'Well, that's all she is to you, Brooke. Be honest. Whatever else you were, you were always that. To the point of brutality.' He paused, and when she didn't answer he said impatiently, 'You can play-act the adoring mother all you like for your public this afternoon, but you don't have to pretend with me, I know you too well. This is just one more ego-trip for you, isn't it?'

CHAPTER FOUR

KNOW her? James Fitzpatrick thought he knew her? Bronte was as near to laughing as she had been in weeks. It was probably hysteria.

She was sitting beside him wearing her sister's clothes, her sister's jewellery, her sister's scent and using her sister's name. He'd even kissed her, for heaven's sake, and he hadn't suspected a thing. That was how well he'd known Brooke.

'Honest?' she repeated, as if she didn't understand what he was getting at. Well, she didn't.

'Yes, honest, damn it. You never wanted Lucy, you handed her over to me and walked away without a backward glance. And, since we're being honest, why don't you tell me why you're doing this, why you're bothering?' His eyes seemed to drill right into her head and any desire to laugh evaporated.

Why couldn't he see the difference? Was he so blinded by her superficial likeness to Brooke that he hadn't noticed the glaring inconsistencies? They were alike—with her new hairdo and wearing her sister's clothes, very alike but they were a long way from being identical. Brooke was an inch shorter, for one thing. Did he think she'd grown? And did he really think that she would still be living at home? Pottering about in the kitchen on her own? If he thought that, he didn't know Brooke at all.

Bron's heart was thumping so loudly that she was sure he must hear it above the sound of the engine. She could have told him the truth, of course. And she would before she left Bramhill. She'd tell him and she'd enjoy watching that arrogant certainty crack apart.

But for the moment she would play her part; she had promised Lucy that her mother would be there for her today and she would do nothing to put that promise at risk.

'It might have had something to do with a threat to call the Sunday newspapers with an exclusive exposé of my wicked past,' she said at last, taking some pleasure in her small private joke. She might not have much by way of a past, but that didn't mean that she was some little nobody whom anyone could walk all over. People had tried. Social workers, doctors, all those people who'd said her mother would be better off in a nursing home when all her mother had wanted was to be left in her own home to die in peace. She had shown them and she would show him.

In the meantime Fitz was smiling, if a little grimly. 'Well, there you are, Brooke. Honesty will do it every time.'

'Do you really hate me that much?' *Me*. She had slipped into her role-playing so easily that for just a moment she wondered if she was more like her sister than she cared to believe.

For a long moment Fitz stared at her, unwilling, or maybe just unable, to answer her. Then a cacophony of impatient horns brought him back to the empty road ahead and he pulled away.

After a couple of miles the continued silence began to grate on her nerves and she glanced across at him, willing him to say something, anything.

He saw her look. 'Wait! Just wait. We'll stop in a few minutes. We can talk then.' *Talk?* She hadn't planned on doing much talking. Had probably already done too much—after all, she was the one who had asked that stupid question. As if she needed an answer. It was quite obvious that he loathed Brooke for what she had done to him. But men did it to women all the time. It took two to make a baby, after all, so why shouldn't he be the one left with the nappies and the sleepness nights and plans on hold for the duration?

Half a mile later, he pulled over into the car park of a public house. 'Come on. We'd better have something to eat, it'll be a long afternoon.'

'I don't... I'm not...' Hungry. Not hungry. How could she be with her stomach knotted up with nerves? She'd thought she was on top of this, having her own little private jokes, even. But Fitz wasn't listening, had already jumped down and was coming around the front of the Range Rover to open her door. She wouldn't have waited, except that her hands were shaking on the door catch and it wouldn't shift. Besides, her legs were like rubber and it was a long way down. Not that she wanted to get out. She had started the day with nothing on her mind but the joy of meeting Lucy, making a little girl happy. Suddenly she realised that it wasn't going to be that simple. Fitz evidently had unfinished business with her sister. That kiss had been a whole lot more than hello. 'I'm not hungry,' she said, drawing back as he opened the door.

'Don't do this, Brooke. I don't want to have a row in a pub car park.'

'You think I do?'

He drew in a deep breath. 'I don't hate you. I should do, but I don't.' There was a long pause and Bron turned to him, couldn't help herself. His face was set, expressionless. 'I thought I did, until yesterday.' His voice was harsh, giving away nothing. And everything. 'As always you have your pound of flesh, Brooke, so you might as well wash it down with a glass of wine and enjoy your victory in comfort.' He wasn't taking no for an answer, and as he took her hand to steady her she quickly eased herself down until she was standing on the gravel of the car park. There was only one problem with that. He hadn't moved back.

For a moment they stood there, Bron backed up against the four-wheel drive, Fitz too close, his eyes a dark slatey-blue that boded nothing but trouble. It was a rerun of the scene in the kitchen—he was going to kiss her again, she thought with the logical, distant part of her mind that was watching the scene as if it were happening to someone else. Well, in a way it was. But in another, much more personal way it wasn't and she stiffened, determined this time to hold him off.

Yet even as he lifted his hand to touch her face, his fingers hovering an inch from her cheek, he seemed to hesitate, instead tracing the faint jagged line of a scar just beneath her left brow.

'Lucy has a scar just like this,' he said thoughtfully.

The tender touch of his fingertip against her skin left her floundering, sinking in quicksand. 'Maybe it's hereditary,' she managed.

'She was six years old, bringing me a cup to wash and she tripped,' he continued, and she could see him remembering. 'There was so much blood…'

She remembered her own similar accident with a glass, her father's panic, her mother's calm matter-of-factness as she had taken control, wrapped her in a blanket, put her in her father's arms while she had driven them to Casualty. It must be so hard to have to do both, she thought. To be both mother and father with no one to say, 'Don't fuss…it just needs a stitch…' No one to hold your precious child while you were driving. No one to hold onto afterwards, when the crisis was over and you could stop being strong and cry your eyes out.

Well, she knew all about that. All about the frights in the night when her mother had seemed so close to death, the moments of joy when the crisis had passed one more time. She had been on her own too. There had been no one to hold her, to tell her that everything

would be all right. But then she had always
known that there would be a time when it
wouldn't be.

'Six years old? Definitely hereditary,' she
said, her voice husky with emotion. Then she
cleared her throat and said, 'Shall we?' in that
same firm voice she had learned at her
mother's knee. And she looked towards the
public house as if she wanted nothing more
than a sandwich and a glass of something to
fortify her against the afternoon.

For a moment Fitz remained quite still, lost
in thought, before he let his hand fall to his
side and stepped back. The danger, whatever
it was, had passed.

It was early and the pub was nearly empty.
Bron hadn't anticipated the likelihood of being
spotted by her sister's eager army of fans, but
maybe Fitz had because he directed her to a
quiet corner well away from the bar before going to order sandwiches, returning with a glass
of dry white wine for her, a cup of coffee for
himself. She would have preferred coffee too,
but he hadn't asked. And he was right, of
course; Brooke would have chosen wine.

If only she knew more. If she knew about his relationship with her sister...

Bron crushed the thought. No. She didn't want to think about that at all. What she really wanted to know was about Lucy. What was she like? How did she spend her time? Who looked after her when he was working? But Brooke would not have been interested in such small domestic things. What *would* her sister have wanted to know after eight years?

'What are you doing these days, Fitz?'

He looked up from the coffee into which he had been carefully pouring a sachet of sugar. 'I'm still making films, but nothing that would interest you, Brooke. You can't take off into the wide blue yonder when you've a child to care for. But of course you know that. You always knew that.'

That was the choice her sister had made? Career before emotional obligations? Fitzpatrick Studios? She remembered thinking that he might be a potter and she found herself staring at the long fingers wrapped around the coffee cup. Long, slender, strong. He would make a good potter, she thought. He would be good at anything he did. Then she felt her cheeks beginning to heat up at the direction her mind was taking. 'What kind of films?'

'You don't know?' Then he shrugged. 'Why should you? I make animated films, Brooke. I wanted... I needed to work from home and when a friend came up with an idea for a children's series for television...' he shrugged again '...it was something to do.'

Until Brooke came back and he could get on with his own life, whatever that had been? Except that she hadn't. Come back. 'If you're still doing it you must have been successful,' she said briskly. 'Would I have seen them?'

He came close to smiling. 'I don't know, Brooke. How much children's television do you watch?'

There was precious little television she hadn't seen, sitting for long hours beside her mother. 'You'd be surprised.'

He shrugged. '*Einstein's Mouse* was the first, then there was *Ginger and Fudge*, *Bellamy's Balloon*...' She stared at him. This man produced those delightful animations? 'No?' He mistook her silence for blankness.

'Maybe you've seen *The Moggles*?' he offered, when she didn't respond. 'They're the latest—'

'*The Moggles?* They're yours? But they're brilliant…'

'You're a fan?' he enquired wryly. 'Well, maybe, if you're very lucky, someone will put one in your stocking this Christmas.'

'A Moggle?'

'We've set up a production unit on the Enterprise Park in Bramhill and we're turning them out as fast as we can for the Christmas market. The books, too.'

'You're doing it yourself? And you still have time to make films? Do you have time for a life?' Brooke was big about having a life. Not that she'd ever worried about her sister having one.

His eyes flashed angrily. 'If you're asking if I have time for Lucy, the answer is that I make time—'

'No, no, really.' She reached out without thinking to reassure him, laying her hand on his forearm. It was darkly tanned, warm, sinewy beneath her fingers and, suddenly realising what she had done, she snatched it back. 'I'm impressed. Honestly.'

'Are you?' He dropped his challenge, stared into his cup. 'Well, it helps the local economy, but it's hardly on a par with saving the earth.'

Lord, but he sounded bitter. Well, he'd been left holding the baby. What man wouldn't be bitter about that? 'It's making a difference, though. To people you know. And Lucy must love it.'

He glanced up at her, clearly surprised by her warmth, her enthusiasm. 'She does make the perfect guinea pig for trying out the prototypes.' He smiled quite unexpectedly and Bron's insides began to quiver in a manner that no slow count could control. She sipped her wine instead. 'Anything that survives in her hands passes the battery of safety tests the toys have to go through with ease.'

'Poor child,' she said with genuine sympathy. 'I know just what that's like.'

'Do you? I don't remember you as clumsy. Rather the opposite, in fact, but then, since you spent most of your time flat on your back—' She blushed furiously and the glass in her hand began to wobble dangerously. She put it down quickly, too quickly, but Fitz moved swiftly to retrieve it as it teetered dangerously on the edge of the table in the manner of a man well used to covering such potential disasters. 'Perhaps pregnancy is a temporary cure,' he said thoughtfully as he set the glass down. She took a deep breath, laid her hands carefully in her lap. *One, two, three, four…* 'All those hormones swishing about.'

Five, six, seven, eight… This was dangerous ground. She knew nothing about Brooke's relationship with Fitz. No, that was a lie. He had kissed her thinking she was Brooke and that told her all she needed to know. A lot more than she wanted to think about it. She also knew that Brooke would not have blushed in that give-away fashion at the image he had raised of them together… This was a conversation she couldn't, mustn't get involved with. She looked around. 'I wonder what happened to the sandwiches?'

'I didn't think you were hungry.'

His tone suggested that he knew she wasn't, knew that this was simply an excuse to avoid his invitation to visit the past. 'I'm not,' she said, edginess lending a sharpness to her voice. 'But I don't relish the thought of sitting here all afternoon waiting for the doubtful pleasure of watching you eat.'

Fitz relaxed. He had almost begun to doubt that this woman could be the same Brooke Lawrence he'd known. He didn't remember a scar and that blush was something else... Oh, he'd anticipated changes. She had been a third-year student then, now she was a celebrity, fêted by the media, loved by millions. He hadn't anticipated that any of these would have made her a gentler, warmer human being. They hadn't. She had simply been trying out her role as mother. Not something he planned on en-couraging.

'Tell me about Borneo,' he said as the food arrived. 'You were there during the forest fires, weren't you?' She'd made CNN, clutching an orphaned orang-utan as she'd made a dramatic plea for international help. How strange that she could feel so strongly about an ape when her own infant had failed to move her.

'I'd rather not talk about it,' Bron hedged.

'It was bad?'

It had been bad. Brooke, tough though she was, had come home and cried her eyes out. Bron had never seen her like that before. Had she cried when she'd given away Lucy? Locked herself away in her room and bawled and then afterwards pulled herself together, put that smile on her face so no one would know what she was feeling? It was what she had done after the Borneo trip, launching a campaign to raise awareness of the problems. Doing what she was supremely good at. 'Yes, it was bad.' And then the sandwiches arrived and saved her from further interrogation.

'What have you told her?' Bronte asked as they neared Bramhill.

'Lucy? About you?' She didn't answer. There wasn't anything else she could have meant. He thought for a while. 'I told her that her mother was someone very special, that you had something important you needed to do. I told her that you were away a lot, living in places where you couldn't take a baby. And because you knew that stability was something

that a little girl would need you had left her
with me.'

That was undoubtedly a lot kinder than
Brooke deserved, but then, he would have
wanted to protect her. A mother's love was a
child's primary need.

'Didn't she want to know why I never came
to see her?' What could possibly be more important than she was?

'No. By the time she was old enough to
think about it, she was old enough to see that
a lot of her friends only had one parent. And
later…well, maybe she thought it would upset
me.' Bron ached for this unknown little girl,
deep inside. It was like a tiny cry in the night
tugging at her so that she longed to reach out
and hold her. It was an entirely new longing…

'You never told who—'

'That was the agreement, Brooke,' he
snapped. 'If I took her, I kept her. You made
your decision, signed the papers…'

What decision? It was so frustrating not to
know. She couldn't believe Brooke could be
so…cold. 'How did she find the birth certificate?'

'They were doing some work on family history at school and she discovered that her mother's name would be on her birth certificate. She took my keys and searched my desk.'

'What a pity I wasn't called Jane Smith.'

'It wouldn't have helped. There were other things…the custody papers…' *custody papers?* '…some photographs…' The muscles tightened in his jaw. 'I thought, later, when she was old enough, she might want to come looking for you. I guess she got old enough when I wasn't looking.'

'Fitz—'

'This is it,' he interrupted as he slowed to turn into a wide gateway. 'Paint on that professional smile, Brooke, and keep it there. This is not the place for anything emotional.'

'No.' Of course not.

Bronte had wondered, briefly, why Fitz hadn't suggested a private meeting first. Now she understood why he had preferred her to meet Lucy for the first time at a school function, why he had come to fetch her. This way he was in control. He would whisk her in, well aware that she would be the focus of attention, and then he would whisk her out again the moment sports day was over. This was no place for a tearful reunion. *No place for anything emotional.*

James Fitzpatrick would have provided his daughter with her heart's desire and she would be the heartless mother who was too busy doing 'important' things to spare Lucy more than a couple of hours. Quite suddenly she didn't like the script she'd been handed. Whatever Brooke had done, she didn't deserve this. And neither did Lucy.

'No,' she repeated, this time with rather more force. But the Range Rover was already scrunching over the gravel driveway and he didn't slow as he glanced at her, a frown puckering his brow. 'This is wrong, Fitz. I can't do it. Not like this.'

'It's a bit late for second thoughts,' he said sharply, pulling over to park alongside the dozens of vehicles that had spilled over from the driveway onto the field. 'Lucy's expecting you and, despite a warning not to say anything, I have no doubt that she'll have told Josie...'

And Josie would have told everyone. It seemed a lifetime since she had been eight years old but Bron could still remember that kind of excitement.

Then Bronte saw her. A tall child in dark shorts and a white T-shirt, flying towards them across the field. Long arms, long legs, a smile that knocked you sideways; despite the tousled chestnut curls she was the image of Brooke at eight years old. And before Fitz could stop her, before she could stop herself, she was out of the Range Rover, arms wide as she stooped to scoop Lucy up in a great hug.

'Oh, Lucy. My dear, sweet Lucy.' She thought she was immune from tears. Her eighteen-year-old self had once cried tears of self-pity, then only tears of relief as time after time her mother had come through each succeeding crisis, each one a little more desperate than the one before it. Now her throat ached so that she couldn't speak; even if she had known what to say, her lips were curled so tightly between her teeth as she struggled to contain the upsurge of emotion that it would have been impossible.

This wasn't the time or place for tears. Fitz had been right about that.

For a moment, as she buried her face in Lucy's curls, it was touch and go but she was finally able to put the child down, folding herself up so that they were the same height and holding her at arm's length so that she could look into her eyes, touch her face. She brushed back an unruly lock of hair. Touched the tiny jagged scar above her eye with the tip of her finger. Her eyes were blue. Not blueberry dark like Fitz's, though. Bright summer sky blue. Bronte recognised the colour. Her mother's eyes had been just that shade. How she wished her mother could have known... She blinked. She must not cry. That was important. She must smile.

'You're so pretty, Lucy,' she said.

Lucy, as close to tears as she was, was startled into a grin instead. 'Am I?' She looked up at Fitz. 'You never said,' she said.

'No, well, I thought you might get bigheaded.' His voice didn't sound quite right and Bronte looked up but he had turned away as a smart woman in her late fifties approached them across the grass 'Claire. I'm sorry we cut it so fine. There were roadworks.'

'No problem, we're running late. The fire bell went off.' She looked beyond him with her face betraying nothing but polite interest. 'False alarm,' she added in a tone that suggested that, come Monday morning, someone would be in serious trouble.

'Claire, may I introduce Lucy's mother—?'

'Introductions are scarcely necessary, Fitz.' As Bronte straightened, still holding Lucy's hand, Claire Graham offered her hand. 'I recognise Miss Lawrence from the television and of course Lucy has mentioned her. I'm Claire Graham,' she said, 'Lucy's head teacher. It's a great pleasure to welcome you here this afternoon, if somewhat unexpected.' She glanced at Fitz, then at Lucy. 'I think you're wanted to help the little ones, Lucy.' Lucy didn't move. 'Now, please.'

Bronte gave her hand a squeeze. 'Your friends are waiting for you, Lucy. We'll have some time later.'

Lucy turned and saw half a dozen girls standing, wide-eyed, a few yards away and she

grinned and bounced away across the field towards them. She wasn't actually punching the
air in triumph, but Bron had a feeling that it
was a close-run thing.

Claire Graham watched her go with an affectionate smile before turning to Fitz. 'You
know it will take more than a bottle of Scotch
and a Moggle to make up for not giving me
some warning that you were bringing a celebrity this afternoon. Our sports day could have
made the front page of the *Bramhill Gazette*
and I'd have been inundated with parents
whose children were desperate to go to the
same school as Brooke Lawrence's daughter.'

'That's why I didn't tell you, Claire. This is
a private visit. We would both prefer that it
stay that way. I'm sure you understand.'

Claire nodded. 'Of course.' Then, 'We're
about to begin, Fitz, maybe you'd like to film
the start?' She turned to Bronte as he reached
through the open window of the Range Rover
to retrieve a hand-held camcorder. 'Fitz is
making a video for us; it's a small fund-raising
endeavour and the more children he can get on
film, the more copies we'll sell.'

'I can imagine.' And Bronte grinned. She couldn't help herself. She felt ridiculously, stupidly happy. She had scarcely allowed herself to think what this afternoon would be like. What thoughts she did have had suggested that there was bound to be a touch of awkwardness. She glanced at Fitz. Maybe he had been expecting that too. 'You'd better get going, Fitz,' she said. 'You don't want to miss anyone.'

'Maybe you'd like to come along and show me how it's done?'

Oh-h-h…*touchy.* 'I don't think so. My *métier* is in front of the camera, not behind it.'

Claire Graham flickered a thoughtful glance from one to the other. 'Why don't you come and meet the rest of the staff, Miss Lawrence?'

Bron didn't look at Fitz, certain that those dark eyes would be full of ominous warnings. Well, he could keep his warnings to himself. Lucy was happy and so was she. There was no reason why she shouldn't thoroughly enjoy this afternoon. 'I'd love to,' she said, and walked away from him, scarcely noticing the swivel of heads turning as she passed the rows of seats set out for the parents, only aware that

the greater the distance between her and Fitz,
the easier it had become to breathe.

Fitz watched her go, deep apprehension
churning in his stomach. He had planned to be
in control today. He'd made sure they'd arrived at the last minute, hoping that by the time
they arrived everyone would be too busy to
notice, that Lucy would be far too involved for
the kind of scene that he had just witnessed
and Brooke would have seemed distant, de-
tached, all glamour and no emotion.

He'd thought he had the whole thing sorted,
under control. It had been going to be simple.
He knew Brooke.

She was selfish, she would be the first to
admit it. She put herself before everything and
the last thing she would want would be to get
deeply involved with a little girl with a world
of need. She would be happy enough to spend
a couple of hours playing the great lady, winning the hearts of the assembled parents, the
teachers, the children. She could turn on the
charm and melt hearts at fifty paces when she
wanted something—he'd experienced it at first
hand and could vouch for its potency—but

there was nothing here that she would want on a permanent basis.

Or was he wrong about that too?

He thought he knew Brooke, what made her tick, but he was uneasily aware there was something different about her. A gentleness about her mouth, a warmth in the depths of those lovely eyes. Something more that he couldn't quite put his finger on. Well, she'd travelled the world and undoubtedly seen a lot of terrible things along with the wonders. That would change a person. At twenty-one she'd been lovely to look at with a practised sexiness that she'd been able to turn on at will. She was a honey-pot and she knew the world was just full of bees. She still had all that, but she had a lot more. Her face had character, strength, compassion.

But she was alone, ploughing her own straight furrow without anyone to distract her. Nearing thirty, could it be that she had suddenly noticed the gap in her life? Could it be that Lucy's letter had coincided with the ringing of the alarm bell on her biological clock?

Brooke was no longer a third-year student caught up in a nightmare. She was a successful woman and a child was the accessory every successful woman wanted these days, preferably without a man to clutter up her life, make demands.

A ready-made daughter, well beyond the messy stages of babyhood, a bright, intelligent child who could talk about most things and had an opinion of her own on all of them had to be an attractive alternative to starting from scratch for someone like Brooke.

He watched her walking across the field, chatting to Claire, laughing, making her feel special. Brooke was good at that. She had already made Lucy feel very special; his daughter was now the centre of attention, surrounded by those same girls who had been giving her such a hard time for the last few weeks, and she was loving every minute of it.

And suddenly he was afraid. He knew how easily Brooke could steal Lucy's heart. He'd been on the receiving end of her charm offensive and knew there was no defence against it, only time. And she was clever. If he wasn't on his guard the whole thing would be accomplished without him ever being aware of the danger.

First she'd just want to take Lucy on holiday. He might have the custody thing all tied up but if he fought her she would go to court and what judge could deny the repentant, heartbroken mother? Not that she would have to go to court. If Lucy wanted it he would have to agree, he could do nothing else. She was her mother. But that would just be the beginning. There would have to be negotiations over school holidays, a tug-of-love over Christmas that he would step back from because Lucy must never be hurt by that kind of dispute and because…

And he had thought he was the one pulling the strings.

He dragged his hand distractedly through his hair, stunned by his own stupidity. Would he never learn?

But what could he have done? Once Lucy knew who her mother was, once Brooke had seen her, the genie was out of the bottle and no amount of magic could ever put it back. He had fooled himself into believing that this afternoon would be enough for both of them. Fooled himself. He was good at that where Brooke was concerned.

Now he had seen them together, he knew it never could be that simple. This was just the beginning and like it or not she was going to be a part of their lives from now on. But how big a part?

Right on cue his mind presented him with a rerun of that moment in her kitchen when, for the second time in his life, he had utterly lost his head and kissed her. The difference being that this time she had kissed him back.

No!

But deep within himself he could feel hot need unravelling his will, he could hear the whisper of *Yes!* running through his veins, heating him from the inside out. He had thought himself immune to Brooke Lawrence…had had no sense of the danger until she had turned and looked at him as if she were looking at him for the very first time and it was like seeing the first dawn…

He didn't know what Brooke's plans were regarding Lucy and she wasn't saying, but as he watched her join the school governors, the flutter of excitement as she was introduced, he recognised that he would do anything to ensure that he wasn't pushed out of Lucy's life. Anything. And, despite his anger at the way she had abandoned her child, he knew he would be kidding himself if he pretended it would be a hardship.

CHAPTER FIVE

'Please, do take my chair, Miss Lawrence.' After a round of introductions, the chairman of the school governors stepped to one side and gallantly offered his seat, but Bron wanted to be sitting amongst all the other parents down on the field, closer to Lucy. Faced with such a dilemma, what would her sister do?

Exactly what she'd been doing since she was old enough to recognise that life was full of choices and that if you didn't make your wishes clear someone else would make them for you. And since she was, as far as everyone was concerned, the famous Brooke Lawrence and not her nobody little sister, there was no reason why she couldn't do the same.

Bron put her hand on the man's arm in a gesture to reassure him that his offer was appreciated and smiled. 'Please, don't let me disturb you. I'm going to join the rest of parents where I can wave at Lucy and cheer like mad without looking foolish. Perhaps we can meet over tea?'

She received a battery of indulgent smiles in return. Bron could scarcely believe how easy it was, or how much she must have absorbed from watching Brooke twist the world around her little finger. That kind of power might quickly go to a girl's head, she realised, and if she wasn't very careful she might just get to enjoy it. But she wasn't being careful today. She wasn't that stay-at-home, caring, terribly nice Bronte Lawrence today. She was Brooke and twisting the world around her little finger came naturally. So naturally that she might just keep on doing it, might even try it on James Fitzpatrick if he didn't behave himself. And she grinned to herself as she made her way down onto the field.

Then she saw Fitz striding across the field with his camcorder, bearing down on her, and her light-hearted reflections were brought to an abrupt halt. He moved with an easy, careless grace, his long legs eating up the space between them, and in that moment she was consumed with a terrible confusion. Despite her wish to be as far away from him as possible, she found herself longing for him to be close enough to touch, close enough to…

She stopped the thought in its tracks. Twist him around her finger? Who did she think she was kidding? James Fitzpatrick, she reminded herself firmly, was the kind of man who spelled trouble for any woman who didn't have her feet planted firmly on the ground. Finger-twisting could lead to nothing but trouble from that particular source. Trouble with a capital T.

'Is this seat taken?' she asked, quickly turning away, not wanting him to see her gawping at him like some infatuated teenager drooling after a favorite pop star, lowering herself into a child-sized chair that pushed her knees up to her chin when the two women sitting either side of the vacant seat shook their heads wordlessly. She raised her hand to shade her eyes and looked towards the start where a dozen or so chubby-legged infants were being lined up. 'What's the first race?' she asked, almost sensing the moment that Fitz came to an abrupt halt, turned away. One moment her skin was prickled with goose-bumps despite the heat, then suddenly she relaxed. It took all her will power not to turn around and check.

Then her neighbour offered her a sheet of paper with the running order and pointed to the first line. 'This is the kindergarten egg and spoon race.'

'Oh, brilliant. I wonder if anyone will have swopped one of the eggs for a raw one? Someone always used to do that when I was at school—' And with that the ice was broken.

Panning slowly along the line of parents, their faces bright, happy that it hadn't rained, to be meeting old friends, to be supporting their children, Fitz was suddenly confronted by Brooke, her laughing face filling the viewfinder. She was laughing at something the woman next to her had said and all around her people were joining in. What was it about her that made people believe she was so damned *nice*?

What would they think if he told them that she'd been hell-bent on a termination? That he'd had to persuade her that having the baby was not the end of the world? That if she was strong enough, she could have it all.

He stared at her through the lens remembering how young she'd been, how scared, that boiling mixture of feelings that had been tearing her apart...

And he remembered too how vulnerable she'd seemed, the horror of morning sickness that had gone on all day. She'd not had a glowing, beautiful pregnancy.

It had been murder making sure she ate properly; he'd had to bully her along to the antenatal clinic, book the natural childbirth classes for them so that he would know what to do, how to help her when the time came. He'd comforted her when she'd found a stretch mark, bought her special oil and rubbed it on her rapidly expanding abdomen, assured her that she was still beautiful, desirable...

He'd even typed her project work during the last months when she'd had problems with her blood pressure and had been warned to rest, driving her to lectures so that she wouldn't fret about missing them, making sure she stayed in bed the rest of the time.

And he'd been there for her through the long hours of childbirth, reading to her, rubbing her back, giving her ice cubes to suck, keeping her concentrating on her breathing when all she'd wanted to do was to let go and scream blue murder. His reward had been to witness the everyday miracle of Lucy's birth. To hold her. He'd looked at the baby lying in his arms and it had been love at first sight.

Then with her daughter lying less than an hour old beside her Brooke had announced that she was going to put her up for adoption, give her away to strangers.

He'd been so sure she would regret it. That within weeks, months, she would wish the deed undone, would come back. He'd even asked Brooke, begged her, to marry him. He'd have done anything to keep that tiny, helpless creature. She'd seen that and used it. Beneath that charming exterior was the toughest woman he'd ever met.

And when she'd had everything she wanted and had signed the papers that made Lucy his, she had told him he was crazy. Maybe he had been, but eight years of loving Lucy, watching her grow, had raised the stakes. Eight years ago he'd been a besotted innocent without a clue how his life would change, the awesome responsibility he was taking on. Now he knew and there was nothing he wouldn't do to keep Lucy.

Nothing.

'You're Lucy's mother?'

Bronte juggled with her cup and saucer as she fished out her wallet, found a ten-pound note. 'Yes,' she said as she paid for the raffle tickets. After all that was why Lucy had wanted her here, so that everyone would know she hadn't been lying.

'But you and Fitz aren't, weren't...?'

'Married?' Bronte had known a second before Fitz's hand descended on her shoulder that he was there, behind her. But she still jumped. 'Brooke considers marriage an old-fashioned concept.' He rescued the cup, rattling on its saucer. 'At least, she did. Maybe you've changed your mind about that, darling?'

Bron's confidence had grown by leaps and bounds during the afternoon. She'd spent years nursing her mother and was used to being treated like a woman with only half a brain. After all, if she'd been *bright* she'd have put her mother in a nursing home and done something with her life, like her sister. Right?

There had even been times when she'd felt that way about herself. Self-esteem was mostly the reflected opinion of others, after all. Today, though, people had treated her with respect, asked her opinion, listened enrapt to her answers.

Well, she knew enough of Brooke's ideas, had seen the videos of the television programmes often enough to handle just about any question that was likely to be thrown at her at a school sports day.

Marriage, though, was something else. It was a long time since she and Brooke had had the kind of sisterly chats that involved 'man' talk and she had no idea what her sister felt about marriage. The subject had just never come up. Now, unsettled by the warmth of his hand heating her skin through the khaki stuff of her jacket, the silk top beneath it, her new-found self-assurance deserted her and she looked up, seeking some clue.

His eyes were unreadable. He was trailing a lure but offering no clue as to what answer he expected, wanted to hear. A lure, or a trap? Did he suspect something? Then it occurred to her that everyone was waiting for her answer, that she was the one in control, and she felt a little surge of power, experienced an unwill- ingness to let him get away with anything— particularly not cheap shots like that.

'Is that a proposal, darling?'

There was a sudden, pregnant pause in which a pin-drop would have been deafening before Fitz, eyes still shuttered, shrugged and said, 'The offer's still open.'

He'd asked Brooke to marry him?

'Mummy?' Bronte turned at the sound of Lucy's voice. Of course he had asked her to marry him. They had a child. One that he had clearly wanted even if Brooke had had other plans. 'Mummy, will you come and say hello to Josie? She's my best friend and she really wants to meet you.'

~~Bronte looked beyond Lucy to where an~~ other little girl was shyly waiting. 'Of course I will, sweetheart.' And she glanced at the still-stunned adults standing around in a semicircle, struggling to pick their chins up off the floor and wondering how quickly they could excuse themselves to pass on this sizzling piece of gossip. 'Please excuse me,' she said as she took Lucy's hand and allowed herself to be led away.

Fitz watched her go, wanting to go with her, flop down with her on the grass beside the two little girls, join in their laughter. Josie's step-mother joined them, glowing in late pregnancy, her little son beside her. Brooke picked him up and cuddled him, her face lighting up with pleasure. The tenderness of the moment cut Fitz to the quick and he turned away to be faced with the group who had gathered about Brooke and who were now all staring at him. He put down Brooke's cup, excused himself and walked away, picking up his camera and inserting a new cassette, or trying to. His fingers were trembling. He had as good as asked her to marry him in front of a dozen witnesses.

What on earth had made him say such a thing?
It was ridiculous. Asking for trouble. Even
supposing she was interested.

And why would she be? But for Lucy he
wouldn't have given the idea a moment's con-
sideration—not now, not then. Brooke had
simply been the girl at the top of everyone's
want list that year—lovely to look at, bubbling
over with life, utterly unattainable. And then
so completely vulnerable in his arms.

He switched off the memory. He wouldn't
allow her to do that to him again. Even if she
wanted to. And why would she? For heaven's
sake, she had to have a string of admirers. Men
with money. Men with power. She had always
liked men with power.

And anyone she chose to charm would be
at her knees in moments. She should have a
health warning tattooed to her forehead. Along
with that scar. He frowned. She'd implied it
was a childhood thing, it was odd that he
hadn't remembered it. He'd thought he had remembered everything...

He picked up the camcorder and panned it
around the field, taking shots of little groups

of parents and children, trying to shut down
the feelings overloading his system. Not succeeding. The way he was avoiding turning the
camera on Lucy and Brooke was a dead give-
away.

'Fitz?' He turned as Claire Graham approached him. 'Do you think Miss Lawrence
would present the prizes for us this afternoon?'

He shrugged. 'Why don't you ask her?'

'Well, you did make the point that this was
a private visit and I don't want to embarrass
her.'

He bit back the sharp reply that flew to his
lips, the suggestion that embarrassing Brooke
would be about as easy as pulling hens' teeth.
At least he had always thought so, yet she had
blushed when he had reminded her about the
weeks of bedrest. Maybe, just maybe, she did
feel a little guilty after all. 'I'm sure Brooke
would be delighted to present the prizes,
Claire, but I think the request would be better
coming from you.'

Claire gave him a sympathetic look. 'Is it
that difficult?'

'What?' She didn't dignify that with an answer and he offered her an apologetic smile. 'I'm sorry, Claire. Does it show?'

She rested her hand briefly on his arm. 'Think of Lucy, Fitz, how happy she is. She's lit up like a Christmas tree.'

'I just hope it's not as temporary.'

'It doesn't have to be. You're adults. You can work something out if you've the will.'

'I'm sure you're right, Claire.'

But what? He watched Brooke jump to her feet as Claire Graham approached, the warmth of her smile making the sun redundant, but then she always had been able to switch it on like an electric light. He had watched her do it, learned to spot it a second before it happened.

But the other morning, in her kitchen, it hadn't been like that. There had been nothing controlled, nothing calculated... Well, maybe she had changed. And maybe he was worrying unnecessarily. In a day or two she'd be off on some lecture tour, or doing the round of the chat shows, signing her books in all the major cities with not a minute to spare to think about

Lucy. And if she hadn't thought about her daughter once in eight years, why should she start now?

Because now that she had met Lucy she would think about her all the time. She wouldn't be able to help herself.

Then the second half of the afternoon's programme began and he was too busy filming to give much thought to Brooke, although he could hear her above the crowd, as if he were somehow tuned into her voice as she cheered Lucy on to win the sprint, as Lucy cleared the high jump bar with what seemed like feet to spare.

Claire Graham was right—Lucy was lit up. Ten feet tall. Glowing. She should be like that all the time, would be if Brooke were part of her life. He didn't want to think how she would be if her mother said goodbye at the end of the afternoon and walked away.

He didn't need to ask. He lowered the camera, aware that he had been using it to keep a distance between them all afternoon. Wasting time. Claire was right, Lucy needed her mother and he owed it to her to see that she had her.

Instead of keeping Brooke at a distance, he should be using this time to make some kind of peace with her. If she really had changed, if they could be friends, anything was possible.

'Brooke?' For a moment she didn't seem to hear him. He repeated her name and suddenly she turned, stared at him.

'Fitz. Sorry, I was miles away.' Her face was lit up too. 'Isn't she amazing?'

'Lucy? I think so, but then I always did.' He could have bitten out his tongue as he realised how his words must have sounded. He offered her his hand. 'Why don't we both go and tell her how great she is?'

She hesitated for a moment and then, almost shyly, placed her fingers in his as he helped her to her feet. He didn't let go, keeping her hand tucked in his as they crossed the field.

'You've done a wonderful job, Fitz. She's a credit to you.' Then, 'Or have you had a fabulous nanny to take care of all the hard stuff?'

'I couldn't afford a nanny. Until the money started to come in from the television series I had to live on what freelance work I could get to fit around babysitters and what I'd saved.

Later, well, I took on someone to do the cleaning, to be there when I couldn't be. Nothing else.'

'Thank you, Fitz.' He stopped, turned to her. 'Thank you for making her happy.' She blinked hard, but not quite quickly enough to stop a tear. He watched as it welled in the corner of her eye. For a moment he thought she had it under control, but then it spilled over on her cheek and without thinking he lifted his hand, scooped it up, felt the wetness against his finger. A tear. He'd seen her angry, he'd seen her depressed, he'd seen her in pain, but he'd never seen her cry. Not once. It hadn't been in her repertoire. Maybe that was why he put his arm about her and held her, offering a moment of comfort for all the lost years. 'I'm sorry,' she murmured into his shoulder. 'This is so silly.'

'No. Not silly.' Understandable. Understandable if it had been anyone but Brooke. He glanced down at her, then frowned. 'Do you know, if I didn't know better, Brooke, I'd swear you'd got taller.'

She blinked. Then with a rather shaky smile said, 'Now that *is* silly. Girls have stopped growing by the time they reach eighteen.'

'Is that right?'

'Give or take a year. I did A-level biology, you know—'

'You've a first-class honours degree in biology—' Lucy ran up to them, distracting him and he turned from Brooke to catch her and swing her up, hugging her while Brooke leaned forward and kissed her cheek giving, for the moment, an impression of the perfect happy family.

'Well done, Lucy. You were brilliant.'

Lucy glowed. 'Did Daddy ask you if you could come to tea?' she asked. 'I made some little cakes last night and Mrs Lamb is making sandwiches, cucumber and smoked salmon—'

'Can you come?' Bronte glanced up, surprised by the unexpected warmth in Fitz's voice. Whatever had happened to the 'you'll-be-too-busy-to-accept' thing? Well, maybe the warmth was for Lucy's sake. 'Just say if you're too busy and I'll take you straight to the station,' he added as she hesitated.

There it was, the reminder that she was supposed to make her excuses and leave. 'Who is ever too busy for smoked salmon sandwiches and home-made cakes?' she asked sweetly. She was disconcerted to discover that he didn't look in the least bit irritated.

'Oh, great! I can show you my room. Daddy painted it for me and it's truly amazing. Maybe you could stay and I could show you how well I can swim, too. Daddy always takes me swimming on Saturday. *Can* you stay?' she asked ingenuously.

'Don't push your luck, Lucy. You asked for an afternoon and you got it. Your mother is a very busy lady—'

'And I don't have a toothbrush with me,' she said, butting in with a look that told him she was quite capable of making her own excuses, thank you very much. When she felt like it.

'But you will come back?'

'*Lucy!*' Fitz warned. Then, 'Hadn't you better run along? Miss Graham wants you for the prize-giving.'

'Then she'll want Mummy, too, won't she?' Lucy said pertly.

'Yes, she will.' Bronte made a move to follow the child while Fitz looked shell-shocked. He clearly wasn't used to that kind of back-chat.

'Little madam,' he said, catching Bron's arm, detaining her. 'Look, do you mind?' She must have looked confused. 'About coming home to tea?'

'Of course not. Just surprised at the warmth of the invitation. I had the impression that you didn't want me around for a minute longer than necessary.'

'And was that the only reason you accepted? Simply to irritate me?'

'Maybe.' Actually, she had thought her presence this afternoon, Brooke's presence, was sufficient to seriously annoy him. But at least if he was irritable he wasn't looking at her with those hot eyes.

'Then I'm sorry to have to disappoint you, Brooke. I'm afraid you'll have to try a lot harder than that.'

Now, despite his bantering tone, the taunting smile, she could tell that he *was* very angry indeed and she was confused. What *did* he want? Oh, well, in for a penny... 'Maybe we could stop somewhere on the way back to The Old Rectory and I could buy a toothbrush,' she offered, obediently trying harder.

His jaw tightened. 'No need, I always keep a spare.'

'I'll bet.' She'd seen the looks he got from the young mothers. A man on his own with a child was always going to be a heart-melter; a man who looked the way he did, kissed the way he did, was a sinful temptation. She turned away before temptation got the better of her, but he caught her wrist.

'You're not going to walk away again, are you, Brooke? It'll break Lucy's heart.'

'You said it, Fitz. An afternoon. I can't come back.' Brooke couldn't come back. And despite her earlier pleasurable anticipation at telling him how easy he had been to fool, she realised that she would never be able to ex-plain why. Not because she was afraid of his reaction, what he might do; she just couldn't bring herself to make him feel that stupid. She pulled free as Claire Graham waved to her. 'Excuse me,' she said, then walked away from him, smiling as Miss Graham welcomed her at a table loaded with coloured ribbons and trophies. But inside, she was shaking. Jelly. How could something as casual as a touch do that? *One, two, three…*

She fixed a smile to her face as she pinned ribbons on the winners, the need to avoid sticking pins into tender flesh keeping her fingers tightly under control. She handed over the little trophies and the house shield without a hitch. Not even the constant flash as proud parents snapped their little heroines receiving their prizes distracted her. Not even when it was Lucy, winning a tall silver cup for being the most successful competitor of the day.

She held it out to her, looking up to smile as Lucy's friends raised a cheer. That was when she saw Fitz with his camera, zooming in on her. It was as if he were boring into her mind with his big black lens, seeking out her secrets, and without warning all that hard-won control slipped and the cup, the lid and the base parted company.

'It's just a *little* dent, Mummy,' Lucy said as they drove away from the school. 'Daddy will fix it. He's really good at that sort of thing.'

'I get a lot of practice,' Fitz said with resignation.

Lucy just giggled. 'I think it's cool that you drop things too. Everyone will know you're *really* my mother now.'

Bronte grinned. 'Well, that's the first time anyone has ever been pleased that I'm clumsy.'

'Tea should be interesting,' Fitz said, glancing sideways at her, a thoughtful look creasing his brow.

'We could have a picnic in the garden with paper cups and plates.' Lucy giggled. 'Then it wouldn't matter what we dropped.'

'And no washing-up,' Bronte added.

'It would certainly be safer. One set of matching scars is quite enough, thank you very much.' He glanced back at Lucy. 'Maybe you should compare notes. It might be useful to know what else we've got in store.'

Lucy clamoured to see and Bronte turned around in her seat and showed the tiny scar beneath her eyebrow. 'Wow! That's amazing!' she said, displaying the results of her own more recent run-in with a cup as Fitz slowed and turned into the driveway of a small Georgian rectory.

Red brick, white-painted lattice porch, blush pink petals showering the drive from a gnarled climbing rose and in the distance the sea shone blue beneath a cloudless sky. 'This is *so* beautiful,' Bron said, jumping down before Fitz could open the door for her. 'What a glorious view...' But Fitz was looking at her rather than the view and the crease between his eyes had deepened. Brooke had been here before with Fitz, she realised with a little gasp. They'd made love, made Lucy... 'I'd forgotten,' she said quickly. *As if anyone would forget.*

'Come on, Mummy.' Lucy tugged at her hand. 'I'll show you my room first. Daddy painted it for me with all his characters...' She

gave Fitz half a smile and followed Lucy into
the house. The hall was papered in a faded
gold and green stripe that looked as if it had
been there for centuries. The curved serpentine
table that stood against the wall was perfectly
in keeping as was the gilt mirror above it. But
there were no ornaments, no flower arrangement to complete the image. Her own home
had been like that—everything put away safely
until she could control her errant limbs.
'Where do you live, Mummy? What's your
room like?'

Mummy. Lucy kept using the word like a
mantra, like a magic talisman, as if to convince
herself that this new person in her life
wouldn't just disappear in a flash of smoke,
and she realised with a sinking heart that an
unknown aunt was going to be a very poor
consolation prize for a mother who was there
for her. Bron swallowed hard on the lump in
her throat and concentrated instead on describ-
ing Brooke's bedroom.

'It's white. There's an antique iron bedstead
with lace drapes and a matching bedcover.'

'And curtains?'

'Matching curtains, too.' Brooke had had it done as a favour by an interior designer in return for publicity when her home had been featured in some magazine. 'They're tied back with thick yellow ribbons. There's a big old squashy armchair with a loose cover—'

'Is that white, too?'

'Everything is white except the carpet. That's pale grey.'

'Doesn't it get dirty?' Lucy asked, astonished.

'No.' Brooke had been one of those children who could play in the coal cellar all day and never get dirty. But it gave her an opening. 'No, it doesn't get dirty, Lucy, because I'm hardly ever there.'

'Oh.'

'I'm away most of the time. You must know that.'

'Daddy said.' Lucy stopped at the top of the stairs and looked up at her. 'He said that was why you left me with him. Because you didn't have time to be a mummy.'

Oh, God. 'Daddy is right.'

Lucy turned away and opened a door. 'This is my room,' she said. But the bounce had gone out of the child. Her shoulders sagged and her little body had lost that impression of being a piece of elastic under tension, a coiled spring. Even her voice sounded flat. Now was the moment to explain that Brooke had a sister, a sister who would have all the time in the world to love her.

'Lucy, I have something to tell you…' Then as the impact of the room hit her, 'Lucy! This is incredible. Did Fitz really do all this?'

Lucy brightened a little as she nodded. 'That's Arthur,' she said, pointing to the brightly coloured cartoon that filled the facing wall. 'He's—'

'He's Einstein's Mouse. I know.' Arthur was casually correcting the famous equation with one hand while holding a thick slice of pizza, its cheesy topping slithering dangerously towards the floor, in the other. Other characters had made themselves at home on the walls. The Moggles—as befitted newcomers—were nearest the door and surrounded by moving crates which they were in the process of unpacking. 'I think I'd want to spend the whole day in bed if this were my room.'

'I've got a present for you.' Lucy opened a cupboard and took out a carefully wrapped gift.

'What is it? Can I open it now?' Lucy nodded and she unwrapped the parcel. It contained a very battered soft toy, scarcely recognisable as a Moggle.

'He's Proto Moggle. That's short for Prototype,' she explained. 'He's the very first Moggle ever made. Daddy gave it to me to test it out.' She made a little gesture that suggested she knew why.

'Proto?' Bron sniffed. She was never going to get through the day without a serious attack of weeping at this rate. 'He's lovely, Lucy. I'll treasure him.'

'He won't look right in your white bedroom.'

She considered the grubby, battered toy. 'A room can be too perfect. He'll make it look like home.' Then, 'Actually I have a present for you, too.' She took a small box out of her bag and opened it. Inside was a delicate silver filigree necklace. Brooke had brought it back from the Far East as a gift for their mother several years ago. She had treasured it, keeping it beside her bed when she could no longer bear even so little weight against her skin. It seemed right that Lucy should have it now. Lucy touched it gingerly with just one finger but made no move to take it out of the box. 'Would you like to put it on?'

'I might break it.'

Bron shook her head. 'No, you won't. It's tougher than it looks. Like Proto. Trust me.' And she lifted it out of the box and fastened it about the child's neck. 'There. Have you got a mirror?'

Lucy gave her a look that suggested she had to be kidding. 'Not in here.' She leapt up, grabbing Bron's hand and tugging her to her feet. 'Come on. There's one next door.'

Next door was not, as Bron had imagined, the bathroom. It was Fitz's room.

As Bron stepped over the threshold, saw the huge antique sleigh bed with its thick, dark green quilt, she came to an abrupt halt as the image of Brooke and Fitz together, the image that had assaulted her earlier, came screaming back, robbing her of breath.

No. This wasn't where she should be. And she stepped back, cannoned into something, someone. Fitz. She tried to turn.

'Hey, steady!'

But it was too late—her bag flew out on its strap, catching a lamp and sending it flying from the walnut lowboy.

'Heavens, Brooke, you're a bag of nerves.' He held on to her while she gathered herself.

'I'm sorry,' she said. 'I'm so sorry.'

'It doesn't matter. It's just a lamp.' He bent to pick it up. 'No damage.' He replaced it on the lowboy. 'See?'

She shook her head. That wasn't why she was sorry. This was all wrong. She shouldn't have come. Fitz took her by the shoulders, looked at her with concern. 'Dear God, you're trembling.'

'She thought you were going to shout at her,' Lucy said, taking her hand. 'It's all right, Mummy. He never shouts.'

'Never?' Bron said shakily.

'Never. He just counts to ten and picks up the pieces.'

She looked up, met Fitz's eyes. They were full of questions. 'Does ten do it every time?' she asked quickly.

'Mostly,' he said, after a moment. 'Mostly.'

CHAPTER SIX

'LOOK, Daddy. Mummy's given me a present.' Lucy innocently cut through an atmosphere that was suddenly treacle-thick as she lifted the delicate necklace to show it to him.

Fitz let his hands fall from Bron's shoulders and hunkered down so that he could admire it properly.

'It's very pretty—'

'It belonged to Lucy's grandmother,' Bron said, cutting off the inevitable follow-up warning that she would have to take great care of it, be careful not to break it. She had so hated that as a child—the attachment of guilt utterly destroyed the pleasure of the gift. She had never broken things on purpose, she had tried desperately hard not to and she was quite sure Lucy did the same. 'She would have wanted her to have it.'

'Belonged?' He glanced up. Then straightened. 'I remember that your mother was an invalid—'

153

Was that the excuse Brooke had given him for not keeping Lucy? That her mother was sick, couldn't cope? But if Brooke had come home, brought Lucy with her, they would have managed. Somehow they would have managed. But then Brooke would not have been able to leave, to take that wonderful job... 'She died last week.'

He threw her a startled look. 'Brooke, I'm so sorry. I had no idea.' She shook her head. 'That was why you were at home? I thought it odd—' He suddenly realised that they had Lucy's rapt attention. 'I've made the tea, sweetheart. Why don't you go down and put the cakes on a plate?'

Lucy, still holding Bron's hand, stood her ground for a moment, but she must have seen something in her father's face that made her think twice about challenging him. 'All right, but don't be *long*,' she warned, before bouncing towards the stairs.

'Slowly, Lucy.' The words had the resigned quality of those often spoken but rarely heeded and he half turned, listening until he was sure she was safely down. Then he turned back to

Bron, 'To be honest I hadn't expected to find you in Maybridge—'

'It must have been your lucky day.'

'Brooke—'

He seemed perplexed, confused, and she realised that he was going to apologise for behaving the way he had when she was undoubtedly grieving. Well, Brooke wasn't grieving and Bron would be ashamed to accept his apology on her own account. 'Fitz, I came to see Lucy.' She made a move to pass him but he didn't give way. 'There isn't a lot of time,' she said, just a little desperately. 'My train leaves at six…'

He fastened his hand about her arm. 'There'll be another at seven.' Had he taken the trouble to check, or was he just guessing? Then, 'Please, Brooke, you must see that you can't just waltz into Lucy's life and out of it again.'

'Lucy said—'

'In her letter. I know. But that wasn't what she meant, you must have known that. We both knew it. Heaven knows I didn't want you in our lives. I was afraid that once you'd seen

her you'd do everything in your power to take
her back—well, it seems I was wrong about
that. But Lucy won't be able to let go that
easily.' His eyes gleamed with the intensity of
a man who knew he was demanding the impossible. 'A card at Christmas won't do it,
Brooke. She deserves more from you.'

And she thought she had been 'showing
him' when she'd accepted Lucy's invitation.
'You've changed your tune since this morning.
Whatever happened to that four o'clock drive
to the station?'

'I was wrong. I admit it. You're good with
her, Brooke. I never expected that.'

No, he'd made that plain enough. And now
he was giving her an opening, giving Brooke
an opening, to admit that she was wrong as
well and miraculously turn into a wonderful,
caring mother overnight. Bron wished she
could wave a magic wand and make it so. She
couldn't do that but it was another chance to
introduce the wonderful, caring aunt routine.
'Would an aunt help?' she offered.

'An aunt?' He stared at her for a moment as
if he didn't quite believe his ears, and for just

a moment she thought he was going to grab the idea with both hands. 'An *aunt*?' he repeated in disbelief, and suddenly she wasn't so sure. 'Good God, Brooke, Lucy has ''aunts'' by the truckload. It's a mother she needs. Someone all of her own. You.'

His reaction was so vehement, so unexpected that Bron's rosy picture of being Lucy's surrogate mother deflated as rapidly as a pricked balloon. She'd had this firm vision in her head, a vision of a little girl with no female relatives, no one but her father to care for her, a child longing for just one person to call her own and who would come to know her and love her for herself. And with that deflation Bron saw another truth: she hadn't just been thinking of Lucy, she had been thinking of herself. She had been the one needing to be loved, wanted. She had been the one looking for someone to fill the aching void.

How could she have been so *selfish*?

How could she have been so *stupid*?

Of course Fitz must have sisters, cousins, a mother in all probability. The only person Lucy needed in this world was her mother.

Brooke. Not some unknown woman who would be just one more female relative.

She had to get out of there. As quickly as possible. And she had to talk to Brooke. Her sister was going to have some tough explaining to do when she finally got home, some really outstanding reason why she couldn't step into the opening Bron had made for her in her daughter's life.

'I know you've a full life, a busy life,' Fitz said, dragging her back from contemplation of what she would do, to the enormity of what she'd done. 'But surely it isn't too much to ask? Surely you can find just a little time for Lucy? She's your daughter, Brooke.'

What on earth could she say? No, she's not? Expose herself to his anger at her deception? Because he would be angry, really angry, and she wouldn't blame him. Eventually he would calm down, maybe even understand what she'd tried to do, but by then it would be too late. Lucy's day would be in ruins and everything she had done would have been for nothing. For the moment she was trapped in a net of her own weaving.

'Stay.' The hand on her arm slid down to hers and he took it, held it. The most innocent of contacts, so why were there charges like tiny electric shocks flickering through her entire body? Her date, that boy at her eighteenth birthday party, hadn't managed that kind of response and he'd had her entire body to play with, but then they had both been virgins; maybe it took practice to make hand-holding seem like sin. He raised his other hand to cradle her cheek. Oh, dear God! *Had she wanted this too?* Brooke's child? Brooke's lover?

The hot burning memory of his kiss singing in her head mocked her. Of course she had.

'Stay,' he repeated, and the dark chocolate voice was melting her resistance, sapping her will. How could he invest one word with such temptation?

Then his lips touched the corner of her mouth. As a kiss it was as innocent as the hand holding, so why were her insides reduced to hot jelly—hot jelly that was demanding she say *Yes!*

'Brooke?'

Brooke. One word. It was obviously the day for charged one word sentences. Life-changing sentences. This one at least had the desired effect of bringing her sharply to her senses. What on earth was she thinking of? Fitz didn't want *her*; like Lucy he wanted, needed, her sister. He needed her to commit to Lucy and, since he clearly knew her sister a lot better than she did, he was using the one weapon in his arsenal that he was sure would work.

She'd never understood about the road to hell being paved with good intentions but suddenly it was all very clear. Her intentions had been good but, overwhelmed by emotion, by her own need, she hadn't stopped to think them through.

It wouldn't have mattered so much if she had resisted a totally reprehensible urge to irritate Fitz by accepting what she had believed to be his wholly insincere invitation to tea. If she had insisted he take her straight to the station when they had left school she would be safely on her way home by now, her good deed done. But she hadn't wanted to leave.

Well, now she must. She had to get out right now. Out of his bedroom. Out of his house. She had to leave as quickly as she could and think of some way to persuade Brooke to come back here with her once she was back in England. Then she could make a clean breast of what she had done and with Brooke there, well, it wouldn't matter what Fitz thought of her.

'Daddy! This tea is getting cold!' Lucy's bossy little voice rose from the foot of the stairs.

'We're just coming, princess,' he said, not taking his eyes off her, and the way he was looking at her was doing unspeakable things to her, turning up her thermostat so that she was beginning to sizzle. Did he want Brooke to stay for Lucy, or for himself? 'Well?' he asked, his voice so soft, so seductive.

She struggled to answer him through a throat stuffed with hot gravel. 'No…' Then she groaned silently. How on earth could she have made that uncompromising word sound so utterly indecisive, so like… yes…

What had happened to her will, the determination that had seen her through the long, lonely years of caring?

Fitz had happened.

He had stormed into her kitchen and kissed her brains out; that had to be it. That had to be why she hadn't been thinking straight ever since. 'No.' She tried repeating the word. Not much better. 'I can't stay,' she added, but she must have been anything but convincing because her words had no effect on Fitz.

He was still looking at her as if he was planning to eat her, very slowly, but hadn't quite decided where to begin. It took a supreme effort of will before Bron could tear her gaze away from his for long enough to marshall her senses, and once she'd managed it she didn't hang about, making a move to push past him.

She'd reckoned without her hand still entwined in his and his grip tightened as he refused to let her go. Bron swallowed desperately, knowing that he wanted her to look at him, knowing that if she did he would kiss her again, and if she kissed him again she would be damned. So she continued to stare at the wall, staring at the faded stripes of the wall-paper until they began to merge and she thought she would faint.

'We'd better go down or we'll be in trou-ble,' he said at last, releasing her, stepping back so that she could pass without touching him.

She couldn't speak for James Fitzpatrick, but Bronte suspected that she was already in trouble. Deep trouble.

Lucy had loaded a tray with a paper plate piled with thinly cut sandwiches, another of little an-gel cakes. Their 'wings' were just a little wob-bly and Bron glanced down, carefully avoiding the tell-tale treacherous smudges of butter-cream that spattered the floor as she added the teapot.

'I'll carry the tray, shall I? It'll be heavy.'

'Wait.' Fitz lifted a mug from a stand, poured himself a cup, spooned in a generous helping of sugar. 'I'll leave you to your pic-nic.' He glanced at his watch. 'You're still catching the six o'clock train?'

He was offering her one more chance. 'Yes.' The first time the word was barely audible. She cleared her throat. 'Yes, I am.'

He nodded. 'Be ready to leave at five-thirty, then. The traffic will be heavy once we get down into the town.'

'I could easily get a taxi…' Her voice trailed away. She'd often wondered what a 'steely glance' was like. Now she knew. Cold and about as much fun as a bayonet. 'Five-thirty,' she repeated obediently. But having made his point he had lost interest, picked up the camcorder and was already halfway across the kitchen. She watched him through the open doorway, long legs carrying him across the courtyard, his dark curls ruffled by the breeze that was coming off the sea. She watched him disappear into a long red-brick building that had once been an old coach house and stables. Only then did she pick up the tea tray and give Lucy a big smile. 'Lead the way, sweetheart.'

Fitz stared at the magazine on the desk in front of him. It was the latest television programme guide and Brooke was the featured cover ce-

lebrity, trailing her new series. She was in
some rainforest, no make-up, her hair clinging
damply to her forehead. Ten minutes earlier he
had been touching that face, holding that arm,
his lungs full of the complicated mixture of
scents that were her personal signature. So
why did he feel as if he were looking at someone entirely different?

He rubbed the back of his neck, eased his
shoulders, looked out of the small window that
overlooked the garden. Lucy was chattering,
nineteen to the dozen as she always did, her
arms, her hands, moving in those great sweeping gestures that were such a danger to anything fragile, but which were so expressive.
She talked with her hands almost as eloquently
as she did with her voice.

He couldn't hear what she was saying but
he knew her so well, had heard her telling anyone who would listen her entire life story, everything important that had happened to her
since the moment she had discovered that she
could talk.

She would be telling Brooke all about Josie
who had been her best friend since the day

they had started at nursery school. Josie, who
hadn't had a mother either, then. Now her father had remarried and she had not only a
brand new mother, but an infant stepbrother, a
dog and another sibling on the way. He wasn't
sure whether Lucy envied Josie the baby
brother or the dog most. He suspected it was
the dog. He hoped it was the dog. Maybe, after
the holiday, he would take her to the rescue
centre and let her choose one of her own. It
wasn't much compensation for not having a
mother of her own, but that appeared to be
beyond him.

She would tell Brooke about school, too,
about the time she'd broken her wrist, about
their first visit to the cinema when she'd tipped
an ice cream down the back of the lady sitting
in front of them and how she'd wrecked the
dancing school performance at the town hall
so that *Madame* had begged him to find some
other way to occupy her Saturday mornings.
At least in the swimming pool her arms were
actively occupied.

He watched Brooke, her face enrapt as Lucy
spilled it all out. What was it? What was it

about her that plucked at something deep inside him? Tugged at his heartstrings—

He turned again to the photograph on the magazine cover. It was plain, unadorned, the lines were undisguised by make-up or artifice... That was one of the reasons women loved her as much as her male admirers. She knew how to look drop-dead gorgeous, but she wasn't afraid to be seen looking tired, sweaty, her age...

He stopped. Could that be it? Could the difference be something as simple as that? Where her youthful beauty had simply been the target of his lustful ambition, was it possible that he was responding to her maturity in an entirely new and unexpected way?

Shaken, he sat back. He had assumed the sweaty scientist bit was pretty much part of the act, but maybe it wasn't. Had she changed that much? Had he? He closed his eyes, letting his mind run back to the first time he'd seen her. He'd been planning a fly-on-the-wall documentary about student life and he'd been walking around the campus with a video camera looking for half a dozen students to feature.

Brooke had been sitting on a bench by herself, bundled up in a thick scarlet coat, tossing crumbs from a roll she had lost interest in to a bunch of half-tame sparrows and glancing from time to time at her wrist-watch, obviously waiting for someone.

Her fair hair had been like sunshine on that cold, grey day and when she had smiled to herself at some secret thought he'd known he'd found his star, the hook, the girl everyone would tune in week after week to watch.

She had started as he had joined her on the bench, for a moment her face lighting up as she'd turned to him, until she'd realised he wasn't whoever she had been waiting for. Not exactly an ego-trip, but he hadn't been there to have his ego stroked. He had introduced himself, given her his card so that she could check up on him, reassure herself that he wasn't simply some creep on the prowl for a pretty girl to lure into something nasty, and he had explained what he'd been doing. And the lights had come back on.

Everything about her had been perfect for the documentary. Her father had died, her mother an invalid and she'd been struggling on a grant with no financial help from home. He'd offered her a fee for the inconvenience of having a film crew following her around, but she'd have done it for nothing, he knew. She'd recognised an opportunity to sell herself and her smile had returned, lighting up the day. That was the moment he had determined that, if he was going to do nothing else for himself that year, he was going to have Brooke Lawrence.

Experience had taught him that it would be easy. He had worked in the magic world of television and the problem had lain not in attracting girls, but in dodging the dull ones.

He pulled a face at the memory of the man he had been, guilt stirring at such careless arrogance. He was a father now, with a daughter of his own to protect. Maybe judo lessons… Then he caught himself grinning. Lucy's elbows were already lethal weapons, she didn't need lessons.

As it happened, Brooke hadn't either. She'd called him, said she'd changed her mind. She'd been too busy, it had been her final year and she'd been desperate for a first—the excuses had streamed out. He hadn't been entirely convinced, and when his camera had picked her out at more than one party he'd sought her out in the Students' Union bar. She might not have been in his documentary but that hadn't meant she'd had to stay out of his bed.

She'd seemed pleased to see him, he'd thought. He'd bought her a drink and she'd flirted with him, but he'd quickly discovered that she'd flirted with everyone, had men standing in line for the privilege, but a mild flirtation was all she'd been interested in. Then, at the Christmas Ball, she'd finally fallen into his arms. Literally. He'd thought it had been his lucky night.

He stared at the photograph, traced her wide, smiling mouth with the edge of his thumb. Just how wrong could a man be? And at the same time wholly right.

His gaze tracked across her face until he was staring at the point below her brow. There was no sign of the scar. Airbrushed out. Except why would they do that? This wasn't a formal portrait; the scar wasn't unsightly. It would have amplified that sweat-stained, fresh-from-the-jungle look she favoured.

Her eyes looked darker too. Well, that could be the light, or the printing. So what was it?

He reached for the camcorder, ejected the cassette and slotted it into the VCR, fast-forwarding it to the point where Brooke was handing out the prizes. He glanced from the magazine cover to the film and back again, ran it a second time. The picture did nothing for him, while the film... Well, the film had movement, action, life going for it. But then so had her television programmes and he hadn't felt this hot, yearning need for the television image.

No. It was something else. He was missing something...

He opened the drawer of his desk and took out the envelope with Lucy's birth certificate, the lawyer's papers giving him sole custody, the photographs he'd taken of Brooke before she'd changed her mind about appearing in the documentary. He tipped them onto the desk, but before he could do more the door behind him banged open. 'Daddy, I've had the most brilliant idea!'

He swept the whole lot back into the drawer and closed it before he turned. Lucy was framed in the doorway, her face alight. Brooke was standing behind her shaking her head desperately. He looked back at Lucy. 'Well, don't keep me in suspense. What is it?'

'Mummy can come to France with us! Tell her she must. There's absolutely loads of room at the farmhouse and it's near the beach and—well…it would be brilliant…' There was a moment of absolute silence. 'Wouldn't it?'

Brilliant. He glanced at Brooke and a stampede of testosterone suggested that it might be very brilliant indeed. But she gave another small emphatic shake of her head. She obviously didn't think so. Fitz discovered he had to clear his throat before he could speak. 'I'm sure your mother has other plans for the summer, Lucy.'

'No.' Eight years old and in no mood to be thwarted, she marched across to the desk and picked up the television magazine. 'There's an interview with her in here. I read it…' she turned to Bron '...and you said you're going to be home all summer. You're not going to Pata...Pata...Pata-somewhere for months.'

'She'll still be busy, Lucy,' Fitz snapped. Then, when he saw her face, he continued more gently. 'Lots of people will want to meet her and talk to her. And trips to Pata-anywhere take a lot of time to organise.'

'She could come for a week,' Lucy said stubbornly. 'That's not long.'

Fitz looked up to where Brooke was pleading silently with him to back her up. Well, he'd pleaded too, but she hadn't listened to him. 'You could come for a week,' he repeated, through with making excuses for her. He'd done everything he could...more perhaps than he should have to bring them together. Now Lucy would have to come to terms with the fact that she'd got exactly what she'd asked for, nothing more, nothing less and that was it. There was nothing else on offer. The sooner she understood that, the better.

Bron stared at the two of them. One face bright with hope, the other, she was certain, taunting her. But maybe it would be all right.

She hadn't read the interview with Brooke—
she never bothered these days, knowing that it
would have been done months ago, long before
Bron had left the country, would be a regur-
gitation of everything she had ever read about
her sister. But according to Lucy she would be
home soon. If that was so then maybe, just
maybe, with the saints on her side and a following wind she would be able to *make* everything all right. 'I'll have to check my diary,'
she said. 'When are you going?'

'The last week of the month.' And Fitz tilted
a dark, sardonic brow at her. He thought she
was simply putting off saying no. Well, he
could think what he liked.

'I'll see what I can sort out and give you a
call.' She glanced at her watch. 'I think I'd
better go now, Fitz. I don't want to miss my
train.'

It wasn't quite half-past five, but he didn't
protest. 'Of course you don't. I'm sure you've
got something desperately important to do this
evening.' He nodded towards the television
magazine. 'Dinner with the Director-General?
Some celebrity do at Number Ten?'

'Actually I have to sort out my mother's things.'

It was a cheap shot, but then his had been bargain basement, Bron thought furiously as she gathered her bag from the kitchen. Then, as she stepped outside, took one more look around her at the view, at the house, storing it all up in case she never saw it again, her anger evaporated. She just felt desperately sad.

When she turned back to the car Lucy was already strapped into her seat belt in the rear and Fitz was standing by the passenger door waiting for her, watching her. His fingers were tucked into the tight pockets of his jeans in a slightly aggressive stance, but it wasn't his stance that bothered her, it was his eyes. They were slightly narrowed, as if he didn't quite believe what he was seeing but didn't understand why. And he was right—Brooke would never have spent an evening sorting out the clutter accumulated by her mother over a lifetime spent in the same house. Not just cheap, but stupid.

'I'll sit with Lucy,' she said quickly. Without a word, he turned and opened the rear door, holding it for her while she climbed in beside Lucy, while she fastened her seat belt. And still his eyes were on her, looking just a little bit too hard, looking just a little bit too thoughtful. 'Fitz?' Her voice was sharper than she had intended but it did the job and he stepped back, shut the door.

As they made their way down into Bramhill, Lucy's hand sought hers, held onto it. 'Can I write to you?' she whispered. 'You don't have to write back.'

Disingenuous was the word, Bron thought tenderly as she squeezed Lucy's hand. 'That would be lovely.' And she had her own agenda, every bit as foxy as Lucy's. What, after all, could be more appealing than a letter from Lucy, a letter full of chatter, full of excitement, full of hope, to demonstrate to Brooke exactly what she was missing?

'And ring you sometimes?' She hesitated. 'Please!'

Bron had nothing to write on but the envelope that Lucy's letter had been in. She quickly wrote down her number and gave it to her. 'You must ask Daddy first,' she warned.

'I will.'

'What are you two plotting in the back there?' Fitz turned as they drew up in front of the station.

'Nothing,' Bron said quickly, but gave Lucy's hand another little squeeze. 'No, don't get out,' she said. 'I hate those long, drawn-out goodbyes, don't you?' She made her voice deliberately bright.

Lucy leaned out of the window as she closed the door behind her. 'You won't forget about coming on holiday with us?'

'No. I won't forget.' She kissed Lucy's cheek and turned quickly away before they were both in floods of tears. But there was no immediate escape as Fitz rounded the front of the car and joined her on the pavement.

'I'll ring you about France,' he said.

'Give me a few days.'

'I'd give you forever if I thought it would make any difference.' Then, while she was still trying to catch her breath, he thumbed away the treacherous tear that had defiantly spilled over onto her cheek, betraying her. 'This is getting to be a habit,' he said. Then, 'Take care, Brooke.' And he held her for a moment, kissed her cheek. It was hours since he'd shaved and the faint stubble grated against her chin. It felt wonderful.

'Oy! That's a no-waiting area.'

Fitz looked up, nodded to the man bearing down on them. 'I'm just going. Try and make France if you can.' He didn't wait for her answer, but jumped up into the Range Rover and pulled away before she could do much more than offer a tentative wave. A last, slightly forlorn goodbye. Then as she turned to enter the station she heard Lucy's voice.

'I love you, Mummy!' She spun around. Fitz had been held up at the entrance to the station and Lucy was leaning out of the back window, waving frantically. 'I love you!'

Bron was frozen to the spot, unable to wave, unable to call out, and while she stood there the Range Rover slipped into the rush hour traffic and was swallowed up. 'I love you, too, sweetheart,' she whispered. 'I love both of you.'

As she turned she saw the man who had shouted at Fitz for parking in a no-waiting zone staring at her. She stared right back before striding into the station.

She bought a first-class ticket and because she had ten minutes to wait before her train, because she was attracting attention and couldn't bear the thought of having to talk to anyone, be polite, be *Brooke*, she went into the newsagent's. If she was looking at the maga zines she wouldn't have to avoid the eyes of strangers as they flickered with recognition, as they plucked up courage to speak to her. She didn't want to speak to anyone.

The magazine covers screamed lurid confession stories of the I - stole - my - daughter's - boyfriend/gambled - my - way - into jail/ had - a - baby - and - I - didn't - know - I - was - pregnant type. Bron stared at them. She wondered how I - pretended - to - be - my - sister - and - fell - in - love - with - the - father-of - her - baby would go down. They'd probably fall over themselves to buy it. If she included the name Brooke Lawrence she probably wouldn't have to worry about money for the rest of her life.

But she did have to worry. Lucy's problems had pushed it to the back of her mind, but she now owned half of a house that she couldn't afford to live in, had no job and no prospects, not even a carer's allowance, pitiful though that had been. It was about time she started worrying about herself, and concentrating on that at least offered the possibility of diverting her mind from Lucy. From Fitz. From the touch of stubble against her cheek.

Bron lifted her hand to her cheek, hurriedly brushed away a tear, blinking furiously. God, she hated women who wept all the time… She took a deep breath, regained control and then, abandoning perusal of the magazines, she bought a spiral-bound notebook and promised herself she would have thought of twenty good ideas on how she would spend the rest of her life before she reached home.

Planning her own future might just take her mind off the fact that she would probably never see Lucy again. She had no hopes of it taking her mind off Fitz.

CHAPTER SEVEN

THE telephone was ringing. Bronte searched through the complex maze of pockets in her sister's bag for the front door key, seething with frustration. For heaven's sake, she'd had the wretched thing in her hand! Then she remembered putting the key in her jacket pocket when she'd paid the taxi driver. *Brooke's jacket pocket, Brooke's bag,* she reminded herself grimly as she slotted the key into the lock.

There was to be no more playing at pretend. She'd promised herself that as Fitz had driven away from Bramhill Station with the warm impression of his mouth sending her heart into overdrive, with Lucy shouting, 'I love you, Mummy' from the back window. If Lucy had been her own child she couldn't have felt more anguish at that moment. If Fitz had been her lover she couldn't have felt the wrench more painfully.

No more games. The edges were getting too blurred.

She opened the door and raced to the phone. It stopped ringing the moment she put her hand on the receiver. She picked it up anyway, dialled one four seven one, but whoever had called had withheld their number. She replaced the receiver with a shrug. It couldn't possibly have been Lucy, it was far too late. And there was no reason for Fitz to call.

She tossed her sister's many-pocketed leather bag on a chair, peeled off her jacket, combed her fingers through her hair and eased her shoulders. She ached from the tension of a long and difficult day, from a train journey with missed connections that had taken forever. As she stretched she caught sight of herself in the mirror.

Brooke or Bronte? It wasn't just the edges that were blurred...the whole image was becoming dangerously smudged. It was scary how much like Brooke she actually looked, she thought. One expensive haircut, a change of clothes, a make-up job that had taken more than her usual cursory thirty seconds with a lipstick, had been all it had taken to transform her into her sister.

Why hadn't she noticed, really noticed, before? Why didn't people ever comment? Because she was just stay-at-home Bron who lived in jeans and T-shirts and whom everyone took for granted? Bron, who no one ever looked at twice? Or was it because next to the real thing she simply faded into the wallpaper?

Well, not any more.

Not that she had any intention of keeping up the lookalike pose—she had no desire to turn herself into a second-best copy of her sister.

'So, what are you going to do with yourself, Bronte Lawrence?' Her reflection had no answer to that. Well, she had never expected it to be that easy and the notebook she had bought at the station was still pretty much blank but for pages of doodles. She had only one thing on her mind. Two things. Lucy and Fitz. Until she had sorted out the problems her foolish meddling had created, how could she think about her own life?

In the meantime what she needed was a long soak in a hot bath rid to herself of Brooke, her scent, her make-up. She needed to give Bronte Lawrence a chance. She was no longer that anonymous creature, a carer, and she had no intention of spending her life being Brooke Lawrence's dull sister. She had brains, too, she was a person in her own right with a life of her own.

The reflection wasn't quite done with her, though. *Sure*, it seemed to say. *Some life*. She pulled a face at it, turned away. She *would* have her own life. She'd have to take a course of some sort, get some training before she could do anything, that much she'd worked out for herself. At eighteen she'd been all set to follow Brooke to university and there was no reason why she couldn't still do that. But the idea of three years studying biology held no appeal now. No one would remember that she had always been going to do that, they would simply think she was trying to copy her sister—*be* her sister.

If she'd been going to do something different it might not have been so bad, but now everything she did would have to stand comparison with Brooke. Short of finding Bigfoot and bringing it back alive, there wasn't anything she could do that would compete.

She yawned and practically dislocated her jaw as the phone started to ring again, making her jump. She picked it up, rattled off the number.

'Brooke?'

'Fitz? Is something wrong?' Her heart was pounding because the phone had made her jump. That was all.

'No. I was just checking to make sure you got home safely.'

He sounded as if he cared. Well, he would. He wanted something from her, something she couldn't give. 'I'm quite capable of catching a train without someone to hold my hand,' she replied sharply.

'I know. I was just—'

Just what? Her stomach had executed a series of perfect somersaults at the sound of his voice. If he could do that with just his voice it might be better not to ask that question. He thought he was talking to Brooke, the mother of his child, not a woman he didn't know. 'Did you ring about five minutes ago?' she asked, just to stop him.

'No.' That wasn't the answer she had expected and she frowned, checked her watch. It was nearly ten o'clock. Who else would be phoning so late? 'Brooke, will you at least think about coming to France? Please. Just for Lucy.'

Ask *me*, she moaned silently and leaned against the wall just to feel the coolness of the white paint against her cheek. Ask *me*. Just for you. 'I'll get back to you, Fitz. Goodnight.' And she swiftly replaced the receiver before she could blurt out her feelings. After all, he was dealing with a mirror image. Those soft words weren't meant for her and she refused to listen to the little devil who whispered that she could go to France, could take the week he offered her and everything that went with it and that he would never know she wasn't Brooke.

She wasn't that lost to common sense. The difference between a woman who had been his lover and a woman who hadn't done more than make the token gesture of losing her virginity as part of the growing-up process would scarcely be lost on any man. And James Fitzpatrick wasn't just any man.

She'd made enough mistakes in the last twenty-four hours without making that one.

Tomorrow she'd phone Brooke's office, find out when she would be home and then try and work out exactly how she was going to explain to her sister what she had done; more to the point, how she was going to persuade her sister to take up where she had left off. Fitz was obviously still in love with her, no matter how unwilling he was to admit it. Maybe, just maybe, it would all simply fall into place.

The empty house didn't exactly rock with hollow laughter at that thought, but when Bronte dropped a jar of cleanser in the sink and it was the sink that cracked it seemed like a very bad omen.

Fitz replaced the receiver. He wasn't sure why he had phoned, only that he couldn't get Brooke out of his mind. And his urging her to join them in France had less to do with Lucy than a disconcerting desire to spend time with her himself, get to the bottom of the way she had managed to stir him up. It wasn't just that careless sex appeal she used on the masses. He wasn't touched by that—he knew her too well for that, knew all the games she played...or thought he did.

He crossed to the sideboard and poured himself a Scotch with hands that were less than steady.

Why?

Lust didn't last. It hadn't lasted five minutes when he had discovered the truth. This was something entirely different, something that engaged every part of him. His mind, his heart...He took a long swallow of the Scotch. It hit the back of his throat, hot and fierce, but it didn't dull the sense of impending heartache, not just for Lucy, but for himself.

He'd looked at Brooke with Lucy today and seen a new woman, someone quite different from the girl whose nails had left marks in his hand for weeks as, in the throes of labour, she'd screamed abuse at mankind in general and him in particular for putting her through such a nightmare.

He carried his glass upstairs, pushed open his bedroom door and reached for the lamp switch. It didn't come on. The bulb must have broken when she'd knocked it over. He ignored the main switch; he didn't want that much light. Instead he left the door open so that the light spilled in from the landing and crossed to his bathroom, put down the glass, turned on the taps.

There was a spare bulb in the cupboard and he took it out, changed the broken one and switched the lamp on. And as he stood there, exactly where she had stood, he caught the ghostly imprint of her fragrance and it raised his skin to goose-flesh. He closed his eyes and he could almost imagine that she was standing next to him, waiting for him to take her in his arms, hold her, kiss her...

He opened his eyes with a long, shuddering sigh. He was behaving like a man lost in love, for heaven's sake, behaving like a fool. He should be grateful that she was behaving entirely as he had predicted. Except that she hadn't behaved entirely as he'd predicted. It hadn't been an act. She had been genuinely moved by Lucy, genuinely loving. And her eyes had displayed none of the mockery he had anticipated, but something entirely different, something that had tugged at a well of need so deep within him that it hurt...

He stopped the thought right there. It would have been so easy to present Lucy with a series of 'aunts,' there had been no shortage of offers, but Lucy had always come first and until he met a woman who genuinely cared about her he had determined that that was the way it would have to stay.

He looked in on her, checked that after the excitement of the day she had finally managed to get to sleep. As the light from the landing fell across her bed he saw that Brooke's necklace was still clasped about her neck and he went in, unfastened it, let the necklace lie for a moment across the palm of his hand. Then he touched it to his cheek.

Nothing. Well, what had he expected? A Bach choral? A crash of thunder? Instant orgasm?

Angry with himself, he dropped the necklace on Lucy's bedside table beside a used and very dog-eared envelope addressed in Lucy's handwriting. Miss B Lawrence… It must have held the letter she'd sent to Brooke and now Brooke had written her telephone number on it and given it back.

He replaced it, then went back to his bathroom. He turned off the taps, picked up the glass and raised it to himself in the mirror over the sink. 'Once a fool, always a fool,' he muttered, but before he could swallow the whisky the glass, wet with steam, slipped from his fingers, shattering in the sink. 'Damn!' He stared at it for a moment and then, quite suddenly, he laughed. 'It must be catching.'

The telephone woke Bron. She'd lain awake half the night as Lucy, Fitz, Brooke, all of them, had tramped in an endless circular procession through her head. It had already been showing light through the chink in her curtains before she had finally dropped off to sleep what seemed like minutes before.

She groaned as the insistent ringing dragged her from sleep, rolled over and looked at the clock. Blinked. It was nearly ten o'clock. Ten o'clock! She hadn't been in bed that late since, since… She couldn't remember the last time she been in bed at that time in the morning. She flung back the bedclothes and, not bothering with a wrap, raced down the stairs.

'Hello,' she said breathlessly, afraid that whoever it was would hang up.

'Miss Lawrence?' Not Fitz. Her stomach caved with disappointment. 'Miss Brooke Lawrence?' And suddenly she wasn't thinking about Fitz. There was something about the oh-so-charming voice that made her cautious. The woman might just be selling double glazing, but she didn't think so.

'No. I'm sorry, you've got the wrong number.'

'Then you must be her sister,' the woman continued quickly before she could hang up. 'Bronte, isn't it? Such unusual names you have.' Definitely not double glazing. It was a journalist. From time to time they called, hoping to get an interview, a 'behind-the-scenes' look at Brooke's family. Maybe they'd heard about their mother…were hoping to dig up something unpleasant… 'Can you spare me a moment? I'm Angie Makepeace from the *Sentinel—* '

That appalling rag? No way. 'I'm sorry, Miss Makepeace, but my sister isn't here and I have no idea when she will be. If you'll excuse me, there's someone at the front door.' And without waiting for permission she put down the receiver. There had been a time when she would have worried about telling a lie like that, but not these days. A couple of years earlier there had been a rumour of romance between Brooke and some television personality and she'd been beseiged by the press who, unable to contact her sister, had been prepared to try any avenue to get what they'd wanted.

She'd finally had to ask for a new telephone number just to get any peace for her mother. It had been the kind of nuisance that had left her without a conscience as far as the press were concerned.

She rang Brooke's office to leave a message on the answering machine but her call was answered by Brooke's secretary. On a Saturday morning? Then she shrugged. Maybe they always worked on Saturdays—what would she know? She explained about Angie Makepeace's call.

'Dear God, how do they find out?'

'Find out what?'

'Oh, nothing...forget it. Have you heard from her?' The woman sounded distracted.

'No. I left messages with everyone I could think of, but she hasn't contacted me. Why, have you mislaid her?'

She laughed, but without much conviction, Bron thought. 'I should warn you that Angie Makepeace might not be the only call you get from the press, Bronte.' Then, 'You didn't say anything, did you?'

A cold, clammy hand seemed to have gripped the back of her neck. 'About what?' she asked.

'Nothing. Nothing. There'll be an announcement later in the week.'

'It's business, then? Not personal?'

'The less you know the better, Bronte.'

Okay. For just a moment she thought that they might have heard about her trip to Bramhill and they'd be saying plenty about that if they knew. This had to be something else.

'I understand, but I really need to talk to her. Urgently.'

'I'll tell her.'

'When you find her.' More unconvincing laughter. 'In the meantime, since I'm even more in the dark than they are, will you kindly get the press off my back?'

Bron replaced the receiver, deep in thought. Maybe it wouldn't be that difficult to persuade her sister to give Lucy some of her time after all—perhaps even go to France with her for a few days. Fitz had shown her the way and her own clammy brush with anxiety had given her a fair indication of just how Brooke would respond to any suggestion of the newspapers being told about her daughter.

The only problem with that solution would lie in convincing her that her thoroughly nice little sister would betray her secret. It just didn't fit the image somehow. Of course, she could always simply pass on Fitz's threat... She could even use that as an excuse for what she'd done. Covering her sister's back would be much more in keeping with the boring old Bronte's goody-two-shoes image. She might even be persuaded to cover Bronte's back in return. Then she could go back as herself, later. A child could never have enough aunts, no matter what Fitz might think.

Fitz.

Suddenly the idea lost its appeal. Brooke and Lucy together she could handle. Brooke and Fitz… As the bile rose in her throat she began to breathe through her mouth. She would not be sick. She was an adult. It wasn't as if she hadn't known they were lovers; they had a daughter, for heaven's sake…

She only just made it to the bathroom.

Fitz enjoyed Saturday mornings, taking Lucy swimming. Most places he took her—Brownies, ballet before he had been asked to find her something more suited to her uncontrollable knees and elbows, the endless round of the birthday parties that small girls loved so much—he was the lone father amongst a host of harassed mothers running taxi services for their offspring. But taking the children to swimming lessons on Saturday mornings, getting the kids out from under their mothers' feet for a couple of hours, was strictly a chore for dads.

'Morning, Fitz.'

'Mike.' Josie's father joined him in the cafeteria overlooking the pool. He was grinning.

'That was some surprise you threw at sports day yesterday. Were you and Brooke Lawrence really...?' He nodded encouragingly but Fitz didn't answer and he shrugged. 'Silly question.'

Having made the point that it wasn't a subject for discussion, Fitz relented. 'I didn't see you there.'

'Oh, I wasn't, but Josie was full of it when she came home. Lucy had told her before but, well, everyone thought she was making it up, you know how kids are...'

'I know how Lucy is,' he said mildly.

'Yes, well... She must have enjoyed it. Lucy. And you'll have people queuing ten deep for the videos, I should think. Of course, we've got our own. Ellie insisted I get a camcorder when we had Jacob—'

'How is Ellie?' Fitz asked, pointedly changing the subject.

'Oh, fine. Josie's over the moon that she's going to have a sister this time. She's already decided on a name for her. Juliet.'

'Won't all those Js be confusing? You won't know which Miss J Castle is which.' And something inside his head seemed to shift, open a door, tantalise him with a glimmer of something—

'Probably,' Mike interrupted and the door slammed. 'But when we were expecting Jacob, asking Josie to name him helped make her a part of it, make her feel that the baby was hers as well, not a threat. You know how it is. You'll do anything. Anyway, she wanted him to have the same initial as she did. This time, well, she just expected it and we're happy with Juliet…'

'It's a pretty name.' Mike was saying too much, Fitz thought, covering his gaff in bringing up the tricky subject of Lucy's mother. But as the conversation drifted to the safer topics of business, the weather, what Mike had said about the video continued to worry at him.

Brooke's visit was supposed to have been private. No publicity. They hadn't discussed it, but he had assumed that she wouldn't want the press sniffing around any more than he did. Was that why Claire had asked him first whether Brooke would present the prizes? Had she been offering him a veto and he'd been too wrapped in his own thoughts to realise it?

Not that it would have mattered. Most parents would have taken some kind of camera to sports day and they would all have at least one photograph of Brooke handing out prizes. And they'd all be talking about it.

For a moment the prospect of publicity horrified him. Brooke would blame him, she would be furious, she would be forced into a situation where she would have to act out the role of doting mother… And with that realisation, the problem of having Brooke mad at him began to be outweighed by the advantages.

With her precious fans wide-eyed at the revelation that she had an eight-year-old daughter, Brooke might be persuaded to do anything to save her reputation—even be prepared to

spend a little time in France playing happy
families. He should be happy about that. So
why wasn't he? Why was he more bothered
about how miserable she'd be, than happy that
he would get what he wanted, what Lucy
wanted?

It didn't make sense. Why should he suddenly give a damn about Brooke's feelings?
When had she ever cared about his?

His lapse into sentimentality quite suddenly
infuriated him. He was almost tempted to send
a copy of the video to the *Sentinel* himself. But
he wouldn't. He wouldn't have to. He gave it
forty-eight hours at the outside before someone
offered their own film to their favourite tabloid, or a sheaf of photographs. All he had to
do was wait and leave Brooke to contact him.
Once he had her in France he'd find out just
how much she had changed, find out why she
had suddenly developed the power to make
him care…

He watched Lucy climb out of the pool, run
giggling with Josie towards the dressing
rooms, and he stood up. 'Time to go. I'll see
you next week, Mike.'

'Actually I'm taking Josie for a burger. Why don't you bring Lucy—'

He didn't have time to answer before a white-faced pool attendant came racing up the stairs. 'Mr Fitzpatrick! It's Lucy, she's had an accident!'

He pushed his way into the first aid room, crowded with too many people flapping about, and felt his blood turn to ice as he saw just how much of Lucy's blood had splashed on the floor, spreading everywhere as it mingled with the water dripping from her anxious friends. He flickered a sharp glance at the assistant who was pressing a wad of surgical dressing over the cut. 'What happened? Have you called an ambulance?'

'It's on its way. She was running by the side of the pool and slipped. I don't think it's serious, just a cut. Head wounds bleed a lot...' She turned away. 'Out, everyone out, right now!'

'Lucy?'

She was white-faced but conscious and she managed a smile as she focussed on him. 'I'm sorry, Daddy. I was running and...' And he'd told her a hundred times, a thousand times, not to.

'Hush, sweetheart. We'll have you stitched back together in no time.'

An hour later she was stitched and tucked up in bed in the local hospital. 'Do I *have* to stay? I'd much rather come home.'

'It's just overnight, princess. Just to make sure you aren't concussed, although how they'll ever know…' Lucy managed a giggle for him.

'I'm going to pop home now and fetch your nightie and toothbrush. Is there anything special you want me to bring? Proto?' he suggested.

'Daddy! I'm not a baby. Besides—' He waited. 'I gave Proto to Mummy.'

For what seemed like ages his mouth was working but no sound was coming out. Finally his vocal cords connected. 'Well,' he said. 'That was nice.' Nice? Dear God, his little girl had parted with her most treasured possession and that was all he could think of to say?

Brooke had better damn well appreciate it, that was all.

'Can I phone her?' He remembered the envelope by her bed.

'She'll just worry, sweetheart. We'll phone her when you get home and you can tell her all about it.' Although why she should be protected from the worry he couldn't have said.

'Miss Lawrence?' Another unfamiliar voice. 'It is you, isn't it?' the woman rushed on before she could answer. 'I'm Staff Nurse Harries at Bramhill General. Lucy asked me to ring you—'

'Lucy?' Bron thought she knew cold clammy hands, but this was on a different plane from anything she had experienced before. 'Tell me—'

'She was brought in half an hour ago. She's had a bit of an accident—'

'What kind of an accident? How badly is she hurt? Is Fitz with her?'

'Mr Fitzpatrick has gone home.' *Gone home?* Left her alone in hospital? Frightened, hurting? 'I don't think he wanted Lucy to worry you, but she was desperate and she asked me if I would call you and I was sure you would want to know. I saw you yesterday, you see, at the school.'

'Of course I want to know. I'm on my way.'

'She's in Ward Five. It's on the first floor.'

The receiver was half-way to the cradle when she snatched it back. 'Thank you!'

She raced upstairs, grabbed Brooke's trousers, the silky sweater, throwing them on, not worrying about her hair, or make-up, not even stopping to do up the laces of the desert boots. Then, picking up the leather bag she had used the day before but hadn't yet emptied and her car keys, she banged the door behind her and opened up the garage.

She jammed her key into the ignition but her battered Mini chose that moment to throw one of its frequent wobblies and refuse to start.

She turned the key, tried to coax the temperamental little monster into life, but it refused to co-operate. Beside her sat her sister's car. Fast, beautiful, not a scratch on its gleaming dark red paintwork. Brooke would kill her if anything happened to her beloved Jaguar.

But this was no time to be worrying about Brooke. Lucy needed her, wanted her.

She returned to the house, collected the keys from the dresser drawer and then had a moment of inspiration. At the foot of the stairs her foot caught on a trailing lace and she stumbled. She stopped, took a long breath. This was not the moment to have an accident of her own. She tied the laces, walked up the stairs, collected Proto and, her mind suddenly functioning on all cylinders, took the time to throw a change of clothing and her toothbrush into a bag.

When Bron slipped the key into the Jaguar's ignition, the engine responded like a kitten to a tickle, purring eagerly as she backed out of the garage and turned towards the coast. Then she put her foot down and the car more than lived up to its name.

She might be clumsy, might have trouble in working out which was her left from her right, but it was only the words that confused her, not the actual directions. There was little traffic, the roadworks were finished and Bron was in Bramhill in little more than an hour, the hospital ten minutes after that.

She reversed neatly into a parking space without thinking twice about it and asked the security guard at the entrance the way to Ward Five.

'I'll have to ask you to sign in,' he said. 'Security, you know.'

'Really?' She looked at the stream of people walking in through the main doors. Then she saw his smile and caught on. This wasn't the time to be squeamish about autographs. 'What's your name?'

'Gerry Marshall.'

She took the notepad he offered and wrote, 'To Gerry Marshall, keeping the world safe for Lucy,' then she signed 'Brooke Lawrence' and handed it to him. 'Now, will you tell me the way to Ward Five?'

He grinned and pointed the way, she thanked him and, suddenly conscious of the attention she was attracting, she tried very hard not to run.

'Mummy!' Lucy saw her the moment she entered the small ward. She sat up and then winced. Fitz, his back to the door, spun around and for just a moment, one precious moment, his eyes betrayed the fact that he was glad she had come.

He was more in control of his voice. 'Brooke! What on earth are you doing here?'

'Nice to see you too,' she murmured as she passed him. Then she bent over Lucy, kissed her cheek, stroked her unruly mop of hair back from her forehead while she checked out the neat row of stitches. On the drive to Bramhill her imagination had been working overtime. Clearly she had been putting herself through torment unnecessarily. 'Hi, angel. You look as if you've been in the wars.'

'I slipped. I was running by the poolside—' Bron sucked on her teeth dramatically '—I know. Daddy's always telling me, but Josie asked me to go for a burger with her and...well, you know...' She said that 'you know' as if they shared some special secret.

'Yes, darling, I know.' Been there, done that. Got the scars to prove it. Taking the child's hand, she propped herself on the bed beside her. 'But you see what's happened, don't you? Because you didn't do what Daddy said you've missed out on that burger altogether.'

Lucy, her eyes huge in her little face, grinned. 'Pretty dumb, huh?'

Fitz, standing behind her, appeared to be choking, but Bron didn't dare look, afraid she might laugh too. 'Pretty dumb,' she agreed solemnly. Then, 'Look, I've brought someone to see you.' She produced Proto from her bag. 'He thought you might need some company.'

Lucy giggled again. 'He didn't.' But she gave him a hug and tucked him down beside her.

A nurse popped her head around the door. 'What's all this? Laughing? I thought you were supposed to be resting, young lady,' she said with mock severity.

'My mummy came,' Lucy said.

'Did she, now?' Her badge said Staff Nurse Harries and Bron silently mouthed a thank you. 'Well, I have to take your temperature, so while I do that why don't you let your mummy and daddy go and have a cup of coffee? It's out in the hall. Help yourself.'

About to protest, Bron was seized firmly by the hand and led to the door. 'We'll be right back,' she called. 'Don't go away.'

Lucy just giggled. Fitz didn't say anything, simply poured a cup of coffee and handed it to her. 'She gave one of the nurses my number and asked her to phone me,' Bron explained.

'That's all it took?'

'She said you'd gone home—'

'And you thought you'd better race to your neglected daughter's bedside?'

'No!' She shrugged, awkwardly, stared into her coffee rather than meet those eyes. 'Well, yes.'

'I just went home to fetch her nightdress, Brooke. I wasn't away more than half an hour.'

'I'm sorry, I should have realised but I just panicked. Have they done an X-ray?'

'Just as a precaution but there's no damage.' He shrugged. 'Well, maybe to the swimming-pool floor... They just wanted to keep her in overnight to be on the safe side. Perhaps it will teach her to be more careful in future.' He didn't sound hopeful. 'How did you get here so fast? Not by train—'

'I drove.'

He checked his watch, lifted his eyebrows. 'And the car is still in one piece?'

'The car is fine,' she declared, then felt a slight wobble of nerves as she recalled the way she had edged the speed limit all the way, the casual manner in which she had backed into a tight parking slot. 'Not so much as a scratch.' Of course, she still had to get home. 'The sooner the better. 'I don't want to be a nuisance, Fitz. I'll say goodbye to Lucy and go.'

'Don't do that. I didn't mean to sound so defensive, it was kind of you to come. Really,' he added, when she looked doubtful. 'You must have a hundred and one things to do clearing up your mother's estate.'

'Not really.'

'No, well, I suppose you've plenty of help. What about family? Is there anyone else?' She glanced up at him. He too was staring into his coffee.

Now. Tell him now. 'I have a sister.'

'Oh? I didn't know that.'

'Bronte. Her name is Bronte.'

'Bronte?' Without warning he raised thick dark lashes over a pair of eyes like laser beams. The paper cup disintegrated in her fingers, spilling coffee everywhere, over the floor, down Brooke's beautiful trousers…

He took the cup from her, took her wet and trembling hands in his, looked at them, turned them over, continued to hold them. 'Did that scald you?' She shook her head. If her flesh had been peeling from her bones she wouldn't be feeling it.

'I'd better go and find someone…mop myself up…'

He didn't let her go. 'Will you stay tonight?' Her heart, apparently no longer content with somersaults, executed a perfect backflip. That kind of stuff made it difficult to speak, difficult to breathe… 'You'll stay and see Lucy safely home tomorrow?' The breath rushed back in. *Fool…idiot…dolt…*

'Lucy has you, she doesn't need me.'

'Yes, she does. That's why she asked the nurse to phone you. She must have memorised your number.' Because she thought he might take away her precious piece of paper? Because she knew he wouldn't phone? 'I suggested we wait until she came home so that she could call you herself and you wouldn't worry.'

'Oh.'

'Besides, you need to get out of those wet trousers, and I guarantee that if you didn't cause an accident getting here, driving half naked will do the job on the way back.'

'We're in the middle of a heat-wave,' she reminded him. 'They'll be dry in minutes.' Then wished she'd kept her mouth shut. Her life had been painfully bereft of men like James Fitzpatrick encouraging her to get out of her trousers; utterly devoid of men like Fitz full stop. And at the first opportunity that had come her way in years she was rushing out excuses. That was lack of experience for you. Okay, so he didn't mean it that way and even if he did she wouldn't...couldn't... Could she? *Stop it right there, Bronte Lawrence! Don't even think it!* Bron dragged her imagination back to heel, but it whined pathetically. At her age she couldn't afford to let these chances to flirt a little pass her by. And *Brooke* would have flirted 'Of course, if I don't get them into soak very quickly they'll probably be ruined,' she said.

'That would be tragic.'

Was he laughing at her? She bridled. 'Well, perhaps that's putting it a little strong…'

'Not from where I'm standing.'

'What?' Then she blushed. 'Oh.'

'I'm glad that's settled. Lucy will be delighted. Shall we tell her?'

Lucy. He was asking her to stay for Lucy. It was nothing to do with his appreciation of the way Brooke's trousers clung to her backside. So long as she remembered that she would be fine.

And she had intended to stay. Why else had she brought a change of clothes with her? They encouraged parents to stay with children in hospital these days, after all. And everyone thought she was Lucy's mother. It was no big deal. 'Yes, let's do that.' She turned back to the ward.

'And you needn't worry.'

She glanced back. 'Worry?' Why should she be worried? Everything was just peachy... 'What about?'

'I'll find you something to cover your...' he lifted one of those dark brows as he considered his next word carefully '...embarrassment.' What had been a simple blush suddenly flamed into a scarlet nightmare. Definitely laughing. 'While they're being put through cycle eight in the washing machine,' he added. Then he threw in the punchline. 'And I've still got that spare toothbrush.'

CHAPTER EIGHT

'ACTUALLY, Fitz, I have my own toothbrush and some spare clothes in the car,' she snapped. 'I came prepared to stay in the hospital if Lucy needed me.' Before he could answer she turned away, walked across to the nurses station and apologised for the spillage, offered to clean up. Then she went to wash her hands.

By the time she returned to Lucy's side she had her blushes firmly under control. Fitz looked up as she joined him at her bedside. 'Lucy is supposed to try and get some sleep. I thought I'd go and get something to eat. Are you hungry?'

'Just a bit,' she admitted, his query immediately prodding her stomach into noisy recollection that she had eaten nothing but a slice of toast since she got up. Food had taken something of a low priority ever since Lucy Fitzpatrick and her father had dropped into her life through the letterbox like an unexploded bomb, a bomb that was ticking relentlessly and could go off in her face at any moment.

'Are you all right?' Fitz grasped her wrist. 'You looked as if you were about to keel over.'

'Faint from hunger,' she said quickly. 'Perhaps ''just a bit'' was something of an understatement,' she added and turned to the staff nurse, busy tucking Lucy's cover tidily under the mattress. 'Is there a cafeteria in the hospital?'

'Yes, but it's a bit hit and miss. You'd do better going into town. There's a lovely restaurant—'

'We'd be quicker going home. You'll be all right for an hour, won't you, Lucy?'

She nodded, fiddling with the radio headset. 'No worries—'

Fitz raised his eyes to the ceiling. 'Where do they pick up these expressions?'

'Television,' Bron said. 'Australian soaps.'

'You're a fan, are you?'

'Never miss.'

'I suppose you pick it up on your satellite dish when you're paddling up the Orinoco.'

'When I'm not using it as a wok to stir fry a few bugs for my supper.'

Lucy groaned. 'That is *so* gross.'

'A woman has to eat.' Then she lowered one lid in a slow wink as she bent to kiss Lucy's cheek. Lucy flung her arms about her neck and hugged her.

'Thank you for coming.'

'We won't be long, Lucy.' Fitz took Bron's arm and Lucy reluctantly let her go. 'Is there anything you want me to bring from home?'

'My necklace.' He hesitated, then nodded. 'And my Walkman,' she added as an after-thought.

'Right.'

'And *all* my tapes.' Still holding Bron's arm he began to back towards the door. 'And my TV...'

'She's got her own television?' Bron was horrified.

'All her friends have their own television sets.'

'Sorry, I've no right to criticise.'

He turned to Lucy. 'Not the television, not for one night.'

'Well, my library book, then.'

'Your library book.' He kept going.

'And a peach.' Her voice pursued them into the corridor. 'And a can of fizzy orange…and some chocolate…the stuff with white swirly bits…'

Fitz and Bron exchanged a glance and then burst out laughing.

'She's going to be all right, isn't she?'

'Not if I let her have all that.'

'They'll be begging you to take her home by morning.'

'We'd better make the most of it, then.' Most of it? Most of what? 'Which is your car?'

She tore her gaze away from his and looked around the car park for her aged Mini. Then she saw Brooke's gleaming monster and, with a sudden unpleasant wobble in her midriff, remembered. 'That one.'

'Good grief.' He threw the car a startled glance. Then, 'With that in your garage why were you catching the train yesterday?'

'Why?' Why? Her brain refused to co-operate—it was out of practice with this kind of stuff. It never had been *in* practice… 'Well, because…because… Because it was in the garage for a service.'

'Oh, I see.' Did he? Really? She didn't care for the thoughtful furrow creasing his brow. Why would she lie?

'Don't you believe me?'

'Why wouldn't I believe you?' And why couldn't she keep her guilty conscience to herself? 'You'd better follow me home.' His eyes narrowed at the tightness of the space she had squeezed into. 'Do you want me to see you out of there?'

'Would you?' The words were heartfelt. She used the remote unlocking device on the keyring, tried the door. It wouldn't open.

'You've just locked it.'

'Have I?'

She looked at the remote. 'No…' Then she realised. She hadn't locked it in her race to get into the hospital and now she had. 'But it might have been stolen.' She groaned, fumbled with the fob, dropped it. The alarm began to hoot and suddenly she was the focus of attention. And as the hospital visitors turned to look they recognised her, began to smile. Bron was unable to smile back. She was transfixed in horror. What on earth did she do now? And what on earth had happened to the ice-cool woman who had reversed into that space without thinking about it twice?

Fitz picked up the fob, unlocked the car, turned off the alarm, removed the small overnight bag she had tossed on the passenger seat, then locked the car. 'Come on,' he said, taking her arm, 'you're not fit to drive a pedal car.'

'It's reaction, that's all.'

'Yes, of course it is.' Why didn't he sound as if he meant it? He led her firmly in the direction of his Range Rover.

'Shock,' she said, holding out her shaking hands. 'See?'

'I see.'

'I'll be fine in a minute.'

'Of course you will.'

She stopped. 'Will you stop agreeing with me?'

He turned to face her. 'You want me to argue with you?'

'No...'

'You want me to tell you that the thought of you driving that monster gives me a cold chill, that it will almost certainly give me nightmares? That I'll probably wake up in the middle of the night in a cold sweat—'

'No! I'm a perfectly competent driver. I got here in one piece, didn't I? Not so much as a scratch—'

'That's the second time you've said that. As if it's something exceptional. Promise me that you won't drive it again.'

'But I have to—'

'Promise me!' Then as she stood before him, unable to do what he asked, unable to explain, he captured a strand of hair that was blowing across her face and tucked it behind her ear. His fingers were cool against the heat of her skin, a heat that had nothing to do with the sun, but came from the fire he was stoking inside her, a fire that without an instant dousing with cold water was in imminent danger of getting out of control.

'Fitz.' Her protest was lukewarm, a waste of breath, and as his fingers laced through her hair, as he cradled her head in his hand, she couldn't quite remember what she was protesting about.

'Promise me, darling...' This time the words were little more than a whisper and he didn't wait for her to answer him. He extracted her promise with his mouth, warm on hers, gentle on hers as his arm slid around her waist, pulling her close.

It was not a moment for lies, for dissembling. She could keep the truth from him with careful words that never said quite what they meant, but her heart didn't know those games. Her heart only knew one way and her lips, her arms, everything that was Bronte threw off the careful deception and followed it without any thought for the consequences, responding with a frankness that shattered any delusions she might have harboured about her feelings for him. There was nowhere left to hide. The moment James Fitzpatrick had stepped into her kitchen and refused to listen to her, melting her brain with the power of his kiss, she had been lost to reason.

He was on loan, she knew that; his kisses were borrowed from Brooke. Well, Brooke could spare her Cinderella sister a few kisses; she'd surely never miss one or two.

Promise me… She would promise him anything if he would just go on kissing her. She wanted the kiss to last for ever, wanted it never to be over. Once it was over he would be able to look at her and she would see in his eyes that he knew the truth.

But when he lifted his head he simply touched her cheek, for a moment looked at her with infinite tenderness before he turned her, put an arm about her shoulders so that she was tight against his side as he walked her across to the Range Rover.

That was it? He *hadn't* noticed? Her heart was thumping along to the swelling strains of a Rachmaninov concerto, the one from *Brief Encounter*, but while her heart was having a sing-along-with-Rach her head wasn't happy at all. Her head was seriously annoyed.

A man should be able to tell the difference between a woman he'd had a serious affair with and her sister. Even if they did look alike. She wasn't in the least bit like Brooke in any other way.

'Fitz?' His eyes were lazily hooded as he turned from the door. They didn't fool her for one minute. There was nothing lazy about Fitz, nothing in the least bit unperceptive. She shouldn't be complaining, she should just be grateful that she'd got away with it. Promise herself that she'd never allow such a stupid thing to happen again.

Promise me… It was almost as if he'd spoken the words. 'What is it?'

There was something about the way he said the words that suggested he was repeating himself.

She swallowed. 'Nothing. Just…well, I'll have to drive home. To Maybridge.'

'I'll have the car put on a transporter and take you home myself.'

Just like that? The relief was awesome. 'But that's silly…'

'Is it? Well, it's been that kind of week.' She looked up at him, not sure what he was getting at, but his face betrayed nothing. He was smiling, but mostly with his mouth. His eyes were not giving away a thing. 'Trust me. I promise you I know what I'm doing.' Just as long as one of them did. 'Come on, up you get, I'm hungry.'

She climbed aboard the Range Rover. 'I *can* drive, you know,' she said as he got in beside her. 'I passed my test first time.'

'Did you?'

'Yes, I did,' she said, slotting home her seat belt, furious that he should doubt her. But not as furious as Brooke had been. It had taken her sister three attempts to get her licence. Over-confidence, her instructor had said. She'd driven with such dash, whizzing in and out of traffic like a Grand Prix driver taking out the back markers, sounding her horn indignantly at a bus driver who had dared to pull out in front of her.

Brooke had been brilliant, of course, where she had been cautious, timid and reduced to jelly when she'd had to reverse around a cor-ner. She still drove like that on her weekly trips to the out-of-town shopping centre, while Brooke had gone on to take a seriously ad-vanced driving course so that she could tackle any terrain, anything that the weather or nature threw at her. And she was a pretty good mechanic too. She called it survival training. Brooke had always taken survival seriously.

The one reason Brooke had left her precious car in Bron's care was because she'd known her little sister would never be tempted to drive it. *Oh, heck!*

Fitz hadn't responded to her indignant affirmation, apparently deep in thought. She threw him an anxious glance. What was he thinking about? Had the difference between her and Brooke finally filtered through to his brain?

It took less than ten minutes to get to The Old Rectory, ten minutes during which neither of them spoke. Well, that was probably a good thing. The less she said, the less likelihood of her getting herself into serious trouble. This thought was followed by seriously hollow laughter.

'Can you cook?' Fitz asked as he stopped at the front door.

He'd lived with Brooke and he didn't know? 'One kiss and you expect me to cook your lunch?' she demanded.

No man's eyebrows should be that expressive. No man's mouth should be able to speak so tellingly without opening. 'I'll rephrase that. Can you cook better than you can count?'

She'd asked for that. Begged for that. What on earth was wrong with a straightforward yes, for heaven's sake? Just because she was all on edge, because her insides were still doing a tango, because…well, *because*… 'Yes,' she said, but only to keep her subconscious quiet.

'Maybe you could rustle up a couple of omelettes or something. I need to check on something in the studio.'

'Omelettes? I don't know. Aren't they tricky?'

'Then you should have no problem. I won't be long.' He dropped her overnight bag on the kitchen floor and kept walking. He unlocked the garden door and then turned on an afterthought. 'The washing machine is through there if you want to do something about those trousers.'

Fitz switched on the scanner, booted up the computer and then opened the desk drawer and lifted out the muddle of papers and photographs that he'd swept in there the day before.

On top was a photograph of Brooke. Twenty-one years old, beautiful, bright, the world at her feet. He stared at it for a moment, then slipped it into the scanner.

He should have known. Right from the first moment he'd set eyes on her he should have realised. That heart-stopping rush of desire the moment he'd set eyes on her should have warned him. He'd fallen in lust with Brooke, then he'd been touched by her vulnerability, then he'd been plain angry with her. But he'd never loved her. She was too self-centred for that. If he'd known she had a sister he might have worked it out sooner. But what on earth was she playing at?

'Would an aunt help?' Her words came back to haunt him. She'd told him. She was going to give Lucy her special day and then she was going to come back as herself. If he'd been thinking with his head instead of... Her image appeared before him on the screen. Brooke's image. He marked the section below her right brow and blew it up. No scar. Well, he hadn't really needed to look. His brain might have been out to lunch, but his body had known, responded, right from the start.

Bron found a basin, took a box of eggs from the larder and some cheese. She found the oil and a suitable pan. Then she looked around for an apron. An apron. It was a bit late for an apron. She stared down at where the coffee had dried in stiff, dark patches on the beautifully cut trousers. It was probably too late to save them, but she had better try. Not the washing machine, though. She would bet her eye-teeth that these trousers hadn't been made for a wash-and-wear existence. No matter how gentle the program.

She walked through into the utility room, put the plug in the sink and turned on the cold tap. Then she kicked off her boots, removed the trousers, folding them neatly so they wouldn't crease, and laid them in the water. Kill or cure. She was beginning to get to the point where she didn't much care about Brooke's precious clothes. There were many of Brooke's other precious possessions needing tender loving care. She wouldn't be averse to a little herself. If Fitz were doing the caring.

And thinking of Fitz, he'd said he wouldn't be long. She'd better get her jeans on before he came back.

Too late. The sound of running water must have masked his return. She came to an abrupt halt in the doorway as she was confronted by his tall figure leaning back against the work surface, arms folded in an attitude that made her suddenly nervous.

'Trousers,' she croaked, stupidly. 'Soaking.' This was not the moment to throw a virginal fit at being seen in her knickers by a man she scarcely knew. Brooke wouldn't... Brooke had shown him more than her knickers... Oh, God! Her knickers!

Beneath the waist-skimming silk sweater, the cost of which would probably have fed the inhabitants of a village in Africa for a year, beneath her entirely naked abdomen, she was wearing nothing but a pair of cotton pants with an unspeakably vulgar slogan written in Day-Glo pink across the rear.

They were part of a set she had bought in Maybridge market because they'd been cheap and she'd been broke and because she had been absolutely certain no one else would ever see them.

Brooke wouldn't have been caught dead in them.

Fortunately, Fitz seemed to have eyes for nothing but her legs. Well, they were long so there was a lot to see, long and brown with a faint, downy covering of sun-bleached hair. After what seemed like a lifetime, he looked up. 'What interesting knees you have.'

She was standing half naked in his kitchen and all he could say was that she had interesting knees? Her knees weren't *interesting*. They were scarred, lumpy things that had suffered horribly in her battle to get to grips with a pair of Brooke's hand-me-down roller skates. She hated her knees. Besides, they were visible any day she happened to be wearing a skirt. Why couldn't he have said something complimentary about her thighs? There was nothing much wrong with them. Or her bottom. Her bottom, like her thighs, had been firmed by years of running up and down stairs. Her bottom was definitely worth a mention… No! Her bottom was encased in the knickers from hell—she had to keep his eyes engaged elsewhere while she worked out how to get to her bag and into her jeans without turning around.

'Knees?' She laughed. Ha, ha, ha. 'Oh, my *knees*—' It wasn't working. Then, casually, 'Could you please pass me my bag?' she said, backing slowly into the utility room. He followed her, put the bag on the draining board and kept on coming.

'I thought you had something important to do?'

'I do. Very important.' But instead of walking away, he took a step closer. The utility room was small, that step brought him close enough to blot out the light from the small window so that his face was shadowed, unreadable, close enough for him to reach out, put his hand on the base of her neck.

She closed her eyes and didn't move. She should protest. She should ask him what the devil he thought he was doing, but simply breathing was hard enough. Words were just too difficult. And just the stirring of his fingers against the sensitive skin below her neck was creating a tidal wave of sensation that made words redundant. She might never have been touched with such exquisite sensuousness before, but she knew exactly what he was doing.

Another step brought him within a hair's breadth of her, close enough to identify the summer meadow freshness his cleaner used in the tumble-dryer. Close enough to smell the warmth of his skin, the faint hospital smell that clung to him. Close enough to know that whatever she was feeling, she wasn't alone.

'Fitz—' The protest was feeble, but it was there.

'Shut up. I'm going to kiss you, Bronte Lawrence. Kiss number four, since you can't count…' Her eyes slammed shut as his lips touched the point, just below her ear, where her jawbone angled. It was bliss, perfect. No…it got better. His fingers at her neck had moved beneath the edge of the sweater and his mouth had begun to travel slowly across her cheek…

Bronte? He'd called her Bronte? She opened her eyes. He knew? Then why was he…?

She let out a little moan of pleasure as his fingers began teasing along her shoulder, as his thumb caressed her vertebrae. His eyes were closed, his thick lashes dark semicircles above cheek-bones that would have made a lesser man vain.

She shouldn't be thinking thoughts like that, she knew, so she closed her eyes again. It didn't help.

Bron was at war within herself. There was the common sense, sensible half who was sternly warning her to stop it right now, telling her to instruct Fitz to stop before throwing herself on his mercy and begging him to never, ever tell Brooke that she'd driven her car.

Then there was the unexpectedly giddy Bron, a girl that she had almost forgotten existed. The half of her who had been thinking with her heart instead of her head ever since she'd opened Lucy's letter, the half that was saying do as you're told, shut up and enjoy this because you might never get another chance.

Common sense had more practice and came out marginally ahead. 'You don't understand, Fitz—' she began.

She broke off as the giddy one moaned when he stopped nibbling at her right eyebrow and said, 'Yes, I do. Believe me, I do—' He moved his attention to her temple and, when she sighed, trailed, warm moist kisses to her cheek-bone while his other hand slid beneath the sweater hem, encircled her waist with a thick forearm while his fingers teased along her ribs and her squirming pleasure drove her still closer so that her cheek was pressed against the soft stuff of his polo shirt, her hips were pressed against the surging heat of his own powerfully expressed need of her.

Under the circumstances it was scarcely surprising that her concentration slipped a little, that common sense decided to give up on a bad job and take a hike, and that she couldn't remember exactly what had been so urgent. But she tried, she really tried. 'Fitz—'

'And I know something else.' His mouth had worked around to hers and he was looking at her now, eyes so dark that she could see herself reflected in them, eyes no longer hiding anything. 'I know that if I don't make love to you right now I'm probably going to die of frustration and how will you explain that to Lucy?'

'That's blackmail,' she gasped.

His slow grin turned her interesting knees to jelly. 'Only if you don't want to play.' His hold was so light that all she had to do was find the will-power to pull away from him and, despite what he was saying, he would let her go. 'But you do, don't you, Bronte Lawrence?'

'Yes…' The word was a tiny little croak that even a frog would be ashamed of so she nodded, just to be sure he understood. Then, 'At least—' His mouth halfway to hers, he stopped, waited… 'How did you know?'

'Brooke never blushed…' Bronte immediately flushed hot pink. 'She has exquisite knees. And she doesn't have a scar here.' He touched the spot with the lips. 'And it took her three attempts to pass her driving test. She told me so herself.'

'Oh.' She swallowed with difficulty. 'Well, so long as we both know who we are…'

'Yes?'

'Could we go somewhere more comfort-able?'

His mouth parted in a slow smile. 'Would you care to suggest somewhere?'

A picture of his beautiful sleigh bed came winging unbidden to her mind, but she couldn't say *that*...

In the event there was no need to say anything. James Fitzpatrick read her mind.

'What will we tell Lucy?' Bron was still shaking with the suddenness of it. The suddenness of loving and being loved in return. Of the miracle of Fitz knowing that she was Bronte and still wanting her...not Brooke. She didn't understand why, but the feelings were too new, too tender to be probed, interrogated. All she knew was that they were racing back to the hospital like a pair of guilty teenagers who had forgotten the time and stayed out late on a date and were going to get it in the neck...

'Nothing.' She turned and stared at him. 'Stick to your original plan, Bronte. Make some excuse about France, then come as yourself. That was what you planned to do, wasn't it?' There had been no time to talk, to explain. Not even time to eat. Just a searing need to know one another, hold one another, feel the warmth of skin against skin, to show the depth of emotions too deep to be spoken. But words, it seemed, were unnecessary. 'If you turned up in France and told her that Brooke asked you to come in her place she'd—'

'She'd be terribly upset.'

'Not for long.' She was unable to take her eyes off him, to stop looking at the creases that appeared without warning at the corner of his mouth when he spoke, or smiled, the way his hair curled over onto the collar of his polo shirt, his neck... He turned into the hospital car park, backed into an empty space. 'You heard her, Bron. She loves you.' *Which was why she couldn't do it.* 'You might have a different name but you'd be the same person so she couldn't help loving you all over again.'

'Do you know you've got your shirt on inside out?'

He unclipped his seat belt. 'No, but if you'll hum it, I'll play it—' He realised she was staring at him. 'What?'

'Here, turn around, let me help you—' She laughed and put her arms around him and tugged on the hem of the shirt, pulling it over his head.

'Good God, woman, what do you think you're doing? We're in a public car park…'

'If you go in there with your shirt on inside out, Fitz, everyone will know what I've been doing.' And then she wasn't laughing any more, but looking straight into his eyes, straight into his heart. He was trying to protect her from Lucy's pain, Lucy's anger. 'We can't start with a lie, Fitz. We have to tell her the truth.'

'You don't know what you're asking. You don't know—'

She put her hand over his mouth. 'Yes. Yes, I do. I did this, not you, and I'll tell her. You are the anchor in her life, she must be able to trust you.'

'I want her to love you, trust you.'

'So do I, but I'll have to earn that, Fitz. For myself.'

'Are you sure?'

'I've never been more certain of anything in my life. Come on.' She leaned into him, kissed him, then she pulled the shirt off him and turned it the right way out. 'She'll be wondering what's happened to us.'

'She's not the only one.' He tugged the shirt over his head, raked his fingers through his hair. 'Stay there, I'll help you down.'

She waited, not because she needed his help, but for the pleasure of feeling his hands about her waist, of sliding her body against his as he swung her from the high seat. 'Bronte.' And for a moment he held her and she clung to him. 'Not now. I don't want to tell her now—we should wait until she's home.'

Every part of Bronte wanted to be rid of the lie, rid of the deception, yet she knew that Fitz was right. Lucy needed to be at home, safe, secure. She needed to be able to shut herself away if she needed to in her own space so that she could come to terms with the truth, to rationalise it.

She groaned inwardly. Rationalise being lied to, deceived by the people she should be able to trust? Lucy was eight years old. She might sound older, she might be able to do that terribly grown-up, terribly cool thing that those 'only' children who spent too much time with adults did so well. But eight years old was not an age for rationalising anything...

'It'll be all right, Bronte. She'll understand.'

'Will she?' She tried to think how it would feel, how *she* would feel in Lucy's shoes... 'I hope you're right.'

'Trust me. Here, can you take these, while I get the television?'

She took the carrier into which they had stuffed everything they thought that Lucy might want. 'Whatever happened to ''not for one night''?' she asked.

'Guilt. I couldn't bear to think of her in hospital deprived of her early morning cartoons while we're at home having so much fun.'

Bron blushed. 'I came to be with Lucy, Fitz.'

'Did you?' He knuckled her cheek. 'Now who's feeling guilty?' She refused to answer that. 'I do understand. I'm a past master at guilt. It goes with the territory, the parenthood thing. It's right there from the beginning, the waking up ten times a night wondering if your precious baby is still breathing, the niggling suspicion that you've never done enough, the fear every time you leave her with someone else for a day because you have to go to some meeting that she'll need you, miss you. I hadn't realised how ingrained it was until I found myself working out how I could per-suade your sister to marry me so that Lucy would have her heart's desire—'

'You asked her to marry you before,' she said quickly, suddenly afraid to look at him, afraid of what she would see, but he hooked his finger beneath her chin and made her face him.

'I asked her to marry me for Lucy's sake and she laughed the idea to scorn, but when I repeated the offer yesterday you didn't laugh, you just looked shell-shocked. If I hadn't been in such a state I'd have realised then that you couldn't possibly be Brooke.' He held her face cupped in the palm of his hand. 'Brooke wouldn't have come to a small school sports day just to make a little girl happy. Brooke was never that kind.

'But you threatened her.'

'Is that why you did it, Bronte? To protect your sister's good name?' He was the one who laughed then. 'Do you really think she'd have been concerned about any threat *I'd* make? She knew me too well for that.'

Of course she did. She was his lover. She had borne his child and even now she held him in some kind of thrall. He was pretending he didn't care, but he did. He had simply been making love to her mirror image, trying to bring back an impossible past, live an impossible future.

That was when Bronte realised that if she was living a dream, it was not her dream and her bright new shining world fell apart.

CHAPTER NINE

SHE was Bronte Lawrence. *Bronte.* Not Brooke. And not even for Fitz would she live a lie, or allow him to live one through her.

'We'd better move before Lucy sends out a search party for us,' she said, turning from him so that his hand slipped away, so that he wasn't touching her. Right now she couldn't handle that.

'Bronte? Wait—'

She left him, hampered by the television, and walked towards the hospital entrance. Was that how it had been for Brooke? That swift, undeniable burst of careless passion that had left her pregnant with Lucy? Were they *that* alike?

Not that she had to worry about being pregnant. Fitz hadn't been so lost in lust that he'd forgotten to take precautions. She'd thought it so loving, so caring, the way he'd held back, taken the time to protect her. Protect himself.

What man would risk being left holding the baby a second time? After all, she was a heck of a lot like her sister and he couldn't be expected to know that deep down, where it mattered, they were worlds apart...

'Hey, slow down!' She turned to him as he caught her up by the entrance, grasped her hand, smiling as if everything in the world was wonderful. 'Wait for me.' Then his smile faded. 'Hey, what's the matter? What's wrong?'

'Nothing.' Well, everything was fine, wasn't it? No point in making a drama out of it. Nothing had happened. Nothing of any great significance. Only to her and she wouldn't tell. She found a smile. 'But Lucy will be waiting—'

'Miss Lawrence?' The voice was familiar and she turned grateful for the distraction. 'Angie Makepeace, the *Sentinel*. I've been trying to contact you all day. Your office didn't seem to know where you were and your sister was too busy to talk.' Then she smiled. 'Or perhaps they just didn't want to tell me.'

The *Sentinel*. That was all she needed. 'I wonder why?' Then, because she knew that antagonising the woman probably wasn't a good idea, 'What's so urgent?' As if she couldn't guess.

'Well, a little bird told me that you were at a school near here yesterday for your daughter's sports day. Lucy? I have got the name right, haven't I?' Bron opened her mouth, but her brain couldn't think of a thing to say, nothing that she would want to be quoted on, and she closed it again. All she wanted to do was slap the self-satisfied smile right off Angie Makepeace's face. She restrained herself—it wouldn't help. 'And now I hear she's had an accident. Is it serious? How long is she likely to be in hospital?' The woman was smiling like a cat who'd eaten a canary, had a mouse tucked up in her larder and was now eyeing a very large goldfish. Slapping her might not help, Bron thought, but it would feel very good. She took half a step towards her, but Fitz tightened his grip on her hand, restraining her. It didn't go unnoticed by Ms Makepeace. 'Would you like to share your thoughts with our readers at this difficult time, Miss Lawrence?'

Fitz stepped into the breach left by her disengaged brain. 'I'm sure you must be aware of the new guidelines on press intrusion, Miss Makepeace. News of a child's very minor accident is scarcely in the public interest.'

'On the contrary, Mr Fitzpatrick—you *are* James Fitzpatrick, aren't you? Lucy's father?' Angie Makepeace didn't wait for him to confirm or deny her supposition. 'I'm sure the public will be very interested—'

It was Bronte's turn to hold Fitz back as her brain finally found gear and moved into overdrive. 'Miss Makepeace, Angie, I'm sure you understand that I just want to see Lucy right now. Perhaps, rather than use this *intrusive…*' she laid only the lightest of stress on 'intrusive' '…piece of journalism…' Fitz snorted '…we could arrange a proper interview when Lucy is home.' The woman looked less than impressed. 'With a photographer?' Fitz looked horrified.

'I've got photographs.'

'Not of Lucy.' Not even the *Sentinel* would be that stupid. Taking photographs of a child in hospital would mean a hefty fine... Or was she the one being stupid? Maybe that kind of exclusive would be worth a fine, no matter how hefty. She couldn't risk it. Nothing was more important than Lucy right now; whatever Brooke was up to, she was big enough to look after herself. Her fingers dug warningly into Fitz's hand as she kept him beside her. 'And of course that's not all. I know you'll be aware that there are all sorts of rumours flying about...' She assumed this to be the case from her conversation with Brooke's secretary. 'I'm sure you'd like the true story.' And she gave a little shrug.

Angie Makepeace's eyes lit up. She'd heard the rumours all right, whatever they were. 'It's true, then?' She could scarcely contain her excitement.

Bron forced a smile to her lips. 'Well, now, that depends on what you've heard.' She hadn't a clue what was going on but she was quite prepared to use anything to get a couple of days breathing space.

'And you're offering an exclusive?'

'In return for complete privacy while Lucy recovers.'

'You'll give me the whole story?' She glanced at Fitz. Bron said nothing, but she knew her silence would be taken as assent. 'You'll call me on Monday?'

'Tuesday.'

'Very well.' And she smiled with the kind of deep satisfaction that made Bron very nervous indeed. She didn't know what she'd committed Brooke to, but she had the feeling that her sister was not going to be pleased with her. But she'd already done enough to make her seriously angry; how much worse could it get? 'And you're wrong about Lucy. I have some charming snaps of her being presented with a big silver cup by her famous mother.' Well, that answered *that* question.

'You should be careful,' Fitz warned and this time when he took a step towards the woman Bron did nothing to stop him. 'Things are not always what they seem.'

'Really?' Angie Makepeace wasn't intimidated. Or if she was, she wasn't letting it show.

'Well, if I don't hear from Miss Lawrence on Tuesday, they'll be on Wednesday's front page and my readers will be able to make up their own minds about that.'

'You have such a charming way with threats, Miss Makepeace,' Bron said. 'Who could resist?' She hooked her arm through Fitz's, her eyes begging him to let it go. 'Come on, darling. Lucy will wonder what's happened to us.' For a moment she wasn't sure whether 'darling' was about to explode. He didn't, but his look put her on warning that it was a temporary reprieve as he pushed open the hospital door and held it for her before letting it swing back into place so that the thick plate glass was between them and Angie Makepeace.

'What the hell was that all about?' He made an impatient gesture as he regained her arm. 'And I don't mean Lucy, it's obvious that someone's called in the story, I expected that…'

'Did you?' Startled out of her suppressed rage, she turned on the stairs and looked at him. Then she realised what that meant. 'And you were prepared to use that to bring Brooke to heel?'

'To bring *you* to heel. At least, not to heel—' The porter called out, 'hello,' Fitz raised a hand, she threw the man a distracted smile.

'You thought I was Brooke,' she hissed.

'No! Yes…' He looked so confused that she would have felt sorry for him if she weren't saving up all her pity for herself. She was going to need it. 'Look, can we talk about this later?'

'Much later. I'm going to be somewhat busy trying to get in touch with Brooke to confess that I've just given first pick on her life to the kind of newspaper she wouldn't use to wrap her potato peelings in.' And with that she turned and swept up the stairs with Fitz close at her heels.

Lucy looked up and grinned as Bron entered the small ward. She was kneeling on the bed doing an old jigsaw that someone had found her. 'Look at this, I've nearly finished.'

Bron looked over her shoulder. 'Oh, good job,' she said, picking up a piece and, after a moment, slotting it into place. 'Sorry we were so long. Have you had any visitors while we've been gone?'

'Just a lady. She knew you were my mother.' She tried to fit another piece that stubbornly refused to go and in an instant the puzzle disintegrated, the pieces flying everywhere. 'Oh...bother!' Then Fitz put the television on the night table. 'You brought it.' Fitz stooped to drop a kiss on the child's head as she hugged him. 'Plug it in, plug it in.'

'Later. What else did she ask you, princess?'

'Oh, where I lived, who looked after me. That kind of stuff.'

'What was her name?' Lucy shrugged and Fitz looked at Bron, who was gathering up the jigsaw pieces and putting them back into the box. 'You know, I think I wasted my time bringing all this. I think you'd be much better off at home.'

'Really?' Lucy, who had been digging around in the bag Bronte had put on the bed, looked up. 'You mean go home *now*?'

'The sooner the better.'

'But I was just going to have tea. I was allowed to choose and I'm having—'

'We'll send out for pizza.'

'Really? Can I choose the toppings?'

'Whatever you like. You can call it in from the car phone.'

'Cool.'

He put his hand on Bron's shoulder, turned her away from Lucy. 'Will you stay with her while I go and sort it out with the doctor?'

'Fitz, is this a good idea? The woman could have been a social worker, anyone.'

'It's the ''anyone'' that bothers me. I won't be long.'

'Any luck?'

She shook her head. 'I can't think of anyone else to call. I've even left a message on my answering machine at home in case she turns up there.'

'Well, you've been on the phone for ages. You need something to eat and all I have is cold pizza.'

'That'll do to be going on with. I'm starving.' Bron helped herself to a slice. 'I've never seen a pizza with triple ''extra olives'' before.'

'Lucy likes olives. Here, have a glass of wine, it'll help it down.' He didn't wait for her answer but handed her a glass of something red and patted the sofa beside him.

She knew she should take the armchair but she was too weary to walk all that way across the room. Besides, it would look too obvious. She wanted to slide out gracefully. Thanks for a really nice time, Fitz. I haven't enjoyed myself so much in...oh, longer than I remember—probably longer than she ever would.

The trouble was, there was still Lucy to consider. She couldn't go anywhere until she'd cleared up the mess she'd made, connected the child to her real mother. At least, that was what she told herself as she sank down beside him and he put an arm about her shoulders. She shouldn't let him do that, either, but it was comforting. Right now she needed comfort and it felt so good to be held. She finished the pizza, wiped her fingers on the hem of her T-shirt. Then she put her head on his shoulder, because it was a really good, dependable shoulder and it seemed a pity to waste it. 'We should have told Lucy, Fitz. You said you would the minute she was home.'

'She was tired.' He dropped a kiss on the top of her head and that was nice too. 'We're all tired. With one notable exception it's been a hell of a day. Here, give me that.' He took her glass and stretched away to put it on the table beside him. It was the moment to make some excuse to move, offer to make coffee or something. But even while she was thinking about it, he'd turned and pulled her onto his lap, settling her against his chest, lifting her feet onto the sofa. And as he began to knead at her instep, using a gentle, soothing pressure that was utterly blissful, making coffee didn't seem like such a good idea.

She sighed with pleasure and somehow, without her ever meaning to let it get that far, his lips were tangling deliciously with hers and the combination was wickedly sensuous, setting off tiny tremors of anticipation throughout her eager body.

'Fitz,' she protested when he released her mouth to pay assiduous attention to the curve of her throat, to curl his tongue in the sensitive hollow at its base. 'Oh-h-h...'

'You like that?'

'Yes... No... Fitz, we can't—'

'Lucy's fast asleep.'

'No...' That wasn't what she'd meant. She'd meant that she couldn't, at least she shouldn't—

'I checked.' And then his tongue was teasing against hers and somehow that was much more important than a few minor scruples about indulging Fitz's fantasies. Wasn't she entitled to a few fantasies of her own?

And then the doorbell rang.

Fitz groaned as he stopped what he was doing and half turned, as if hoping that if he didn't answer whoever it was would go away. Bronte, though, sat up abruptly and her head collided with his chin. She heard the painful snap as his teeth jarred together. 'Oh, God, I'm sorry! Are you all right? I'll get some ice to put on that...' But as she scrambled to her feet she collided with the table, sending it flying. It hit the carpet with a crash of plates and glasses, sending a splatter of pizza and red wine across the carpet, while the bottle emptied itself into a dark, spreading stain that Bron knew, from long experience, would never come out.

There was a soft chuckle from the doorway. 'I seem to have arrived at an inopportune moment. Sorry, darlings. But your message sounded desperate and, since no one answered and the door was on the latch, I let myself in.'

'Brooke!'

'You might well look guilty, wretch. What have you done with my car?' She lifted a hand. 'No, don't answer that. If it's in a ditch somewhere I need something sustaining inside me before you tell me about it. Just sit down over there, knees together, hands in your lap the way Mother taught you, while I clear up this mess. Hello, Fitz.' She dropped a kiss on his cheek. 'I see you've met Calamity Jane.'

Calamity Jane. No one but Brooke had ever called her that. How she'd hated it!

Maybe Fitz saw that because he grasped her hand, keeping her by his side. On second thoughts it was probably so that she could witness the development of the bruise on his jaw at close quarters. He moved it gingerly before he said, 'Bronte has been leaving messages everywhere for you.'

'So I gathered.' Brooke picked up the wine bottle and shook her head. 'Bron and red wine. A fatal combination.' She handed the bottle to Fitz, straightened the table and picked up the plates and glasses. 'Have you got a soda siphon? That will shift the wine from the carpet if you give it a good squirt straight away.'

'Forget the carpet,' he said. 'We've got a real problem. Or rather you have. The *Sentinel* know about Lucy.'

'Is that why Angie Makepeace was trying to contact me?'

'You know about that?'

She turned to Bron. 'I know nothing except that when my taxi dropped me in Maybridge this evening you weren't there and my car was missing, and then I heard your message on the answering machine and recognised Fitz's number.'

'So why didn't you phone?'

'Believe me, darling, I was tempted. I've been travelling for days and then I had to face a press conference at the airport… But something warned me that I'd better make the effort to come in person.' Brooke's gaze lingered on the way Fitz was holding onto Bronte's hand. 'My instincts never fail me.' Then she looked at the wreckage of their supper and said, 'I'll put these in the kitchen while you pour the Scotch, Fitz. Then you can tell me exactly what the pair of you have been up to.' She paused in the doorway. 'On second thoughts, perhaps you'd better make that the expurgated version.'

'It's all my fault, Brooke. Lucy wrote to you, asking you to go her school sports day, and I opened the letter by mistake.'

'But why didn't you tell Fitz who you were?'

'I didn't give her a chance,' he said quickly. 'Lucy told me about the letter and I went charging in like a bull in a china shop demanding that you do as she asked.'

'Or?'

He shrugged. 'Or I'd tell the world about Lucy.'

Brooke grinned. 'And Bron *believed* you?'

'She had no reason not to. I wasn't exactly... Well, let's say that I didn't make a good first impression.'

Brooke laughed. 'You mean you did all this to keep my name pure for the great British public? For heaven's sake, Bronte, get real. We have the touching reunions of adopted children and their newsworthy parents all over the front pages these days. Who gives a damn?'

'I did it for Lucy, too.' Then she glanced at Fitz. 'And if I'm honest, just a little bit for me.' She knew she was blushing, but she didn't care about that. 'The problem is, I've made things worse. For you that is. Someone must have contacted the *Sentinel* and sold them the story.'

'I should think there was a stampede for the phones.' Brooke didn't seem particularly bothered. 'Let's face it, you weren't exactly discreet.'

'No.'

'So why isn't it all over the news?'

Bron told her. 'Angie Makepeace wants the whole story. She called the house this morning and she's obviously been in touch with your office. Then she got lucky. Lucy had a bit of an accident today and she went to the hospital and I suppose the local stringer who called in the first story must have followed it up. We bought some time by promising her an exclusive about Lucy, about your plans. I sort of hinted that there was something interesting afoot.' They were sitting around the kitchen table and Fitz covered Bron's hand with his. 'When I phoned your office this morning your secretary seemed to be in a bit of a dither.'

'You obviously haven't seen the evening news.'

'We haven't had time to watch television, Brooke.'

'Pity.'

'We've been trying to contact you.'

'So, how much time do we have?'

'Until Tuesday.'

'Tuesday? You held her off until Tuesday? My God, what did you promise her?'

'Everything.'

'Oh, dear. Poor woman.' Brooke chuckled. 'It must be like having the Holy Grail right there, in your hands, and then have it disintegrate.'

'Would you care to explain what the hell you are talking about?' Fitz was getting to the edge of his patience, but Brooke just laughed.

'Think about it, darling. While Bron, as me, was promising Angie all my dark secrets, with pictures to prove it, I was giving a televised press conference at Heathrow.'

'But she'll be livid, she'll think we did it deliberately. She'll—'

'No, she won't. She won't know what to believe and she won't dare print a thing in case she looks a complete idiot.' She gave a little shrug. 'I suppose I'd better call her tomorrow and make my peace, let her publish a story about how I had a baby when I was a student and had to give her up but now we've been reunited. I'll do it right after I've taken out an injunction preventing the publication of any photographs of Lucy.'

'Can you do that?'

'She's a minor, Bron. Anonymity is her right.'

'It's that easy?'

'Probably not. It might be a good idea if you all disappeared for a couple of months, until the excitement has died down.'

'What excitement? What was the press conference about?'

'I've drawn a line in the earth, Bron. I'm making a stand. You haven't been able to get hold of me because I've been one hundred per cent occupied raising the cash to outbid some cattle barons for some land on the edge of the rainforest. I'm planning to buy up a lot more. All I need is the money, lots of it, so I'm offering people the chance to buy a share in the future of the planet, their own acre of rainforest to be held in trust.' Then she grinned. 'Can I sign you two up?'

'Make it three. Lucy will want her own piece of earth.'

'Will she?'

'She thinks you're amazing.'

'Really? Then instead of buying her an acre of land, Fitz, why don't you let me call the trust after her? The Lucy Trust? The Lucy Fitzpatrick Trust? You decide.' She downed the remaining whisky in her glass and stood up. 'Look, I've been travelling for what seems like for ever and then driven further than anyone should be obliged to in Bron's wreck of a car. I'm bushed. You don't mind if I take a shower and then crash out, do you? I have to leave really early…'

'Help yourself.' Fitz waved a hand in the direction of the stairs. 'You know where everything is. And, Brooke—' she looked at him '—I think you're pretty amazing, too.'

Bron felt like a volcano was about to erupt inside her head. Brooke had walked right in without so much as a by-your-leave and was making herself right at home. And Fitz was letting her. Was he going to take her back just like that? Hadn't he been listening? Brooke wasn't going to hang around and play mother. Well, he might not know what was good for him, but she did and she wasn't about to let her sister mess up his life again.

She stood up abruptly. 'Wait for me, I'll make up the spare bed for you while you take that shower.'

'Thanks, Bron.' Brooke's smile was infuriatingly knowing. She knew everything. Always had. 'Making beds was never my thing.'

'Or lying in them once made,' Bron muttered.

'Excuse us, Fitz. I think I'm about to get the ''behaving responsibly'' lecture.' She grinned at him as she took Bron firmly by the arm and headed for the stairs.

'For God's sake, Brooke, this isn't a laughing matter. Don't you care about Lucy?'

'Sufficiently to leave her with Fitz. He's a carer, darling. Like you. He cared for me and I knew he would care for my baby.'

'You should have brought her home.'

She made an impatient little sound. 'You had enough to do.'

'You're missing the point. There was nothing to stop *you* looking after her.'

'I'm not made that way, Bron. I'm the selfish one, remember? It's not something I'm proud of, but I knew I wasn't ready to surrender my life because of a few stupid weeks of infatuation. I would have gone through with that bloody termination if Fitz hadn't stopped me.' Brooke pulled a face. 'Then I thought, well, okay, I've done my duty, now I'll have her adopted, but Fitz... Fitz took one look at her and...well...'

Bron saw the betraying glint of tears that belied the hard words and from being furious with her sister she quite suddenly felt nothing but sadness for her, for all she'd thrown away. 'Oh, come here.' She opened her arms and Brooke came into them and for an age she simply held her.

'I wish I were like you, Bron.'

'No, you don't. And I'm glad you're not. You're special, different. Some of us were born to change nappies and some of us to change the world. I understand. Truly.'

'Do you?' Brooke pulled back, dashed the beginning of a tear from her eye. 'Maybe you do. You always understood me better than anyone, even Mother. I'm sorry I wasn't there for you, Bron. I should have been, but I was having to chase down the money to buy this land

and, honestly, I thought it was just one more crisis. And then it was too late and I thought, What's the point? What can I do in Maybridge? I was needed there…'

'Nothing. There was nothing you could do, truly. You were right to stay where you could do most good.'

'Was I?'

'She understood, darling. She was so proud of you.' She glanced down at Fitz, standing at the foot of the stairs, looking up at them both. What was he seeing? His lost love returned to him? How big a mistake he'd made that afternoon going for second best? 'We're all proud of you. Come on, you're tired. Have your shower—'

'What's she like, Bron? Lucy?'

Bron hesitated. Then she said, 'She's beautiful. She looks so much like you. And she has Mother's eyes.'

'Really?'

'And my delicacy of touch.'

'No!' She grinned. 'Poor Fitz.'

'Calamity Jane mark two. The genes will out.'

'And her hair? Is she fair, too?'

'No. She's darker. Not as dark as Fitz, more chestnut. She has his curls, though.'

'Ah.' And Brooke turned and looked down at Fitz. 'She doesn't know. You haven't told her.'

'Know what?' Bron felt a sudden premonition of something awful as she stared at her sister. 'What hasn't he told me?'

'Fitz isn't Lucy's father, Bron.'

CHAPTER TEN

'DOWNSTAIRS! Now!' Fitz had taken the stairs three at a time, stabbed an angry gesture towards Lucy's door which he'd left standing slightly ajar so that he could hear her if she cried out.

He was glaring at Brooke, who had turned deathly pale beneath her sun-darkened skin. 'Oh, my God!'

'Not another word!'

'She's in there...' He turned to Bronte, pleading silently with her to move Brooke away from the door. 'My little girl.'

'Not now, Brooke.' Then he watched in horror as Brooke seemed to shrink before his eyes, collapsing against Bron as she put her arm around her. 'Come on, darling. You're tired. I'll put you to bed.' She glanced at him and he realised that, unlike Brooke, she didn't know which was the guest room.

He led the way to the back of the house and opened the door for her. Feeling utterly helpless as they disappeared into the bathroom, he dragged his hand through his hair. 'Stay with her, I'll make up the bed.'

'Thank you.' And then Bron closed the door, but not before he heard the terrible low keening as Brooke Lawrence let out the years of bottled up grief for the daughter she had so casually given away.

All those years ago he had waited, hoping that she would realise her mistake and return to claim the little girl he had been holding in trust for her. Well, now she was back and his only feeling was a deep and terrible fear that what he had so devoutly wished for would finally come true.

Up to his eyes in nappies, with bills piling up, unable to get out and work, he would have welcomed her back to relieve him of the burden he had taken on without for a moment considering the problems.

Now Lucy was so much a part of his life that he couldn't imagine being without her. She was his daughter in every way but for that careless moment of conception.

For a moment he continued to stare at the door that muffled, but did not completely block out, the sound of weeping. Then, unable to bear it for a moment longer, he turned away to fetch sheets from the airing cupboard.

He glanced at Lucy's door, took a step towards it, then stopped himself. If she'd woken, heard voices, she would have called out. If he went to check he might just disturb her and this was not the moment to reunite her with her real mother. Brooke was in no state to handle that.

Instead he returned and made the bed to the sound of quiet weeping from beyond the bathroom door, to the quiet gentling of Bron's voice as she tried to comfort her sister. If only she'd phoned, or waited until tomorrow…

Tomorrow. The word mocked him. That was what he'd been doing for years: putting it off until tomorrow. Even today, when it was perfectly obvious that there were no more tomorrows left, when Bron had been pushing him to tell Lucy the truth, he had still baulked at confronting it.

He straightened the cover, glanced again at the bathroom door and after a moment tapped on it. 'Bron.' It opened a crack and she looked at him, her face unreadable in the gathering twilight. 'I'll be downstairs if you need me.' He made an awkward gesture. 'Would she like a cup of tea or something?' Good God, what was he thinking of? Offering Brooke the universal panacea, as if a cup of tea could make up for eight lost years. 'I'll be downstairs.'

'Fitz.' He turned back. She'd been shedding tears along with her sister and her eyes were shining. She looked so beautiful. Not beautiful like Brooke, not that slick, polished beauty that came with the careful use of cosmetics, careful camera angles; Bronte's loveliness shone from inside her. Seeing them together had been a revelation. He couldn't believe how he'd ever been fooled into thinking she was Brooke. Then he realised that he hadn't been, that somewhere deep inside he'd always recognised the difference. He wanted to hold her and tell her that, but she was keeping the door like a barrier between them. 'Look in on Lucy, make sure she's asleep, that she didn't hear...' She struggled with the words. 'That she didn't hear what Brooke said.'

He nodded and she closed the door again.

He wanted to hammer it down, explain, tell her everything. He should have done that this afternoon instead of sweeping her off to his bed. Now there were more secrets standing between them. He tightened his fist but instead of beating at the door he lay it silently against the wood before turning abruptly and walking away.

He paused outside Lucy's door. There was only the quiet sound of her breathing but he pushed it open a crack wider so that the light fell upon her still figure, needing to reassure himself.

Her cover was its usual messy tangle, her arms were flung wide. She was not a quiet sleeper.

He stood for a while, just watching her breathing. Life. It was a precious magic. Infinitely fragile, infinitely tenacious. He knew every moment of her life, had seen it all, from her first angry yell at being pitched headlong into a hard world. It was all there, in his head. Her first smile, her first word, her first step. The first panic-stricken dash to Casualty…

'Why are you crying, Daddy? Have you hurt yourself?' She'd opened her eyes and was looking up at him.

'No.' He rubbed his palm across his cheek and crossed to her bedside and sat beside her, scarcely able to speak for the ache in his throat. 'I was just remembering how you were when you were little.'

'Bad things or good things?'

'Everything. How you cried when you had your first tooth. How cute you looked when you lost it. Stuff like that.'

She moved over to give him some room and he kicked off his shoes and put his feet up. 'Josie's going to have a baby sister, did you know?' She snuggled up to him. 'I was thinking, maybe we could have a baby to play with if Mummy stays.'

This was it. No more tomorrows. 'Lucy—'

'I wouldn't mind if it was a boy, even.'

'That's just as well, because you have to take what you get.'

'Oh, well. You can always have another...'

'Lucy.' He stopped her before her imagination ran riot. 'I have something to tell you. It's important so I want you to listen carefully.'

She waited, her face eager, expectant. 'It's about the lady who came to sports day. About the lady who came today '

'Mummy?'

The road to hell, he thought. But there was no easy way to say it. No gentle way. No way to soften the blow. 'She isn't your mother, Lucy.'

Lucy's kittenish little face puckered up in a frown and there was a long moment while she tried to understand what he was saying. 'But you said…when I asked you… You said Brooke Lawrence was my mother.' She was clearly baffled. He had never lied to her. He might have kept some things from her but… but it was a fine distinction.

'She is, angel. Brooke Lawrence is your mother, but the lady who came to see us, to see you yesterday, and today, well, she isn't Brooke. Her name is Bronte. She's Brooke's sister and she's your aunt.' The last words came out in something of a rush as he made himself say them before he cracked up.

Her mouth made a little 'o' of surprise. Then the sound followed. 'Oh. My aunt.'

'She opened your letter by mistake, you see, and then—well, because Brooke was away and she didn't want you to be disappointed, she decided to come in her place.'

'Are they twins?'

'What? Oh, no. Just ordinary sisters but they are very alike to look at.' *Not in any other way.* 'And it is a long time since I saw your mother. But that's no excuse, I should have told you the minute I realised. Bronte wanted me to. I said it would be better to wait until tomorrow. But something happened tonight and I didn't think I should wait until then. Not now you're awake.'

'Oh.' That was all and her disappointment cut to his heart. Then, 'She's really nice. Bronte.'

'Yes, she is.'

'She laughs a lot and I liked the way she hugged me.' *He'd second that.* 'But I suppose she'll go away, too, if she's not my mother.' Now it was Fitz who was confused.

'Would you like her to stay, Lucy?'

'Oh, yes!' There was a seemingly endless pause, then she said, 'I mean, Brooke Lawrence doesn't have time to be my mummy, does she? She's far too busy saving the animals and stuff and I would like to have a mummy. A real one. Who stays at home and makes cakes and things…'

'Are you suggesting that they swop places?' There was such childlike logic to Lucy's solution, such a sweet simplicity that Fitz wasn't sure whether he wanted to laugh or cry.

'Don't be silly, Daddy, they can't change places. Brooke Lawrence will always be my mummy.' *Right.* 'But if you married Bronte she could be my mummy as well. Like Ellie is Josie's mummy, now.' *Right!* 'And then I could have a baby sister, too.'

'I think you'd better slow down a bit. First we have to ask Bronte if she'd like to be your mummy.'

'When?'

'Tomorrow. And you can meet Brooke as well. That's the thing that happened, Lucy. She arrived this evening—'

'Brooke Lawrence is here!'

'Yes, but she's very tired. You can see her in the morning.'

Lucy's eyes lit up with excitement. 'That's so cool! Can I call Josie?' She flung back the bedclothes but Fitz caught her, tucked her up firmly.

'Josie will be asleep and so should you be. You can call her in the morning.'

'Right. I'll ask Bronte about the baby then, too.'

He cleared his throat. 'I think perhaps you'd better leave that to me, sweetheart.' It was a task he was looking forward to.

'Is it true?'

Bron was standing in the doorway, looking at him with an almost desperate intensity. His answer mattered very much and as he stood up, walked towards her, he thought he knew why. He hoped he knew why. 'What has she told you?'

She looked up, but not far. She was taller than Brooke. Her watered-silk eyes were darker than Brooke's. He wanted to hold her so much, but not yet. Not yet.

She crossed to the armchair and lowered herself into it wearily. 'She told me that she was having an affair with a professor at her university, a man who should have known better. That when she told him that she was pregnant he wrote her a cheque and told her to get an abortion. And that she was getting very drunk prior to doing just that when she passed out in your arms at the Christmas Ball.'

He crossed to the window, stared out over the town towards the dark steely sheen of the distant sea for a moment, then turned back. 'That's about the way it was.' But not entirely and he wasn't pretending any more. 'Of course, I had been lusting after her myself for weeks.' He heard the sharply indrawn breath of the woman behind him, but didn't allow that to deflect him from the whole truth. 'I really thought it was my lucky night when she collapsed into my arms. I brought her here, but then I realised that it wasn't just alcohol that had made her faint and I sent for the doctor.' He shrugged. 'He gave her a good ticking off for drinking and told her to look after herself and her baby. And since he thought I was responsible for her condition, I got an earful too.'

'Oh, dear.' Her voice sounded very much as if she was close to a giggle and he allowed himself to hope. 'Poor Fitz.' Definitely a giggle.

'When he left, she told me the whole story It was obvious that she didn't want an abortion and, fired up by me, she went into college the next day and tore up his cheque in front of the man—kidding herself, I suppose, that the wretch would realise the error of his ways. He told her she could do what she liked, but that if she breathed so much as a word about his involvement he would have her thrown out of college.'

'Could he do that?'

'She wasn't prepared to risk it. It would have certainly put paid to any chance of a first.'

'I suppose so. And how about you, Fitz? How were you kidding yourself?'

'Not that way. Pregnancy has a very sobering effect on a man's libido. And I have to tell you that as an expectant mother your sister was not particularly nice to know. She was demanding, petulant, tearful and sick in turn. But I promised I'd help if she wanted to have the baby.'

'Why?'

'Guilt first. I wouldn't have treated her like that creep, but I wanted the same as he did with no strings attached.' He lifted his shoulders in an awkward, slightly defiant gesture. 'Then, fascination. There was this child growing practically before my eyes. One day Brooke put my hand against her waist and I felt Lucy moving. She was only...' he held his finger and thumb apart '...only this big. The power of life is awesome, Bron.'

He saw her swallow with difficulty. He knew exactly how she felt. 'I went to the antenatal classes with her and everyone assumed I was the father. I felt like the father. I found myself looking in baby shops, choosing a buggy, working out whether disposable nappies were better or whether I should get terry ones.' He saw her smile to herself at the image he presented of himself. 'And I was there when Lucy was born. The midwife let me cut the cord... She's mine, Bron, in every way that matters.'

'And my charming sister let you keep her in exchange for a job in television.'

'I thought she'd be back.'

'Kidding yourself,' she said.

'No, Bron. I hadn't planned on playing happy families. I just thought she'd be back to claim her precious baby. I didn't understand how she could walk away.'

'That's Brooke. Easy to love, hard to understand.'

'How is she?'

'Jet-lagged, exhausted, or she would never have broken down like that. She's sleeping now and tomorrow she'll be herself again.' She finally reached out a hand to him. 'There's no need to worry, Fitz. She won't try and take Lucy away from you.'

He pulled her onto her feet and then sat down with her in his lap. She didn't protest. 'Talking of Lucy, I've had a little chat with her. She knows the truth.'

'What?' Bron sat up hurriedly, but this time Fitz was too quick for her. 'Sorry.' And she touched the darkening bruise on the edge of his jaw. 'Does it hurt?'

'You could always kiss it better.' Bron touched the place tenderly with her lips. 'And there hurts a bit, too,' he said, touching his chin. She kissed his chin. 'And there,' he added, hopefully, pointing to his lower lip. She covered his mouth with her hand.

'Tell me about Lucy.'

'Lucy's only concern was that you would leave.'

'But Brooke's here now.'

'Mmm. Lucy isn't stupid. She knows Brooke won't be staying, and she thinks you're pretty useful in the hugging department. She'd rather have a full-time mother than a one-day celebrity.'

'And Brooke?'

'Brooke can drop in any time she's got a moment to spare from saving the earth.'

'Lucy's got it all worked out, then.'

'Just about. Even to the fact that if you stay she could have a baby sister, like Josie.' His lips sought out the tender spot just below her ear. 'Will you stay, Bron?'

'For Lucy?'

'For me. For you.'

'You're sure you know who you're asking?'

'I think I must have always known. I lusted after Brooke. You do something else to me entirely.'

Nestled in his lap, Bron had her doubts. 'It feels a lot like lust to me.'

'If that's all it was, I wouldn't be sitting here holding you, I'd be doing something about it.

But this time I think we'd better get the details
out of the way first. Will you stay?'

'Are you sure you want me to?' She was
lying back in his arms, smiling up at him. 'You
do know that everyone will think you're a sad
man who couldn't have the real thing so you
settled for second best?'

'Is that a fact, Bronte Lawrence? And do
you think I give a damn what anyone thinks?'
Her throat was pale in the deepening gloom of
the long, midsummer evening. He trailed a line
of tender kisses from her chin to the point just
above her breastbone where her T-shirt began.
He would have removed it, but there was no
rush, she wasn't going anywhere. Ever. 'You
know it's not true, don't you?'

Bron gave a little shrug. 'Maybe you'd like
to prove it?'

'Here? Now?'

'Well…'

He laughed. 'It's a good thing I can read
your mind so well.'

'Oh?' Her lips parted softly, her lids flut-
tered down so that her lashes hid her eyes.
'Then how come I got away with pretending
to be Brooke for so long?'

'I couldn't ever read Brooke's mind. It was when I realised I could read yours that I knew you were someone else entirely. Someone very different.' It was his turn to grin. 'Now we've settled that you're staying, there's just one more problem.'

'Oh?'

'Where you're going to sleep. With Brooke in the spare room…'

'This is a big house, surely there are other bedrooms?'

'Yes, there are other rooms. One was Lucy's nursery. One is full of junk and one used to be my study before I converted the barn. Lots of rooms, but no beds…so it's just as well I can read your mind, darling.'

'And I can read yours. You are not telling the truth, James Fitzpatrick.'

He grinned. 'Maybe not. Did you want me to?'

They woke to a scuffle and a giggle and a tap on the door. Fitz grabbed for the clock on the night table and groaned. 'Bron, sweetheart, we've overslept.'

There was another tap. 'Can we come in?' The door opened a crack and Brooke grinned around it. Bron, flushing a deep pink, sat up clutching the sheet about her. 'I'm sorry to wake you, but I have to get back to London...' she eased the door open to let Lucy in '...and I wanted you to know that Lucy and I have been getting to know one another. She's been giving me the low-down on parenthood, but unfortunately I can't stay for the full course.' Her hand was resting lightly on Lucy's shoulder. 'She understands how it is—rainforests to conserve, species to save.' They exchanged a look, a conspiratorial smile. 'So, there's a vacancy for full-time mother around here. But not for much longer, by the look of things.' Her smile widened. 'Good interview, Bron? Fitz?'

Bron forgot her embarrassment and reached out to her sister, grasped her hand. 'Do you mind?'

'Mind? Good heavens, no, I think it's a wonderful idea. I get all of the fun, but none of the responsibility. You always were better at that than me. But I do have my uses, see? I've organised breakfast in bed for you.'

'That was kind,' Fitz murmured from somewhere deep beneath the bedclothes.

Brooke raised a sharply defined brow in his direction. 'Just send me an invitation to the wedding and we're quits.' Then she grinned. 'In the meantime I have a meeting at ten in London, so I need to know where you've hidden my car. If it isn't in a ditch, that is?'

'It's perfectly safe and without a scratch on it in the hospital car park.' Fitz sat up. 'If you'll wait while I get dressed, I'll run you down there.'

'No, darling, you stay and play happy families. I'll leave Bron's Mini there with the keys under the seat. Not that anyone would bother to steal it.' She was back to her usual self this morning, Bron realised. Bright, exquisitely groomed and in total control. Then as Fitz tensed beside her she forgot all about Brooke and instead grabbed his arm, warning him to keep silent, well aware of the damage any sudden movement could cause as Lucy staggered towards them under the weight of a tray laden with juice and tea, a plate piled high with toast.

Lucy made it without spilling a drop, carefully placing the tray on the bedside table, and the tension evaporated as Bron took a mug of tea and passed it to Fitz. 'This is nice,' she said, helping herself to a slice of toast, patting the bed, inviting Lucy to scramble up beside her.

'It was Brooke's idea,' Lucy said, wriggling down beside Bron.

'Brooke?' Fitz queried.

'It's all right, Fitz. It's what we decided,' Brooke reassured him. 'I don't think ''Mummy'' is quite me.'

'When I told Brooke that you were going to make me a baby sister,' Lucy continued, helping herself to a piece of toast from the plate, 'she said we'd better bring you breakfast in bed because, if that's what you were doing, you'd be worn out.'

And Fitz, for the first time in his life, discovered exactly how a cup could disintegrate, without warning, in the hand.

CONTENTS

WARNING

These are powerful practices. The techniques given in this book can profoundly improve your health as well as your sexuality. If you have a medical condition, however, a medical doctor should be consulted. People who have high blood pressure, heart disease, or a generally weak constitution should proceed slowly with the practices in this book. If you have questions about or difficulty with the practice, you should contact a Universal Tao instructor in your area (see appendix 2 on page 281).

Practice makes pleasure. Because this book is based on a three-thousand-year tradition of actual sexual experience, the authors are well aware of the effort that is involved—pleasurable as it might be—in changing your sex life. Learning sexual secrets is one thing, but using them is quite another. The techniques in this book have been tested and refined by countless lovers over thousands of years in the laboratory of real life. We have tried to present them in as clear and simple a way as possible, but the only way to benefit from them is to really use them.

PREFACE

Many people wonder why a modern, Western-trained medical doctor would choose to write a book on ancient Taoist sexual practices. The reason is simple: As a physician who is passionate about female health and sexuality, I am interested in what works for women. As a woman, however, I'm amazed by the incredible pleasure and harmony I've experienced through Taoist lovemaking techniques. I first encountered Taoist sexuality during my medical training when my husband, Doug, began working on a book with Master Mantak Chia on male sexuality. Initially I was skeptical of the traditional claims that the Taoist sexual practices would improve one's health, but they are the most powerful techniques for sexual healing and transformation that I have encountered in both my personal and professional life.

As the demands of my life increased, including medical residency and the birth of our three children, I began to explore Taoist sexual and energetic principles specifically for women. The benefits for my energy level and well-being, both inside the bedroom and out, were tremendous. I was extremely grateful for the joy and pleasure that Taoist practices brought to my life. Then, once I established my practice as a family physician specializing in women's health, my interest in Taoist sexuality became professional as well as personal. As I witnessed the enormous suffering and frustration that so many women experienced in their sexual lives, I saw the need for a healthier and more holistic understanding of women's sexual energy and sexual pleasure.

I have learned these practices from Master Chia, who began studying Taoist practices as a child and has studied with many great Taoist masters (as well as Yogic and Buddhist masters). He is the founder of a comprehensive system of Taoist practice and healing called Universal Tao (previously called the healing Tao). Within the Universal Tao, he has distilled the essence of Taoist sexual wisdom into a unique system he calls Healing Love, which he has taught to hundreds of thousands of people around the globe over the last thirty years. Master Chia initially coauthored *The Multi-Orgasmic Man* with my husband to introduce men to a wiser and more satisfying understanding of men's sexuality. After that book's wide reception, Doug and I coauthored *The Multi-Orgasmic Couple* with Mantak Chia and Maneewan Chia to offer couples an opportunity to explore the more intimate and profound lovemaking that men had discovered in the first book. I realized, however, that it was impossible to address women's varied, subtle, rich, and sometimes difficult sexuality in the depth that it deserves in a book for couples. It has since become clear to me from numerous readers, patients, and friends that many, many women have a difficult time accepting and cultivating the fullness of their own desire, let alone experiencing multiple orgasms. It is my hope that this new book, specifically for women, will help them—and you—to experience a level of joy and satisfaction in their lives that they may not have known was possible.

Taoist sexuality reminds us that we can only live truly healthy, dynamic, and meaningful lives if we connect to the source of our overall desire and vitality—that is, our sexual energy. Our sexual energy is not some optional luxury. It is nothing less than a major source of the energy we have in our life as a whole. It is a wellspring of incredible power and joy for us if we cultivate it. The simple practices will teach you how to use your body's own energetic resources to augment your sexual pleasure and profoundly heal your body. You will be able to enhance and expand your orgasmic ability and then use your pleasure and sexual energy to bring joy and vitality to your whole life.

Throughout the book I will be weaving in the stories of my patients and students on their journeys to greater pleasure and fulfillment through Taoist sexual practice. Although the insights and exercises come from both a Taoist master and a western doctor, we have decided that I should write this book in the first person. We believe that this is important for the kind of directness and intimacy that is essential for a subject as personal and profound as sexuality. While I am a physician and a student of the Tao, I hope you will see me simply as a friend and as a companion on your journey to experiencing your full desire, pleasure, and vitality.

By making time to explore your pleasure and to unleash your sexual energy, you will give yourself a most precious gift. You will also be giving a gift to everyone else in your life—not only your partner, if you have one, but also everyone that you care for and who cares for you. The more fulfilled you are sexually, emotionally, and spiritually, the more energy and joy you will have to share with everyone in your life. *The Multi-Orgasmic Woman* is written to help you embrace your passion and explore the potential that every woman has to experience sexual and personal fulfillment.

Rachel Carlton Abrams
December 2004, Santa Cruz, California

ACKNOWLEDGMENTS

I wish to express my gratitude for the many generations of Taoist masters who have passed on their knowledge to me. I would also like to express my thanks to Universal Tao instructors Sarina C. Stone, Saida E. Desilets, and Jutta Kellenberger, and many other Tao instructors, for their insightful contributions to this book. And especially I thank coauthor Rachel Carlton Abrams, M.D., for her invaluable efforts in assimilating and integrating these personally sensitive and important contents through her writing of this book.

—M.C.

I would like to acknowledge all of the wonderful women who shared their sexual experiences and challenges with me in workshops, interviews, and in my clinic. Their stories inspired me to teach these practices, and their words fill this book with unique insight and humor. Special thanks to the Sunday morning women for their love, laughter, and willingness to try just about anything. Many thanks as well to Heather, Victoria, Molly, and Charlea for their invaluable (and ruthless) editing, advice, and support. And I don't know how I would have finished all of the preparations without Janet's footwork.

I would especially like to thank the Universal Tao instructors who contributed their wisdom and invaluable experience to the book—Angela Wu, Dena Saxer, Lee Holden, Marcia Kerwit, Raven Cohan, Sarina Stone, Saida Desilets, and Saumya Comer—as well as the many other instructors who have worked over many years to simplify and perfect the exercises presented here.

I would like to thank our gifted agent, Heide Lange, whose excitement for the book persuaded me to write it. Many thanks to our editors at Rodale Press, to Stephanie Tade for her great enthusiasm and support, and to Jennifer Kushnier for her detailed editorial work and unflagging commitment to make this the quality book that it is. I would also like to thank the top-notch team at Rodale, who have worked so hard to make this book a success and launch it into the world.

Most importantly, I want to thank my family—my children, Jesse, Kayla, and Eliana, for their patience during the hundreds of hours of writing as well as for the many hugs of encouragement. For my sister, Lisa, the sane voice in my head and my heart when things got a little crazy. For Dad, who loves me no matter what. And for Mom, my saving angel, how can I thank you enough?—for your undying support of me and my family under the duress of deadlines and your insistence that I can do whatever I set my mind to. And most of all, for Douglas, the love of my life, my inspiration, my best editor, and my greatest support in writing this book. Thank you for your love, your passion, and your companionship on the spiritual path.

—R.C.A.

THE POWER OF PLEASURE

A woman's pleasure is as powerful and intoxicating as any force on earth. You may not yet feel it, but within you is a wellspring of vitality that can transform your sexual pleasure and illuminate your life. We often think of sex as separate from the rest of our lives, but nothing could be further from the truth. Our sexual lives mirror our general health, our relationships, and our emotional well-being at the deepest level. It is certainly true that who we are and what we have experienced affects our sexuality, but it is also true that making changes in our sexual lives can transform the other parts of our lives, including our relationships.

Taoism, an ancient Chinese system of healing and spirituality, has always understood the fact that sexuality is an integral part of our health and wellness. The ancient Taoist physicians would ask about desire and sexual activity as a routine part of assessing one's health. They might even prescribe lovemaking at certain times of day or in certain positions to treat illnesses. In this book, Mantak Chia and I will combine this Taoist knowledge with insights from modern medicine to offer an effective program that will kindle your desire and magnify your sexual pleasure.

As a holistic physician, I am committed to offering the best of traditional and complementary medicines to address the issues that are most pressing in women's lives. I have repeatedly seen that a woman's overall health and well-being is dramatically affected by the quality and frequency of her sexual experiences. And sadly, too many women are not experiencing the pleasure and sexual satisfac-

1

tion that they need and deserve. According to surveys, one-quarter of all women in the United States have never had an orgasm, more than half are not regularly orgasmic, and even fewer women, only one in five, are multi-orgasmic.

Some of us experience our most profound joy, connectedness, and spiritual oneness during lovemaking. Many of us may have had only rare glimpses of what is possible in intimate sexual union. And still others of us may have been blocked from claiming our full sexual potential by painful sexual experiences. This book will lead you on your own personal journey to discover your sexual power and pleasure, and it will show you how to use this power to transform your life.

In chapter 1, you will develop a personal sexual satisfaction plan that will help you to focus on the chapters, techniques, and exercises that will be of greatest help to you. In chapters 2 and 3, you will learn to cultivate your desire and balance your energy. In chapters 4 and 5, you will discover what prevents you from having the full pleasure of your orgasms and learn the best techniques for you to orgasm easily—and often. In chapters 6 and 7, I will show you how to expand these orgasms into whole-body orgasms and to extend them with your breathing into longer and more intense multiple orgasms. Finally, in chapters 8 and 9, I will help you to maintain your sexual health and healing over the course of your life and show you how you can begin to use it for your emotional and spiritual growth.

Cultivating your multi-orgasmic ability requires that we explore your sexual energy and your pleasure anatomy. By "sexual energy," I simply mean your desire, your passion, or your libido, as doctors sometimes say. The more sexual energy or desire that you have, the easier it will be for you to orgasm. The Taoists see sexual energy as the most powerful source of our overall vital energy, or *chi*, which is responsible for our health and livelihood. If your energy is being drained by demanding work, family responsibilities, financial stress, ill health, or addictions, it will be harder for you to have the sexual energy you need for satisfying lovemaking.

Not only does low sexual energy make it harder to orgasm, it makes it less likely that you will even want to have sex. A recent in-depth study determined that the number one reason that couples don't have sex is fatigue. This is certainly the case for the women who come to my medical practice. In part due to their physical and emotional exhaustion, many of these women are less interested in sex and when they are, they cannot orgasm regularly or at all. The Taoist practices that Mantak Chia and I will teach throughout this book will teach you how to draw energy and inspiration from the desire within your own body.

As an expert on the various medical and complementary options available, I can say that Taoist sexual practices, called Healing Love, are uniquely able to help women with low energy and low libido to have satisfying multi-orgasmic lovemaking and to increase their overall vitality. Carol, a 44-year-old nurse from Pittsburgh, talked to me about her experience with the practice. "I began doing the Healing Love practice several months ago, and I can't remember the last time I felt so alive! I feel so sensual, womanly, and juicy. Even my friends have noticed that my color looks better. I have rosy cheeks!" For women who already have high levels of sexual energy, the Healing Love practices will help them to channel this energy and to access it when and how they like as a source of vitality in all aspects of their lives.

But while Healing Love sees orgasm as an important source of joy, energy, and health for women, it does not minimize or in any way overlook the rest of your sexual experience. The Healing Love practices offered here will allow you to enjoy your pleasure before, during, and after orgasm. As you'll see, orgasm is not the goal of sex. It is simply one of the highlights on a journey of personal pleasure and discovery.

Another part of this journey to sexual satisfaction involves exploring your "pleasure anatomy"—that is, your body's particular sensual response pattern—and learning what arouses you. In chapters 4 through 7, I will show you how to intensify your sexual enjoyment all along the way to orgasm and from crescendo to crescendo. You will discover what your unique "hot spots" are and use the latest—and some of the oldest—techniques from both Western and Eastern traditions to guide you in your pleasure. Whatever your current experience with orgasm—whether never having had one to already being multi-orgasmic—the techniques and exercises throughout this book will help you to enjoy the ever greater bliss in your body that is your birthright.

TAOIST SECRETS OF SEXUALITY

Taoism is the foundation of Chinese philosophy and medicine. It is a comprehensive physical and spiritual system that helps individuals to reach their highest potentials. Taoism is perhaps best known in this country as the basis for Traditional Chinese Medicine, which includes acupuncture, herbal therapy, nutrition, massage, the energetic meditation called Chi Kung (pronounced "chee kong"), and the martial art called Tai Chi Chuan ("tie chee chwan"). The Universal Tao system was developed by Mantak Chia to teach Taoist meditative and exercise techniques to balance the body and increase one's vital energy, or chi ("chee"). The sexual practice, or Healing Love, is an essential part of this system.

"Chi," the Chinese word for life energy, is the force within our bodies and within the universe that engenders life. The word itself has many translations, such as energy, air, breath, wind, or vital essence. I will be using the word "energy" throughout the book when referring to chi, as it is the closest approximation in our language. But chi is not equivalent to energy; it is more subtle, akin to the force behind all life and movement. There are 49 cultures around the world that understand the concept of chi in one form or another; examples include Ki (Japanese), Prana (Sanskrit), Lung (Tibetan), Neyatoneyah (Lakota Sioux), Num (Kalahari Kung), and Ruach (Hebrew).

Western culture and allopathic medicine, often called Western or conventional medicine, is one of the few cultures that does not have a similar concept, although it recognizes the role of energy at the molecular level. Western medicine is extremely effective for treating acute disease and traumatic injuries. However, I believe that it is, in part, the absence of this concept of life force that limits Western medicine's effectiveness in treating chronic illnesses. Western medicine is just beginning to recognize what the Taoists have known for more than 2,000 years—that directing the flow of our life force, our chi, can improve our health and vitality. One such method of directing this life force is with acupuncture, a Taoist healing tradition that uses fine needles to direct the flow of chi in the body. In the past decade, standardized clinical trials have demonstrated the effectiveness of acupuncture for a large number of illnesses. We've even begun to explain just what it is that happens in the body when chi flows; acupuncture modulates subtle body processes, such as blood flow, hormone release, nerve activation, and immune system stimulation.

You will probably be relieved to hear that we will *not* be suggesting that you use acupuncture needles in your sexual practice. It is possible to control the flow of chi in your body and have these energetic and health benefits without using needles. Mantak Chia and I will teach you, with simple exercises, to use your concentration and your breath to activate and move your energy; this practice is called Chi Kung. It involves both concentration exercises and simple movements to facilitate the flow of chi. Used throughout China and now widely practiced in the United States, Chi Kung is an ancient and effective practice. I often refer to the Healing Love sexual practice as "Chi Kung for the bedroom."

Once you become aware of your chi, you'll find that it's rather easy to notice and feel it. Try this simple exercise. Briskly rub your palms together until you produce heat. Now slowly separate your palms until they are about an inch apart. You should feel a "cushion" of air between them that may feel like pressure, heat, or tingling. This sensation is the chi passing between your hands.

As you increase and move your chi, you will also be able to move your sexual energy, called *jing chi*, as well. The ability to expand and move your sexual energy is what allows you to increase your pleasure and intensify your orgasms. It will also give you a great deal more energy out of the bedroom as you live your life in the world.

Mantak Chia has refined the Healing Love practices that are in this book over the course of three decades teaching students. I encourage you to try all of the practices and exercises as written. The purpose of this book, however, is *not* for you to perform all of the exercises correctly. It is to experience and adapt these teachings so that you feel the luxurious joy of your own life force, your sexual energy, streaming through your body and so that you are able to use that energy to find fulfillment in your life. To do this, you need to be aware of your own responses as you practice these exercises. You should take from the practices what you need and add whatever feels right to truly make them your own. The purpose of doing these Taoist practices is not to become a Taoist expert, but to become more fully who you are.

The practices use the natural energy of your own body and are safe when performed in a balanced way with loving attention. I'll teach you the Inner Smile and Healing Sounds practices because they encourage loving self-regard and will help you to refine your energy. These practices improve the *quality* of your chi, while the sexual practice helps you generate a greater *quantity* of chi. If you learn and practice the Inner Smile and Healing Sounds, you are much less likely to have difficulties with the sexual practice because your chi will be more refined and will flow more smoothly.

I give instruction throughout the book on how to keep the practices fun and effective. But because each human body is different and we all bring our own experiences to the practice, different people will struggle with different parts of the practice. In the book, I provide a "troubleshooting guide" for the most common problems, from "I can't feel my chi" to "My chi is keeping me awake at night." If for any reason you have trouble with the practice, it might be helpful to have an instructor to guide you in the practice and to consult if problems arise. A resource for Healing Love instructors is available at the end of the book. There are hundreds of instructors throughout North America and Europe and in most countries around the world.

You can integrate the insights and practices in this book in whatever way suits your needs and your life. Since you will be learning a variety of practices throughout the book, I encourage you to try each of them to find what works for you. They are rich and powerful enough to do for hours each day, but flexible enough to energize you or help relieve physical or emotional stress in minutes. The sexual practices initially take some time to understand and feel in your body, but they can then be seamlessly integrated into lovemaking with astounding results: more pleasure, intimacy, and vibrancy than you've ever experienced.

No matter where you are in your sexual unfolding, the insights in this book will help you to feel more desire and more satisfaction and to have as many orgasms as you wish. We begin our journey by taking a sexual personality quiz to help you design your own personal path to sexual fulfillment.

CHAPTER 1

YOUR OWN SEXUAL FINGERPRINT

Who are you sexually? Our sexual selves are as colorful and varied as each of our unique personalities or fingerprints. Our sexual preferences are influenced by our past experiences, our relationships, the culture in which we live, and the biochemical reactions in our bodies. No two women share the same experience of desire or even the same orgasmic pattern. Misperceptions about the "right" way to have an orgasm and expectations about "normal libido" leave many women feeling inadequate. With this book, I want to assist you in finding *your* ideal sexual self. No matter who you are and no matter what your experiences have been, your body is whole and fully capable of giving and getting great pleasure just as it is. The purpose of this book is not to fit your body into someone else's experience of pleasure, but to awaken your own natural desire and energy so that you can have a fulfilling sexual life that is truly your own.

Your preferred pattern of pleasure may be to have long hours of intense lovemaking once every 2 weeks or "quickies" twice a day. Or you may practice self-cultivation (as the Taoists refer to masturbation) that is so satisfying that partnered sex is enjoyable but not absolutely necessary. There is no "right" way to be a sexual woman. The sexual personality quiz in this chapter is meant for your perusal alone, to help you explore where you are sexually and identify the sexual self that you would like to manifest.

Taking a quiz on something as subtle and ever changing as sexuality can be difficult. As one of my students pointed out, while our sexuality may be as unique as a fingerprint, it is not nearly as permanent as one! The way in which we experience desire changes throughout our lifetimes and even throughout our weeks. Think of this quiz as simply a snapshot of you at this moment. When you're able to understand who you are in the present, it is possible to take the steps toward who you want to become on your sexual journey. Not all of the responses will fit perfectly for you, so choose the one that seems closest to your truth right now.

Please do your best not to judge yourself about your responses. It is easy to imagine that you are the only person with sexual challenges, but I assure you that this is far from the truth. I spend a good deal of my medical practice talking with my patients about their particular difficulties around sexuality. As we grow and change physically and emotionally, our sexual lives will undoubtedly offer us some challenges, *no matter how sexually confident or capable we feel we are*. If, for example, you rarely have sex and have never had an orgasm, this is not another opportunity to feel bad about it, but rather, a chance to be proud. You are choosing to read this book and ask for some assistance with your sexuality, something that might not have come easily for you. I hope this chapter and this book will help you to get excited about the sensual world that can unfold within your body.

Take the quiz, circling the answers that most closely approximate your experience. Add the numbers of your answers and put them in the subtotal space at the end of each section. If you wish, you can put your answers on a separate piece of paper. Refer to your subtotal as you read the two discussions that follow each of the five sections. Each discussion is targeted to those who scored within a certain range for that section. I encourage you to read both discussions, however, as many things discussed in the alternate section may apply to you as well.

If you do not wish to take the quiz, please read the discussions

anyway. In them, I establish the "ground rules" for lovingly supporting yourself during your sexual exploration. And remember, this
quiz is a gauge and not a grade. Approach it with a sense of curiosity
and without self-judgment.

Your responses to the quiz will help you identify the roadblocks that prevent you from experiencing your full pleasure. Your
answers will also help me guide you to the sections of the book
that will be most helpful on your journey. It might be interesting
for you to take this quiz again after you have read the book and
integrated some of these practices into your life. Where are you
starting from now, and where might you go? The possibilities are
as endless as the vast landscape of your imagination. As the Taoists
say, "The journey of a thousand miles begins with one step." So
let's begin.

SEXUAL PERSONALITY QUIZ

SEXUALITY

1. How frequently do you make love with a partner or masturbate?

    1. Almost never.

    2. One to two times a month.

    3. One to two times a week.

    4. Three times a week or more.

2. Compare the frequency of your sexual experiences now (either partnered lovemaking or masturbation) to a period of your
life when you felt the most sexual desire. Your sexual frequency
now is:

    1. Much less frequent than at the height of your desire.

    2. Somewhat less frequent than at the height of your desire.

    3. Almost as frequent as at the height of your desire.

    4. The most frequent that it has ever been.

3. After lovemaking, what percentage of the time do you feel completely satisfied?

    1. Less than 25 percent.

    2. About 50 percent.

    3. About 75 percent.

    4. Almost 100 percent.

4. What best describes your orgasmic pattern?

    1. I am never or rarely orgasmic.

    2. I sometimes orgasm.

    3. I usually orgasm but cannot regularly have multiple orgasms.

    4. I have multiple orgasms whenever I desire them.

Add the numbers for each of your answers and put the subtotal here.

Sexuality: _____

SEXUALITY

If your subtotal is less than 10:

Congratulations. This book is a wonderful place to begin discovering or re-discovering your sexual pleasure. There is no perfect number of times that one needs to make love per week to be a fully satisfied sexual being. Our desire for lovemaking will change throughout our lives and depending on our daily experiences. It is possible, however, for everyone to have a vibrant level of sexual energy and desire, which is part of the fullness of our human expression, our passion for life itself. It is our passion that allows us to fully engage in the world, to do good work, and to enjoy ourselves. We can use the tools of Western psychology and health in combination with Taoist principles to find and expand our sexual energy. In order to nurture your passion, I suggest you explore in full the exercises and recommendations in chapter 2 on stoking the fire within. The Taoist exercises that teach you to identify and expand your sexual energy—the Microcosmic Orbit and the Orgasmic Upward Draw in chapter 6 and Ovarian Breathing in chapter 8—are enormously useful in increasing the fullness and presence of desire.

Lack of satisfaction with lovemaking, on the other hand, can often be due to difficulty with your partner (see "Partner Profile" on page 21) or not enough knowledge about what it is that you need for pleasure. In chapters 4 and 5, I'll discuss at length how to get to know your own body and its responses. If it's orgasm that is sometimes difficult, I reveal in chapter 5 specific techniques that have been proven to help women orgasm, either alone or with a partner. Then in chapter 7, I divulge the secrets to multiple orgasms.

   If your subtotal is 10 or more:

Your sexual journey is unfolding, and I can help you enhance and embolden your sexual pleasure. If you have been capable of great desire but are currently lacking your full desire, chapter 2 is devoted to discovering what may be blocking the flow of your passion. I will teach you how to nurture your passion and keep it full throughout your life. If your desire is raring and ready to go, begin learning the Taoist practices that will help you refine your sexual energy for more ecstatic lovemaking. The Healing Sounds in chapter 3 prepare you for learning the Taoist sexual practices in chapter 6. If you have difficulty with orgasm, chapter 4 discusses some of the physiologic and energetic gifts of orgasm and common roadblocks that prevent women from being regularly orgasmic. If you are already orgasmic, go to chapter 5, which teaches you how to discover your own hot spots (some of which you may not yet have found) and to orgasm easily. In chapter 6, I show you, step by step, how to use your sexual energy to expand your orgasms and to feel their tingling pleasure from your nose to your toes (and a few places in between). Chapter 7 teaches the secrets to multiple orgasms, how to have pleasure that expands beyond orgasm, and, for those of you who are interested, the "how-tos" of female ejaculation.

BODILY COMFORT

5. How comfortable are you being naked with a lover?

    1. I prefer to be partially dressed or have the lights out when naked.

    2. I am somewhat comfortable being naked with a lover.

    3. I am usually comfortable being naked with a lover.

    4. I almost always enjoy sharing my body with a lover.

6. How do you relate to your body?

    1. I hate my body and/or regularly consider extreme means (surgical or other) by which to make my body acceptable to me.

    2. I sometimes feel good in my body but often criticize myself for how I look.

    3. I usually feel good in my body but sometimes criticize myself for how I look.

    4. I love being in my body and appreciate all it can feel and do.

7. How comfortable do you feel touching your genitals?

    1. I touch myself only when it is absolutely necessary.

    2. I am somewhat comfortable touching my genitals but have rarely touched myself for pleasure.

    3. I occasionally self-pleasure or masturbate.

    4. I frequently self-pleasure and enjoy touching myself alone and when with my partner.

Add the numbers for each of your answers and put the subtotal here.

Bodily Comfort: _____

BODILY COMFORT

If your subtotal is less than 8:

If you live in the United States or Europe (and increasingly, the rest of the world), the cultural ideal of what is beautiful is so far from the average female that most of us feel inadequate by comparison. It can be a tremendous challenge as a woman to feel good about and enjoy one's body. In addition, the cultural and religious traditions from which many of us come teach that the body and its pleasures are dangerous and that masturbation is sinful. In truth, your body is the most precious treasure you have, *no matter what you look like.* Every body is capable of giving and receiving pleasure. Taoism teaches us that the body is sacred and that sexual pleasure is a necessary part of our aliveness and our wholeness. The first step in reclaiming the enjoyment of your body is to love yourself as you are.

You will explore your body in detail in chapter 5, so that you can get to know your own pleasure spots. And although you do not *have* to masturbate (or self-cultivate, as the Taoists prefer to call it) in order to have a fulfilling sexual life, it certainly helps. It allows you to pleasure yourself or to teach a lover how best to pleasure you. You will practice loving regard and loving touch toward yourself in chapter 5.

If your subtotal is 8 or more:

Loving your body and being willing to share your pleasure are the cornerstones to ecstatic lovemaking. Even those of us who enjoy our bodies immensely sometimes criticize how we look or how our bodies function. How would it affect your sexual pleasure if you felt at all times that you were an incredibly beautiful, luscious woman? How would it affect your sexual pleasure if you trusted that your body knew exactly what it was doing and that you could relax and fully surrender to your pleasure during lovemaking? Our bodies are precious gifts, no matter what they look like or what challenges they may have.

In my clinic, I care for women of every age, every shape, and every color, and I can tell you that the degree to which a woman is in possession of her sexual desire and confidence has nothing to do with her body type. Many of the most desirous (and desirable, according to their partners) women that I know are overweight, so-called "flat-chested," or over 55. A recent study explored the sexual satisfaction of women who were more than 50 to 100 pounds over-weight. The study showed that women were sexually satisfied, re-gardless of their weight, as long as their body image was positive and they had good communication with their partners, *just like everyone else*. Being significantly overweight did not impair their sexual en-joyment; feeling bad about their bodies or having difficulty with their partners did. Women are desirable when they experience and feel entitled to their own pleasure. Sex appeal is not all about body type; it is about how you move, how you speak, and how you ex-press yourself when you *feel* desirable.

I suggest that during your reading of this book you take a break from body criticism. Do not speak critical thoughts about your body out loud, to yourself, or to anyone else. Undoubtedly, you will still have critical thoughts, but when they arise, try to express your ap-preciation for whatever it is that you're criticizing. For example, you might look in the mirror and think, "I have such a fat ass." Instead, try to find a way to appreciate it: "What a lovely, soft rump for my lover to sink his (or her) hands into!" When we replace negative thoughts with positive ones (even when we are *stretching* ourselves to be positive), new associations begin to form. So the next time that you are with your lover and he or she is gazing at your arse, you just *might* think, he or she "can't wait to get their hands on my gorgeous ass." Positive regard about your body feeds your desire rather than extinguishing it, *because it helps you feel desirable* and, therefore, rightfully entitled to feeling your sexual desire. In short, your ability to feel desirable directly influences your ability to feel desire. And a woman who feels her own desire is inherently more desirable. She shines from within with the power of her passion.

If you are somewhat hesitant about self-cultivation (masturba-tion), know that it is absolutely essential to discovering what you like and to meeting your own sexual needs. Many of us are taught to expect that only our partners are allowed to stimulate us sexually. The ability to touch ourselves, however, allows us to have our pleasure independent of our partner. If only your partner can pleasure you, that means that you need to control him or her in order to get your sexual needs met. And your partner is unlikely to enjoy being controlled. When you and your partner have different levels of desire in the relationship (and you always will at one time or another), each of you needs to be able to satisfy yourself or there will inevitably be conflict. And contrary to common assumption, self-cultivation does not decrease the frequency of partnered sex. If anything, it stokes the fire and keeps it burning for later. As I will discuss in chapter 5, touching yourself during partnered lovemaking is also one of the best ways to become multi-orgasmic.

SEXUAL PAST

8. **My family or families of origin educated me about sexuality in an open and loving way.**
   1. This is not at all true.
   2. This is somewhat true.
   3. This is mostly true.
   4. This is completely true.

9. **My family or families of origin had appropriate boundaries around sexual discussion and behavior so that I felt safe developing as a sexual being.**
   1. This is not at all true.
   2. This is somewhat true.
   3. This is mostly true.
   4. This is completely true.

10. **In my life:**
   1. I have been raped or been the victim of incest.
   2. I have often agreed to sex when I didn't want to.
   3. I have occasionally agreed to sex when I didn't want to.
   4. I have almost never had sex when I didn't want to.

11. I have enjoyed:

    1. Very few of my sexual encounters.

    2. Some of my sexual encounters.

    3. Most of my sexual encounters.

    4. Almost all of my sexual encounters.

Add the numbers for each of your answers and put the subtotal here.

Sexual Past: _____

SEXUAL PAST

If your subtotal is less than 9:

Our past experiences influence who we are and also how we live in our bodies. The study of neuropsychology is just beginning to appreciate the ways in which our past emotional and physical experiences influence the sensations that our bodies currently feel. It is well known that women who have had traumatic sexual experiences, such as rape or incest, often struggle to feel safe and emotionally present during lovemaking. There is also good evidence that women who have experienced sexual trauma have more *physical* ailments of the genital area such as chronic vaginal pain, painful menstruation, or frequent infections. Taoism teaches that when the body is injured physically or emotionally, the flow of life energy in that area is blocked, leading to dysfunction. For example, if you were taught by your family of origin that your sexual organs were "dirty," it is possible that your negative associations with your sexual organs partially block the flow of chi in your genital area.

Negative experiences around sexuality can contribute to low desire and difficulty with orgasm, but there is much hope to be had. Many of my patients have experienced extensive sexual trauma and, through their own psychological and spiritual work, now have extremely fulfilling sex lives. The key to this process is becoming aware of what your experiences have been and to get help from friends, partners, or therapists in processing all of the confusing and some-times terrifying feelings that these experiences can bring up. If you have been raped or been the victim of incest and have not discussed it with anyone, I encourage you to contact a therapist with whom you can process the many feelings that will undoubtedly arise as you go through this book. If you are in a relationship with a trustworthy person, it is also important to share with your partner what you have experienced. Exploring these experiences is hard emotional work, but getting free of their hold over your vital sexual self can be exhilarating and even miraculous.

For many of my clients who have had negative experiences around their genital area, using the Healing Sounds as described in chapter 3 has been a very transformational practice. It can be par-ticularly effective when combined with the Jade Egg practice in chapter 8. From a Taoist point of view, these practices allow the trapped emotions and energies of anger or fear to be released and for the sexual energy in the genital area to flow freely.

If you have not been raped or been the victim of incest but have had sex when you really didn't want to, the same processes can occur. Sex when one isn't feeling desirous can be painful or can make one feel numb physically or emotionally. In either case, your body "learns" to associate the stimulation of your sexual organs with pain or fear or emotional withdrawal. This can also block the flow of chi to the genital area and make arousal and orgasm more diffi-cult. It is possible, however, to reverse this process by changing the choices and experiences that you have. Begin by *never* having sex unless you want to. Your body needs to learn that all genital touch is now safe and that you get to choose when genital touch occurs. In this circumstance, it is even more important to learn to touch your-self for pleasure so that you can feel sexual sensation in an entirely safe environment where you have control over what is taking place. It will help you to do the Body Exploration exercise as described in chapter 5.

If your subtotal is 9 or more:

In most societies, it is the rare woman who has had solely positive sexual experiences. Processing whatever difficult experiences you may have had can unleash your natural desire and enjoyment. If you have been the victim of rape or incest, you might want to refer to the discussion above, but also think back to the conceptions of your body that pervaded your youth. Were your sexual organs seen as "naughty" or "dirty" or simply ignored? What did you call them? The word "vagina" comes from the Latin word for "sheath"—meaning the place to put one's sword (in this case, a man's penis). It seems strange for a woman's powerful sexual center to be named only in reference to a man. And "vagina," although anatomically accurate for the vaginal passage, does not begin to describe the whole of our sexual organs, which include our clitoris, the opening to our urethra (where the urine comes out), and our vaginal lips. (For a fuller discussion of our genital treasures see chapter 5.) Taoism, in contrast, refers to the vagina as the "jade gate" and the clitoris as the "black pearl" (a precious stone). Tantric[1] texts refer to a woman's external genitals as her "yoni," which means "sacred place." Given that a woman's genitals are the gateway to all human life, these names seem more appropriate. What name would you give to your sexual organs? If you were to have daughters, how would you like them to view their genitals? One of my colleagues fondly refers to her vagina as "Viv." You certainly don't have to name your vagina, but can you begin to think of your sexual organs as the sacred source that they are?

It is always helpful to understand the cultural assumptions about sexuality with which we are raised. Once we understand the origins of our feelings, we can begin to reshape them. It might be helpful to talk to a woman from a similar cultural background about

---

1. Tantra refers to the spiritual and sexual practices native to India. The Tantric tradition also has a long history of meditative and healing practices

her experiences. Alternatively, hearing about a different cultural experience highlights what is particular about our own. A friend from a Mexican Catholic family told me that she learned never to touch herself "down there" and that if she did, she had to go to confession and tell the male priest—a fairly direct message that her genitals were reserved for the man in her life. A white, Protestant friend recalled that she had no word for her genitals because they were simply never mentioned by anyone in her family (just as sex was never discussed). She internalized the impression that her genitals, and sex in general, were wrong and should be avoided. Exploring your familial and cultural heritage can help you understand your feelings about sexuality and your body.

If you have had largely positive sexual experiences, you have received a great gift. If desire and affection are your usual associations with physical intimacy, you will not need to address your sexual past and can focus fully on your present. Consider, then, what you would like your current sexual life to look like. Are you able to fully abandon yourself to your desire? How much pleasure are you capable of? Is there anything holding you back from your full sexual potential? Keep your answers to these questions in mind as you practice the exercises in this book. Your ability to surrender completely to your pleasure is equivalent to your ability to expand your orgasmic energy.

PARTNER PROFILE

12. My current or previous partner and I discuss(ed) our sexual life in an open and constructive way.

1. Never
2. Rarely
3. Occasionally
4. Regularly

13. The following best describes my current or past relationship(s):

1. I am often afraid that I will be hurt by my partner and do not trust him/her with my body or emotions.
2. I sometimes trust my partner with my body and pleasure but am afraid of being hurt physically or emotionally.
3. I can usually trust my partner with my body and pleasure.
4. I completely trust my partner with my body and pleasure.

14. The following best describes myself in my current (or most recent) relationship:

1. I almost never ask for or show (with my body or sounds) what I want from my partner sexually.
2. I have difficulty asking for or showing what I want sexually.
3. I can usually ask for or show what I want sexually.
4. I almost always ask for or show what I want sexually.

Add the numbers for each of your answers and put the subtotal here.

Partner Profile: _____

PARTNER PROFILE

If your subtotal is less than 8:

The foundation of any relationship is trust, and the most fundamental aspect of this trust is the belief that the other person does not wish to harm you. All relationships, sexual or not, will at some time bring up fear and emotional pain in the natural process of growing. But if you fear that your partner wishes to intentionally harm you, either physically or emotionally, it is almost impossible to do the tender work of awakening your sexual fire together. It is sometimes the case that we do not trust our partner because he or she is not trustworthy and has physically or emotionally abused us. If this is your situation, please seek the good counsel of friends, family, or a therapist. Living in physical or emotional fear of one's partner will stunt your growth in many more ways than in your sexual life, and both of you will need help finding alternative ways to communicate if you are to be together. Organizations and literature on domestic abuse are listed in appendix 2.

It is also the case that we sometimes do not trust our partner, not because he or she is untrustworthy, *but because we have lost our ability to trust due to prior hurts.* All of us have experienced emotional or physical injury from another person during our development, whether it was a friend who betrayed you, a sibling who demeaned you, or a past love who rejected you. Once you have been "burned," it is easy to become emotionally guarded to protect yourself from further pain. In an intimate relationship, however, this emotional defensiveness will prevent the closeness you need in order to connect and experience your full passion. If you know your partner to be safe, it may be in your best interest to openly discuss your fears and express what it is you need from him or her to relax into trust.

Jean is a woman in her late fifties whose husband, Charlie, loves and is attracted to her, but who would often look at or talk about other women when they were out together. Jean grew up with a mother who was always critical of how Jean looked, and Jean felt self-conscious about her own looks in comparison to these other women. Because of Jean's fears that she was not attractive enough, she was reluctant to be naked or sexual with her husband. Charlie, in turn, felt rejected as a lover and was angry about their deteriorating sex life. Jean's hurt (fearing that her husband found other women more attractive) was making her withdraw affection from her husband, and he in turn withheld the appreciation and affection that she craved. As a result, the integrity of their marriage was threatened. If both of them had continued to "defend" against the other's perceived "attack," their marriage would have dissolved.

Fortunately, Jean and her husband both found the courage to express their fears and to ask for what they needed. They acknowledged that they both loved each other and wanted the marriage to work, which began the process of reestablishing trust. Jean asked that Charlie not look at or talk about other women in her presence and that he show, by his words and his affection, his attraction to her. Charlie asked that Jean also be affectionate with him and that they reestablish their sexual connection. This honest coming to terms with each other of their fears and needs sparked an entirely new level of commitment in their marriage, and this was reflected in greater communication and willingness in their sexual intimacy. Their sexual play since then has never been more satisfying or more intimate.

Consider your current relationship or, if you have more than one, consider the one that is for you most significant. What is holding you back from full closeness and intimacy with this person? Could you discuss it with him or her? What do you need from him or her in order to be lovingly present in your sexual connection? As I will discuss throughout the book, your sexual life is not separate from the rest of your life or your relationships. Increasing your sexual energy will only magnify what is already happening in your life emotionally. It is important to engage in whatever emotional work you need to do with your partner as you progress in your sexual practice.

If you feel connected to your partner but are simply embarrassed about discussing sexuality, this is a great opportunity to take the risk of asking for what you want. If you can't do it verbally, consider writing a letter to your loved one. How do you think your partner would respond if you asked for *just what you wanted* sexually? Some partners might initially be afraid that they cannot perform as you desire, but the majority of partners find great satisfaction in truly meeting their lover's erotic needs. If you make an honest, loving, and patient request, you just might get what you want.

If you are not sure what it is that you need or want to be sexually fulfilled, chapter 2 will help you find your desire, and chapter 5 will guide you (and your partner, if you wish) to explore your body's responses in detail. Even if you do know what you want, the idea of asking one's partner for it can be scary. It may be helpful to have your partner read chapter 5, as well, to become familiar with a variety of sexual techniques that you can try together. There is really no replacement, however, for communicating to your partner what you like and what you don't. If it is difficult to do this with words, ooohs and aaahs as well as the grinding of your hips or the encouragement of your hand can be very successful means of expressing your wants and needs. Try to focus on what you want your partner to do rather than criticizing what he or she is doing. Everyone feels vulnerable when they are naked, whether they are receiving or giving pleasure.

If your subtotal is 8 or more:

If you have chosen a partner who you can trust most of the time and with whom you can discuss what you want sexually, this will be a great gift as you explore your sexual potential. For most of us, there continue to be ways in which we can improve our ability to be honest with our partners about what we are feeling. These skills are basic to the functioning of any relationship but are particularly important when it comes to the vulnerable area of our sexuality. An improvement in communication at any level will contribute to the clarity and enjoyment of your sexual relationship, as was illustrated in Jean and Charlie's relationship. Facing our deepest fears around relationship and sexuality, whatever they are, can flood the relationship with a resurgence of love and passion.

Being honest with your partner about how you're feeling sexually is particularly important. In the discussion earlier, I encouraged women to avoid having sex when they truly do not want to; this is especially important if they've experienced sexual trauma. It is likewise important never to pretend desire or fake an orgasm for the sake of your partner. When you do this, you "trick" your body into experiencing the physical sensations of lovemaking without the warmth of desire. The result is that your genitals learn to become "numb," to be touched and feel nothing. This is a dangerous practice for women who are seeking to cultivate their desire and pleasure because it makes one's sensitive sexual organs less responsive.

If you stop having sensation in your genitals or experience pain during lovemaking, stop and change the stimulation. If you also feel emotionally disengaged from your partner, stop and try to reconnect before continuing. A simple way to do this is to face each other (lying or sitting) and look into each other's eyes. If you are able to talk about what you are feeling—"That position hurt and I got scared," or "I remembered that I forgot to pay the phone bill and got distracted"—it will be helpful information for you and for your partner. Reconnect with gentle touching until you are ready to resume lovemaking. It is important to be honest, even with yourself, about what you are and are not feeling. Only then can you really begin to explore what you need for satisfaction. Remember to discuss with your partner your intention to change the pattern of lovemaking when your sensation wanes so that he or she understands what you are doing and can support you in finding your desire.

I encourage you to discuss lovemaking with your partner and ask for exactly what it is that you need to be present and fully pleasured. Reciprocating and asking your partner what it is that you can do to help him or her sexually will facilitate the process of your finding passion together. In situations where your partner has a difficult time understanding and meeting your needs, it can be helpful to write down exactly what it is you are asking for. Remember to be patient, as real change takes time.

In some cases, your partner may not be able to give you what you want, for whatever reason. You must then meet your own erotic needs to whatever extent you can using self-cultivation. When you honor and make time for self-cultivation as a legitimate sexual path, it can be extremely fulfilling and allow you to integrate the Taoist practices in this book on your own terms. You will also need to decide whether your partner's inability to engage you sexually is a "make or break" issue in your relationship. No one relationship can fulfill all of a person's needs. You need to decide which of your needs are so important that you cannot have an intimate relationship unless they are met.

When we first begin to explore our needs for intimacy and sexuality, it is frightening because we never know for sure whether our partner will choose to accompany us on our sensual journey. Most of the time, partners are grateful for the fresh insight and passion that this growth brings, as doing this work will certainly "stir the pot" of any stagnant relationship. I sincerely hope that the result for you will be a more dynamic and exciting partnership. If you are afraid that your relationship cannot sustain the power of your new growth, I believe that it is still important to do this work. If you are meant to grow and blossom into a more complete, vibrant you and you deny that growth in order to "save your relationship," the result will be your own stagnation and dissatisfaction. You are growing at every moment of your life, and if you stop growing, you begin the process of dying. Your growth may spur your partner to overcome his or her fears and embrace his or her whole, sensual selves as well. Your partner would benefit from reading *The Multi-Orgasmic Man*, *The Multi-Orgasmic Couple*, or a second copy of this book while you read yours. When both of you are engaged in cultivating Taoist sexuality, the results can be profound. If your partner is not interested, it is still possible for you to do the energetic sexual practice alone or even during lovemaking, with his or her support. Use the Taoist practice to cultivate your compassion for his or her feelings. If they witness your new development into a more vital, loving partner, they are much more likely to become interested in the practice.

Communicating with one's partner can be a complicated and sometimes exasperating experience. If you'd like further assistance dealing with your own emotional complexity as you negotiate all of the rich and sometimes difficult relationships that we have (in and out of the bedroom), chapter 3 teaches the Healing Sounds practice. They are an almost miraculous way to calm one's raging emotions when reason does not suffice. They utilize an ancient Taoist knowing about the places that we store our emotions and give practical ways to release and balance them. The Healing Sounds are a vital accompaniment to the sexual practice as they help balance and ground the sexual energy.

PHYSICAL HEALTH

15. I consider my physical health to be
   1. Poor.
   2. Fair.
   3. Good.
   4. Excellent.

16. I exercise for at least 20 minutes
   1. Almost never.
   2. Once a week to once a month.
   3. One to two times a week.
   4. Three times a week or more.

17. The optimal diet for each person is somewhat different, but nearly everyone needs a balance of fresh fruits and vegetables, lean protein sources, and whole grains. Most of us need to limit sweets, saturated (solid) fats, cholesterol (animal fat), processed foods (which usually contain the above), and fast food. Given these guidelines, I consider my diet to be
   1. Poor.
   2. Fair.
   3. Good.
   4. Excellent.

18. Many medical conditions and normal hormonal changes can affect one's libido and orgasmic ability. After reviewing the list of these conditions on page 277, I have
   1. Four or more conditions that can affect my sexual health.

2. Two or three conditions that can affect my sexual health.

3. One condition that can affect my sexual health.

4. None of the conditions on the list.

19. All of the drugs listed on page 278, both recreational and prescription, can affect one's sexual and physical health. After reviewing the list, I note that I am taking

1. Four or more drugs that may affect my sexual health.

2. Two or three drugs that may affect my sexual health.

3. One drug that may affect my sexual health.

4. None of the drugs on the list.

Add the numbers for each of your answers and put the subtotal here.

Physical Health: _____

PHYSICAL HEALTH

If your subtotal is less than 12:

If you are struggling with libido or orgasm, it is highly likely that some of your difficulty arises from your physical health. No matter what your age or physical condition, some degree of physical exercise can improve your health. Moderate exercise, by which I mean 20 minutes of aerobic activity at least three times a week, has been shown to increase libido, decrease depression as effectively as Prozac, improve heart disease, improve or eliminate diabetes, decrease osteoporotic bone loss, decrease arthritic and muscle pain, boost metabolism and weight loss, and overall just make you feel more vital. Most of us "on again/off again" exercisers have noticed that it's hard to start regular exercise once we have been sedentary, but that after the first month, it becomes so pleasurable that the body craves it. Almost any body type can find a suitable exercise, from walking and yoga to bicycling and water aerobics. If you're not exercising now and you want to boost your sexual health, consider adding exercise to your schedule in any way that you can. Simply being more active during your day can help: taking the stairs instead of the elevator, walking instead of driving, or doing your own yard work.

When your body feels well, your chi flows and your sexual energy is more available to you. Even small changes in your diet or activity level can make a difference. Many of the medical conditions listed at the end of the book can be treated, and even cured, with lifestyle changes. If you suffer from hypertension, heart disease, diabetes, high cholesterol, chronic fatigue, fibromyalgia, or osteoarthritis (all of which can affect sexual satisfaction), your condition can be improved or reversed by exercise, a healthy diet, and stopping addictive behaviors (cigarettes, excessive alcohol, and other drugs). If you are pregnant, nursing, menopausal, or post-menopausal, you can read about the sexual issues that are particular to your life stage in chapter 8. The sexual effects of hormonal shifts can often be improved and balanced through Taoist practices. The practice of Ovarian Breathing in chapter 8, for example, is a natural and effective way to improve menstrual pain and irregularities and menopausal symptoms, including low libido. I also explore genital health in detail in chapter 9.

Many medications can also influence sexuality, and many doctors simply do not know the sexual side effects of all the drugs that they prescribe. Speak with your doctor about whether there are any alternatives to what you are taking, and feel free to take the medication list on page 279 into your next appointment to see if together you can find any alternatives. If you do not ask the questions, your physician may assume that all is well and that you are perfectly happy with what you are taking. In the meantime, please continue your current medications, as they are contributing to your overall health, but try maximizing the other "libido friendly" behaviors that I discuss in chapter 2.

If your subtotal is 12 or greater:

You have reasonably good health, which is a great blessing in every aspect of your life. As I've discussed, your sexual vibrancy and your overall health are intimately entwined, especially as you age. Taking good care of yourself now with regular exercise, a healthy diet, and avoiding addictive behaviors can mean that you are more sexually responsive today and will remain so as you get older.

Developing good health habits is important for your physical well-being as well as your psychological health. Besides preventing depression and anxiety, exercise and good life habits mean that you are *loving and taking care of yourself*. We use many of our poor health behaviors (eating junk food and sweets, smoking cigarettes, watching excessive TV, using drugs) to try to escape what we are feeling in the moment, be it anger, sadness, self-hatred, or boredom. We add to the burden of our "dis-ease" by heaping self-destructive behaviors onto negative emotional experiences.

I discuss the basics of sexual health in chapter 9. If you feel that you are already doing a pretty good job at maintaining your physical health, you may want to learn the Ovarian Breathing and Jade Egg practices in chapter 8 that are designed to enhance your vaginal, breast, ovarian, and uterine health. These have been used by women in China for millennia to finely tune their hormones and their sexual pleasure. If you suffer from painful or heavy periods, PMS, or are going through menopause, the Ovarian Breathing practice can be very helpful.

GROUND RULES FOR A SATISFYING AND SUCCULENT SEX LIFE

I hope that this quiz has given you some insight into the areas of your sexuality that you can focus on to increase your pleasure and enhance your orgasmic ability. Use the results of the quiz to guide you to the places in the book—whether that's the next chapter or a section near the end—that can be most helpful for you. I suggest that you retake the quiz several months after integrating the practices in this book into your life to see how you have grown in your sexual fulfillment.

It may also be helpful for your partner to take the quiz as well so that you can compare your experiences. All of the questions are also relevant for men, including the one about multiple orgasms. If your partner is interested in having multiple orgasms and expanding his own sexual pleasure, refer him to *The Multi-Orgasmic Man*; the basic practices are very similar, and it is much more fun to do them together. Having a partner who supports you in doing this practice is great, but having a partner who is willing to learn the practice with you is extraordinary.

During the discussions throughout this chapter, I laid down some of the "ground rules" that I hope you follow while learning the sexual practice. They bear repeating since they should help you stay on the path of developing a satisfying and succulent sexual life.

1. Do not verbally criticize your body.
2. Affirm your body whenever possible.
3. Never have sex unless you want to.
4. If you feel pain or a lack of sensation in your genitals during lovemaking or self-cultivation, stop, change the stimulation, and reconnect with your partner.

Think of these as promises to your unfolding sexual self. If you are able to keep them, you will have created a safe space for your desire to blossom into its fullness. Let's start the process by learning to stoke the fires of your passion.

CHAPTER 2

STOKING THE FIRE WITHIN

Can you recall a time when you felt infused with the strength of your passion, when you felt a warm ache pulsing between your thighs, your breasts tingling or swelling in anticipation of someone's touch? Desire is a rich and potent part of our human experience. As we learned in the introduction, the Taoists think of desire, called sexual energy or *jing chi*, as part of our life energy, or chi. To be passionate is to be full of chi. The English words "desire" or "passion" connote a feeling of yearning and fervor that includes sex, but they also reflect our strongest feelings about life. When we are passionate about anything—our family, our work, our spirituality, an important social cause—we are investing our chi in this experience. Our passion is what moves us to action and ultimately is what gives us joy. We are passionate about the things that matter most to us.

When I ask the women I teach to describe how desire feels in their bodies, they use a variety of words (and sounds) to describe their experiences. The list in the table on page 34 includes an array of experiences that reflect the complexity of our humanness. Many of the words express pleasure, but some also express irritation. Because desire compels us to action, when it is frustrated, it can also feel irritating. Our sexual energy is much more than the force that lands us "in the sack." We often speak of "getting horny" as if we were being invaded by some lewd, demonic (notice the horns) force, but the powerful energy of arousal is basic to our humanity. It is not, as some religions have taught, a dark force that separates us from God, but is the essence of what can compel us to live dynamic and fruitful lives. It is the fact that sexual energy *is* so powerful that it has prompted most major religions to control and restrict sexual behavior, especially the behavior of women. Reestablishing our connection with our desire is part of recovering our personal power.

It is true that sexual desire can be used in a harmful and exploitative manner. But it is also true that someone who understands the nature of sexual energy can use its power in her body and in the world to do great good. The Healing Love practices can teach you how to direct and refine your sexual energy so that you can benefit from its gifts. Though our modern world suffers from ignorance about sexuality on the one hand and blatant exploitation of sexuality on the other, Healing Love offers a several-thousand-year-old wisdom about how to live in our bodies as sexual beings and to use our passion to become the people we want to be.

HOW DOES SEXUAL AROUSAL FEEL IN YOUR BODY?

Flushed	Buzzing	Awake
Alive	Deep	Earthy
Open	Mm, mm, mmmmm	Driving
Connected	Yummy	Warm
Energy shock waves	Full	Juicy
Tingling	Singing	Moist
Dense	Vibrational	Horny
Expressed	Poignant	Frustrated
Mindlessness	Appreciated	Irritated
Confident	Complete	Magnetic
Freeing	Real	Prayerful
Powerful	Pleasure	Happy
Purposeful	Gathering energy	Light

WHAT INHIBITS YOUR DESIRE?

The most common sexual complaint I hear from women in my medical practice is that they have very little interest in sex. Some women have never had a great desire for sex, and others are concerned that the desire they used to feel is now somehow missing. Low sexual desire is the most common sexual complaint, according to the National Health and Social Life Survey, the largest and most well-conducted survey of sexual behavior in the United States. In this study, 43 percent of women said that they had had sexual problems within the previous 12 months. The most common problem was a lack of interest in sex (33 percent), followed by an inability to orgasm (24 percent), and sex not being pleasurable (21 percent). Another survey of women seeking routine gynecological care in the United States found that 87 percent had problems with low sexual desire and 83 percent had difficulty reaching orgasm.

Why is sexual desire so difficult for so many women? Probably because sexual desire is a barometer for many aspects of a woman's well-being. When you are happy, well-rested, relaxed, healthy, and in a supportive and loving relationship, it is a whole lot easier to feel sexual desire. Most of us, however, live lives where we are challenged in at least one, and often many, aspects of that list. In addition, many physical factors can affect your desire, no matter how fabulous you feel otherwise.

If you were to come see me at my clinic complaining of chronically low libido, or a loss of a previously healthy libido, I would first look at what physical factors might be decreasing your desire, particularly hormonal factors. In fact, I spend a great deal of time counseling menopausal and post-menopausal women with low libido. (This is so important for so many women that I have included an extensive discussion of libido and other issues of menopause in chapter 8.) Nursing moms also have a reduction in their desire due to hormonal influences. Thankfully, most women have a return of their libido once their babies are weaned.

I would also ask you about any chronic illnesses and any medications or herbs that you might be taking. So many medications affect libido that I have listed them in appendix 1, where I also note physical conditions that interfere with sex drive. If you find that one or several of the items on those lists pertains to you, I encourage you to discuss it with your health provider as you begin the practices in this book.

Two of the most common issues affecting desire that I see in my office are depression and anxiety. Decreased sex drive is such a common manifestation of depression that it is included among the defining criteria for diagnosis. Depression is eminently treatable today with both psychotherapy and medication. I have witnessed women practically "return from the dead," as they describe it, within a month of getting proper attention for their depressive symptoms. Often, the improvement of mood is accompanied by an increase in sexual desire. Many common antidepressants, however, can decrease sex drive and orgasmic ability. If depression is an issue for you, by all means get appropriate treatment. Be sure to discuss with your health provider if you feel your antidepressant medication may be affecting your sex drive. There are antidepressants available, such as Wellbutrin, that are less likely to have that effect.

Chronic vaginal pain or infections, for obvious reasons, keep women from wanting to be sexually active. These conditions are so common and so misunderstood, by patients and clinicians alike, that I have devoted chapter 9 to discussing holistic approaches to maintaining your sexual health and pleasure.

After exploring what might be physical and emotional challenges that decrease your desire, I would encourage you to take a look at your life as a whole. How do your work and daily schedule affect your ability to feel your desire? Are you chronically fatigued? Do you feel stressed much of the time? If you are in a relationship, how does your interaction with your partner support or detract from your desire? How do you feel about your body and sharing it with a lover? We began to discuss these issues in the quiz in the previous chapter, and we will be discussing each of these in greater detail as we explore your passion.

We all have life experiences that dim our capacity to feel desire. Sometimes life is so overwhelming or so monotonous that it may feel like you will never again experience desire. I believe that every person is capable of feeling desire, no matter what her physical or emotional barriers may be. The next section will lead you through a visualization that will help you remember the desire inherent in your own body.

PASSION IS IN ALL OF US

No matter how frazzled, overburdened, or bored you may be, there is within you the seed of desire. Our capacity for desire and passion is intrinsic to our human nature. Before you can feel your desire, you need to relax your body and mind. A good place to start is with a simple, but effective relaxation exercise called Belly Breathing. There is extensive scientific research (and millennia of Eastern wisdom) that demonstrates that deep breathing can induce relaxation. Belly Breathing is a technique to use any time you feel anxious, particularly as you experiment with your sexuality. As for all the exercises in this book, it is helpful to do this exercise in a comfortable space that supports your sensual self (such as in a bedroom with candles lit). If, however, hiding from the kids behind a locked bathroom door is as good as it gets, then go for it. Most of these exercises can be done just about anywhere.

You will notice in this exercise and nearly all the exercises to come, that you'll do repetitions in multiples of nine. We do this because in Taoism, nine is the number that means "no end." Although it is fine to do the repetitions as many times as you wish, it often

---

EXERCISE 1

BELLY BREATHING

1. Sit in a comfortable position and relax your shoulders.

2. Place your hands on your abdomen just below your belly button.

3. Breathe deeply through your nose and into your abdomen so that your belly gently pushes your hands out.

4. Slowly exhale, through your nose or mouth, allowing your belly to return to its normal position.

5. Inhale and exhale 9 or 18 times (or as many times as you need), feeling your body relax. As you breathe out, imagine that you are releasing your tension with your breath.

---

helps to have a number to define the beginning and end of your practice.

Once you are relaxed, follow the Guided Meditation exercise on the next page. Find a private place where you won't be disturbed for 15 minutes. This guided meditation works best if you can listen to it and let your imagination flow. I know that it can be difficult to do this exercise and those that follow while reading the steps from a book. To help you, I've prepared an audio CD that will guide you, step by step, through the exercises in this book. You can order a copy at www.multiorgasmicwoman.com. Alternatively, you can record the words of the meditation on a tape and play them back to yourself. If this is not possible, try to keep yourself in a free and imaginative mindset while you read the text and do the exercise. Try to let your mind wander and be free. Let images come to you regardless of what judgments you may have about them in your current life. This exercise is about feeling your desire in whatever context it might appear. If you are able to record the meditation and play it back for yourself, relax and close your eyes. If not, close your eyes periodically as you read the text so that you can better focus on your visualization.

After the Guided Meditation exercise, recall the particularities of the encounter you visualized. Where were you? What time of day was it? Were you with a longtime lover or a stranger? Was it planned or unplanned? Was it a part of your normal life (including work, family, etc.), or were you away from home? Most important, how did you feel—naïve or sexy, vulnerable or confident, loving or lusty, gentle or assertive? Who were *you* in this encounter? How does the emotional and physical environment differ from, say, the last sexual encounter you had? How does it compare to your "typical" sexual encounter, either with someone else or with yourself?

On a separate piece of paper, I want you to list, in as much detail as you are able, the particular qualities that made this encounter erotic. Consider the setting, your partner (if you had one), your

---

EXERCISE 2
A TIME OF FULL DESIRE: A GUIDED MEDITATION

Begin by allowing a memory to come to you of a time when you felt passionate and sexually alive. Allow your mind to wander over your history until you find a memory that you can connect to and see clearly in your mind. It may be that several memories come to you. You don't necessarily have to choose one. You might be with a partner or you might be alone. If you're having trouble remembering a time when you felt passionate, it's fine to imagine what your finest sexual fantasy would be.

Now I want you to tune into that memory.

Are you alone or with a partner? If you're with someone, who is it?

What does your environment look like? Describe it in the most detail that you can. Are you inside or outside? What does the room or outdoor environment look like? What colors do you see? What is the quality of the light—soft or shining brightly? Is it cool or is it warm? Is it quiet and still or are there sounds around you?

Now I want you to notice how you feel inside your body. Notice the sensations of your skin, your lips, your genitals. Allow yourself to feel your desire. Do you feel warmth, tingling, or vibration? Where in your body do you feel your passion? I want you to hold on to the energy of your desire. And, remembering all of the details of this experience, come back to the present.

emotional state, how you felt about your body, and what you had done prior to lovemaking—anything that contributed to your experience. Think about which of these qualities you could incorporate into your life right now. Some experiences cannot be duplicated, such as being a teenager in the backseat of your parent's car. But recall what was erotic about the encounter instead: the thrill of being discovered or having sex outside. Some of the qualities—a previous partner, perhaps—you may not want to integrate into your life now, but there may be something about it that you want to include: your response to that partner or his or her particular attention or skill, for example.

I suggested this exercise to one of my patients, Sharon, a bright 40-year-old woman who is a salesperson, wife, and mother of two children under age 6. Sharon and her husband had much less time alone together and less frequent lovemaking since their first child was born. In the past year, in particular, they had been fighting more over responsibilities at home and their lack of sexual intimacy. After visualizing her erotic experience, Sharon made a list that included the following erotic qualities.

EROTIC QUALITIES

Trust in my partner
Vacation (time out from life)
Liking my body

You've filled in the erotic qualities from your encounter on your piece of paper. Now I want you to think about and include on the list any erotic qualities that you know would enhance your current sexual life but were not necessarily a part of this particular encounter. Sharon added getting a massage from her husband, which always helps her to relax and enjoy lovemaking more.

Now I want you to consider how often, in your present life, you would need that particular erotic quality in order to fully support your libido. Then list the things that keep you from having this quality as often as you would like. Sharon's list looked like this:

EROTIC QUALITIES	HOW OFTEN DO I WANT THIS?	WHAT KEEPS ME FROM HAVING IT AS OFTEN AS I WANT?	
Trust in my partner	Always	Infrequent communication	
Vacation (time out from life)	Four times a year for a weekend	Making the effort, money, getting child care	
Liking my body	Always	Lack of exercise, self-criticism	
Getting a massage	Twice a month	Afraid to ask (because then I'll owe him a favor)	

Next, I want you to consider what it will mean if you don't have this erotic quality in your life. What will happen to you, to your desire, or to your relationship, if you do *not* have that particular quality as often as you want it? And lastly, what might happen if you *do* have this erotic quality in your life as often as you want it? What might develop for you, for your relationship, or for your sexual passion? Fill these in on your sheet of paper.

EROTIC QUALITIES	HOW OFTEN DO I WANT THIS?	WHAT KEEPS ME FROM HAVING IT AS OFTEN AS I WANT?	WHAT IS THE CONSEQUENCE OF *NOT* HAVING IT?	WHAT WILL I EXPERIENCE IF I HAVE IT?
Trust in my partner	Always	Infrequent communication	Losing my relationship	Peace, a solid foundation
Vacation (time out from life)	Four times a year for a weekend	Making the effort, money, getting child care	Low sex drive, being irritable	Intimacy, harmony and passion
Liking my body	Always	Lack of exercise, self-criticism	Feel dumpy and non-sexual	Feel explorative and expansive
Getting a massage	Twice a month	Afraid to ask (because then I'll owe him a favor)	Not relaxed during sex, don't feel cared for	Gratitude towards my husband, more ease in our sexuality

Finally, I want you to make a list of priorities for your sensual self that will help you include more libido friendly behaviors in your life. Use the list of erotic qualities and brainstorm what it is that you need to do to make them happen. Sharon's priorities list looked like this:

PRIORITIES

1. Make time to talk to Michael about our relationship and sex life.
2. Call Mom to see if she can watch the kids for a weekend in the next month.
3. Start walking in the mornings twice a week.
4. Ask Michael for a massage this weekend.

Sharon realized that not only her erotic self, but perhaps her marriage as well, might be at stake. Her concern fueled her motivation to make changes. Your list may look very different from Sharon's. For example, Sasha, a 28-year-old visual artist, described her erotic memory as a spontaneous encounter with an ex-lover who was not emotionally intimate but had allowed her raw sexual energy to flow. Sasha found that with her husband, whom she loves deeply, she has difficulty turning off her mind and accessing the same powerful sexual drive. Her list of erotic qualities included connecting with her basic, physical desire for sex. Sasha had unwittingly set boundaries around her sexual expression with her husband. One of her priorities was to explore fantasy and role play that might let her access her powerful sexual energy in her current life. We discuss the importance of fantasy (and some healthy guidelines) later in this chapter.

I want you to consider your list of erotic qualities and integrate at least one of them into your life this week. This is easier to do with some items than with others. You may not be able to find a willing and loving partner by Thursday afternoon, but you can choose to get enough sleep or create a number of hours to devote to lovemaking. Sharon, for example, chose to call a babysitter for a Saturday night date, and Sasha enrolled in an erotic dance class to access some of her raw sexual energy.

I want you to also pick an item that seems absolutely essential to reaching your erotic potential but that perhaps might take some time to accomplish. You may need to find a partner, change your work, or love your body. Think carefully about one smaller step you can take this week to move toward that goal, such as checking the personal ads or letting friends know you're looking for someone (and *whom* you're looking for). Start doing job searches or set aside time to create a list of characteristics that you need in a new job. Commit to refraining from body criticism for a week or to taking a relaxing bath at least one night a month.

After doing this exercise, Jill, a vibrant 49-year-old who was looking for a new female partner, committed to talking to all of her friends about exactly the kind of woman she was looking for. As often happens when we put our intentions out into the world, Jill met an exciting new lover 1 week later. Having the intention to nurture your erotic life and taking even small steps toward doing so will greatly magnify your chances of getting the passionate, charged self that you deserve.

It is most important that you expand your passion using erotic qualities that work for you. As a physician and teacher, I have witnessed many women rediscover and augment their passion in a variety of ways. Some of these are so important and successful that I will discuss them in detail: the use of our erotic imaginations, the lure of novelty, and the importance of self-nurture.

KINDLING YOUR PASSION WITH YOUR IMAGINATION

One of the most direct ways to increase our sexual desire is by the stimulation of what sex therapists often call our most important sexual organ—the brain. Women, in particular, have active imaginations about intimacy and relationships. This is why soap operas and romantic novels and movies are considered "women's entertainment." Sexual fantasy has such a potent effect that some women can orgasm simply from fantasy alone. Studies show that sexual fantasy helps many women achieve arousal and orgasm during part-nered sex.

Because we live in a society still bound by strict social conventions about sex, many women are ashamed or afraid of being aroused by sexual fantasies. Our sexual fire, however, does not obey the moral codes that we live by. In fact, our sexual imaginations are most frequently fueled by situations that *flaunt* traditional moral codes: public sex, group sex, adultery, or S&M sex. Every woman must make decisions about how she wants to *physically* express her sexual self in life, but I want to encourage you to loosen the reins a bit on your sexual imagination.

When we censor our sexual imaginations, we limit full access to our sexual energy. One of the keys to stoking our libido is freeing up our sexual imagination, and there are many ways to do so. Consider writing down some of your fantasies. If you have a partner, you may want to share or act them out with him or her. Change your environment so that it inspires your sensual self. If you enjoy reading erotica or renting erotic movies, do so. If you like playing roles with your partner, go for it. It may seem silly, but your erotic imagination is actually very powerful, and you will be surprised by what "realistic" responses you may get. There is good evidence to show that our brains and hormones respond similarly to imagined reality as they do to lived reality.

Some of our sexual fantasies may challenge our boundaries. Many of us are afraid that if we even *think* about having sex with a forbidden person (or persons), we will act on it. I would argue that, in fact, the opposite is true. When we suppress our fantasy lives and refuse to acknowledge them, our fantasies become even more powerful. And we have less control over the power our fantasies exert because they are now *unconscious* fantasies. When we explore our fantasies, we access the sexual energy that they possess. We also make them *conscious*, thus increasing our decision-making power over them. If you are in a relationship, sharing these fantasies with your partner in an environment that is safe can be an incredible turn-on and also quite liberating.

That's what happened with a couple I know, Sarah and Caleb, who have been married for 8 years. After prodding her, Caleb found out that one of Sarah's sexual fantasies was to be with two men. In the beginning, he felt threatened by this. Would Sarah ever pursue her fantasy outside of their marriage? After a few years, feeling confident that Sarah was as committed to monogamy as he was, Caleb acted out her fantasy with her, using fingers and props and his own imagination. Their lovemaking was unusually intense. Afterward, Sarah said she felt closer to him than ever before because he had helped her accept and even integrate a part of herself about which *she* had felt embarrassed. As a result, their marriage and commitment were stronger.

The purpose of fantasy is to uncover your own erotic possibilities so that you can play with them with yourself or with a trusted partner. I cannot emphasize enough how important trust is for this process. If you have been hurt physically or emotionally in a sexual context, you need to establish that your partner has your best interests in mind before playing with sexual fantasy. If this is not the case for you or if you do not have a partner, using fantasy in self-cultivation is also safe and fun. Many women enjoy reading erotica as part of their self-cultivation. Suggestions for woman-friendly erotica selections can be found in appendix 2.

It is worth emphasizing that the goal of role play in sexuality is not to disconnect from your lover, but to include your lover in the fantasy. There is a large difference between fantasizing about *someone else* while making love with your partner and playing out a fantasy while being *with* your partner. As was true for Sarah and Caleb, having the courage to incorporate fantasy into your lovemaking can feel very emotionally intimate. On the other hand, if you are fantasizing about another person while with your lover, you will be emotionally and energetically absent. If this is the case, it is impossible to harmonize and exchange your sexual energy with the partner you *are* with.

I was discussing the use of fantasy and imagination with a class in Santa Cruz, and one of the women commented, "I have plenty of experience using fantasy to create a 'screwing' kind of sexual energy, but I also feel like it's a crutch, like it's not even the best kind of sexual energy, the kind that is most nourishing." I assure you that even "screwing" energy can be nourishing, and you'll be learning in this chapter and the next how to channel your sexual energy and refine it so that it can be. The Healing Love practices teach us how to fuse our lust with our love—how to channel our energy from our genitals and transform it so that it nourishes our hearts. But I want to stress that there is not good, sensitive sex, and bad, screwing sex; all sex can be meaningful and profound. Taoist sexuality, however, does believe that sexual energy is most stable and nourishing when it is fused with the loving energy of the heart. Taoist sexuality allows us to draw all of our sexual energy—sensitive or screwing—up from the genitals to the heart, where it can nourish our bodies and lead to our emotional and spiritual growth.

I would suggest that you consider the use of fantasy as one of the many possibilities in your sexual repertoire. Exploring your imagination is important in that it expands the myriad ways that you feel comfortable expressing yourself sexually. But the idea is not that you need to constantly express yourself within a fantasy to feel desire. When you play out a fantasy that you have chosen, even within your own mind, the desire and the feelings become yours. It is really no longer a fantasy because it has become a part of your sensual wholeness. When we feel comfortable with ourselves and deeply connected with our partners, we can be free to express exactly what we're feeling in the moment of being intimate. We can ask for what we want, whether it is tender touch or wanting to "be screwed," because we have explored those feelings before and know how to access our desire through them. Lovemaking is one of the few places that we can express some of the contradictory and uninhibited aspects of our humanness in a loving context. When we act on our deepest desires with our partner, we foster a connection that is profound.

KINDLING YOUR PASSION THROUGH NOVELTY

When we widen the scope of our sexual play, we are experimenting with *novelty*. Our minds and our bodies—both our own and our partner's—respond with interest to things that are new. When we learn new information, our body rewards us with pleasurable sensations. Change and learning actually feel good. Most of us are aware of our need for safety and security—in fact, we go to great lengths to provide them for ourselves. What is more challenging to understand is that we have a need for change that is just as strong as our competing need for security. In no area is this desire for change more evident than in the pool of desire itself.

No matter how skilled we or our lovers may be, using the same techniques or styles of lovemaking will become less interesting and less powerful over time. So how do we introduce novelty into relationships that may be far from new? Using some of the erotic qualities that you generated in the previous pages will help. The most potent sexual tool that you possess, however, is your imagination and your own changing being. There is nothing more exciting than seeing new growth or change within oneself or one's partner. It is also often terrifying because it challenges your competing desire for security—for things to remain the same. But in lovemaking, as in the rest of life, excitement and fear are often paired. What's exciting about novelty and change is that you don't know what to expect. Have you ever happened upon your partner in an entirely new situation, perhaps at a party or at their work when he or she didn't know that you were there? It can often feel exciting to see them in a different context, *as if they were someone new*. Part of that excitement is also the fear, "How will he or she acknowledge me in this new context?" You probably don't experience the same excitement (or fear) when you are flossing together before bed.

Creating mystery and novelty was the appeal of costume balls a century ago. But it is not necessary to dress up to access the power of novelty in relationship (though if you enjoy it, you certainly should!). Most of us are growing and changing every day. Do you share with your partner your new insights about the world or yourself? Are you seeking growth or change in your life? I assume that since you are reading this book, you are. It's a wonderful gift to yourself and to your relationship, either now or one you'll have in the future. If you are single and you live a life of passion, committed to personal growth, you will, I assure you, have many partners seeking to be with you because passion is magnetic. It is inherently interesting. Haven't you known women or men who were not attractive by conventional standards but had many lovers because they had personal magnetism? They were in touch with their passion. We want to be around others who are excited about life because it helps us access our own passions.

What are some ways that you can introduce novelty into your lovemaking? Consider varying your usual environment. Make your bedroom into a sensual palace, adding candles, scents, wall hangings, low lighting, or music. I strongly suggest that you reserve your bedroom for lovemaking and sleep, while minimizing other activities. Watch television, read the paper, and pay the bills elsewhere. Or, if you always make love in the bedroom, consider trying other places. The ancient Taoists, by the way, were great fans of having sex out in nature, as it allowed them to absorb the chi from the environment directly.

If you enjoy sexual props (lingerie, dildos, vibrators, plugs, balls, harnesses, etc.), you can use these aids to the degree that they help you stoke your own sensual fire. Many are available at local stores and online, and I give suggestions for women friendly vendors in appendix 2. Remember that we want to use our sexual energy to increase our overall vitality and love of life. Your aids should be your friends in the process. If any erotica, movie, or sex play makes you feel uncomfortable or bad about yourself, doesn't add to your feeling sensuous and whole, or in any other way feels like it is depleting your energy, please avoid it.

Perhaps the most fundamental aspect of nurturing your desire—whether you're buying sex toys or taking a hot bath—is that you nurture yourself in the process. While nurturing ourselves may not sound sexy to us, from a Taoist point of view it is the key to enhancing our passion, as I'll show you next.

KINDLING YOUR PASSION BY NURTURING YOURSELF

In my clinical experience, the major issue for most women who are struggling to feel their desire is that they are living stressed lives and are physically and emotionally exhausted. Women in most cultures have been the primary providers of physical and emotional support for their families and community. The modern "superwoman" phenomenon has increased the amount of "giving" that women do by adding work responsibilities outside the home to the burgeoning list of things women are *still* supposed to accomplish at home and in the community. Despite sharing the responsibility for providing economic security, most women feel that they are primarily responsible for maintaining the home and caring for the personal and educational needs of their children. Even women who choose to remain single or who do not have children often give to others through multiple activities at work and in the community.

Giving of oneself is a vital act that can itself be rewarding. Giving of ourselves in a context where we feel a sense of autonomy and appreciation can enrich our personal lives and can give us back just as much love and energy as we put in. Many women, however, give out of what they see as necessity in situations where they feel drained, rather than energized. Most of the women I see spend very little time engaged in activities strictly for their own enjoyment or spiritual or emotional growth. The balance of giving and receiving is tipped so far toward giving that many women live their lives feeling physically and emotionally drained. I was recently struck by a medical definition of well-being: "The balance each of us strikes between our own enrichment and depletion, which is critical to our own physical, emotional, and spiritual health." I'd add further that your *sexual* health depends on the vibrancy of these three, your physical, emotional, and spiritual health.

The ancient Taoists offered a nuanced understanding of our overall life energy and sexual energy that reflects this balance between the giving and receiving of chi. They believed that there are three major divisions of chi within the body. Our sexual energy, or jing chi, is part of the first division, called principal energy. Principal energy derives from the forces of heaven and earth and is instilled in our bodies through the love and sexual union of our parents. We are born with plentiful amounts of principal energy, which is one of the reasons that children are so active. Our principal energy is associated with our sexual organs and is the basic, sustaining force in our bodies. It is depleted as we live our lives. The second division of chi is the vital energy that circulates in our bodies and supplies energy for our organs, referred to simply as "chi" in this book. The secret of the Healing Love practice is that you can transform your sexual energy into chi and invigorate your body. The third major division of chi is spiritual energy, or *shen*. When our chi is plentiful and our minds and emotions are clear, our chi is then transformed into spiritual energy. Sexual energy is transformed into chi, which is then transformed into spiritual energy, shen.

As we live and work, we routinely derive chi, the "fuel" to power our bodies, from the chi sources all around us: relationships (or not!), exposure to the natural world, nutritious food, satisfying work, art and beauty, creative pursuits, spiritual practice, love and affection, and especially lovemaking. When we are not being nourished by these sources of chi, our bodies are forced to draw on our stored principal energy to do their work. Our principal energy is like the backup generator that we drain when we are not connected to

EXERCISE 3
THE BALANCE OF YOUR WELL-BEING

1. In the spaces below, list those activities or pursuits that give you energy and joy, even if you are not currently doing them.

2. Then list those activities that drain your energy, joy, or optimism. If an item, such as your work or childrearing, both gives and drains energy at different times, list it in both columns. Try to be specific about what particular activities at work or home decrease your energy or joy. Many activities in your life may be simply neutral.

3. Now list how much time, in an average week, you spend on each of the items. If an item appears in both columns, list the amount of time that is energizing in the first column and the amount of time that it is draining in the second column. This is, obviously, a crude simplification of the "balance" in your life, but it is meant to give you a symbolic representation. It is certainly the case that a horrendous 5-minute conversation with your mother can be much more draining than a grueling hour at work.

4. Total the amounts of time in each column and consider the outcome.

ACTIVITIES THAT INCREASE ENERGY (CHI) AND JOY	TIME PER WEEK	ACTIVITIES THAT DECREASE ENERGY (CHI) AND JOY	TIME PER WEEK
TOTAL TIME PER WEEK			

our power supply—those things in life that excite us, give us energy and joy, and help us feel love. Think about the things in your life that excite you and help you feel joy and love. How much time do you spend in 1 week on these pursuits? And how much time do you spend in activities that drain your energy? When we are drained by stress or overworked, we need our power supply to literally fill us back up and keep our engines running. If we don't nourish ourselves with love, good food, and creative juice, we have to rely on chi from our backup generator—our principal energy.

Unfortunately, many of us push ourselves hard in our lives on a regular basis without refueling from our power supply. In order to function, we are forced to consume our principal energy, our basic life force, and because of this can experience chronic illnesses, sleep disturbances, depression, or low libido. According to the Taoists, our principal energy is present from conception and when it is fully depleted, we die. Whenever we drain our principal energy, we're diminishing our life force. In order to stop draining this life force—and our libido—we need to increase our chi by nurturing ourselves: taking time to love, play, create, and care for our spirits.

Earlier, you listed the erotic qualities that support your desire. As you may have already discovered, things that support your desire can also enhance your overall energy and joy. In the next exercise, I want you to picture the balance in your life between those activities that nurture you, or give you chi, and those that drain your energy. (Some activities, such as work or childrearing, may do both at different times.)

What kind of balance are you striking in your well-being? Remember that if you give much more than you receive, you are diminishing your own vitality and therefore even your "gifts" do not come from the highest qualities in yourself. How do you work, parent, or relate to others when you're drained? What is sexual intimacy with yourself or a partner like when you're drained? Imagine how your life might be different if you had a little more time each day to connect with your power supply—that is, your sources of chi. Consider carving out 1 hour more a week in which to nurture yourself.

I know how difficult this can be, especially for women who are struggling financially to provide for their basic needs, handling demanding careers, or caring for small children. I had my twin daughters toward the end of my medical residency. Just taking a shower when they were newborns was a major accomplishment. But even small changes in how you attend to your own needs can have a big impact. It can shift your attitude, and therefore your energy, remarkably when you feel that your own needs are taken into account. Consider using break time at work or time in the car or shower to do a brief Taoist meditative exercise to ground your energy, such as the Inner Smile at the end of this chapter. Nurturing yourself will benefit you, but it will also benefit all of those whom you love. When you are charged with your own joy, you are able to give to the world in a much more profound way.

Your ability to care for yourself will change throughout your lifetime, but it is absolutely never too late to begin to honor your own needs. One of my patients, Danya, a creative 63-year-old, told me that she is having the best sex of her life with her new 79-year-old partner. When I asked Danya why this was the case, she explained that she has finally been able to give up the notion of having to be there for everyone else and having to be *someone* in particular. As Danya put it, "When I peeled away all the other layers of who I felt I had to be, I found the most exquisite desire at the core of my being." At 63, Danya is choosing to nurture herself, and her desire and sexual fulfillment have never been more poignant.

Most sexologists would agree that self-nurture contributes to a greater capacity for sexual desire.

The Taoist understanding offers us another profound insight. Sexual energy itself can, in turn, increase our principal energy. This is a very important point. Instead of your principal energy being steadily depleted throughout your life, you can replenish it by transforming your sexual energy into chi through the Taoist sexual practices. By cultivating your passion, you can increase your basic life force and therefore replenish your overall health and vitality. The *only* other energetic force that can increase your principal energy is the vital force of real love and compassion. When we combine these two—sexual energy with real love—we have the most potent force for healing and happiness that we as humans have access to. This is why we call these practices Healing Love.

As I will be reminding you throughout the book, sexual energy is a powerful force, and it is vital that you cultivate the energy of love and compassion for yourself and your partner prior to doing the sexual practices. Taoism teaches that emotional energy is simply another form of life energy, or chi, and that when we understand how to sense and move our chi, we can direct our chi and our compassion to facilitate our healing. Let's begin our exploration of the Healing Love practices by learning how to sense and move our own life energy, our chi.

THE MOVEMENT OF CHI

Your chi travels in paths throughout your body known as channels, or meridians. The subtle movement of chi can cause many sensations—some of the most common are tingling, heat, expansion, an electrical sensation, a magnetic feeling, pulsation, or effervescence (a bubbling feeling). Not surprisingly, many of these sensations are similar to those we feel with arousal or desire, since arousal is simply the movement of sexual energy. These sensations are not the actual chi itself, but the signs of increasing chi in a particular area. You can think of the movement of chi as an electrical or biochemical charge moving through the tissues of the body.

There is a saying in the Taoist classics, "The mind moves, and the chi follows." Wherever we focus our attention, the chi will tend to gather and increase. Western science has shown that simply focusing your attention on an area of your body will cause increased activity in the nerves and muscles, as well as an increase in blood and lymphatic flow. Traditional Chinese Medicine understands all of these systems to be moved by chi. Your increased attention shifts the flow of chi, which then influences blood flow.

The stronger your focus, the greater will be the movement of chi. For example, if you focus your mind on, say, your pinky fingertip on your left hand, more chi (and more blood) will move to that area. You may even sense some sensation in that fingertip as you read this, simply because you focused on it. This awareness is the basis for the Universal Tao's meditative and sexual practices, which help you to sense and move your chi through major meridians to benefit your sexuality as well as your overall health and vitality. These concepts are shared by other great traditions, such as the Indian practices of yoga and Tantra, which also focus on creating and moving life energy.

OUR BELLY MIND

Most of us in Western societies today locate our awareness and our sense of self in our heads—what we think in our brains, see with our eyes, hear with our ears, and speak with our mouths. One of the major teachings of the Universal Tao practice is that we need to shift our awareness (and thus, our chi) from our heads down to our bellies. The navel is where all nourishment flows into our body while we're in the womb, and, according to the Taoists, it remains the *energetic center* of our body throughout our lives. Eastern martial arts masters are successful at performing incredible feats of strength and flexibility because they locate their awareness in (and thus, draw their chi from) their bellies, the same place that is our center of gravity.

Modern research has confirmed the complexity and importance

of our "abdominal brains." Our intestines alone have 100 million neurons—more than in our spinal cords—and there is good scientific evidence that the abdominal brain has an independent ability to process thoughts and feelings. For example, we in the West speak of love residing in the heart or refer to having "gut feelings." These common phrases are recognition of the natural association between our feelings and organs. Often our gut feelings represent our best intuition. The Taoists have always believed that our feelings are actually energies that arise from different organs, not just from the brain.

All of the parts of the body work together to maintain balance and harmony, and each part has its particular abilities. The brain is superb at transforming and projecting our energy out into the world through our actions and our creativity. It is not, however, very good at generating or storing energy. For this reason, it is never good to leave energy in the brain for very long. (When we do, we tend to become irritable and often discharge our excess brain energy through yelling at the people we love or other, not so constructive outlets.) The energy should always be brought down to the abdomen, where the organs are ideal for energy storage. The organs then release energy to the body when it is needed, almost like timed-release capsules. As we'll discuss in later chapters, although the genitals are capable of generating an enormous amount of energy, this sexual energy also needs to be brought to the abdominal organs to vitalize our bodies.

THE HEALING LOVE PRACTICES

You will be learning all of the basic Healing Love practices throughout the book, beginning with Laughing Chi Kung on page 58 and the Inner Smile on page 61. You can think of all of the Healing Love practices as active meditations. Some of the practices, such as Laughing Chi Kung, involve moving your body in order to stimulate the movement of chi. Some basic guidelines, which can be used with any meditative practice in the book, can help your practice to be most successful. Remember that these are only suggestions and that if you feel more comfortable in a different position, you should do what feels best to you. The important thing is that you are able to move the flow of energy within your body, not that you sit in a certain position.

PREPARING FOR MEDITATION

From a Taoist point of view, certain positions (usually standing or sitting) will benefit your ability to do Laughing Chi Kung and the Inner Smile, as well as all Healing Love practices, because they align your head with the heavens and your feet with the earth. Keeping your feet in contact with the earth grounds your practice by allowing any excess or negative energy to pass harmlessly into the earth. I would suggest that you begin doing the practices sitting so that you can fully concentrate on moving your chi. If, later, you would like to do the practice standing, that is certainly fine. Here are a few suggestions (refer to the illustration on page 60).

1. Choose a quiet spot where you will not be interrupted.
2. Dress warmly enough so as not to be chilled. Wear loose fitting clothes and loosen any belts. Remove your glasses and watch.
3. Sit comfortably on your "sitting bones" at the edge of a chair.
4. Place your legs hip-width apart and your feet solidly on the floor.
5. Sit comfortably erect with your shoulders relaxed down your back and your chin slightly tucked in, as if a string were gently pulling up the crown of your head.
6. Place your hands comfortably in your lap, the right palm on top of the left. You may find it easier for your back and shoulders if you place a pillow under your hands.
7. Breathe normally.

EXERCISE 4

LAUGHING CHI KUNG

1. Sit in meditation position with your hands on your abdomen.

2. Begin making the sound "HA, HA, HA." Let your laughter begin to emerge, laughing with your mouth open, letting your chest shake and become warm. Laugh for several minutes if you can.

3. Now laugh with your mouth closed, really shaking your belly and hands. Laugh for several minutes.

4. Take deep breaths into your abdomen and feel the chi, warm and vibrating.

5. Rub your hands in a spiral around your abdomen to help the chi absorb.

LAUGHING CHI KUNG

In order to increase the chi in your abdominal center, we begin our practice with one of my favorite Taoist exercises, Laughing Chi Kung. Laughing has been shown to be a powerful, natural stimulator of positive emotion and endorphins, our "feel-good" hormones. Laughter activates our chi and stimulates the immune system. In fact, Norman Cousins, the editor of the *Saturday Review*, famously cured himself from a fatal illness by watching Marx Brothers movies and laughing a lot. After a good belly laugh, you can sense the warm chi in your abdomen, and it's a fun way to begin your Inner Smile meditation. There are many kinds of laughter. From a Taoist perspective, the open mouthed "Ha ha ha!" or "Hee hee hee!" stimulates the chest area—lungs, heart, rib cage, and thymus gland. Belly laughter, done through the nose with the mouth closed and the belly shaking, sounds more like "hm hm hm!" It stimulates the organs of the abdominal cavity and awakens the chi at the abdominal center.

It may sound strange to simply begin laughing for no reason at all, but I assure you that it is so fun that you will have a hard time stopping once you really get going. It is much easier to start this practice with a group of other people, because amused or not, you eventually begin to laugh at everyone else for laughing so much. It is a great pleasure to laugh in a workshop with a large group of people, but it is just as possible to crack yourself up at home.

THE INNER SMILE

Like laughter, smiling can be a powerful tool for inner healing. I'm not talking about the smiles that we feel obligated to show in order to be polite. I'm talking about a genuine smile, a smile that is gentle but shines from the eyes or a real mouth-stretching, toothy, eye-wrinkling grin that seems to go hand in hand with laughter. It is true that the smiles we enjoy the most are the spontaneous ones that erupt from the feelings of love or laughter, but it is also the case that smiling, *regardless* of how you feel, can improve your mood. Smiling actually stimulates the immune system and releases endorphins. In a study conducted at the University of California at Berkeley, a group of chronically depressed people who had been resistant to multiple antidepressant medications were asked to do one thing: They were to smile at themselves in a mirror for 20 minutes a day. Remarkably, a majority of these people had a significant or complete remission of their depressive symptoms. The Taoists believe that when we smile our organs release powerful secretions that nourish our whole bodies. On the other hand, when we are angry, fearful, or under stress, our organs produce toxic secretions that block the energy channels, settle in the organs, and cause illness and negative emotions.

In a remarkable series of experiments, Masaru Emoto, a holistic physician from Japan, photographed water crystals just as they were forming under different conditions. When he placed water in jars with the words "Love and Appreciation," beautiful crystals formed overnight. When he placed the same water in jars with the words "You make me sick. I will kill you," the crystals were distorted and an ugly image appeared.[1] If a written thought can have that much ef-

---

1. Masaru Emoto, *Messages from Water: World's First Pictures of Frozen Water Crystals* (Tokyo, Japan: HADO Kyoikusha, 1999). The front cover of this beautiful collection of photos and text reads, "The messages from water are telling us to look inside ourselves." Dr. Emoto tries in his work to demonstrate the effect of chi on water.

fect on water, imagine what effect our active thoughts and intentions have on our bodies, which are two-thirds water. If we smile and send loving attention to ourselves, the healing and transforming power that we have is awesome.

We can send loving attention and smile inwardly to ourselves by practicing the Inner Smile meditation. The purpose of the meditation is to nurture the quality of love that you might feel when you see a baby, a beloved animal, or a beautiful sunset. Whatever image brings up the quality of precious caring in you can be used to activate those same healing feelings toward yourself. The Inner Smile helps us to use our energy for our own pleasure and healing. When we smile to ourselves in this meditation, we use a subtle inner smile from the eyes to direct our loving attention and chi to our heart and sexual or-

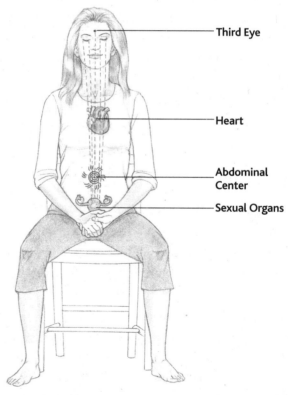

Third Eye

Heart

Abdominal
Center

Sexual Organs

The Inner Smile

gans. I taught Jeanette, a 23-year-old student, the Inner Smile, and 1 week later she confided, "When I got really frantic this week, I started smiling down to my belly, and it completely changed me. It's so good for me because I'm really up in my head thinking a lot."

In this meditation, you'll visualize your own smiling face or warm sunshine or whatever engenders a quality of love for you, and then you'll feel the loving energy or warmth shining into you

---

EXERCISE 5

THE INNER SMILE

1. Sit comfortably in the meditation posture as described on the opposite page. Relax and take a deep breath.

2. Close your eyes and focus on the soles of your feet and their connection to the earth. Feel yourself supported and energized by the earth energy coming through your feet, up your legs, and into your abdomen.

3. Visualize a smiling face 3 feet in front of you. Smile and feel this loving energy entering through your third eye.

4. Smile gently down to your navel and feel the smiling energy move down the front of your body to your abdominal center, located 1½ inches behind the navel. It may help you focus on moving the energy down if you hold your hand open at your navel as if it were a cup receiving the waterfall of energy from your smiling face.

5. Touch your fingertips to your heart and smile down to your heart, feeling the loving energy soften it. You can imagine your heart opening like a red rose, blooming with love and appreciation. Feel the heart radiant and shining, sending its loving energy throughout your body.

6. Bring this loving energy back down to your navel, feeling it flow from your heart to your navel center.

7. Touch your hands to your pelvic belly and smile to your sexual organs. Feel your uterus, ovaries, and clitoris glowing and warm within your pelvic belly. Feel love and appreciation for your sexual organs.

8. Bring the loving energy of your sexual organs to your navel center. Spiral the energy of the sexual organs with the energy of the heart, starting at the navel center and spiraling outward and then inward (see illustration). If you like, rub your open palms around your abdomen as you spiral the energy to help it absorb.

through your "third eye." The third eye is located midway between and just above your eyebrows and is considered an important energetic point in all Asian traditions. In Taoism, it is considered the center of happiness. In the Indian tradition, it is the center of intuition and "inner seeing." The Inner Smile calls forth your compassionate and healing intention toward yourself. This is vital, as it sets the "energetic tone" for the Microcosmic Orbit and the sexual practices that will come later in the book.

SPIRALING THE ENERGY

In many of the practices, we "spiral" the energy at our heads to help the chi distribute itself throughout the brain or at our bellies to be stored in the abdomen. The essence of the spiraling practice is to begin at the center, spiral the chi with the power of your mind outward and then back inward. You should spiral the energy however it feels natural for you. The practice works no matter which direction you spiral or how many times. In the beginning it can be helpful to use your fingers to trace the spiral on your belly or head, in order to assist in your concentration. Eventually, you will control the energy with your mind alone. If you want more specific instruction, here's what the traditional female practice teaches us.

Imagine a clock on your abdomen facing forward, with the three at your left hand, and the nine at your right; and imagine a clock on top of your head facing up, with the three at your left ear, and the nine at your right. Spiral in the counterclockwise directions first, spiraling from the center outward. Then reverse the spiral back inward in the clockwise directions. (These directions are reversed for men.) Traditionally, you spiral out from your navel 36 times (the travels of the earth around the sun in a year) and back inward 24 times (the travels of the moon), ending back at the navel. Your spiral should not extend beyond your pubic bone at the bottom or your rib cage at the top.

Cultivating your compassion and desire is a loving practice that

Spiraling the Energy

you can do over your lifetime—like tending to your inner hearth. The Inner Smile helps us to take the warmth of our sexual fire and refine it with loving intent so that the energy we generate heals us. But most of us do not feel loving all of the time. What do we do with the irritation and anger and self-pity that we experience in real, daily life? In the next chapter you will learn the secret to transforming negative emotions into positive energy, which will make the sexual energy that you generate a truly healing force.

CHAPTER 3

HEART, SOUL, AND SEX

Sexual desire is a wonderful gift, but many women find it difficult to achieve the clarity of desire amongst the anxieties and irritations of their everyday lives. It is often necessary to balance our emotions in order to fully experience our passions. It is also true that the passion we may feel when we are angry or impatient is not as nourishing and can even be destructive to our relationships. Taoists seek harmony and balance in everything, and they explain that our sexual energy is most profoundly satisfying and nourishing when it is joined with the loving energy of the heart. The Taoist practices help us to create harmony between our body and mind, between our mind and spirit, and between ourselves and the people and places around us. When we find harmony within us and come into harmony with all that surrounds us, we are increasingly becoming one with the Tao—the underlying creative and sustaining force in the universe.

Taoism has an interesting insight into emotional health that is quite different from our Western medical understanding. Each of our five major organs and their related meridians—lung, kidney, heart, liver, and spleen—is associated with a particular emotion. Though this is not common thought to those of us in the West, it is a common human awareness: We associate hearts with love and stomachs with worry. When our organs are in balance and the chi is flowing, our emotions come and go and do not cause us much trouble. When the chi in our organs is congested, however, whether from a poor diet or chronic stress, the chi does not flow well and the

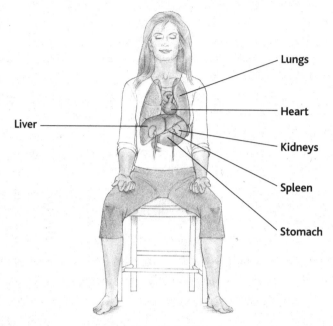

Liver

Lungs

Heart

Kidneys

Spleen

Stomach

Beginning Position for the Healing Sounds

organ can "overheat." When this occurs, the emotions that are associated with that organ become prominent in our emotional landscape. For example, many people in industrialized countries are under constant stress from strict time schedules, perpetual stimulation, and long work hours. These stresses affect the liver, which is responsible for the smooth movement of chi through the body. Liver dysfunction, in turn, manifests emotionally as increased anger, which is an emotion associated with the liver.

Taoism, like many holistic medical paradigms, teaches that repeated stresses to a body first cause emotional symptoms. After repeated exposure to stressors, not only are our emotions unbalanced, but the organs themselves become ill and we manifest physical symptoms of disease. For example, under chronic stress, the liver cannot perform its function in directing the smooth movement of chi through the body, and digestive problems occur as a result. The Healing Sounds practice reverses the harmful effects of stressors to the body by releasing emotional stagnation and balancing our organs and emotions. Most Taoist practitioners come to love the calming and healing effects of the Healing Sounds. My friend Collette, a 56-year-old practitioner from Canada, expressed what I often feel. "The Healing Sounds keep my energy in balance. I feel like a calm lake after doing this practice." It's as if the turbulent waters of your emotions become clear and still. And when we release and balance our emotions, we prevent the ongoing stagnation of vital energy that can lead to illness and disease.

By doing the Healing Sounds, you can also improve your intimate relationships. You'll stop taking out your unbalanced emotions on your partner and instead listen and share from a more loving point of view. Lee Holden, a Universal Tao instructor, explains it this way, "The Taoist practice builds from the foundation of a healthy body. A healthy body leads us into balanced emotions. When you have better emotional balance, your mind is clear. When your mind is clear, you have access to your spiritual consciousness." In other words, balancing our organs and emotions is necessary in order to access our spiritual selves. You may know of spiritual seekers who have not been able to balance emotions of anger or jealousy, and that imbalance impairs their ability to reach the spiritual life that they seek. Strong vitality and balanced emotions create a clear mind. A clear mind creates spiritual consciousness.

Emotional and energetic balance is particularly important when doing the sexual practice. Sexual energy is so powerful that it will enhance the intensity of negative (or unbalanced) emotions. Imagine that your car had a wheel that was out of alignment, causing the car to vibrate. The last thing that you'd want to do is get on the highway and accelerate because it would exacerbate the vibration, worsen the alignment, and be inherently more dangerous. The same is true when our bodies, our organs, and our emotions are "out of alignment." Adding the "rocket fuel" of sexual energy to an imbalanced system will cause physical and emotional distress. Because they prepare and harmonize the body, the Healing Sounds are vital to the sexual practices so that the sexual energy can heal and enliven us.

Most of the Healing Tao instructors I interviewed and the students that they teach say that the Healing Sounds is their favorite practice. I think that this is because the results are so immediate and tangible. Heather, a 28-year-old single mom of a 5 and a 1 year old, uses the Healing Sounds regularly: "I do it in the car before I drive and when I lose my temper. It helps me regain a sense of calm in my family if I take a break and do the practice. Sometimes it *creates* the calm." One of the gifts of the Healing Sounds practice is that it helps you realize that your emotions are just manifestations of energy; they are not actually you. *You* are not nervous, angry, or afraid; those feelings are simply moving through you. The Healing Sounds teaches you how to let emotions move on through and then get the heck out. Saida Desilets, a Healing Tao instructor from Canada, told me, "My emotions used to go through *huge* pendulum swings: When I was happy I was *really* happy, and when I sad I was *really* sad," she said. "And now what I notice, after doing the Healing Sounds regularly, is that I'm still emotional, but the pendulum swing is not so severe. I still feel things very intensely, but they don't take me over. They're not me."

WHEN TO USE THE HEALING SOUNDS

The Healing Sounds are a very important part of an active Healing Love practice, as they balance and refine the energy created by the sexual practice. If you are doing the sexual practice regularly, it would be wise to do the Healing Sounds regularly as well. Most of us know when we are out of balance, emotionally or otherwise. The Healing Sounds are a gentle way to love ourselves back into balance, instead of say, having a chocolate bar or a glass of wine. There is nothing wrong with chocolate or wine, but anything that we use to avoid feeling what we are feeling, be it anger or loneliness, simply buries those feelings and furthers our imbalance and the stagnation of our energy.

I'm going to present the Healing Sounds in the optimal sequence to take your body through each of the seasons: Lung (autumn), Kidney (winter), Liver (spring), Heart (summer), Spleen/Stomach (Indian summer), and Triple Warmer. Triple Warmer is not actually an organ, but a method of balancing all the organs' energies. This sequence is known as the Creation Cycle, as the organs help and support each other in their healing. If, however, you are suffering from a condition associated with one of the organs—such as chest pain or impatience, which is associated with the Heart—do greater repetitions of that sound in the sequence. The particular sounds can also be used individually in times of acute distress. For example, the Spleen/Stomach Sound can be used for indigestion and stomach upset.

Many people find the Healing Sounds extremely helpful for insomnia. Doing the sequence before bed will help empty your head of busy thoughts and relax you into restorative sleep. Insomnia is one of the most common problems I treat in my medical practice. My friend Calla, a 48-year-old Healing Tao instructor, said that, amazingly, "the Healing Sounds completely cured me of my insomnia."

To summarize the relationships of each organ and emotion, refer to the chart on page 70. It's a quick reference to the colors, emotions, seasons, elements, and animals associated with each organ in Taoist belief. All of the major organs of the Healing Sounds are considered the yin organs of the body. Each has an associated yang organ, which is also healed and balanced by the sound. For example, the lungs (yin) are associated with the large intestine (yang), and doing the lung sound will also heal and balance the large intestine. As I mentioned above, each organ is associated with a particular season, and as such can often get "overheated" during that season. Doing the sound more frequently when you are in that season will help prevent overheating of the organ. For example, the lungs are associated with autumn. During this season, you'd want to do more repetitions of the lung sound to prevent manifestations of lung disease such as cough, bronchitis, or asthma.

Every organ has a related color, and visualizing or actually viewing that color will stimulate that organ. Each organ system is further also associated with a particular animal. This is sometimes helpful in visualizing the energy of that particular organ. For example, the kidneys are represented by the sea turtle. The sea turtle is a lovely way to imagine both the water quality of the kidneys and the emotional quality of gentleness.

The major organs are also linked to the elements. The kidneys,

THE ORGANS OF THE HEALING SOUNDS AND THEIR ASSOCIATED QUALITIES

YIN ORGAN	YANG ORGAN	SOUND	COLOR
Lung	Large intestine	SSSSSSS	White
Kidney	Bladder	CHEWWW	Dark blue
Liver	Gall bladder	SHHHHH	Bright green
Heart	Small intestine	HAAAAW	Red
Spleen	Stomach, pancreas	HOOOOO	Yellow
Kidney	Uterus, ovaries, clitoris	CHEWWW	Violet
Triple Warmer	—	HEEEEEE	—

for example, are associated with water, as is appropriate for their function of filtering blood and producing urine. The heart is associated with fire, as befits its role in providing energy to the body and its quality of perpetual movement. In the chart, the primary emotions are listed first, but I've listed many related emotions so that you can choose those that seem most relevant to you at the time. There is no need to try to encompass all of them in your meditation. Indeed, it would be impossible!

Finally, it is most important to relax, breathe deeply, and have fun. Remember that your intention and focus is much more important than reproducing the correct hand movements. Do what feels natural to you. If you need to shorten your practice due to time con-

NEGATIVE EMOTIONS	POSITIVE EMOTIONS	ANIMAL	ELEMENT	SEASON
Sadness, grief, sorrow	**Courage**, righteousness, surrender, letting go	White tiger	Metal	Autumn
Fear	**Gentleness**, alertness, stillness	Sea turtle	Water	Winter
Anger, aggression	**Kindness**, identity self-expansion	Dragon	Wood	Spring
Impatience, arrogance, hastiness, cruelty	**Joy**, honor, spirit, enthusiasm, radiance	Pheasant	Fire	Summer
Worry, guilt, pity	**Compassion**, fairness, centering, Music making	Phoenix	Earth	Indian summer
Pain or whatever emotions you need to release	**Personal power**, creativity	—	Water	Winter
—	—	—	—	—

straints, simply doing the lung and kidney sounds will help balance your energies in a pinch. (Although each of our organs is important to our health, in Taoism, the kidneys, which contain our principal energy, and the lungs are particularly vital to our basic well-being.)

PREPARING FOR THE HEALING SOUNDS

When you are first beginning this practice, make time alone or with like-minded friends to do the exercises. As I explained, it is best to do the series in the order described to optimize the calming and balancing effects of the practice. You'll see that each organ has associated with it both positive and negative emotions. For example, the liver is associated with both kindness and anger. As the Taoist practice avoids judgment and moralism about sexuality, it also avoids it with our emotions. What we often see as negative emotions (anger, fear, worry) to be gotten rid of, Taoism sees as simply energy that can be recycled in the body and cultivated into more productive and nourishing energy. Rather than dumping our emotions on others or out into the world, the practice of the Healing Sounds allows us to transform our negative emotions into more positive ones.

I need to make one more point about negative emotions. We all experience the so-called negative emotions, and in fact, *need* those emotions from time to time. For example, if Helen is being treated unfairly at work, anger is an appropriate response and may motivate her to change her situation. When we are dealing with our emotions healthfully, we experience them, decide whether and how to act on them, and let them go. Helen might act on her anger by filing a complaint with her human resources department. A problem, however, arises when our negative emotions perpetuate themselves in our consciousness, long after they have served their purpose: Helen is still extremely angry when leaving work, cuts off and nearly collides with another car on her commute, yells at her partner when she gets home, and kicks the proverbial dog. This use of anger is no longer helpful and in fact is disturbing her safety and relationships, not to mention her poor dog. The Healing Sounds exercise helps to rid you of negative emotions that you are holding onto and to cultivate the emotions that we all generally need more of: kindness, patience, and joy.

I will discuss each of the organs and emotions in turn. The chart on page 70 summarizes all of the characteristics associated with each organ. You will learn to integrate hand movements, breathing, sounds, emotions, and visualization in order to feel the balancing effect of the practice. This is a lot of information to absorb at first, but with time it will become quite natural. Start slowly and integrate each aspect of the practice as it becomes more familiar. In the beginning you may find it helpful to follow a summary sheet, such as the one I have included at the end of the chapter on page 84, for easy reference. When you have done the Healing Sounds four or five times, it will be familiar enough that you can choose which emotions and visualizations work best for you at a particular moment and emphasize those. Above all, relax and enjoy the parts of the practice that work for you. (This practice is depicted more fully in *Taoist Ways to Transform Stress into Vitality* by Mantak Chia.)

THE HEALING SOUNDS PRACTICE

To begin, sit on the edge of a chair in meditation posture. Rest your hands on your thighs, with your palms up. Alternatively, you can do the Healing Sounds in the horsewoman stance that I'll describe on page 225—in this case, start with your hands hanging loosely at your sides. The hand movements of this practice are used to gather the chi from the space around us as well as direct it in our own bodies. The Healing Sounds are, therefore, even more powerful when performed outdoors, as you have access to the livelier chi of the living world. For example, when breathing in prior to the liver sound, we visualize breathing in vibrant green light. The experience can be heightened by gazing upon the undulating green leaves of a nearby tree and imagining pulling their peaceful strength into your body.

It is nice to do the Healing Sounds outside when you have the opportunity, but you can literally do them anywhere (and I suggest that you do!). When I feel particularly sad, I use the lung sound, SSSSSSS, to help me release and process my feelings, which most frequently takes place while I am driving or at work. You'll do each sequence three times. The third time, do it very gently, as your organs will be almost full of chi and positive emotion and just need a little topping off.

THE LUNG SOUND: FROM SADNESS TO COURAGE

The practice begins by visualizing the organ that you are trying to heal and balance. Become aware of your lungs resting within your chest. Take a deep belly breath to slowly fill the full extent of your lungs, as we learned in Belly Breathing on page 38. As you breathe in, raise your arms up in front of you, with your elbows slightly bent outwards. When your arms are at eye level, begin to rotate the palms away from your face and raise your hands above your forehead. Follow the movement of your hands with your eyes. Keep your elbows rounded. Keep your palms open and stretched upward so that the stretch extends through your arms and shoulders to the pleura, or tissue, surrounding your lungs. The arms should be lifted in one sweeping movement, lifting up from the thighs and stretching above your head as you take in one deep breath. You should feel a stretch that extends from the heels of your palms, along your forearms, over your elbows, and along your upper arms and into the shoulders, where it pulls up on the chest cavity. With your eyes focused upward between your palms, breathe out slowly and evenly making the "SSSSSSSS" sound quietly. The sound is made in a normal tone of voice and is heard more internally than externally. With the sound,

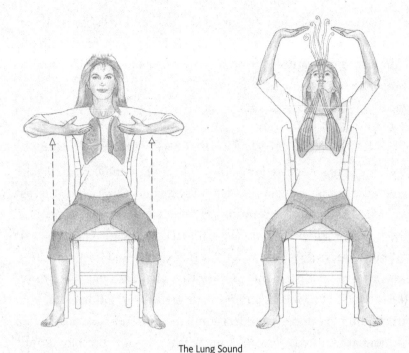

The Lung Sound

imagine that you are releasing feelings of sadness or grief from your lungs.

When you have fully exhaled, float your arms down, rotate the palms forward and rest them gently on your lap, palms up. Close your eyes and breathe in to the lungs to strengthen them. When you breathe in (both during the exercise and after), imagine that you are breathing in a brilliant, white light and the qualities of courage and surrender, letting them fill your lungs. Smile down to your lungs. As you rest and breathe, continue to release sadness and grief as you breathe out. As you breathe in, continue to fill the lungs with white light, courage, and surrender. You may want to imagine that you are breathing in the pure white of star light or sunlight that is always around us. Often the exchange of energy and emotion takes place best when we are in the resting phase between movements. When you are breathing normally, repeat the sequence two more times.

As I mentioned above, the lung sound can be used at any time to release sadness. The lung sound is also useful to release nervousness and can be performed without the hand motions to help you calm down in front of a crowd or any other nerve-wracking situation. The lung sound and movement is further useful in the treatment of colds, excessive mucus, or asthma.

THE KIDNEY SOUND: FROM FEAR TO GENTLENESS

Your kidneys are located on either side of your spine, just where it meets the bottom of your rib cage. We generally think of the rib cage as being located in the front of our bodies but it actually wraps all the way around to the back where it meets the spine. Become aware of your kidneys. Place your legs together, ankles and knees touching. Take a deep breath as you bend forward and clasp one hand in the other. Hook your hands around your knees and pull back on your arms. Round your back and feel a pull in your mid-back where your kidneys are located. Now look up gently, without straining. Round your lips and quietly make the sound "CHEWWWW," beginning with "CH" and ending with the sound one makes in blowing out a candle. At the same time, press the middle abdomen, between the sternum and the navel, toward your spine. This compresses the area of the kidneys. As you make the sound, imagine that you are releasing fear from your kidneys that travels up and out of your body with your breath.

When you have exhaled, sit up slowly with your palms face up on your thighs and your legs hip-width apart. Breathe in to the kidneys, imagining blue energy and the qualities of gentleness and stillness entering them. Continue to let go of fear with each out-breath. The kidneys are the organ associated with water. You can imagine breathing in the cool blue light of any source of water that surrounds you or simply the clear blue light of the sky above.

When you move your arms in front of your knees, gather the gentle blue energy of your environment with your hands and let it flow up your arms into your torso and kidneys. Repeat the sequence

The Kidney Sound

two more times. The kidney sound helps treat back pain, fatigue, and dizziness. You can use it any time to dispel feelings of fear.

THE LIVER SOUND: FROM ANGER TO KINDNESS

Your liver is vital to your health because it detoxifies chemicals that we are exposed to as well as toxins that we produce. The liver is a large organ in our right, upper abdomen. Smile down to your liver. Place your arms at your sides, with your palms facing up. Take a deep breath as you slowly swing your arms up and over your head. Follow your arms with your eyes. Interlace your fingers over your head and rotate the palms to face the ceiling. Push out at the heels of your palms and feel the stretch through your arms and into your shoulders. Bend slightly to the left, exerting a gentle pull on the liver. Exhale slowly making the sound "SHHHHHHH." Imagine that with your out-breath, you are expelling excess heat and anger from the liver.

When you have exhaled completely, breathe into the liver, return to sitting up straight, unlock the fingers, and press out with the heels

The Liver Sound

of the palms as you gently lower your shoulders. Bring your arms to your sides, with your palms face up on your thighs. As you gently breathe in and out, imagine that you are breathing green light into the liver and filling it with kindness. Smile down to your liver and continue to imagine letting go of anger with your out breath and breathing in kindness and green light. It is sometimes helpful to imagine that as you breathe out you are releasing anger as a darker green light. If you are out in nature, you can imagine breathing in the verdant green of whatever surrounds you. You may want to imagine as you raise your arms that you are gathering the energy of the greenery that surrounds you and letting it flow down from your upraised arms into your liver. Repeat the practice two more times.

You can use the liver sound to treat red and watery eyes or a sour or bitter taste that won't go away. The liver sound can be used at any time to dispel anger. A Taoist axiom about controlling anger says, "If you have done the liver sound 30 times and you are still angry at someone, you have the right to slap that person." I'm not sure about that, but certainly if you *want* to slap someone, it is worth trying the liver sound first. It is the sound that mothers traditionally use to calm their angry babies, and it works equally well for the child in all of us.

THE HEART SOUND: FROM IMPATIENCE TO JOY

Shift your focus to your heart. Take a deep breath and raise your arms from your sides exactly as you did for the liver sound. Clasp them over your head but in this case lean slightly to the right. This stretches the connective tissue (or pericardium) surrounding your heart. Look up, open your mouth, round your lips, and exhale the sound "HAAAAAAW" as you picture the heart releasing impatience, arrogance, and hastiness. If you make the sound "HA" as in laughter, you will not feel it so easily in the heart. The sound "HAW" is made

The Heart Sound

deeper in the throat and is more like the "caw" of a blackbird. This sound can be felt vibrating in the heart space.

Relax and lower your arms as you did for the liver sound. As you breathe in, imagine a bright red color and the qualities of joy and honor entering the heart. Breathe out impatience, arrogance, and hastiness. Remember to rest and breathe between movements, as this is when much of the energy exchange takes place. When you raise your arms, visualize that you are gathering the red energy of joy from your environment and allowing it to flow into your heart. Repeat the exercise two more times. The heart sound is useful for sore throats, heart disease or pain, and moodiness.

THE SPLEEN/STOMACH SOUND: FROM WORRY TO COMPASSION

The spleen is associated with the stomach and anatomically is located just behind it. The spleen is important to proper immune function.

The Spleen/Stomach Sound

Become aware of your spleen and stomach just below your left rib cage. Take a deep breath as you place the fingers of both hands on your abdomen, just below your rib cage on the left. Press in with your fingers as you push out the middle of your back. Exhale using the sound "HOOOOOO," imagining yourself releasing worry and pity (including self-pity!). The HOOOOOO sound is made deeper in the throat than the Whooo of an owl, giving it a quiet, but raspy tone.

Relax, place your hands, palms up, on your thighs, and breathe into the spleen and stomach imagining yellow light filling them. Imagine the qualities of compassion and fairness filling your spleen and stomach while you release worry and pity with your out-breath. Repeat the exercise two more times. The spleen/stomach sound is good for the treatment of indigestion, nausea, and diarrhea. It is the only sound that is recommended for right after eating.

THE UTERUS AND OVARY SOUND: FROM PAIN TO PERSONAL POWER

In Taoism, the uterus and ovaries are the yang organs, which are related to the kidneys, the yin organs. We therefore use the same sound for the uterus and ovaries as we do for the kidneys. They are traditionally included implicitly in the kidney exercise of the Six Healing Sounds, but we are giving them their own emphasis here because of their importance to most women's health. The uterus and ovaries are energetically very powerful but can also hold much emotional and physical pain for many women. I have found it helpful to do a separate exercise and visualization for the uterus and ovaries to energize them and to help clear any stagnant energy that remains from past experiences that were painful or unpleasant.

Place your hands, palms up, on your thighs, as you did for the other sounds. Become aware of your uterus and ovaries. Now take a deep breath and place your hands on or just in front of your pelvis with your palms toward your body. As you breathe out, pull your pelvic belly inward as if you were bringing your navel to your spine.

The Uterus/Ovary Sound

This will compress your sexual organs. With your exhale, make the sound "CHEWWWW" as you did with the kidney sound. Imagine that you are releasing any pain or negative experiences that you have had from your uterus and ovaries.

Relax and keep your hands in place or bring them back to your thighs. As you inhale, imagine that you are filling your uterus and ovaries with glowing lavender light and the qualities of personal power and creativity. Repeat the movements two more times. This exercise is good to do at any time that you experience pain, or the fear of pain, in your sexual organs—for example, menstrual cramps or painful memories of sexual abuse or rape.

THE TRIPLE WARMER SOUND: CALMING YOUR MIND

The Triple Warmer is not an organ. It refers to the three warmers, or energy divisions, of the body. The upper warmer, which consists of the brain, heart, and lungs, is hot; the middle warmer, consisting of the liver, kidneys, stomach, pancreas, and spleen, is warm; and the lower warmer, containing the large and small intestines, the bladder, and the sexual organs, is cool. The Triple Warmer Sound balances the temperature of the three warmers by bringing hot energy down to the lower warmer and cool energy up to the upper warmer, through the digestive tract. As we discussed, it is important to be able to bring the "hot" energy of our active (and sometimes overactive) brains down to our abdomens to refine our attention and the clarity of our thinking. This exercise is specifically designed to "cool" our brains and "heat up" our sexual center, which makes it an optimum exercise for the end of the day. Many Healing Tao practitioners do this exercise just before sleep and have significantly reduced their insomnia. There is no season, color, or emotion associated with the Triple Warmer.

(Continued on page 86)

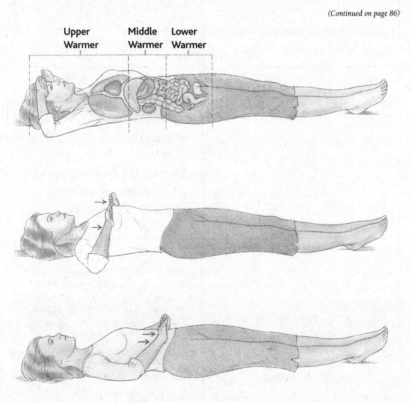

Upper Warmer   Middle Warmer   Lower Warmer

The Triple Warmer

	Lung Sound: From Sadness to Courage Raise arms overhead and stretch your lungs. Breathe out SSSSSSS as you release sadness, grief, and sorrow. Breathe in the white light of courage. Do 3 times.
	Kidney Sound: From Fear to Gentleness Pull back on hands, round back, and pull in abdomen. Breathe out CHEWWWW as you release fear. Breathe in the blue light of gentleness, alertness, and stillness. Do 3 times.
	Liver Sound: From Anger to Kindness Raise arms and clasp above head. Lean to the left. Breathe out SHHHHHH as you release anger. Breathe in the green light of kindness, self-expansion, and identity. Do 3 times.
	Heart Sound: From Impatience to Joy Raise arms and clasp above head. Lean to the right. Breathe out HAWWWWW as you release impatience, arrogance, hastiness, and cruelty. Breathe in the red light of joy, honor, spirit, radiance, and enthusiasm. Do 3 times.

	Spleen/Stomach Sound: From Worry to Compassion Press your fingers into your left abdomen and breathe out HOOOOOO as you release worry, guilt, and pity. Breathe in the yellow light of compassion, centering, fairness, and music making. Do 3 times.
	Uterus/Ovary Sound: From Pain to Personal Power Place your hands in front of your lower abdomen. Breathe out CHEWWWW as you release any pain or negative experiences from your uterus or ovaries. Breathe in the lavender light of personal power and creativity. Do 3 times.
	The Triple Warmer Sound: Calming Your Mind Lie down, raise your hands to your forehead, and breathe in to your abdomen. Breathe out HEEEEEE and move your hands down your body, like a roller pressing out your breath from your chest to your lower abdomen. Do 3 times.

Lie down on your back. Elevate the knees if you feel any pain in the small of the back. Lay your arms at your sides. Close your eyes and take a deep breath, expanding the stomach and chest without strain. As you inhale, lift your hands up your sides, palms up, and round your elbows as you reach your head, bringing your fingertips together over your forehead with your palms now facing down towards your feet. As you exhale, you will push your hands down the length of your body ending at your pelvis. Exhale using the sound "HEEEEEEE" as you picture and feel a large roller moving with your hands and pressing out your breath, beginning at the top of the chest and ending at the lower abdomen. Imagine that your chest and abdomen are as flat as a sheet of paper and feel light, bright, and empty. Rest and breathe normally with your hands at your sides. You may find it helpful to feel the "hot" energy of your mind being "rolled" down into your abdomen and pelvis as you breathe out. Imagine sending your erratic brain energy down into your abdomen, as we do in the Inner Smile. As you breathe in, feel the cool energy of the lower warmer rising up to calm and refresh your mind. Repeat two more times. If you are doing this before bed, you can do the Triple Warmer sound as many times as needed to induce sleep. At other times the Triple Warmer Sound can be used to simply relax.

In the past chapter, you learned how to cultivate your desire. In this chapter, you've learned how to balance the emotions and energies of your organs so that your energy can flow freely. Now it's time to use the sexual energy that you've generated and to let it flow freely through you into that great celebration of pleasure: orgasm.

CHAPTER 4

THE GIFT OF ORGASM

Now that you have kindled your desire and balanced your emotions, in this chapter you will learn the insights you need to experience one of the peaks of your sexual energy—orgasm. Many sex therapists and Taoist practitioners argue that orgasm should not be the focus of lovemaking. I would agree that orgasm should not be the *only* focus of lovemaking. In fact, it is possible to greatly benefit from the Taoist sexual practice by channeling your sexual energy without ever having an orgasm. Still, knowing how to help your body surrender to the ecstatic rush of pleasure that is orgasm is an important part of gaining mastery and fulfillment in your sexual repertoire. Making love with your own style and full expression is more satisfying if you know the basic response patterns of your body. An improvisational jazz musician needs to learn all the basics of classical jazz before she can improvise successfully to her own rhythm. Your sexual response is no different. In this chapter, we are going to learn about the basics of your individual sexual response so that you can become a virtuoso of your own pleasure and crescendo at any time that you would like.

Enhancing your sexual energy and being able to move that energy through your body is vital to experiencing orgasm. Women who use the Taoist practices that you will learn in this book find that their sexual energy is stronger and more available to them when they want it. Debra, who has been a Healing Tao instructor for 20 years, told me, "My arousal, and that of my students, is much quicker when doing the Healing Love practice. It takes much less time to become aroused and orgasm because you are consciously cultivating your sexual energy." The Healing Love practice gives you clear and simple access to your desire. When you do the practice, it's as if you are keeping your sexual energy simmering in a pot. It then takes much less additional energy to make that pot boil over into orgasm. If you do not do the practice, you may be starting with a pot that is cold, and it'll take much more energy and attention to make that pot boil. It is helpful to understand just what happens in our bodies when we orgasm so that we can guide the energy in our body as it builds and explodes into the exquisite release of orgasm.

WHAT IS ORGASM?

We now have extensive research on female sexual response that divides the continuum of sexual pleasure into sexual desire, sexual arousal, and orgasm. In general, desire leads to sexual thoughts or activity, which cause arousal. Orgasm is a peak experience that follows intense arousal. It is helpful to have desire (or sexual energy, as I discussed above) and necessary to have some degree of arousal in order to orgasm. Arousal, either from thoughts or from physical stimulation, causes increased blood flow to the genitals, resulting in the engorgement, or swelling, of the clitoris, labia (the lips around the vagina), and vagina as well as the secretion of lubricating fluid from the walls of the vagina. Orgasm is the pleasurable contraction of the pelvic floor, or pubococcygeus (PC) muscle, and the smooth muscle the vagina and uterus. Extreme arousal and orgasm also cause an increased heart rate and breathing rate, flushing of the chest and neck, increased blood flow and swelling of the lips and breasts, and dilation of the pupils. These observations may demonstrate how orgasm can be measured in the laboratory, but they give no voice to the singular, sublime, and transcendent experience that is orgasm.

Julie, a 34-year-old physical therapist, describes her orgasmic experience this way: "When I orgasm it feels different every time.

Sometimes it moves through my center in gentle waves, melting my insides like warm honey. At other times it's as if I've been overtaken by an avalanche of pure pleasure, almost painful in its intense release, and shaking me to my core. I can't help but cry out in surrender, and I'm left warm and glowing and tingling from head to toe."

Orgasm feels different to every woman. It can be as intense as Julie's avalanche or as gentle as a sigh of sensuous gratification. I have had a number of patients who thought they didn't orgasm, but when we discussed their sexual experiences, they were having orgasms, just not the earth-shattering ones that they expected. Women who orgasm easily and regularly will note a wide variety of orgasmic pleasures, from continuous gentle waves to the classical "peak" orgasm that is modeled on the male experience of singular orgasm.

Researcher Helen Kaplan has proposed a model of single orgasm that corresponds to the three stages we've discussed: rising desire, physical arousal, and orgasm. Men who are not multi-orgasmic experience arousal similar to the graph: peaking in orgasm and then "resolving," returning to the baseline, of not being aroused. For men, this resolution phase is then followed by a "refractory phase," during which they cannot have another erection for a period of time. The refractory phase is shorter in younger men and longer in older men.

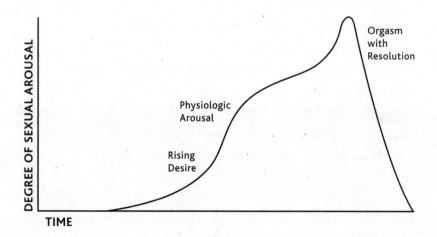

The female sexual response, like many medical models for women, was modeled on the male sexual response. Some women, like Shanti, a 26-year-old massage therapist, have an orgasmic response that fits this pattern: "I take awhile to get aroused, and when I concentrate I can have an intense orgasm. It leaves me feeling relaxed and relieved but also hypersensitive. I don't want my boyfriend to touch me after I orgasm. We sometimes continue lovemaking, but it is only for him, not for me." Shanti has what sexologists refer to as a "terminal orgasm." No, it's not lethal, it just ends the lovemaking session because she loses all of her desire, or sexual energy. She has a female "refractory period." This pattern of orgasm is very similar to the male pattern of orgasm with ejaculation. Since many women—and men—are not aware that men can have orgasms without ejaculating, it is worth emphasizing that this is possible. Discussed at length in the book *The Multi-Orgasmic Man*, men who learn to separate orgasm from ejaculation are able to have multiple orgasms that are as varied and as numerous as those of many multi-orgasmic women.

More recent research shows how truly varied women's orgasmic patterns are. Women may have a number of less intense orgasms or a less intense orgasm followed by a stronger one, or simply a long, undulating plateau of pleasure, which challenges our traditional assumptions and definitions about orgasm.

If you already have orgasms, consider your pattern of arousal and orgasm. Is it usually the same, or does it change depending on the experience and circumstances? Many of us find a scenario or series of stimulation that works and then stick with it, like a good friend. It is important to have a trusty arrangement of stimulation that will reliably bring you to orgasm. But it can also be fun to mix it up a bit and see what other avenues may work for you.

Most sexologists have concluded that sex and orgasm are largely learned responses, which means that, like many elements of our lives, what we feel is often what we expect to feel. Because women have been expected to have orgasms like men, many do. If you have not yet had an orgasm, the good news is that you can influence your orgasmic response by opening up your mind to the wide range of orgasmic pleasure that your body is capable of. If you already orgasm, imagine what it might be like to allow your orgasmic pattern to change—to allow the pulsations of orgasm to go on for 5 minutes or more, to have six orgasmic waves in a row, to feel your orgasmic energy surging through your whole body. *Your expectation of how you are able to experience orgasm will influence how your orgasm unfolds.*

An analogy from the field of neuropsychology will help explain why our expectations and intentions are so important. Have you ever been driving or cycling for several hours and then stopped and noticed that the road continued to look as if it were moving under you? This happens because your brain is telling your eyes that you are still traveling. Our minds are constantly interpreting our world and actually telling our senses *what it is that they are sensing.* There are almost as many nerve fibers traveling from the visual part of the brain *to* the eye (to tell the eye what it is seeing) as there are fibers traveling from the eye to the visual part of the brain (to tell the brain what it is actually seeing). What this means is that *what we see is enormously affected by what we expect to see.* The same is true for sexual sensation. *What we feel sexually is strongly influenced by what we expect to feel.*

As you are making love with a partner or stimulating yourself your brain is giving your body feedback on what it *should* be feeling. This can work in our favor when we have had, let's say, outrageously wonderful sex under an overhanging roof during a rainstorm. Now when we see storm clouds gathering, we begin to feel our sexual energy rising. It is also the case, however, that having low expectations of our pleasure or limited expectations of our orgasm will cause our body to limit its responses. For example, Marly, a 21-year-old patient of mine, has difficulty orgasming with her partner, Tatiana. When I spoke with Marly about what she felt during their encounters, she said, "Tatiana tries and tries, but my body just doesn't work right. I know I won't be able to orgasm and my body feels numb." Marly's low expectations of herself impede her ability to feel pleasure with her partner. As you learn new stimulation and energetic techniques to improve your orgasmic experience, I want you to begin to shift your expectations of what you are capable of feeling. Try to make it your intention that you will surrender to the full scope of orgasmic pleasure that your body is capable of.

ORGASM IS GOOD FOR YOU

As you may have already intuited from how amazingly *good* you feel after having an orgasm, orgasm is in fact good for you and your health. Since many of us were taught by our religions or our parents that something so good had to be bad for us, it is worth taking the time to explore this point. For those of you who are fitness minded, sexual activity burns quite a few calories and boosts your metabolism. Regular sex improves your immune function, helps you to sleep better, relieves menstrual cramps, and reduces stress. Studies over many years have confirmed a correlation between regular sex and longevity; sexual activity is associated with better health among sexually active older adults when compared with their similar peers. Though we don't yet understand all of the reasons that sex and orgasm are good for us, there is mounting (no pun intended) evidence of the tremendous ability of sex and orgasm to "tone" our hormones—which many of us could use some help with—and improve our emotional state. Let's take a closer look at the hormones that sex and orgasm tone.

Our bodies produce a natural form of amphetamine (or "uppers"), called phenylethylamine (PEA). It is nicknamed the "romance hormone" because it is high during early courtship, but it also peaks with orgasm. High PEA is associated with giddiness and excitement; low PEA is associated with depression. When PEA is too high, it can cause psychosis. (Now you finally understand why it

was you stayed in that lousy, but exciting, relationship. It was romance psychosis!) The "high" of PEA is one of the reasons that we
crave early romance. But it is possible to get this natural high,
whether or not you're in a new relationship, through orgasm! Orgasm helps feed the fire of romance in a relationship, no matter how
old your relationship is. And, ladies, guess how we can artificially
increase PEA? That's right. Chocolate. Thus the post-romance "I
must eat a box of chocolate because I am in PEA withdrawal" syn-
drome. So if you're watching your waistline and need a little pick-
me-up, pick up your vibrator (or your lover) instead of the
Hershey's.[1]

Touted by many in the alternative health field as the "anti-aging"
hormone, dehydroepiandrosterone (DHEA), is the precursor to all
of the sex hormones. It peaks in humans at age 25 and then declines
thereafter. Low DHEA is associated with chronic disease, bone loss,
and weight gain, whereas higher DHEA levels protect the immune
system and may lower cholesterol. Although I cannot recommend
supplementation with DHEA, as we do not yet know whether this is
safe, it does—you guessed it—peak at orgasm. And there's no evidence that "natural stimulation" of DHEA has any untoward effects.
It may be one of the major reasons that sexually active adults live
longer and feel better.

Our "bonding hormone" is called oxytocin. It is produced in
large amounts during birth (when it stimulates uterine contractions)
and breast-feeding and assists in maternal and child bonding, hence
its nickname. It is also increased by nipple stimulation in women
and men. Oxytocin helps us feel connected to one another, and it
promotes touch and affectionate behavior, as well as relaxation. Interestingly, it also increases with giving or receiving loving touch

1. Much of this discussion is informed by the brilliant work of Theresa Crenshaw in her book the
Alchemy of Love and Lust: How our Sex Hormones Influence Our Relationships (New York: Simon and Schuster,
1996).

(that includes our pets), genital stimulation, and intercourse. Oxytocin also decreases cognition and impairs memory, contributing to that befuddled "milky mind" that new moms often experience. Oxytocin is important in that it stimulates the release of all of the other sex hormones, and, like the hormones above, it peaks at orgasm and contributes to that lovely, "let's cuddle" afterglow. The feedback loop of oxytocin—loving touch increases oxytocin, which stimulates more touching—helps to explain why affection and sexuality often have that "use it or lose it" mentality. When we are sexual or affectionate, it drives us to more sex and affection. When we are distant (literally) from our partner for prolonged periods of time, we are less inclined to sex and affection. When touch is abruptly withdrawn (a business trip or, in the worst case, the death of your partner), skin hunger ensues. We crave the person—and the touch—who we have been missing. I regularly recommend to the women in my practice who have lost relationships to continue to self-pleasure and consider getting regular massages to try to boost their oxytocin levels, and their corresponding level of well-being.

Testosterone is the sex hormone with which you are likely most familiar. I'll discuss more fully in chapter 8 in its relationship to female sex drive and changes with menopause, but for now, know that it is a potent contributor to sex drive in both women and men, increasing sexual thoughts and fantasies. It is also *increased* by sexual thoughts and activity, a feedback loop similar to oxytocin's. The more sexual thoughts or activity that you have today, the more that you will *want* to have tomorrow.

Estrogen is considered the quintessential female hormone, and indeed we have much more of it than our male counterparts. Synthetic estrogen has been in the news of late because of new evidence that it increases health risks when given to post-menopausal women. I will discuss estrogen, its importance, and its difficulties, in chapter 8. Estrogen influences our seductive sexual behavior and is released into the body with intercourse.

Orgasm also releases endorphins into the bloodstream. Endorphins are those feel-good, pain-blocking, natural morphinelike substances that flood our bodies when we need them. Endorphins are responsible for that "runner's high" that you get just after exercise, when you feel great and your legs don't yet ache. It's because endorphins are blocking the pain. I have had several of my patients with chronic pain attest that when they found a new relationship and were having a satisfying sex life, their need for chronic pain medications dropped considerably.

The release of these hormones is only one of the reasons that sex and orgasm help us feel good, and are good for us. We do not yet have any research on the relationship between Taoist sexual practices and hormonal or physiological responses, but it is the experience of practitioners that the Taoist sexual practices *prolong* the feelings of wellness, vitality, and bonding with one's partner that follow sex. Debra, a long-time practitioner and instructor, told me, "After doing the practice for years, the level of the energy is so high that you don't need to go on forever. The feeling of orgasms can last for several hours. You can still feel the vibration while making dinner, and you wake up energized." Because sex and orgasm are so beneficial to our bodies, I'm going to discuss in full what might be preventing you from having an orgasm as often as you want.

WHAT IF I CAN'T HAVE AN ORGASM?

If you do not orgasm regularly or at all, take heart. More than 90 percent of women who have never had an orgasm can learn to with the right information and motivation. If you're reading this book, that means you! We will explore the common roadblocks to orgasm in the following pages, which will help you identify the elements in your life that may keep you from your orgasmic pleasure.

If you have had orgasms in the past but do not currently orgasm, or do not orgasm in particular situations (with your partner, during intercourse, etc.), you are experiencing what we call "orgasmic disruption." This is different than when the answering machine clicks on to the sound of your parent's voice just as you are getting in the mood. Orgasm requires that we weave a delicate web of psychological, physical, and energetic awareness, and as such can be "disrupted" by many events. In Bernie Zilbergeld's book *The New Male Sexuality*, he describes occasional impotence as often reflecting the "wisdom of the penis"—that a lack of erection may represent a man's intuition that this is not a good time to have sex. In my experience, orgasm in women often acts as the same kind of indicator. Its occasional absence signals that we need to pay closer attention to our bodies and our emotional balance. Is our relationship in turmoil? Are we physically drained? Do we need a good cry rather than an orgasm? Is a new medication affecting our sexual energy? Often orgasmic disruption reflects a disturbance in the multifaceted web of our being. We are going to explore what some of your roadblocks to orgasm might be.

ROADBLOCKS TO ORGASM

The women in my medical practice who struggle to have orgasms all have individual stories, but they share some common challenges. These roadblocks keep them from their full pleasure. When a woman is able to confront and resolve what is blocking her pleasure, her sexual energy flows more freely and orgasm is easier. Sometimes physiologic factors can inhibit arousal and prevent orgasm.

PROBLEMS WITH AROUSAL

As I discussed, research on sexual health is divided into the processes of desire, arousal, and orgasm. While desire is what compels us to seek sexual satisfaction, arousal refers to the physiologic response of the body—the swelling of the clitoris, vulva, and vagina and the re-

---

COMMON ROADBLOCKS TO ORGASM

- Problems with arousal
- Medication that inhibits orgasm
- Stress and anxiety
- Relationship challenges
- Bodily comfort and knowledge

---

sulting vaginal lubrication; tension in the pelvic musculature; as well as the swelling of breasts and nipples and increased blood flow to lips and ears. For most of us, the "plumbing" (the nerves and vessels that supply these areas) is intact, and we simply need to further develop our sexual desire and techniques in order to increase our arousal. Some of the time, however, the plumbing is not working adequately, due to disease or injury, and women are unable to orgasm because of a problem in the physiology of arousal.

Blood flow and nerve supply to the genital area (and elsewhere in the body) can be diminished by chronic diseases that affect the nerves and blood vessels—such as diabetes, high blood pressure, heart disease, and kidney disease—as well as many medications. For example, women taking high blood pressure medications, particularly at high doses, may experience difficulty with arousal, including reduced clitoral and vaginal swelling and lubrication. The diseases and medications that may affect arousal and orgasm are listed in appendix 1.

The swelling, lubrication, and sensation of the genital area can also be impaired by injury to the pelvic nerves or blood vessels. This can happen from pelvic trauma or be an unwanted result of genital or pelvic surgery—such as hysterectomy (removal of the uterus), oophorectomy (removal of the ovaries), or surgery on the vagina or vulva. Groundbreaking research on this subject is being done by Drs. Jennifer and Laura Berman at the Female Sexual Medical Center at UCLA. When women have clinically detectable problems with arousal (impaired blood flow to the genital area, causing decreased genital swelling and lubrication), many women at their center have responded well to the first of the popular medications for erectile dysfunction in men, Viagra.[2]

Hysterectomy is the most common pelvic surgery in women, and several decades ago it was performed without much regard to women's sexual pleasure. Today, many gynecologists are becoming aware of the possible ill effects of pelvic surgery on women's sexual response. In particular, the newer "supracervical" hysterectomies that leave the cervix intact likely spare the plexus of nerves near the cervix that are responsible for vaginal sensation. For most women who have hysterectomies, clitoral orgasms are preserved, but some women will note a loss in vaginal sensation, which is particularly distressing to those women who have enjoyed vaginal orgasms. This happens because two separate nerves supply the vagina and clitoris with sensation. The pudendal nerve supplies the clitoris, PC muscle, inner lips, and the skin of the perineum and anus. The pelvic nerve goes to the vagina and the uterus and can be injured by routine hysterectomy. Techniques for removing the uterus without injuring the pelvic nerve have been developed; if you're considering a hysterectomy, discuss this with your gynecologist.

You may have an arousal problem if, after sufficient desire and sexual stimulation your labia and clitoris do not swell and you have difficulty with lubrication. Some of these changes occur naturally with menopause, which we will discuss in full in chapter 8. It is also quite common to be aroused and have labial and clitoral swelling but no lubrication. The reasons can be many, from hormones (nursing, menopause, oral contraceptives) to medications (antihistamines) or simple dehydration. In general, difficulty with lubrication alone is no cause for alarm. Be sure that you are getting adequately stimu-

2. There are now two other drugs on the market for male erectile dysfunction that have not been studied in women: Cialis and Levitra. Studies on the use of these medications in women with general sexual dysfunction have not shown any benefit. This is likely due to the fact that they improve arousal but do nothing for the many other factors that influence orgasm in women.

lated and use one of the lubricants listed on page 262. In order to naturally improve or maintain your arousal, look after your cardiovascular health. Get regular exercise, which will increase and maintain the blood flow to your genitals. Eat a balanced diet of fresh fruits and vegetables, grains, and lean proteins. Avoid smoking, which restricts the blood supply to the genitals as well as to everywhere else.

It is worth mentioning that extensive cycling can be a problem for some women (and men) because the traditional, narrow cycling seats can compress the pudendal nerve and arteries that supply the clitoris, leading to decreased clitoral sensation and blood flow. These changes are reversible if the pressure is decreased by reducing cycling or using a different cycling seat. Over a long period of time, however, the changes can become permanent. Do yourself a favor and get a gentler cycling seat (one of the wide, comfy ones) rather than a hard, narrow one.

From a Taoist viewpoint, anything that slows the flow of chi will also impede arousal. Emotional and physical trauma to our sexual organs can result in tension in the pelvic area and blockages in the flow of chi. The Healing Sounds that we discussed in the last chapter and the Jade Egg practice that we will learn in chapter 8 are helpful for releasing the blockages in the genitals.[3]

MEDICATION THAT INHIBITS ORGASM

There are many medications that can inhibit your orgasmic ability. Please consult the list of medications on page 279 to see if you are taking any of them. Any changes in dose or type of medication can

---

3. Taoist genital health massage, Karsei Net Sang, performed by a well-trained and safe practitioner can also be helpful for freeing up blockages in the flow of sexual energy. Direct pressure with small circular massage movements are used to break up and dissolve the sedimentation in the circulatory system, release toxicity, and remove the physical and emotional blockages in the pelvic area. Genital health massage addresses the common problems associated with our sexual organs, painful menstruation, painful intercourse, frequent and difficult urination, and low sexual libido. Currently, an advanced practitioner of Karsei Net Sang, Khun Ni, offers genital health massage at the Tao Garden Health Resort (see appendix 2) and instructor Soumya Comer (appendix 2) travels throughout the world and offers genital health massage.

also interfere with orgasm. It is important to note that not all of these medications cause orgasmic problems in all women. If you note a change after starting or changing the dose of one of your medications, it is worth considering it as a cause. Sometimes there are alternative medications available, so please discuss this with your physician.

One of the most common group of drugs that affects orgasm in women are the SSRI antidepressants (Prozac, Paxil, Celexa, Lexapro, Zoloft, and Luvox). As one of my patients once expressed, "Orgasm on Paxil is like the ah, ah, ah, without the 'choo.'" In other words, she would experience arousal but could not reach orgasm. I prescribe these medications in my practice because they are generally safe and effective antidepressants, but I always discuss the sexual side effects with my patients. For those of you who need to remain on your SSRI, take the lowest dose that is effective for you. You may want to consider adding Wellbutrin (another antidepressant) to the SSRI in order to decrease the sexual side effects or talk to your doctor about whether your depression could be treated by Wellbutrin alone. Some holistic physicians have found it helpful to add the herb ginkgo biloba at a dose of 120 milligrams twice a day to the SSRI to decrease the sexual side effects. I would try this for at least 3 weeks to see if it improves your symptoms. Ginkgo is safe for most people but can thin the blood and interact with other medications, so please check with your physician before trying this.

STRESS AND ANXIETY

We discussed the importance of self-nurture to decrease stress and increase our desire in chapter 2. Here I want to address the anxiety that arises particularly during sexual encounters. Anxiety during sexual play can stem from shame, embarrassment, previously painful experiences, or fear that one cannot "perform" adequately. Whatever the cause, stress and anxiety induce a "fight or flight" response in the body that causes a cascade of stimulating hormones—epinephrine, norepinephrine, and cortisol—as well as the activation of the sympathetic nervous system. What this means in simple terms is that your body changes from being in a relaxed state to an "on guard" state. When this occurs, the body shifts all blood flow *away* from the sexual organs and toward the muscles in order to "fight off" the suspected enemy, making orgasm nearly impossible.[4] The "enemy," unfortunately, is usually ourselves.[5] Because of our fears and discomfort, we short-circuit our orgasmic capability.

We all have fears that arise during physical intimacy, but it is very important that you take the time you need to address your fears and relax. When you are trying to build towards orgasm and fear or anxiety begin to enter your body, pause your sexual play. If you are emotionally intimate with your partner, it is useful to share your feelings and reconnect with him or her emotionally before continuing. It is also helpful to do a simple calming exercise, like Belly Breathing (page 38). Deep breathing into your belly can reverse the stress response. You can also use the Healing Sounds to calm and center yourself; the kidney sound is particularly useful in dispelling fear and can be used during lovemaking or at any time.

RELATIONSHIP CHALLENGES

It is, of course, the case that difficulties in life or in a relationship can impair the ability to orgasm because they erode two of the fundamental foundations of orgasm: trust and relaxation. The tenor of your relationship will have a profound affect on whether

---

4. Some women enjoy, and find erotic, the suggestion of danger, or even some degree of physical pain, during sexuality. This is an extremely individual response, and most women who enjoy some level of sadomasochism within their sexual play only enjoy it within a context where the boundaries and safety of the "play" have been agreed to beforehand. That is, the women have given their consent to the sadomasochistic play. This is in stark contrast to women who experience violent sexual acts against their will, such as rape.

5. I have mentioned previously that, of course, if you are actually in danger of physical or emotional abuse from your partner, it will likely be impossible to reach orgasm with him or her. In this case, please do your sexual cultivation alone and consider getting help for yourself and/or your partner.

you can orgasm with your partner. If you are not "in synch" with each other outside of the bedroom, it will be difficult to synchronize your efforts with physical intimacy. Lily, a 44-year-old artist, relates her experiences, "In my twenties my orgasms happened occasionally, if I was with the right partner to really 'let go,' but I often just couldn't relax enough. In my thirties I was married to a great sexual partner and could orgasm if we were getting along, but if we were fighting, forget it. Now, in my forties, I'm finally in a sweet and supportive relationship, and I orgasm many times, every time we make love."

Honest communication and an open and loving heart will go a long way toward healing relationship rifts. As you cultivate your desire and orgasmic ability, use the practice of the Inner Smile to open your heart and fuel your compassion. If you continue to be in a difficult phase in your relationship, you may want to first cultivate your orgasmic ability through self-pleasuring and share it with your partner when you feel more relaxed and trusting.

BODILY COMFORT AND KNOWLEDGE

It is of primary importance on this journey into your orgasmic experience that you focus on loving and appreciating your body. If you don't feel good about your body, it is hard for your body to *feel good*. As you continue on this journey to fully experience and expand your orgasmic ability, do your best to refrain from criticizing your body. When we criticize ourselves, we send negative energy to those body parts and interrupt the good flow of chi. That's right. Those sweetly dimpled thighs that you hate are a waste dump repository for the negative chi that you send there. This makes it very difficult to abandon yourself to using those strong thighs to draw your partner closer to you. In order to enliven and adore your body, you need to begin blessing yourself—all of yourself.

The Inner Smile that we learned earlier is a wonderful way to send our precious loving attention to ourselves where we need it

EXERCISE 6

BODY BLESSING

1. Sit or lie in any comfortable position.

2. Take three deep breaths into your abdomen and let your body relax.

3. Begin the Inner Smile practice, seeing an image of love (your smiling face, your partner, your child, the sun) in front of you. Take in the loving, warm energy through your third eye and direct it, in turn, to each part of your body. Begin with your head and continue down your body to your face, neck, arms, hands, chest, breasts, back, belly, sexual organs, buttocks, legs, and feet.

4. Observe your judgments about each of your body parts as you send them loving energy. Your judgments often present themselves as blocks when you try to send smiling energy. For example, smile to your arms and let any judgments that you may have come to your consciousness—"weak, flabby, skin is dry and scaly, ugly elbows, too hairy."

5. Send smiling energy to the body part and shift your intention to see all of the strengths that she possesses, using words silently or aloud to enumerate her positive qualities—"my arms are capable of expressing love, carrying my children, writing, and praying and are a beautiful dark brown."

6. Imagine the energy of your judgments being released and sent out of your body through your hands or feet. It is helpful to imagine that your judgments have a particular color or texture. As you breathe in, send smiling, warm energy to your body part. And as you breathe out, imagine the smiling energy filling that part and the judgmental energy flowing out and down your arms or legs and out of your body into the ground.

7. Continue to each body part that you wish to address, becoming aware of your judgments and sending loving energy to replace the judgments. The more specific you can be about your judgments and, in particular, your affirmations, the more "clearing" will take place.

8. When you are finished, shake your hands and feet to release any of the trapped negative emotions that you may still hold.

most. If you struggle with orgasm or have difficulty feeling your desire in your genitals, you may want to use the following exercise, the Body Blessing, to increase the flow of chi there. If you hate your so-called "flabby" belly, use this exercise to love and appreciate your belly and enliven it as your energetic center. Use the Body Blessing exercise to reclaim those body parts that you'd just as soon trade in and help your entire being to glow with the chi of self-love.

The first time you do this practice it is useful and interesting to go through your whole body. It may surprise you how vehement some of your judgments are and how many you have! Likewise, you may be amazed at the many loving and appreciative feelings you can have about your body. It is not necessary to go through your whole body each time. It may be that you have a particularly hard time loving your buttocks or your breasts or your vagina. You can do the exercise with just these few areas in order to "reprogram" your thinking and feeling. Doing this exercise before body exploration (coming in the next chapter) or at any time before self-cultivation helps align your intention to *love yourself*.

Now that you have identified your roadblocks to pleasure, it's time to find your own path to orgasm.

CHAPTER 5

THE PATH TO ORGASM

How can you find your own path to orgasm, easily and whenever you want? Using the insights of the Taoist practices that you have already learned and the power of your sexual energy, you can explore the terrain of your own pleasure and find the places and touches that will inspire your own orgasmic energy. If you are learning to orgasm, I will take you through a five-step process that will allow you to surrender to your body's orgasmic celebration of itself. You will learn to align your intention, use your sex muscle, stoke your sexual energy, know your pleasure anatomy, and surrender to the waves of orgasm. If you already orgasm, this chapter will help you to intensify your orgasms and enhance your body's capacity for pleasure. For those of you who orgasm easily, I encourage you to read the sections that follow on strengthening your sex muscle and exploring your pleasure anatomy so that you can expand the pleasure you are already having during lovemaking. Understanding the keys to pleasure will help you a great deal when you want to cultivate your multi-orgasmic ability.

INTENTION

I discussed at length in the last chapter how our expectations guide our sexual experience. I suggested that you set your intentions for sexual play in order to expand the sensual repertoire of your orgasmic experience. An intention is a wish or aspiration for what you would like to experience. It acts as a guiding principle so that when you lose your way—"Here I am, holding my vibrator, feeling guilty about the items I forgot on the grocery list"—you can find your way back to your path—"Oh yeah, I'm exploring my body and honoring my pleasure." There is a subtle but important difference between an intention and a goal. Typically, we in Western society think of a goal as a target that we need to meet. If we do not meet our goals, we fail, and then get to feel bad about ourselves. The purpose of setting an intention is to open yourself up to greater possibility, not to criticize yourself for not having fulfilled your intention. Your intention is *supposed* to be something that is not currently easy for you to do.

When considering your intention, think about a general aspiration for exploring your sexual pleasure. From that general aspiration, you may want to have specific wishes for a particular lovemaking or self-cultivation session. I would suggest that you write down your general intention in a journal or perhaps somewhere that you can see it regularly. It may pertain specifically to sexuality or to some of the emotional roadblocks that keep you from your full desire. In chapter 1, we met Jean and Charlie, a couple in their late fifties who were struggling in their marriage. In particular, Jean felt self-conscious about her physical appearance and withdrew from her partner sexually because of this. Jean's statement of her general intention read, "I will practice loving regard for my body, share my body generously with my partner, and surrender to my pleasure." Jean's intention helped guide her in making the emotional shifts she needed so that she could fully experience her pleasure.

When we set out intentions for ourselves, we inevitably will have both conscious and unconscious thoughts that will make it hard to keep to our intention. Gabriella, a 32-year-old accountant who had never had an orgasm, had an intention to "trust my body, use everything in my power to cultivate my desire, and to experience orgasm." When she was self-cultivating, however, she would have critical thoughts: "What's wrong with me?" "Why can't I orgasm?" "I'm such a hopeless case." These thoughts deflated Gabriella's sexual energy, and she continued to have a hard time reaching orgasm. Self-criticism makes it almost impossible to relax into your pleasure. Most of us choose to distance ourselves from people who are unreasonably critical or insulting towards us. But it is often the *inner critic* that it is the most brutal *and* the hardest to escape.

I discussed the importance of loving and not maligning your body in the last chapter. You can use some of those same techniques to stem your inner critic and align yourself with your intention during sexual play. When you find yourself drifting into a critical frame of mind, take several deep breaths and do the Inner Smile exercise, focusing on your heart. Gently pull your attention back to pleasure and self-love. This can be quite difficult at first, but the practice of marrying self-love to self-pleasure can give extraordinary rewards, both inside the bedroom and out.

Aligning oneself with one's intentions is a lifelong spiritual challenge, but one well worth the effort. The focus of your practice needs to be on self-love. When you stray into critical thoughts, do not add to your difficulty by berating yourself for *having* those thoughts. Gently bring your mind back to your intention using the Inner Smile and Belly Breathing to relax you and gently guide you back to your pleasure. If this description sounds suspiciously like a meditation practice, where one gently brings one's mind back from worldly distractions, it is. It is a meditation on the limitless capacity of your body for love and sensual joy, a potential that is nothing short of miraculous.

What is *your* intention on this sensual journey? Where do you want to go and what do you want to experience? Spend a few moments considering your intention and then write it down. Use it as a guiding principle as you explore your body's potential.

YOUR SEX MUSCLE

The one muscle in your body that is essential to your sexual pleasure is your pubococcygeus (PC) muscle, also fondly known as your sex muscle. Strengthening your PC muscle will help you to have orgasms whenever you wish, improve your ability to have multiple orgasms, and give you the strength to pleasure a male partner intensely during intercourse.

Your PC muscle is actually a collection of smaller muscles that surround your urethra, vagina, and anus and support your pelvic organs. It extends from your pubic bone in the front to your coccyx (tailbone) in the back, which is where its name comes from (see the illustration on page 117). Learning to effectively contract and relax your PC muscle will increase the pleasure you feel and the ease with which you can have orgasms from both clitoral and vaginal stimulation. When you contract your PC muscle, you improve the blood flow to the entire pelvic area, which increases your sexual energy and lubrication.

Most women learn about their PC muscles when their doctors or midwives suggest that they do Kegel exercises. Prior to and after childbirth, Kegel exercises improve the pelvic support of the uterus and bladder and help treat and prevent urinary incontinence (passing urine when you don't want to). For now, though, I want to focus on how getting familiar with your PC muscle can enliven your sex life.

STRENGTHENING YOUR PC MUSCLE

It's relatively easy to locate your PC muscle. The next time you go to the bathroom, start peeing and then stop before you are finished. It is your PC muscle that you use to stop urinating. A basic exercise is to stop the stream multiple times during urination to feel the muscle working. But to get a better sense of where the PC muscle is in the *vaginal* area and how to contract it, it is helpful to feel the muscle itself. The vaginal squeeze exercise will teach you how to sense and assess the strength of your PC muscle.

Once you have the feel for where your PC muscle is and how to contract it, you can begin to strengthen it. Begin by contracting your

---

EXERCISE 7

VAGINAL SQUEEZES

1. Lie down or sit down on the edge of a chair and insert two fingers into your vagina up to the second knuckle.

2. Squeeze your PC muscle around your fingers. You should feel a slight contraction of the walls of your vagina around your fingers.

3. Spread your fingers apart as if you were making a peace sign. Now relax your fingers, but keep them spread, and contract your PC muscle again to see if you can bring your fingers together. With practice, you will be able to squeeze your fingers together with more and more force.

PC muscle and try to keep it contracted for 10 seconds. If the muscle is weak, it may be hard to hold it for this amount of time. If you feel the muscles letting go, just let them go. After contracting for 10 seconds, relax for 10 seconds. If relaxing is difficult for you, try putting two fingers back in your vagina and making the peace sign again, only this time, widen your fingers with gentle force as you breathe into your vaginal area, feeling it soften and relax. Now tighten your muscles again around your fingers, holding for 10 seconds, then and relax for 10 seconds while widening your fingers. Like any muscle, your PC may feel tired after exercising. Do three repetitions of contracting and relaxing when you start. You may want to increase the number of repetitions as you gain strength, until you're performing up to 10 repetitions twice a day. This may seem like a lot, but remember that you can do these while driving, watching television, or sitting at work (probably without the fingers!). If contracting your PC muscle gives you a little surge of sexual energy, as it does for many, it will make the workday much more interesting. You can draw this sexual energy into the Microcosmic Orbit, which you'll learn in the next chapter, and use it to enliven your mind, open your heart, and rejuvenate your organs.

When you first begin contracting your PC muscle, it is almost impossible to contract it and not contract your buttock or abdom-

---

EXERCISE 8

PC PULLUPS

1. Inhale and relax your PC muscle.

2. Exhale and contract your PC muscle, pulling it up into your body.

3. Repeat 9 or 18 times.

4. Now, contract your PC muscle for 10 seconds while you continue to breathe easily.

5. Repeat three times.

---

inal muscles at the same time. While there is nothing wrong with contracting other muscles, it will be easier to specifically strengthen your PC muscle if you can identify and isolate it from the other muscles. One of the best ways to contract the PC muscle and *not* the buttocks or abdomen is to do the contraction as you breathe out and relax the rest of your body. If you relax the PC muscle while you breathe in and contract it while you breathe out, it makes for a lovely brief meditative exercise as well.

Some of the women who are referred to me for PC muscle training do not have PC muscles that are weak; rather, they have difficulty because they are chronically tensing, or contracting, their PC muscles. If the muscle is contracted, it may be painful to have sex that involves penetration or a vaginal exam because the tense PC blocks the entrance to the vagina. It is interesting to note that the PC muscle includes the anal sphincter. Both Eastern and Western culture acknowledge a seemingly universal phenomenon of anxiety and emotional reserve associated with a tight PC muscle and anus. Think of the implications of the phrases "tight ass," "anally retentive," or "stick up the butt." These all suggest someone who is withholding, anxious, and perfectionistic. These qualities are the opposite of the open, relaxed, and accepting emotional state that each of us needs in order to have profound sexual pleasure. If you can learn to relax your PC muscle and anus, it will be much easier to experience orgasm, and especially expanded orgasm, which you will learn about in chapter 7. It is just as important to learn to relax a PC muscle that is too tight as it is to strengthen a PC muscle that is weak. The exercises that follow will help you to consciously relax your PC muscle. And who knows? You may just relax a bit more in your life in general!

When you begin, try doing this exercise 9 or 18 repetitions at a time at least once a day. It takes time to reverse old patterns of body tension. It may take several weeks until you can relax your PC muscle at will.

Once you can easily relax your PC muscle, change your breathing pattern so that it is similar to that in the PC Pullups exercise. Contract your PC muscle as you exhale and relax it as you inhale.

Once you become familiar with using your sex muscle, use it to stoke your own fire during self-cultivation or lovemaking. When you contract your PC muscle during sexual play, it will increase your arousal. It may be more fun for you to do your PC exercises using a dildo to contract against or with a male partner during intercourse. As you stimulate yourself, or your partner stimulates you, contract the muscle rhythmically, and it will help you build your arousal toward orgasm. If you have a male lover, he will also appreciate your

---

EXERCISE 9

RELAXING THE PC MUSCLE

1. Empty your bladder prior to this exercise.

2. Take a deep breath into your belly and focus on your PC muscle.

3. Inhale and lightly contract and pull up your PC muscle.

4. Exhale and push out your PC muscle.

5. Continue the above steps until you feel that you can sense what it feels like to relax your PC muscle, as opposed to contracting it.

6. Again, inhale and lightly contract your PC muscle.

7. Now, exhale and "let go" of your PC muscle, feeling it broaden and relax without pushing out.

new skills; as your PC muscle gets stronger, the contractions against his penis become intensely pleasurable. If you wish to further develop your vaginal muscle control and ability, the Jade Egg exercises in chapter 8 will teach you more subtle techniques for vaginal toning.

SEXUAL ENERGY

In chapter 2 you explored what erotic qualities support your desire. Now is the time to put that knowledge into action. Make time for self-cultivation in an atmosphere that you find sensuous and seductive. If you enjoy fantasy or erotica, create a scene in your mind, read your favorite passages, or watch a few scenes of an erotic film to fire your sexual imagination. Remember that the more intense your desire, or sexual energy, the easier it will be to orgasm.

For this practice you will need a loose fitting shirt and no bra, or you can be naked if you prefer. It is best to be in a room that is comfortably warm. Begin by finding a comfortable sitting position. Place the heel of your foot or a firm ball or rolled up cloth against your clitoris and vagina to keep them stimulated and help them hold their chi. Use the Inner Smile and smile down to your heart, sending loving energy to soften and open it. Now smile down to your sexual organs, feeling them become warm and come alive. Draw the chi with the intention of your mind to your labia and clitoris, feeling them swell with increased blood flow—the beginning of arousal.

Now rub your hands briskly together until you feel heat. Put your hands over your breasts, blessing them with your loving intent and sending them chi from your hands. Hold your breasts and smile down to them. Your breasts are connected to your heart center. If you do not enjoy touching your breasts, simply keep your hands over them and imagine their awakened energy traveling down to your sexual organs and clitoris, further awakening their chi. In chapter 8, I'll discuss Breast Massage practice in full, but here I'll show you a simple version to feed your desire.

Using your fingertips and oil if you like (and you're naked), circle around your breasts, moving around the nipple from the middle of your chest to the outside of your breasts. Your left hand will be moving from the center of your chest, down and to your left; your right hand will move from the center, down and to your right. Circle lightly with your fingertips at least nine times. Then caress all of the fullness of your breasts, gently circling your fingertips over your skin and pressing your flesh against your rib cage. Caress your nipples, at first lightly and then with more pressure. As your breasts fill with chi, your nipples will swell and harden. Feel the awakening of the breasts awaken your sexual center and feel the connection between your breasts and your sexual organs, particularly your clitoris, which often will tingle or swell. Hold your breasts and send their awakened chi down to your clitoris and vagina. Even if you do not feel the chi in your genitals, sending loving energy there and increasing your focus on your genitals will still assist with your sexual energy.

EXERCISE 10

AWAKEN YOUR SEXUAL ENERGY

1. Sit in a relaxed position.
2. Place your heel, a firm ball, or rolled-up washcloth against your clitoris and vagina.
3. Smile down to your heart center, feeling your heart warm and open.
4. Now smile down to your sexual organs—uterus, ovaries, vagina, clitoris, and lips—feeling the loving energy enliven them.
5. Rub your hands together and place them over your breasts, smiling down to them and sending them chi.
6. Begin Breast Massage (see page 207), rubbing in circles from the middle of the chest to the outside of the breasts.
7. Caress your breasts and nipples, sending their awakened chi to your sexual organs and clitoris.
8. After exploration or self-cultivation, circle your chi at your abdominal center.

You can use your awakened sexual energy for self-cultivation. It is lovely to do this exercise prior to exploring your pleasure anatomy, as your clitoris and vagina will be more sensitive to your touch if they are filled with sexual energy.

YOUR PLEASURE ANATOMY

Sexual energy is vital, but to get the pot of water that is your arousal from hot to boiling over with pleasure, you need to intimately understand your pleasure anatomy. I am going to lead you on a step-by-step tour of your intimate pleasure zones so that you will know exactly what it is that you need for orgasm. Recently a woman asked me for some advice about a new sexual relationship. She said, "I'm having a problem. I had a lover with whom I had an orgasm every time through oral sex. And then I had a second lover with whom I could orgasm through finger stimulation and with vaginal stimulation, but not with oral sex. Now I am with a man that I feel deeply connected to but I can't orgasm at all." I asked her if she ever masturbated. She said, "Yes, and I can always orgasm with my vibrator. What's wrong with me?" I said, "It sounds like you had one lover who knew what to do with his tongue, a second who knew what to do with his finger, and now a third who hasn't yet figured out either." We know that she can orgasm because she does so easily by herself. She simply needed to figure out what techniques for oral and manual stimulation really work for her and teach them to her new lover. It is also the case that some women who use vibrators on a regular basis will find that their clitoral area is somewhat "numbed" to the touch of fingers or a tongue. This is usually taken care of by decreasing or eliminating vibrator stimulation to "resensitize" the area.

None of us grew up knowing what it was we needed for orgasm. We have had to figure it out through experimentation. There is a bias in many countries in the world that in heterosexual couples it is the man's job (and prerogative) to please the woman. Women are discouraged from pleasing ourselves, especially during intercourse. This means that a woman's orgasm is dependent on finding a partner who can "figure her out" and "give her an orgasm." Although this is prevailingly a heterosexual issue, Carmen, a 48-year-old lesbian woman in a committed relationship, complained that "because we are both socialized to be stimulated by a man, it creates a problem in lesbian relationships. If we're both women and we've both been socialized to wait to be stimulated, how do you get started?" Assuming that someone else is responsible for initiating sex and giving you pleasure can lead to many long nights spent at home with no one initiating sex.

When discussed in these terms, it seems ridiculous to expect that another person should understand your intimate sexual organs better than you. No one can *give* you an orgasm. You need to create it yourself. It happens in your body and is, therefore, *yours* to give yourself. There is no more surefire way to have regular orgasms than to know, exactly, what it is that turns you on and gets you off. You or your lover may be insecure, at first, when you touch yourself or ask for what you need during lovemaking, so reassure your partner that your giving a helping hand does not mean that he or she is not a skillful lover. Let him or her know that you have discovered what gives you the most pleasure and you want to share that.

Some women feel uncomfortable touching themselves sexually at all, and if this is the case for you, you can certainly share these exercises with your partner and let him or her stimulate you. But I *really* encourage you to consider trying self-touch and self-cultivation. It is by far one of the most important steps in learning how to have regular, satisfying orgasms. Some women fear that if they masturbate they will have less desire for partnered lovemaking. Studies show that this is not at all the case. Many women who are regularly sexually active with their partners *also* masturbate frequently. Remember that the hormones that are released with sexual activity *increase* the likelihood of future sexual activity. Getting hot and bothered by

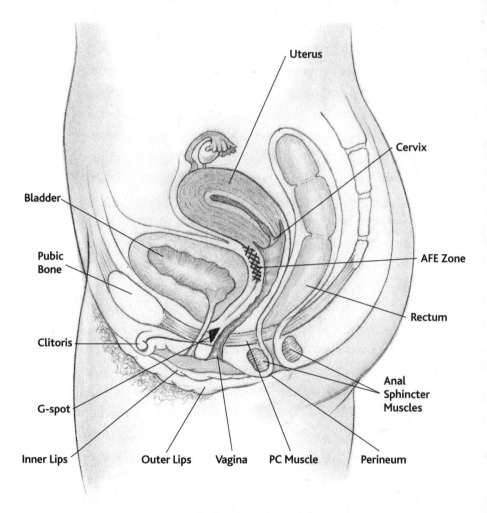

Uterus

Cervix

Bladder

Pubic Bone

AFE Zone

Clitoris

Rectum

G-spot

Anal Sphincter Muscles

Inner Lips   **Outer Lips**   **Vagina**   **PC Muscle**   **Perineum**

The Sexual Organs

yourself will keep you hot and bothered for your partner. And if you do not have a partner, self-cultivation is vital to maintain your healthy tissues and hormones, not to mention that it's a gift when you need to release sexual tension.[1]

I'm going to start your exploration with a detailed discussion of your sexual anatomy. You'll then do a full body exploration designed

1. If you're shy about touching yourself, Betty Dodson's classic book *Sex for One* is an entertaining guide to the pleasures of self-loving.

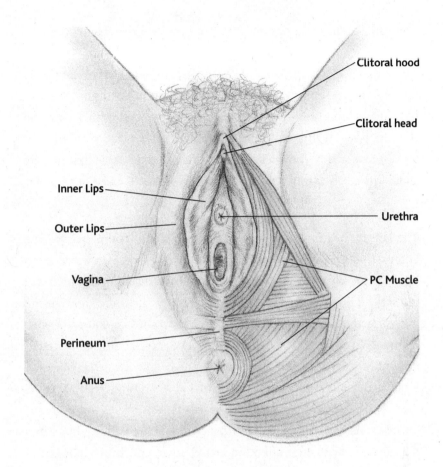

Clitoral hood

Clitoral head

Inner Lips

Outer Lips

Urethra

Vagina

PC Muscle

Perineum

Anus

The PC Muscle and External Genitals

to make you tingle from head to foot. I suggest that you read the following sections when you have some time alone to "check yourself out" as we go. You will need a mirror to see your vulva and vagina, unless you are *very* flexible. If you have any hesitation, relax, take a deep breath or several, and please follow along. It will help tremendously to improve your sexual enjoyment if know "what's going on down there."

LABIA

If you look at your genitals from the outside, two larger "lips" with hair (labia majora) surround two smaller hairless lips (labia minora).

The color of the labia minora varies in every woman, from brown to gray to peach to pink, depending on the color of your skin. They also vary tremendously in size and shape. Some women have long labia minora, others quite short. Most are uneven in their contour and have many small folds, which allow them to swell (along with the labia majora) during arousal. In general, they tend to shorten after menopause and become less prominent.[2] Both the large lips and the small lips can be quite sensitive when stroked or sucked during sex.

CLITORIS

The clitoral head is generally hidden partially or completely by the clitoral hood, a small flap of skin. To see the clitoris, you will need to use your fingers and draw back the skin above the clitoris, which will retract the hood. The clitoris is, remarkably, the only organ in the human body that solely exists for pleasure. If she is not already, your clitoris is likely to become your good friend, as she is instrumental to orgasm. The clitoral head is the anatomical equivalent of the head of a penis but has a greater number of nerve endings (8,000, to be exact), in a much more compact space. The clitoris is therefore intensely sensitive, sometimes to the point of being painful, but when handled with care and affection can yield an enormous amount of pleasure.

The clitoris is actually 10 times larger than we thought a decade ago. The clitoral head is the only part that we can see, but the clitoral shaft, bulb, and arms extend much further (see the illustration.) This is one of the reasons that the entire vulvar area can be exquisitely sensitive to touch. The clitoris swells and becomes much more prominent during sexual arousal. From a Taoist point of view, stimulating the clitoris is important, as it is related to all of the glands of the body and stroking it can improve your hormonal balance.

---

2. If you are interested in seeing the variations among women (and you're not a gynecologist), a beautiful collection of photos of various women's vulvas is available in the book *Femalia*, edited by Joani Blank.

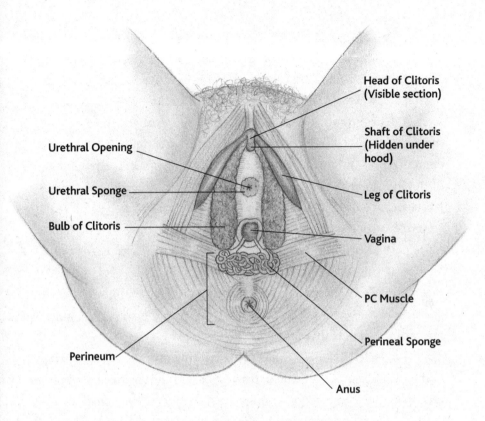

Head of Clitoris
(Visible section)

Shaft of Clitoris
(Hidden under
hood)

Urethral Opening

Leg of Clitoris

Urethral Sponge

Bulb of Clitoris

Vagina

PC Muscle

Perineal Sponge

Perineum

Anus

Full Size of the Clitoris

URETHRA

If you spread your inner lips, you will be able to see the urethral opening. In some women it can be very subtle, but it is usually seen as a dimple in the tissues midway between the clitoral head and the vagina. Some women find stimulation of the urethra arousing and can even orgasm from urethral stimulation, usually with gentle to firm pressure directly on the area. If you suffer from frequent bladder infections, you may not want to stimulate this area directly, as outward pressure may drive more bacteria into the urethra and cause swelling of the urethra—both of which can predispose women to bladder infections.

VAGINA

The vaginal opening is sometimes obscured by the lips and the soft tissues that surround the vagina. If you bear down (as if you were having a bowel movement), the tissues will part and you will be able to see the beginning of the vaginal passage and perhaps some of the hymenal ring. The hymen is a membrane that partially, or in some circumstances, fully, covers the entrance to the vagina. The breaking of the hymen with first penetration, and possible bleeding, is what has been touted as "evidence" of virginity in our patriarchal culture. In modern society, with vital, active girls and the use of tampons, there may or may not be any hymen, or bleeding, with first penetration. In all of us, however, the remnants of the hymen, the hymenal ring, still exists as small pieces of tissue surrounding the opening of the vagina. This area is sensitive to touch and contains many of the glands that lubricate the vagina.

PC muscle: Just inside the vagina is a ring of muscle that is part of the PC muscle. This is the narrowest part of the vagina and when it is tight, due to anxiety or simply never having been stretched, penetration can be uncomfortable. Fortunately, we have control over this muscle and can learn to relax it and flex it using the PC exercises from earlier in this chapter.

G-spot: Beyond your PC muscle is the area of the famed "G-spot," which was named by sex researchers John Perry and Beverly Whipple after the physician who first described it in the medical literature, Dr. Ernst Grafenberg.[3] The Taoists have referred to this area for thousands of years as the black pearl. If you feel along the front wall of the vagina, on the belly side, approximately one to two knuckles in, there is an area of ridged tissue that swells with arousal. It is not always easy to find, but most women have more luck when they are aroused, as the spot can swell to the size of a

---

3. Some women like to refer to their G-spots as their "Goddess" spots, rather than in reference to a man who has little familiarity with their particular anatomy.

quarter. When you or your partner stimulates your G-spot, it may initially feel like you need to urinate. This is because the G-spot consists of a collection of glandular tissue that surrounds the urethra, also referred to as the "urethral sponge." The G-spot is the area of the urethral sponge that can be felt through the anterior (belly-side) vaginal wall. When a woman is highly aroused and consistent, firm pressure and strokes are applied to her G-spot, the "need" to urinate can change to a deep, pleasurable fullness. Many women who have vaginal orgasms do so from stimulation of their G-spots.

As is true with all vaginal spots, G-spot stimulation can feel not just physically, but emotionally intense. Monique, a 36-year-old student, relates, "I just discovered my G-spot 2½ years ago, and I felt a lot of emotional release, like he was touching places that had never been touched before. I find that squeezing and bearing down helps it not be so painful. Now it feels very releasing." It is worth mentioning that not all women may *have* a pleasurable spot in this location, so if you can't find it, don't worry. It is also true that each woman may have her own pleasurable spots that are just not yet famous. One of the Healing Tao instructors I spoke with told me that her entire vagina is "a tube of pleasure" and that she has sensitive areas everywhere. A number of women note increased sensitivity at the same depth of the G-spot, but on all walls of the vagina—less like a spot and more like a ring of pleasure. The only way to discover your own pleasure landscape is to explore.

Anterior fornix erotic zone: This area was researched and named by Malaysian sexologist Dr. Chua Chee Ann. It is located deep on the anterior, or belly, side of the vagina, close to the cervix (see illustration on page 116). You will need long fingers or a dildo to touch this spot yourself. The AFE zone is longer and less defined than the G-spot. You can try light strokes or firm, undulating pressure in this area. Like the G-spot, women experience a deep, pleasurable sensation that can result in orgasm. Unlike the G-spot, however, the AFE zone is an area that can be easily stimulated with intercourse. Positions for reaching this are described at the end of the chapter.

"**Spots**": From a Taoist perspective, any part of your anatomy is capable of great pleasure, and even orgasm, if you are able to concentrate your sexual energy there. The experience of many Healing Love teachers is that the entire genital area is capable of exquisite pleasure leading to orgasm. Within the vagina are represented acupressure points for the healing of all the internal organs. Stroking the entire length of the vagina will stimulate the flow of chi to the body (see the illustration on page 219).

PERINEUM

The perineum refers to the area of skin and muscle that stretches the centimeter or two between your vagina and anus. Underneath the perineum is a dense network of blood vessels, which is sometimes called the "perineal sponge" or the "perineal body." During sexual arousal, these blood vessels engorge like the other erectile tissues of the vulva and become sensitive to light stroking, pressure, and licking. The collection of muscles felt at the perineum is a part of the PC muscle that I discussed earlier.

ANUS

The anus is a strong sphincter of muscle, which, in addition to the anal canal, has the body's second highest concentration of nerve endings. Anal stimulation, either by gentle touching or penetration, can be very arousing to some women. Many of the same nerves that innervate the vagina innervate the rectum as well. If you are just beginning to experiment with anal penetration, be sure to use plenty of lubrication and go slowly at first. The anal canal does not secrete its own lubrication and can be injured by rough penetration without lubrication. Start with one finger and add more fingers or toys or body parts if it continues to be pleasurable. It is often popular to do anal stimulation along with clitoral stimulation or vaginal penetration to multiply the sensations. Some women can orgasm from anal stimulation alone. If you enjoy anal stimulation, be sure to wash all hands, toys, and body parts that touch the anus *prior* to touching the rest of the genitals, as the bacteria from the anus can cause vaginal infections. Some women who anticipate anal play and are concerned about fecal content use enemas beforehand.[4]

BODY EXPLORATION

Now that you are familiar with your pleasure anatomy, let's spend some time learning just what it is that you like. For the next exercise, you are going to need privacy and a warm comfortable place to be intimate with yourself. If you want to experiment with a vibrator, be sure that one is handy. If you have trouble reaching orgasm, a vibrator is often the easiest way for most women to orgasm. Stores at which you can purchase vibrators online or in person are listed in appendix 2. If you want to explore your vaginal spots, you may need some lubricant and a dildo or other long smooth object. Different women prefer different lubricants. The advantage of water-soluble lubricants is that they easily clean off with water and get washed from the vagina with your natural secretions. Oil-based lubricants remain in the vagina for a longer period of time. There are now many water-based lubricants on the market that are widely available; lubricants and their various properties are discussed in chapter 9.

Before starting the Body Exploration, prepare your space with whatever helps you feel sensual and comfortable. Music, candles, incense, and essential oils can be nice. If you wish, have body oil or massage cream available to rub into your skin. Lying in a comfortable place, with your back propped up with pillows works well. I would highly recommend that you do the Body Blessing or simple

---

4. For those of you who want detailed instruction on anal play and penetration, see Tristan Taormino's book *The Ultimate Guide to Anal Sex for Women.*

Belly Breathing to focus and relax before doing this exercise. I also encourage you to focus and send your sexual energy to your sexual organs, as described in the Awaken Your Sexual Energy exercise. It will also be important to empty your bladder prior to the vaginal stimulation exercise so you do not have to urinate.

When you touch yourself, remember that there are many kinds of touch to explore. Tantric teachers talk about seven levels of touch, from barely felt (blowing) to hard enough to draw blood (scratching). While I am not recommending that you draw blood during this exercise, I do want you to experiment with how different touch feels. Try licking, blowing, scratching, biting, and sucking your skin, as well as simply moving your fingertips over your flesh. You can also experiment with different textures and materials, such as silk, scratchy materials, feathers, and even ice. Touch awakens your skin and increases the chi and blood flow. It is a common Taoist practice to slap one's skin all over to awaken the chi. Developing your repertoire of touch is really important because it's what keeps lovemaking interesting and alive. It keeps you interested and alive, too.

Finally, the purpose of this exercise is to explore your body and not necessarily to orgasm. In fact, if you are someone who experiences a significant drop in desire after orgasm, delay your orgasm until the end of your exploration so that you can feel your desire as you explore your body. If you are just learning how to orgasm and feel orgasm approaching, then by all means, go with it! And though I'll discuss techniques for pleasure with your clitoris and vagina, the purpose of this exercise is to unlock the sensual potential in your whole body. I gave this exercise to Jill, a 49-year-old hairstylist, as homework. When Jill returned to class the following week, she explained how it had affected her perceptions: "I have always defined my sexuality in the genitalia and the breasts. And this exercise reminded me that the sensual-sexual part extends out to the fingertips and down to the toes. That was really full body." Some women can orgasm from non-genital stimulation—nipples, ears, or nape of the neck, so don't underestimate the sensual power of your whole body! And take your time. Jill added, "Last night I just relaxed and did my body exploration and self-cultivated. I was just exploring and I loved the sensation of touching my outer lips for a long time before I even got near my clitoris. I was thinking, 'God, that's like 20 minutes, is that too long?' No, because at 25 minutes I was rocketing to outer space!" It takes time to find out what fuels *your* rockets. Go at your body's own pace. And have fun!

BODY EXPLORATION

1. **Relax.** Do Belly Breathing and then the Awaken Your Sexual Energy exercise to awaken your sexual energy. Now let go of your thoughts and focus on your sensations.

2. **Head:** Begin by stimulating your scalp, running your fingers through your hair and running your nails along your skin. Gently pull at the roots of your hair to further stimulate your scalp. Using the pressure of your hands, rub your fingertips over your scalp. Move your fingertips or other materials over your lips and face. Notice where the skin gets softer and warmer. Spend some time outlining your ears with very soft feather touches, then rub the lobes between your fingers vigorously until they're warm. Since the ears represent the whole body in Chinese medicine, you can awaken the chi by rubbing them. Experiment with putting your fingers inside your sensitive ear canals.

3. **Neck:** Move your hands or a cloth down to your neck. Gently scratch the nape of your neck (cats love this!). Circle your neck with your hands and also use your nails. What kinds of touch make you arch your neck in sensual surrender?

4. **Arms:** Using silk or a scratchy material or your palms and nails, slide down the slope of your arms, feeling their strength and weight. Notice the different feel on the inside of your arm (the yin part) and the outside (the yang part). Try slapping or pinching and

see if it further awakens your chi. Your hands and fingers are exquisitely sensitive. Scratch the insides of your wrists and fingers. Bite, lick, and suck your palms and fingers. What feels good to you? Now transition to your other arm.

5. **Belly:** Stroke down your chest and belly with broad hands, feeling the lovely softness of this center of your being. Use different materials or ice to see how your skin responds. Play with your navel.

6. **Buttocks:** Use your fingernails to scratch down and across your buttocks. Hold them in your hands and appreciate their strong weight. Feel where your buttocks end and your pubic hair begins . . . but don't go there quite yet!

7. **Legs:** Stroke down the length of your thighs, feeling the difference between the strong outer thighs and the soft inner thighs that merge with the pubic area. Squeeze or slap your flesh, feeling the nerves awaken. Slide your hands down to behind your knees and use light, tickling touches or scratches on the tender skin. Cup and squeeze your calves. Stroke your lower legs down to your feet. Run your hands over the tops of your feet and then gently slip your fingers between your toes. The skin is very sensitive. Like the ear, the foot represents every part of your body, so leave no skin untouched! Use your nails or cloth on the arch of your foot or between your toes. Now run your hands in a sweeping motion all the way up your legs and belly to your breasts.

8. **Breasts:** Cup and hold your breasts. No matter what size they are, they are capable of generating an extraordinary amount of chi and pleasure. Bless your breasts and circle around the outsides with your fingers or material. Squeeze them gently and feel their weight. Experiment with light touch or other materials around the areola and nipple. Gently (or not so gently, if you like it!) squeeze your nipples and roll them between your fingers. Try pulling slightly on your nipples. Try scratching softly over the surface of the nipples. If you have a vibrator, see how the vibratory touch feels on them. You can

continue to involve your breasts and the rest of your body as you move your touch down to your pubis.

9. **Pubis:** Run your fingers and nails through your pubic hair, tickling the skin. Feel how soft and padded the skin is under your hair. Pull gently on the hair as you move down your genitals to awaken your chi.

10. **Lips:** Run your fingers down and over your outer vaginal lips. Gentle scratching, rough materials, or feathers can feel good here. These lips will swell with arousal. Part your outer lips and begin to feel your inner lips. If you are not wet, you may want to use a lubricant or dip a finger into the vagina. Rub your inner lips between your fingers and gently pull them. They, too, will swell and darken with your arousal.

11. **Clitoris:** Find your clitoris at the top of your inner lips. Start by rolling the shaft of the clitoris underneath the skin of the lips and pubis. If you slide your index finger down your pubis toward your clitoris and rub back and forth, you will feel the shaft of the clitoris, like a cord under the skin, slipping under your finger. The shaft is not as sensitive as the head but is also pleasurable. Slide down the left side of the shaft to the clitoral head, which will probably still be covered by the hood. Try a few different strokes on the clitoris through the hood. You can rub side to side, letting the clitoral head slip under your finger back and forth. Try making little circles over the clitoral head. Anchor the clitoral head with one or two fingers by pressing it against the inner lips and try short up and down strokes.

All of these strokes can be soft and light or can be more firm. Try vibrating your finger against your clitoris as well. See what feels best to you. The more variety that you are able to enjoy, the more fun you can have. Most of these moves can be done with one hand, leaving your other hand free to touch the rest of your body, caress your breasts—or to hold this book open. When one particular stroke feels good, stay with it and don't let up until your pleasure peaks in orgasm or begins to wane. If it becomes less pleasurable, change the stimulation in location, intensity, or rhythm and build up your pleasure again.

Now let's try some two-handed techniques. You can place a finger of each hand on either side of the clitoris and rub up and down or around in a circle for doubled sensation. You can also use one hand to hold the clitoris still (she is a slippery little pleasure bud) by placing your second and third fingers on either side of the clitoris (like an upside down peace sign) with your non-stroking hand (most of us have a favorite) and use your other fingers to play with the clitoris. Some sex experts (and many women) strongly recommend stroking the clitoris with the foreskin withdrawn, as the sensation is much more acute. Remember that your pressure needs to be *very* light (think butterfly), and I would recommend lubricant.

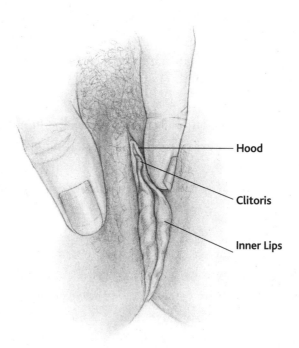

Stimulating the Clitoris through the Hood

You may find that some of the thicker lubricants make your motions smooth but not impossibly slippery.

Your non-stroking hand will need to draw back the hood to expose the clitoris. There are various ways to do this. The simplest is to place your hand on your pubic bone and pull up, withdrawing the hood. Alternatively, some women find it easy to withdraw the hood with their thumb and then caress the clitoris with the finger of the same hand, which allows for a one-handed approach to the naked clitoris.[5]

Remember that since the clitoris is so sensitive, small movements can be felt in a big way. Try short up and down strokes and circular strokes. Many women have a special spot that sends them into ecstasy. If you find your "spot," stick with it for awhile. It takes time for the sexual energy to build, but it is a wonderful ride into orgasm. Steve and Vera Bodansky, teachers who have researched female orgasm for a total of 50 years, confirm in their book *The Illustrated Guide to Extended Massive Orgasm* what I have experienced in my teaching: Many women are most sensitive at the left upper quadrant of the clitoral head (see the illustration on page 130). You may or may not enjoy stimulation here, but it is certainly worth giving it a try.

You can do any of the stimulation techniques that we have discussed using a vibrator as well. If you have never or rarely had an orgasm, I strongly suggest that you experiment with a vibrator. Use it at whatever speed seems to arouse you most to stimulate the clitoris through the hood or directly. Or stimulate the clitoris with your finger and place your vibrator against the stroking finger to transmit the vibration. You can combine vibrator stimulation of the clitoris with vaginal stimulation or vice versa for a powerful orgasmic combo. As I mentioned earlier, using a vibrator regularly may de-

5. Some of these techniques are derived from Steve and Vera Bodansky's excellent discussion in their book *The Illustrated Guide to Extensive Massive Orgasm*.

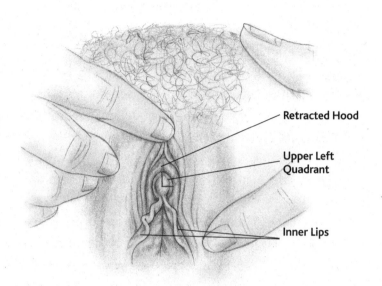

Retracted Hood

Upper Left
Quadrant

Inner Lips

Upper Lift Quadrant of Clitoris

crease clitoral sensitivity to manual and oral touch. Using a water jet (shower massage, tub faucet, bidet, or Jacuzzi jet) may give you the same orgasmic result without quite the numbing effect. Your bathroom may become your favorite room in the house.

12. **Vagina:** We all vary in the sensitivity of our vaginas, but if you can awaken your vaginal pleasure nerves, the rewards can be great. It is also true that many women who orgasm only with clitoral stimulation may have more profound orgasmic experiences if the clitoral stimulation is combined with vaginal penetration. If you are already lubricated from the preliminaries above, go for it. But if you are not, you will need some lubrication to keep this pleasurable and comfortable.

Begin by circling one or two of your fingers around the opening of the vagina. Dip your fingers inside one to two knuckles deep and curl them upward, toward your belly, to find the area that I described as your G-spot. It may feel ridged and, when pressed, may make you feel as if you need to urinate. Exert rhythmic, moderate pressure by pressing into the area while stroking forward in a "come hither" fashion (see the illustration on page 133). Make circular motions around the spot. Try vibrating your fingers against your G-spot by rapidly "wagging" them forwards and backwards, hitting the spot on the forward motion. If the desire to urinate does not fade to pleasure with further stroking, try opening your fingers into a "V" and stimulating the same area, just not exactly in the middle, where the urethra is. With your other hand, try pushing down on your pelvic belly just above your pubic bone as you push up on your G-spot with the fingers in your vagina. This "sandwiches" the spot and gives it more stimulation. It also sandwiches your bladder, so do it only if it is comfortable. Explore the sides and back of your vagina, too, at the same depth. This is a ring of pleasure in some women.

Using a curved dildo or vibrator made for this purpose allows you to stroke your G-spot in a less cramped position. The G-spot is best stimulated by fingers or a dildo because it is so close to the entrance of the vagina. Possible positions for G-spot stimulation during partnered intercourse with a penis or strap-on are discussed at the end of the chapter.

Depending on the length of your fingers and vagina, you may or may not be able to reach your AFE zone with your fingers. Most women need to squat or put one leg up on a chair to do so. Though this is not a terribly sensual position, it may help you to feel the area with your hands at least once. Press your fingers to the back of your vagina and feel for your cervix, a firm nub that feels a bit like the end of your nose. Some women experience pleasure and even orgasm from cervical stimulation. Most women are not aware of their cervix unless they are getting a Pap test or when it gets accidentally gets "bumped" during vaginal penetration, causing a very non-sexual, deep, crampy pain. The AFE zone is located in a fairly broad area just on the anterior, or belly side, of the vagina, right next to the cervix. This spot can respond to light, tickling strokes, or to more forceful pressure, like the G-spot. Slide a dildo, vibrator, or other long, thin object along the belly side of your vagina until you reach the top. It will help to angle the dildo so that it presses more forcefully against the belly side of the deep vagina. For most women, this means that the hand holding the dildo moves back toward the anus so that the vaginal end of the dildo angles forward toward the AFE zone.

Try rhythmically pressing the spot or pressing with a circular motion. Keep in mind that both the G-spot and the AFE zone are best stimulated and enjoyed after high arousal and/or clitoral orgasm. It may take some experimentation to find the areas that are most pleasing to you.

To intensify your vaginal sensations, try contracting your PC muscle against your fingers or a dildo as you move them in and out. This pushes the vaginal walls against your fingers and also creates a "vacuum" in the vagina as you withdraw, which can be very pleasurable.

If you are still aroused and wish to orgasm, combine whatever touch is most arousing to you, breathe deeply, and begin the ascent to orgasm. Often using a clitoral stroke combined with vaginal penetration is a climactic combination. Don't forget about nipple stimulation or other bodily touch that arouses you. Try rhythmically contracting your PC muscle as you stroke your vagina and clitoris. This mimics the contractions of orgasm and can help launch you into orgasmic bliss. These techniques may be quite enough to send you over the edge. If they are not, it may be that you are having trouble with surrendering, which is the fifth step on the path to orgasm.

SURRENDER

Now that you've focused your intention, strengthened your PC muscle, kindled your sexual energy, and explored your pleasure anatomy, it's time to surrender to the orgasmic wave. You can have the perfect setting and all the right strokes, but if you can't let go of

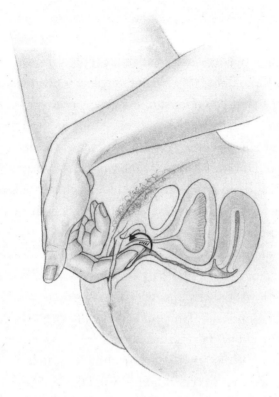

Stimulating the G-Spot

conscious control and surrender to the orgasmic process, you can hover at the edge of orgasm forever. If you are someone who likes to be "in control" in your life, this may be the hardest part of becoming regularly orgasmic. But think of this as an incredible opportunity. This is the one place in your life that is completely safe and extremely fun to let go and surrender to your body's pleasure. This is your own sensual free fall, ladies, and it's the best ride you'll ever go on.

Despite our best intentions, most women cannot orgasm by focusing on orgasm. When we focus on getting to our *goal*, we stay in our heads and do not fully inhabit our bodies, thereby making it more difficult to orgasm. To orgasm, relax into the enjoyable sensations in your body and don't stop yourself. As the pleasure builds and intensifies, don't resist. Surrender to your body's celebration.

When reaching for orgasm, it's not so much about "climb, climb climb," it's more about *slide*. I like to think of it as "falling back" into orgasm and letting the orgasmic wave move through you.

My patient Jill told me, "My block to orgasm is my internal dialogue that I can't shut down most of the time. So instead of trying *not* to use words, I use the right words of "letting go" and the word "surrender," and now the only time I do completely surrender is in the bedroom. But I do still have to use the word." Use whatever tools work for you to surrender to your pleasure. Jill actually tells herself in that moment to "surrender." You can also try Belly Breathing or doing the Inner Smile to your genitals to focus your attention and energy before continuing.

During partnered sex, it may help to focus on the eyes or attentive face of your lover. Other women need to close their eyes to focus on their own sensations. A fair number of women use fantasy to "transport" them and help them surrender. If you enjoy erotic books or movies, try self-cultivating while reading or watching. Some women simply fantasize in their minds during the build to orgasm.

If you have difficulty in your relationship with your partner outside of the bedroom, or if you have a new partner, it may be more challenging to surrender during lovemaking. Lily, a 44-year-old artist, describes her history with surrender and orgasm: "I have a really old history of not surrendering. During my thirties I never really had any control over orgasm, not until many sexual partners and many, many years of not wanting to let go. I enjoyed sex, but I was completely unable to orgasm because I was unwilling to let go. I didn't feel safe enough with any of those people." Lily adds that what finally allowed her to start having orgasms was, "getting over my shame and owning my sexuality. I was able to feel proud that I got to have an orgasm and that I could actually know my body—that someone didn't have to do it for me. And then I got to the next stage of just really loving myself and feeling that I got to be a fully sexual human being—that it was okay as a woman."

Learning to surrender will take practice, so be patient with yourself. It may take quite a long time for you to find the pattern of touch that you need and to stay with it long enough for you to be able to surrender to your pleasure. Many women feel that they need to be on their partner's time schedule—that they need to "hurry up" and have their orgasm. For most women, orgasm does not accommodate your schedule and trying to hurry makes it run away faster. Serena, a vivacious 66-year-old woman, told me, "Somehow I have this preconceived notion that it's somebody else's time frame that I should be on, that I should focus on my partner and pleasing them. And so the person, the environment, and the time are so interconnected. We have to give ourselves that time and teach our partners the time that we need." Ask for your partner's help in giving you all the time you need to reach orgasm or explore all the facets of your pleasure. If you have trouble surrendering with your partner, then try to orgasm during self-cultivation instead. Many women find it much faster and easier to orgasm alone than with a partner, at least as they are developing their orgasmic ability.

PUTTING IT ALL TOGETHER: THE PATH TO ORGASM

If this was your first orgasm, congratulations! If this was one of many you have had in your life, congratulations on taking the time to honor your body and experience that pleasure in your life now. If you still have difficulty with orgasm, be patient. It takes time to overcome old patterns of response. Search out and focus on your pleasure. The more that you relax and simply follow what feels good, the sooner the orgasm will come. If you have never before had an orgasm, it will be useful to try stimulating yourself regularly, even daily, for a few weeks so that your awakening nerve endings can build on the sensations from the day before.

EXERCISE 11

THE PATH TO ORGASM

1. **Set your intention.** Read your statement of intention from page 107 or create your intention for right now at this time. For example, "Today I want to treasure my body as I touch myself," or "I want to stimulate myself more intensely and experience as much pleasure as I am capable of."

2. **Kindle your sexual energy.** Prepare yourself and your location with whatever erotic qualities support your desire, relax you, and turn you on—candles, oils, pillows, massage. Explore sexual fantasy or erotica if you enjoy it. Play sensual music and dance. Rocking your hips sensuously will awaken your sexual center. Dress in what you find inviting or wear nothing at all. Take a bath and emerge relaxed, hot, and ready to get hotter.

3. **Awaken your sexual energy as we did in the previous pages.** Using the Inner Smile, smile down to your heart and feel it soften and open. Smile down to your uterus and ovaries, to your clitoris, lips, and vagina, feeling them warm with chi. Massage your breasts and nipples and send their awakened sexual energy to your sexual organs, as we did in the Awaken Your Sexual Energy exercise.

4. **Caress your pleasure anatomy.** Use silky or roughened touch to caress your nipples and any other sensitive spots that you discovered in your exploration. Use your fingers or a vibrator to stroke your clitoris, pulling back the hood if you enjoy it. Use your fingers or a dildo to penetrate your vagina and stimulate your hot spots with shallow and deep strokes. Try stroking the G-spot or AFE zone.

5. **Squeeze your sex muscle.** Contract your sex muscle, squeezing and holding rhythmically as you fondle yourself.

6. **Surrender to your pleasure.** Now stroke your clitoris, finding a rhythm that pleases you while pressing your vaginal spots or caressing your nipples. Let go of control and allow your pleasure to build. Move or make sounds as the sensations intensify, sliding into your pleasure, and falling back into a delicious and satisfying orgasm.

SHARING YOUR ORGASM WITH YOUR PARTNER

Now that you've found your path to orgasm, you may want to involve your partner, who can lend a helping hand, or two. Trying new positions can sometimes be helpful for finding new sources of pleasure in your sensitive vagina. I discuss oral techniques and positions at greater length in the book *The Multi-Orgasmic Couple*, but I've included some positions on the following pages that are particularly good for stimulating different parts of the vagina and bringing women to orgasm. If your partner can get to know the rhythms and pleasures of your body, he or she can caress you to orgasm while you truly surrender to your pleasure. Have your partner read this chapter, or at least the section "Your Pleasure Anatomy" beginning on page 114 as well as this section. It is then important that you share with him or her exactly how and where you like to be touched. You can certainly discuss it, but by far the best way for him or her to understand exactly how to touch you is to watch you touch yourself. You may feel embarrassed, but a loving partner will likely be fascinated by your pleasure—and probably turned on as well. It is important that this sharing session be focused on you, however. If you can, bring yourself to orgasm while your partner watches. This can end your "date" or, if you feel comfortable, your partner can then try to stimulate you.

After you have stimulated yourself or on your next "date," your partner will try to bring you to orgasm using the techniques you showed him or her. It is vital that he or she try to touch you *the way that you touch yourself*, not the way that *he or she* wants to touch you. Most women who are learning to orgasm regularly find it easier to orgasm with a partner's finger or tongue stimulation to the clitoris and/or vagina. For the purpose of this "show and tell" session, your partner needs to focus on giving you pleasure and avoid intercourse. There is obviously nothing wrong with intercourse, but most women orgasm more easily with the "other" aspects of lovemaking, and we want to hone your and your lover's skill in bringing you to orgasm.

If you can orgasm without a vibrator, it is easier to translate to partnered lovemaking. But if you need a vibrator to orgasm, there is no reason that it cannot be integrated into lovemaking. If, however, you want to learn to orgasm without a vibrator, take a vibrator "holiday" and focus on manual (and oral, if you like) stimulation of your clitoris and vagina. Usually, with enough persistence and experimentation, you will be able to orgasm with manual stimulation using the techniques in the previous pages.

Once your partner is able to bring you to orgasm with fingers and/or tongue, you can try having an orgasm during penetration. You can do this most easily by stimulating your clitoris during lovemaking. You can touch yourself in almost any position, but at first it is probably easiest when you are on top and can control the rhythm and flow. Then experiment with your partner stimulating your clitoris during lovemaking to bring you to orgasm.

EXPLORING THE JADE CHAMBER: POSITIONS FOR VAGINAL STIMULATION

Every woman is different in terms of which positions she likes best and which bring her the most pleasure. Sometimes we want the emotional connection of the face-to-face positions, and at other times we crave the vigorous animal quality of the "from behind" positions. Sometimes we want to relax and be on the bottom, and at other times we want to take charge and be on top. It's good to have a variety of positions that you like in your repertoire so that you can express what you need in the moment. Some positions, however, will optimize your chances of stimulating the G-spot and AFE zone.

The position of your uterus and the angle of your vagina vary throughout your lifetime and even throughout your monthly cycle. And the "flexibility" of your vagina will vary depending on how old you are and whether you have ever delivered a baby vaginally. This means that there are no generic positions to reach vaginal spots for every woman. Certain positions, however, maximize the possibility that vaginal penetration will stimulate its intended "target." Do remember to start gently, as any new position may take some getting used to. And thrusting strongly at a new angle can hit the cervix— a very painful experience. It can sometimes be challenging to find

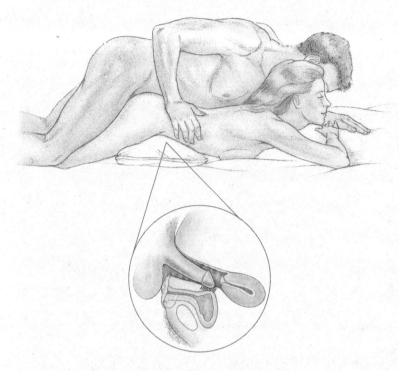

Position for AFE Zone Stimulation

sensitive vaginal spots, and when you happen upon them, to find them again. This was the experience of Julie, a 34-year-old physical therapist, who confided to me, "My husband and I had been having satisfying lovemaking for 7 years when he hit some incredibly pleasurable area deep inside my vagina during intercourse and I couldn't get enough. I had the strongest orgasm that I had ever had. It took us several weeks to find it again but since then, we know just how to hit it: I lie on my stomach and he lies over me thrusting down. It gives me the most intense, deep orgasms; I completely lose control." What Julie describes is a position that is usually good for stimulating the AFE zone during intercourse with a male partner or with a female partner wearing a strap-on.

It is also possible to reach the AFE zone with the woman on top and leaning back. You can lean back while facing your partner, or

Alternative Position for AFE Zone Stimulation

you can face your partner's feet and lean back, achieving a slightly different angle of penetration.

Some women enjoy stimulating the AFE zone by having the man on top with her lower torso lifted at an angle so that his entry hits her deep anterior vaginal wall (see illustration). She can put her knees or heels on his shoulders, or he can hold her under the knees. You can adjust the angle at which your vaginal wall is being stimulated by lifting your buttocks higher or lower. This position can be somewhat strenuous for your partner and a little more complex to coordinate since it can be more difficult for your partner to stay inside.

Stimulating the G-spot during intercourse can be difficult for some women as it's only an inch or less inside the vagina. Fingers are really the ideal instruments by which to stimulate the G-spot, unless your G-spot is further inside your vagina. In that case, the same positions that work for the AFE zone also work for the G-spot, just at a shallower angle of penetration.

Using fingers to stimulate the G-spot rhythmically while stroking the clitoris with the tongue is as close as many women get to heaven. During intercourse, thrusting shallowly in and out will sometimes stimulate the G-spot, especially if you angle upward. The best position that I have come across to stimulate the G-spot during intercourse is when the female lies on her back on a bed or other raised surface. The partner enters shallowly and grips the penis at the base to angle it sharply upward toward the G-spot, thrusting upward. Alternatively, the woman can grip the penis at the base and angle it herself to use for her own pleasure.

Experiment with what feels good to you. You never know; you may find a new treasure spot all your own. Even if you still have difficulty with orgasm, remember that the sexual energy you generate can still benefit your health and increase your vitality. We are going to explore in the next chapter how to transform that sexual energy or orgasmic energy into vital energy, chi, to energize your whole body and expand your pleasure from head to toe.

CHAPTER 6

WHOLE-BODY ORGASM

Orgasm that leaves your hands and feet tingling, your heart warm and open, and your mind expanded and clear—this is whole-body orgasm. If you have never felt it, it is an ecstatic expression of human potential that you don't want to miss during your lifetime. The fact that you can experience it on a weekly or even nightly basis is one of the great and often undiscovered possibilities of human sexuality. When I asked Julie, a 34-year-old who has been practicing Taoist lovemaking for 8 years, what whole-body orgasm feels like in her body, she described, "It allows me to access a state of expanded awareness and contentment that I have only felt after hours of meditation combined with an incredible feeling of bliss that stays with me for hours—sometimes all day!" It is possible for all of us to experience this ecstatic state with the methods I will teach you in this chapter.

We reach the experience of whole-body orgasm by circulating our orgasmic energy through a basic energetic pathway of the body that the Taoists refer to as the Microcosmic Orbit. When you circulate sexual energy through the Microcosmic Orbit, you transform your desire into your energetic "rocket fuel" and enhance your vitality. Sexual energy combined with the healing energy of love is the most powerful force within the body. Drawing on this source of energy increases your life force tremendously and nourishes your body, mind, and spirit.

Though the information may seem overwhelming at first, with time these exercises will become as natural as breathing. Your chi is already flowing in the Microcosmic Orbit. In the first exercise I will teach you how to understand the natural flow of your chi so that you can consciously control it, and thereby improve the quality and the quantity of your energy. Doing this will enable you to really be the person that you want to be in the world. After Lily, age 44, had been doing the Microcosmic Orbit for three weeks, she said, "I think that the orbit is giving me a lot of extra energy. And the way I'm seeing that energy manifest itself in my life is that I'm having a lot more time to be present with other people. I'm finding myself supporting other people, drawing people out, and being the intermediary in situations. It's allowing me to go to another level of being present in a healing way." What would *you* do if you felt calm, focused, and invigorated on a daily basis?

You'll begin your exploration of the Taoist sexual practice, or Healing Love, by learning to circulate chi within the Microcosmic Orbit, which is like an energy superhighway in the body. As I've explained, there are many reasons to learn the Healing Love practices. To begin with, they're fun, but you will also experience more pleasure than you may have ever imagined. They can also deepen the intimacy of your relationship with your partner. And finally, from a Taoist perspective, these practices will increase your principal energy, improve your health, and possibly prolong your life. First you will learn to do the Microcosmic Orbit using chi to establish familiarity with the circuit and open up the flow of energy. After you can easily circulate your chi through the Microcosmic Orbit, I will teach you how to use the Orgasmic Upward Draw to transform your sexual energy into chi. Sexual energy is hotter and more volatile than chi and, therefore, more difficult to control, which is why we first learn to do the Microcosmic Orbit with the clarity of chi. If you practice the Microcosmic Orbit, the Orgasmic Upward Draw will become easy because you'll have trained your body and your nervous system and will be able to tune in to the subtle flow of your energy.

THE MICROCOSMIC ORBIT

In all Eastern traditions, meditative practices calm and focus the mind. The Healing Tao meditative practices do this by focusing on the movement of chi. When you circulate your chi in the Microcosmic Orbit, you refine and distill it, creating a better quality of energy, or chi, for your body. The Microcosmic Orbit is made up of two channels, the Back Channel and the Front Channel (traditionally called the Governor Channel and the Conception Channel, respectively, in Chinese medicine). These channels are formed during the earliest development of the fetus in the womb. The fetus, which resembles a flat disk, folds over to create a seam, which becomes the midline along the front of your body, or the Front Channel. The fold opposite the seam forms our spine and spinal cord, or the Back Channel. The front seam is not as noticeable, but when a woman is pregnant a dark line, called the linea nigra, often appears up the center of her belly, which is why the Front Channel is referred to as the Conception Channel.

The Back Channel begins at the perineum and runs from the tip of the tailbone, up along the spine to the crown of the head and then over the forehead, ending between the bottom of the nose and the upper lip where there's an indentation (see illustration on page 146). The Front Channel runs from the tip of your tongue to your throat and along the midline of your body down to your pubis and perineum. Touching your tongue to the roof of your mouth completes the Microcosmic Orbit. There is an indentation approximately a quarter-inch behind the teeth as the roof of the mouth curves upward, and it is through here that the energy descends most easily from your brain and moves through your tongue and down your throat and chest to your abdomen.

We begin the Microcosmic Orbit by bringing the energy from our brains down the Front Channel to our abdominal center using the Inner Smile exercise on page 61. At this point, you might be

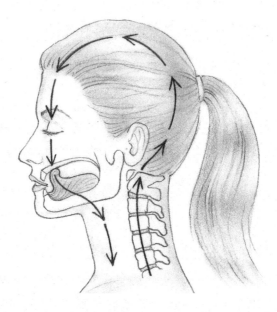

Completing the Microcosmic Orbit

thinking, "What brain energy? I don't have any left up there!" You may not have the clear-thinking and feeling energy that you need, but the great majority of us in this sped-up, always-on world have plenty of erratic energy. We sometimes have obsessive energy in our brains that continually compiles our to-do list and berates us for the things we have not yet accomplished. Or our minds may narrate our every experience with critical and evaluative feedback about our worth or the worth of others. *This* is the energy that I want you to *empty* from your brain so that you can fill your mind with the clarity of vital chi.

Chi is flowing through your Microcosmic Orbit even as you read this. Sometimes it moves like a free-flowing river, and sometimes it moves only in a trickle. When we open our Microcosmic Orbit and consciously circulate our chi, our energy flows through it with more ease, which contributes to our overall health. However, there are "energy centers" along the orbit where the energy gathers and can be multiplied or where energy can slow down or become "stuck," if

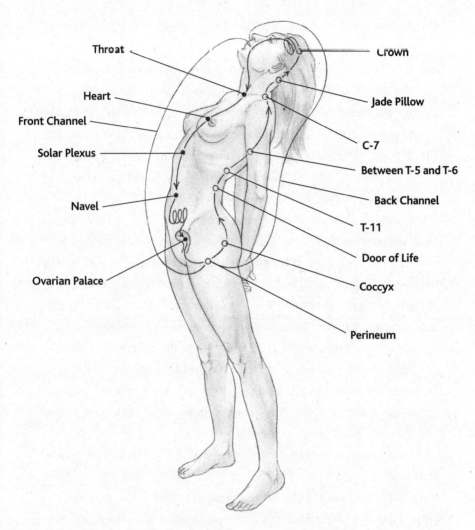

The Microcosmic Orbit with Front and Back Channels

that center isn't open. Some of these, such as the navel and the third eye, we have already discussed. The other "rest stops" along the chi highway are noted in the illustration above.

Let's look at the locations of each of the energy centers. Keep in mind that these are not finite points, and that if you're in the general vicinity, you will be able to feel and collect the energy there. Also, they are not located at the surface of your skin, but underneath your skin approximately 1 to 1½ inches. For example, the Back Channel doesn't travel up the surface of your back, but actually through the inside of your spinal column, where the spinal chord is located.

The Back Channel, as I've said, begins at the perineum, which is a short, muscular area between your vagina and your anus. The next center is your coccyx, or tailbone, which is at the tip of your sacrum. The sacrum forms an upside-down triangle at the base of your spine. The next center, called the Door of Life by the Taoists, is located at the small of your back, directly across from your navel. The T-11 center, which is the 11th thoracic vertebrae, is located midway along your spine, directly across from your solar plexus. The next center is located between the fifth and sixth thoracic vertebrae, just across from your breasts and your heart center. The C-7 center, which is the seventh cervical vertebrae, is located at the base of the neck. You can sometimes feel a prominent bone in your spine where the neck meets the upper back; this is C-7. The Jade Pillow can be found at the base of the skull in a central, natural indentation. The next center is the crown of the head, which is the very apex, or highest point, of your skull. The third eye, then, as we've seen, is midway between and just above your eyebrows.

Though not an energy center, per se, the Front Channel begins at the upper palate, or the roof of your mouth. The first energy center of this channel is the throat center, located at the indentation at the base of your throat. The heart center is in the middle of your chest, over your sternum, or breastbone, and between your breasts. The solar plexus is located several inches below the sternum, midway between the lowest ribs. Your navel center, with which you are already familiar, is, of course, just behind the navel. Below your navel is an important center for women, the Ovarian Palace. This center can easily be located by placing your thumbs over your navel and letting your fingers fan over your abdomen, as shown in the illustration. Where your forefingers meet is just over your Ovarian Palace, which overlies the main body of the uterus.

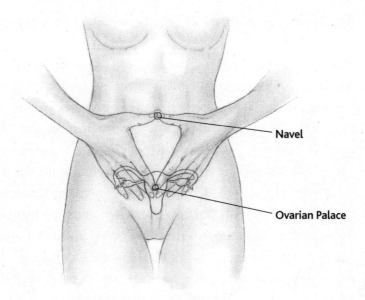

Navel

Ovarian Palace

Finding the Ovarian Palace

Although it is helpful to know exactly where each center is, it is not necessary for your practice. Remember that the chi flows naturally from one point to another. If you're not sure of the exact spot for the center, focus on the general area while moving your chi. For many beginning students, however, learning the points along the Microcosmic Orbit are important in order to fully sense the movement of their chi. For others, the points are confusing or overwhelming. I would suggest that you try doing the Microcosmic Orbit by moving from point to point since this will help you learn the energy route in detail and make sure that there are no blockages along the way. If it is difficult or distracting, it is fine to abbreviate the practice as I demonstrate in the Basic Microcosmic Orbit exercise. In this abbreviated orbit, you focus on the crown of the head, the heart center, and the abdominal center. After you are able to sense the flow of your chi through the orbit using these three points, it may be easier to feel each of the points on the full Microcosmic Orbit.

When you first begin your practice, it is often easier to visualize the energy moving from center to center along the front and back channels. For this reason, the exercise directs you to visualize each of the points in order. While the Upward Orgasmic Draw follows the sequence that we have just discussed, the Microcosmic Orbit begins and ends at the navel center, as it is an important point from which to gain chi for the orbit and to store your chi at the end of the sequence. During the exercise, you will circulate the chi around the entire orbit several times, beginning and ending at the navel center.

It may help you to touch your body at the energy center at which you want to feel the chi. This helps focus your mind and also passes chi from your fingertips into that area. Chi flows easily from the fingertips and also radiates from the palms of our hands. Another way to stimulate the flow of chi is to hold your open palm or palms several inches from your body over the point at which you are concentrating your chi. If you put your right hand on one point and your left hand on the next point, you can visualize the energy moving between your hands.

It also helps to imagine the energy flowing down the front of your body with your out-breath—as if the energy is falling down with gravity, while your chest relaxes and you exhale. To move the energy up the Back Channel, focus on "sipping" the energy up the back with the in-breath. Inhale, in small sips, as if you were sucking in your breath through a straw, and imagine your energy being pulled up your spine with your breath. At first this practice seems complex, but with experience, the chi can circulate through the entire orbit in a few seconds using only the intention of your mind.

Before doing any of the exercises in this book, it is also important that we cultivate loving intention toward ourselves with the Inner Smile so that the chi we circulate has loving and life-giving qualities. You shouldn't do the Microcosmic Orbit, or any of the exercises, if you are feeling angry, sad, impatient, or otherwise out of sorts. Use the Healing Sounds to balance and tonify your emotions and then do the Microcosmic Orbit. In this way, the Microcosmic Orbit can be healing and balancing.

EXERCISE 12

BASIC MICROCOSMIC ORBIT

1. Using the Inner Smile, smile down to your navel center and feel the chi awaken. Now smile to your sexual organs at the Ovarian Palace and feel the chi move from the Ovarian Palace through your sexual organs to the perineum.

2. Squeeze your PC muscle in order to pump the chi from the perineum into the sacrum and spine.

3. Feel the energy rise to the crown of your head.

4. Touch your tongue to your palate and smile again down to your abdominal center, allowing the chi to fall like a waterfall from your crown, through your tongue, and into your navel.

Begin the Microcosmic Orbit meditation by warming up your spine so that the energy can flow more smoothly. Many of us sit much of the day and therefore have chronic stiffness or pain in our backs, which, in addition to being uncomfortable, can impede the flow of energy.

First, sit comfortably in the meditation position that I described on page 60, with your feet on the floor and the crown of your head stretched toward the ceiling. Then, starting at the bottom of your spine at your sacrum, rock from the hips, left and right. Move up your spine to your lower (lumbar) and middle (thoracic) vertebrae, rocking each one in turn, back and forth. Rock each vertebra in your neck as well. As you do this, your head will naturally rock side to side.

Now move back down the spine from your neck to your sacrum, rocking each in turn. Repeat this three times. Then rest and smile, directing joy, love, and healing to your spine. Feel it warm and loosen. Once your spine is open and warm, you're ready to start moving energy through your body.

TOOLS TO HELP YOUR MEDITATION

Almost everyone has difficulty when they first attempt the Microcosmic Orbit. Some of these problems are so common that I will ad-

EXERCISE 13

THE MICROCOSMIC ORBIT

1. Sit comfortably in meditation posture.

2. Using the Inner Smile, smile down to your heart center, feeling it soften and open. Bring that loving energy down to the navel center. Touch your navel with your fingers and breathe deeply into your belly. Smile down to your navel center, feeling it warm and the chi awaken. Doing Laughing Chi Kung (see page 58) may help energize your navel center. Feel the chi gather at your navel as warmth, pressure, or tingling. If you cannot feel anything, simply visualize a glowing ball of chi behind your navel.

3. With the power of your concentration, move the chi, or the glowing ball, from your navel to your Ovarian Palace. If it is helpful, place your left fingers on your sexual center while keeping your right fingers on your navel. Feel the chi running from your right to your left fingers. As you exhale, feel the energy running down into the sexual center.

4. Now move your chi to your perineum. Feel the energy radiating from the navel and Ovarian Palace to the perineum. Imagine a channel between your navel and perineum opening wide with the flow of chi.

The Back Channel

1. Move the energy from your perineum to your sacrum. It is helpful to place your left palm over the sacrum and your right fingertips over the Ovarian Palace. Feel the energy flow down from your Ovarian Palace and through your perineum to your sacrum. Contracting your PC muscle in order to "pump" the energy to the sacrum is very helpful. (I explain this in detail in the Pumping the Energy Up exercise on page 156.)

2. Breathe in, in short sips to draw the energy from your sacrum up the spine to the Door of Life center and let the energy gather.

dress them by topic. If you have not had any difficulty feeling or circulating your chi, it is still helpful to review each topic as the discussions can add depth and strength to your practice.

What if I can't feel my chi? When you first begin the meditative practice, it may be difficult to feel your chi. Remember that the sensations of the movement of chi can be subtle, sensed as tingling, heat, bubbling, or expansion. The more you focus your attention on

3. Move the energy to the T-11 center and feel it concentrate there.

4. Let the energy rise to the center between T-5 and T-6.

5. Now move the energy to the C-7 point at the base of the neck.

6. Let the chi flow to the Jade Pillow at the base of the skull.

7. Move the energy to the crown at the top of your head. Feel the energy flowing all the way from the sacrum up to the crown.

8. Now move the energy through your brain to your third eye and feel the energy accumulate there. Touching the third eye with your fingers can help you concentrate.

The Front Channel

1. Touch your tongue to the roof of your mouth at the top of the palate behind the teeth and connect the Front and Back Channels (refer back to page 146). Feel the energy moving down from your third eye through the tip of your tongue.

2. Move the energy to the throat center and imagine the energy flowing down from your tongue into your throat center. It may be helpful to visualize the chi moving into your saliva and swallowing it down to the throat center.

3. Move the energy down to the heart center and feel the heart softening and opening.

4. Now move the energy to the solar plexus and feel the energy collect there.

5. Put your fingers on your navel, opening it slightly, and allow the energy to return there. Imagine that a waterfall of energy is falling from your third eye down to the cup of your navel. It might be helpful to stroke from your third eye down to your navel with your hand, helping the energy to move.

6. Spiral the energy just behind the navel to help it absorb into your abdomen, counterclockwise and then clockwise if you wish.

a particular point, the easier it will be to sense the chi that is present. It is also the case that we all *sense* chi differently. Some women will feel it, but others will never feel a sensation but can visualize it moving. When I taught Desiree, a 54-year-old writer, the practice, she said, "I haven't ever really felt it moving around, but I can visualize it. I just picture it, and that's getting easier. When I'm done I feel really good. I feel cleansed, I feel relaxed, and I feel connected, so I think it's probably happening, and I'm just not aware of it." If you cannot feel your chi, but can visualize moving it with your mind, you will still benefit from the practice.

If you are having trouble feeling your chi, you may want to begin your meditation by simply focusing on the navel point,[1] which is located about 1½ inches behind the navel. Bellows Breathing (opposite) is designed to help you activate your chi at that point. After Bellows Breathing, you can use the chi that you created to start the energy moving in the Microcosmic Orbit.

For many people, it is easier to sense your sexual energy than it is to sense your chi. Practice the Microcosmic Orbit simply visualizing the pathway for now.

What if I can't move my chi? It is the natural character of chi to flow, but sometimes we have blockages that impede the flow of chi. When the chi is "stuck" or moving slowly through an area, you may experience pain, tingling, or burning. Rubbing the area where the chi feels stuck can be helpful. Some people try to force the chi to flow, which is a little like trying to move a lake with a Ping-Pong paddle. Relax, breathe deeply into your abdomen, and visualize a free-flowing river without blockages (or whatever image works for you). It is much easier to remove the dam (which may be the obstacles of your mind) so that the water can freely flow than trying to move the lake itself. It may sometimes happen that the chi will flow spontaneously to areas that you did not intend. For now, just stay relaxed and assume that the chi went to where it was needed. Remember that the more you practice, the more deeply your "chi river" will mark its bed, and the easier it will be to move and control it. The exercises in this chapter have many steps, but soon you will be able

1. Some Taoist practitioners locate the central abdominal point, the Tan Tien, 1 inch below the navel and about 1½ inches into the body from there. It doesn't matter if you use this point or the navel point, as both are energetically powerful. If you are used to locating your abdominal point below the navel, it is fine to continue doing so. In Traditional Chinese Medicine, the "boiling cauldron" is located just below the navel and the "steam" or chi that is created is located at the navel. You can use either point.

EXERCISE 14

BELLOWS BREATHING

1. Sit in meditation posture.

2. Lay your hands on top of each other over your navel.

3. Inhale and expand your lower abdomen at the navel region, feeling your lungs expand. Keep your chest relaxed and focus on breathing with your belly.

4. Exhale with some force, pulling the navel back in toward the spine and keeping your chest relaxed. Feel your sexual organs pull up toward your navel at the same time.

5. Repeat the inhalation and exhalation 9 or 18 times.

6. Relax and feel the warm chi that you have created at your navel center.

to move your chi through the Microcosmic Orbit at any time in only a few seconds.

What if I can't remember all of the points? You can begin by practicing the Basic Microcosmic Orbit (see page 151) and then work your way up to the full orbit. Each point has its own special qualities and associations. If you cultivate your ability to sense each point and let the chi flow smoothly through it, it will benefit your health and well-being. One way to amplify the strength of the sensation at each point is to pause to spiral the energy at that specific point, as we did in our abdominal center. This will allow points that are "weak" to become stronger. For example, if you have trouble feeling your chi at your heart center, cultivating your ability to spiral the chi there and feel the heart soften and open will help you feel more love and joy in your life.

What if I can't move my chi up my spine? If you are having a problem drawing the energy up your spine, you can help the energy rise by using your spine's natural pumps. Your cerebrospinal fluid bathes the brain and spine. Pumps at your sacrum (the back of your pelvis) and at the base of your skull help this fluid circulate and can also help you draw energy up your spine. These pumps were well

---

EXERCISE 15

PUMPING THE ENERGY UP

1. Rock your hips forward and back. Activate your sacral pump by squeezing your anus up toward your tailbone while you rock your hips forward and flatten the curve of your back. Then rock your hips back and release your anus. This should feel like you are riding a horse. Imagine that with each squeeze of your anus that you are pumping chi from the perineum to and through the sacrum and into your spine (see opposite).

2. Draw in your chin. Activate your cranial pump (at the base of your skull) by drawing your chin in and up and then back out in a soft, gentle circle. Keep the jaw and neck muscles relaxed. Look up to the crown of your head and feel the energy rise.

3. After activating the sacral and cranial pumps, rest and then begin drawing the energy up your spine into your brain. Looking up with your eyes toward the top of your head will also help direct the energy up to your crown. Activate the sacral pump to move the energy from the perineum to and through the sacrum and into the spine. Use sipping breaths through your mouth to suck the chi up the spine. Activate the cranial pump to draw the energy into the base of the skull and through to the brain.

---

known to the ancient Taoists and are still used today. Osteopathic physicians manipulate these pumps using craniosacral therapy to improve the flow of cerebrospinal fluid. You can do the following Pumping the Energy Up exercise standing or sitting.

What if my back hurts? It is sometimes a little difficult to draw the energy into the base of the spine, and some people experience a little pain, tingling, or pins and needles when this energy first enters the spine. If this happens to you, do not be alarmed. You can help pass the energy through by gently massaging the area. If you have pain in other parts of your spine, it is likely that the energy is blocked there. Do the spine rocking warm-up on page 151 to loosen up your spine and mobilize the energy. It may also help to rub it or have someone else massage the area.

What if I feel pain or pressure in my head? If your head hurts, you feel wired, or you are having difficulty sleeping, you may be

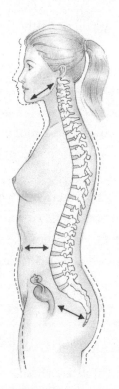

The Cranial and Sacral Pumps

leaving too much stagnant energy in your head. The energy can over-heat if it stays in one place. Remember that the brain is good at trans-forming energy, but not at storing it. It is important to keep the energy moving through the head during the Microcosmic Orbit. An easy way to do this is to circulate the energy in a spiral fashion once it reaches the brain. Spiral the energy from a central point outward nine times. Imagine that the energy is revitalizing and reinvigorating the brain. Then reverse the flow and spiral nine times back into the center (see page 62).

It also helps to spiral your eyes as a way to direct the energy. Keeping your head in a normal position, look up with your eyes to-ward the ceiling or sky. Then move your eyes, still looking up, to-ward your left ear, then up and backward as far as you can, then toward your right ear, and then forward again in a fluid motion. You will be making a spiral that will be on the same plane as if a clock or Frisbee were sitting on top of your head. By "spiraling" your eyes, you help the energy in your head to spiral as well. Now spiral your eyes in the reverse direction, as you spiral the energy back in toward the center of your head.

While the energy is still mobile, move it directly to your third eye and down through your palate and tongue to your throat center and down to your abdomen.

What if I can't bring the energy down? For many of us who spend too much time "in our heads," it can be difficult to bring the energy down. Too much energy can make you feel wired or cause pain or pressure, as discussed above. The Bringing the Energy Down exercise will help.

EXERCISE 16

BRINGING THE ENERGY DOWN

1. Sit in meditation position and place your hands on your abdomen.

2. Relax your body and take a deep breath into your belly, releasing any blockages.

3. Touch your tongue to your palate.

4. Smile, gently curving your lips and smiling with the corners of your eyes, directing your smiling energy down to your navel center.

5. Breathe deeply in and out and visualize that with your out-breath you are draining all of the excess energy and frenetic thoughts down through your tongue to your abdomen.

6. Bring the energy down. Imagine the energy descending down the front of your body like a waterfall and pooling in your abdomen. Cup your left hand within your right just below your belly button, as if you were catching this waterfall of energy. If the energy feels thicker and more viscous than water and harder to move, imagine that the energy is like molasses or a thread and that a spiral wheel at your abdomen is turning like a spindle and drawing the energy down.

7. Swallow your saliva. Imagine that you are draining the energy from your head into your saliva and then forcefully swallow your saliva down, moving the energy directly into your organs.

If you still feel that you have too much energy in your head, the Venting exercise that follows will allow you to drain the energy from your head down and out your legs and into the ground.

Once you've learned to move your chi in the Microcosmic Orbit, you can use the same principles to circulate sexual energy in the Orgasmic Upward Draw.

EXERCISE 17

VENTING

1. Sit in a chair in meditation position or lie down on your back. If you're lying down, elevate your knees with a pillow if you feel any pain in the small of your back or lumbar area.

2. Place your hands in front of your mouth so that the tips of your fingers touch and so that your palms are facing toward your feet.

3. Close your eyes and take a deep breath. Feel your stomach and chest expand gently.

4. Smile and exhale quietly, making the sound *HEEEEEE*. As you are exhaling, push your hands toward your feet. Picture your body as a hollow tube of blue light that you are emptying with your hands from your head down past your chest and your abdomen, through your legs, out the soles of your feet and into the earth.

5. Repeat the sound and movement nine times.

THE ORGASMIC UPWARD DRAW

Once you have mastered the Microcosmic Orbit, the Orgasmic Upward Draw is a simple exercise, but it's extremely powerful for increasing your overall energy and concentration. Many of us are exhausted by the many demands of modern life. Finding time for lovemaking or self-loving feels like just another drain on an already taxed system. But I will teach you how to easily increase your sexual energy and use it regularly to give yourself an energy "espresso." This one, however, will not make you irritable or give you the shakes, although it can be addicting.

When we use our own creative juices to increase our life passion, we don't "crash" after the high. Instead, we increase our capacity for vibrancy. In the same way that a mother's love is not halved when she has a second child, our body's capacity for multiplying our energy, our concentration, and our joy is limitless. I'm not talking about the kind of verve that one gets from artificial stimulants. A healthy and generous flow of chi leaves us awake, alert, calm, and content. We are in the ideal mind-space to work, to create, to parent, and to love.

In the Orgasmic Upward Draw, you draw your sexual energy from your genitals up to your brain and back down to your abdomen to rejuvenate yourself. This exercise uses the same techniques and pathways that we discussed in the Microcosmic Orbit. Remember that sexual energy is part of our principal chi, our generative life force. It is uniquely capable of nourishing our bodies and refreshing our minds. Though sexual energy is often easier to feel than chi, because it is so powerful, it is also harder to control. This is why we try to learn the Microcosmic Orbit using chi alone before trying it with sexual energy.

Orgasmic energy is simply a more potent form of sexual energy. If you have ever had an orgasm (and I sincerely hope that by the time you finish this book, the answer to this will be a resounding

"Yes!"), you understand that the fall into orgasm is a process of letting go. At first, it can be challenging to surrender to that spontaneous rush of pleasure while still remembering to pump the energy from your genitals up your spine. With time and practice, this will become as natural as breathing. The Orgasmic Upward Draw allows you to spread the sexual energy throughout your body to vitalize your organs and senses. Collette, a 56-year-old woman from Canada, says that "with the Healing Love practice, my orgasms are stronger and longer and go to all levels of the sexual organs, internal organs, and senses."

Most women draw the aroused energy up their spines several times prior to orgasm. Doing so actually expands the orgasm, as we will discuss in the next chapter, increasing the capacity of the body to experience and generate more and more pleasure. You can do the Orgasmic Upward Draw at any level of arousal and benefit from the circulation of that energy so that even if you do not orgasm, this practice can expand your pleasure and your energy. Ultimately, you will learn to fall over the brink into orgasm and to simultaneously send that orgasmic energy pulsating through your body. I'm going to teach you how in this chapter and the next.

The muscles of your sacral pump (the PC muscles), which we used in the Pumping the Energy Up exercise to pump the energy from the perineum to the spine, are the same muscles that are naturally contracting with the throes of orgasm. In fact, when you are able to consciously guide the contractions of your PC muscle in the rhythmic pulse of orgasm, feeling the orgasmic energy flow through you, your pleasure will be more acute and more prolonged. I think of this *conscious orgasm* as analogous to conscious dreaming. You are still in the fulsome pleasure of orgasm, but you have a subtle control over your energy and your response. Instead of being an orgasmic dreamer under the spell of the orgasm itself, you can prolong and intensify the pleasure of orgasm *because you can guide the orgasmic energy*. Sarina Stone, a Healing Tao instructor in St. Paul, Minnesota, says that "the difference between releasing orgasm energy outward and drawing the chi up and into the body is comparable to the difference between a shower at the gym and a luxurious bath with rose petals at a five-star resort, followed by a different relaxation therapy every time you do it."

When we arouse and circulate our sexual energy, it is, as you might expect, *hotter*, and more difficult to control. Practicing the Microcosmic Orbit will make it easier to focus and guide your sexual energy in the same path. It is helpful to begin moving your sexual energy when it is only mildly aroused, and as you feel able, progress to higher and higher levels of arousal. In the beginning you will need to pause from continued stimulation to do the Orgasmic Upward Draw, but as you develop you will be able to circulate your sexual energy simultaneously with continued stimulation.

I've found that it's easier to learn the practice while self-cultivating simply because you can easily control your own arousal. It will also enable you to get a feel for the speed and intensity of your own arousal. Many female Universal Tao instructors use self-cultivation and the Orgasmic Upward Draw as one of the foundations of their spiritual practice. When I spoke with Julia, a 56-year-old psychotherapist from Mexico, she was very exuberant about self-cultivation and the Healing Love practices. When I asked how they had affected her, she replied, "They opened a whole different world. I learned to contact a part of my feminine power I had never even imagined. When you learn to cultivate, value, and enjoy your own sexual energy, you no longer need a relationship to keep you satisfied." It is also true that the self-cultivation practices stoke the fire of any relationship that you have.

Regardless of whether you currently have a lover, I would suggest that you develop your ability to cultivate and circulate your own sexual energy on your own. Saida Desilets, a Healing Tao instructor from Canada, notes that, "Now I can be a woman whose sexual energy is fully activated even without a man. Usually, when I'm celibate, I get sexually frustrated. But when I did the practice, this didn't happen. It became more and more exquisite—the feelings in my body and the subtleness. I would have constant orgasms all day long. They were so subtle that I hadn't noticed them before. They were like little bubbles, always rising." You can, of course, also do the Orgasmic Upward Draw while making love with a partner; I'll show you how later in this chapter.

The practice of circulating sexual energy through your body is powerful. Because it is so powerful, it is important to use some caution in doing the practice. It is best to practice when you are in a calm and balanced state of mind. If you are feeling angry or impatient, the practice will simply amplify your emotions. It is helpful to do the Inner Smile to your heart and sexual organs prior to beginning the Orgasmic Upward Draw to focus on doing the exercise in a spirit of self-love and love toward your partner, if you're practicing together. I would also suggest that you do the Healing Sounds practice several times a week when you are actively practicing the Orgasmic Upward Draw to help balance your emotions and assist in the clear flow of your sexual energy. This will help to keep the sexual practices safe and make them much more effective in boosting your health and vitality.

BEGINNING THE SEXUAL PRACTICE

You will need time alone in a nurturing sensual atmosphere to practice the Orgasmic Upward Draw. As I mentioned, it is usually easier to learn the practice alone, but if you prefer to do the practice with your partner, then go for it. It is best, especially in the beginning, not to do the Orgasmic Upward Draw while lying down, as the energy is more likely to get "stuck" in the chest. Sitting, reclining at an angle, or standing are fine. Try to keep your spine in a relatively straight position, not bent to the right or left, as this, too, can impede the flow of energy. Begin by practicing the Inner Smile to your heart and

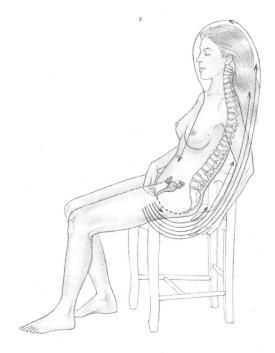

The Orgasmic Upward Draw

sexual organs to awaken your chi. Smile to your heart until it softens and you can feel it radiant and shining. Now smile to your sexual organs—uterus, ovaries, and clitoris—and feel them warm and glowing within you. Send the loving chi from your heart down to your sexual organs, feeling love and appreciation for them.

Use any of the techniques of mind and body that work for you to kindle your desire. Begin the practice by lovingly touching yourself. This is an ideal time to massage and caress your breasts, as the breasts are directly connected to the clitoris, energetically and hormonally. (Taoist Breast Massage, which will be taught in chapter 8, is ideal for this purpose). Lovingly stroke your clitoris and labia, feeling the warm sexual energy gather there. Most women feel the sexual energy around the clitoris, labia, and vagina. Focus your mind on that sexual energy and move it from your sexual organs to your rectum and through your sacrum to your lower spine. Once again, use the power of your concentration and the squeezing of the perineum and rectum. Try placing one hand on your clitoris, vulva, or perineum and another on your sacrum and try to pass the energy between the two points. As with the Microcosmic Orbit, these techniques and hand positions are simply tools that you can use to help move the energy. Eventually you will be able to move the energy with the power of your mind alone.

Draw the energy from your sacrum up your spine to your head. You can stop at each energy center, if you wish, or simply let the energy rise up the spine to the crown of your head. If necessary, you can also use the sacral and cranial pumps from the Pumping the Energy Up exercise (see page 156) to help move the energy up. To nourish and energize your brain, spiral the energy in your head from a central point outward 9 or 18 times. Then reverse the direction and spiral it in toward the center of your head again. Touch your tongue to your palate and draw the energy through your third eye and down the Front Channel to your abdomen, as in the Bringing the Energy Down exercise (see page 158). Spiral the energy at the abdomen from the center outward and then reverse the direction and spiral it back in to help it absorb.

The sensations that you feel doing the Microcosmic Orbit with sexual energy may feel different, warmer, or more pleasurable. It may be harder or easier for you to move the energy. With practice, you will be able to draw sexual energy up your spine with a single thought, which will make getting through the day a lot more fun. For many women, sexual energy moves more quickly; for example, it might shoot from your pelvis straight to your head. It is also common for the energy to rise up from the genitals straight to your abdominal organs. Pay attention to what feels good in *your* body. The reason we send the energy through the sacrum and into the spine is so that the sexual energy is transformed into chi and refined so that it can nourish our bodies. If it seems that the energy is going straight into your abdomen, concentrate on keeping the energy in the area around your perineum. Use the contraction of the anus and the sacral pump to "pick up" the energy and send it through the sacrum to the spine.

Some women experience the Microcosmic Orbit traveling naturally in the opposite direction: The energy moves up the Front Channel to the head and down the Back Channel to the perineum. This is considered the traditional yin, or female, direction of energy. Mantak Chia and I choose to teach the Microcosmic Orbit in the yang direction because it is easier for most people to move the energy in that direction. If, however, the energy moves more naturally for you up the Front Channel and down the back, experiment with moving the energy in this way and notice how you feel. If the energy flows easily and you feel calm and refreshed after practicing, it is fine to practice in this direction. As with the yang direction, placing the tongue against the palate connects the Front and Back Channels. It is likewise important not to leave the energy in your head, so if the energy goes up the Front Channel, it therefore *must* come down the Back Channel (a sometimes more difficult direction). If the energy feels "stuck" in your head and you can't move it down the Back Channel, try the Bringing the Energy Down exercise on page 158 and the Inner Smile to help bring the energy back down to the abdomen.

Once you are able to draw up the sexual energy, try arousing yourself more and more. You can use any techniques that you enjoy: clitoral or vaginal stimulation, breast stimulation, or your erotic imagination. If you use a vibrator, do remember that it has its own electrical, "energetic" charge. For some women, this makes it harder to do the practice. Also, because clitoral stimulation with a vibrator is so intense, it can also be more difficult to control your arousal. If you enjoy using a vibrator and can easily do the practice using it, then go ahead. Experiment with what feels best for your body.

USING ORGASMIC ENERGY

You can do the Orgasmic Upward Draw practice using sexual energy at any level of arousal. The practice, however, is even more powerful and beneficial if you circulate *orgasmic* energy through the Microcosmic Orbit. As your arousal increases, continue to circulate your energy. Some women need to pause from "the action" to do this, and others can circulate while continuing to stimulate themselves. If you are someone who cannot orgasm or has difficulty doing so with self-stimulation, simply arouse yourself as much as possible and circulate the energy. The practice is still very beneficial, regardless of whether you orgasm.

If you do orgasm, pay attention to the moment that you crest over into orgasm. Contract your PC muscle and anus rhythmically and pump the energy through your sacrum and into your spine. Usually when we orgasm, a small amount of our sexual energy goes out of our bodies through the perineum. If you were able to circulate

---

EXERCISE 18

THE ORGASMIC UPWARD DRAW

1. Set the mood with a sensual atmosphere and assurance that you will not be disturbed.

2. Smile down to your abdomen, letting any distracting thoughts drain from your head to your belly.

3. Arouse yourself by any method you choose and feel your desire gathering in your pelvis.

4. Pump the energy from your perineum to your sacrum by contracting your PC muscle and anus. Then move the energy through the Microcosmic Orbit, using your tongue on your palate to connect the Front and Back Channels.

5. Now arouse yourself to orgasm, and when the waves of orgasm begin, contract your PC muscle and anus to move the energy into the sacrum and the Microcosmic Orbit. Try to keep the PC muscle lightly contracted throughout orgasm.

6. Circulate the orgasmic energy in your head 9 or 18 times, spiraling out and then in.

7. Touch your tongue to your palate and let the orgasmic energy flow down the Front Channel to your abdomen.

8. Smile to your navel and spiral the energy at the navel outward and then inward 9 or 18 times.

energy in the orbit during your arousal, but are unable to move the orgasmic energy, you will still, overall, increase your chi and keep the life-giving orgasmic energy in your body by *holding the energy at the perineum* with the power of your concentration until you are able to pump it through your sacrum. This requires that as you abandon yourself to the pleasure of orgasm, you maintain some concentration at your perineum and pump those lovely waves of pleasure right into your sacrum and spine.

It is easiest at first to concentrate on moving the energy into the spine during orgasm. After orgasm, move the orgasmic energy up your spine and into your head and spiral it. Then smile down to your navel and bring the energy down to your abdomen to spiral and store it. With practice, you may be able to do all of these steps during the orgasm itself: Pump the energy up, move it into your head, touch your tongue to your palate, and let the energy flow to your abdomen. As you practice, the energy will naturally flow from your perineum to your brain and back down your front to your perineum in orgasmic cycles. In fact, some women experience a rapid cycling of their sexual energy through the orbit right from the beginning. You can then choose to end the cycles when you are ready and bring the energy down to the abdomen to store it.

Several of my students have had a hard time "letting go" enough to orgasm yet still maintaining some conscious control over their sexual energy. "I feel a resistance to moving the energy up during orgasm," commented Lily. "One of my favorite things in the world is to have an orgasm. I feel like that is really the time to let go and not think about anything." The intention here is not to turn orgasm into a chore but simply to channel the energy, as and when it feels joyful and nourishing to do so. Do what feels comfortable to you. As you become more familiar with the practice and integrate it more into your lovemaking, it will feel more natural. Try to do the Orgasmic Upward Draw sometimes and at other times simply "let go." Remember that if you do develop the ability to control your sexual energy during orgasm, you can much more easily have multiple and extended orgasms. This small loss of spontaneity now will be well worth the rewards of ecstatic expanded orgasm that the practice allows.

Some Taoist practitioners arouse themselves almost to the point of orgasm and continue to move the energy in the Microcosmic Orbit without orgasming. They do this because it can sometimes be very tricky to enjoy the release of orgasm and still hold on to all of your energy. If you find it difficult to do this, it is fine to do the practice and not orgasm. It is also the case that if you circulate the energy during your arousal and then orgasm without circulating it, you still benefit from the practice. The key to enjoying orgasm and keeping your energy is to gain mastery over your PC muscle. Doing the PC exercises from chapter 5 and the Jade Egg practice I'll describe in chapter 8 will help you develop more control over this important muscle.

Some women may be blessed with *so much* sexual energy that it feels as if it overflows the Microcosmic Orbit. If this is the case for you, there are other channels in the body that you can involve in your meditative practice to distribute the energy. The simplest of these is an extension of the Microcosmic Orbit that involves the legs in a figure eight. After bringing the energy through the Microcosmic Orbit, allow the energy to cross over at your sexual center and run down the backs of your legs and up the front of your legs to join the Microcosmic Orbit again.

For some women, the Orgasmic Upward Draw comes easily, but for most of us it takes a bit of experience for it to feel natural. Have heart. If you do the Microcosmic Orbit practice regularly, the Orgasmic Upward Draw will be easier because you have opened up your channels for the energy to flow. If you continue to have difficulty, please contact one of the Healing Tao instructors listed in appendix 2, and they can help you. This book is written to help guide you on the path of Healing Love, but there is no replacement for an instructor who can lead you through the practice, answer questions, and address problems with you. If it is at all possible, I suggest that you establish a relationship with a Universal Tao instructor in your area.

Above all, have fun. If you can't quite get it and, darn it, you had another orgasm without circulating your chi, *relax*. Having an orgasm is in and of itself a joyful celebration of your desire and a gift to your body. It is important to keep in mind that according to the ancient Taoists, most women lose very little energy during orgasm, so they do not have to worry too much about this release. The point is not to obsess about how much energy you have or lose but simply to share the nourishing sexual energy that you experience—before or during orgasm—with the rest of your body.

The practice is best learned with an open heart and a sense of humor. It is better in the beginning to do the practice when you feel inspired. Once again, do not let the practice become another chore that you have to do, or, God forbid, another voice telling you how your sex life should be. You need to make these practices *your own*. Practicing Healing Love is really more akin to *playing* with energy. And when you feel playful, your chi will flow easily.

In my experience, by far the most common difficulty is that the hot sexual energy gets "stuck" in the head, which can cause headache, head pressure, a "spaced out" sensation, or an experience that the mind is racing, as if you had too much caffeine. After the Orgasmic Upward Draw, you should feel energized, but calm and grounded, not "buzzed" in an unpleasant way. If this is a problem for you, please use the Bringing the Energy Down exercise on page 158 to bring your energy down to your abdomen. The Healing Sounds are also helpful in grounding your energy, and the Triple Warmer exercise (see page 82), in particular, is effective in calming the mind and inducing sleep. If these ideas still do not help, or if you have energy "stuck" in other parts of your body that feels unpleasant, it is possible to clear the excess energy from your body using the Venting exercise, which we discussed on page 159. If you feel that you have too much fullness or sexual energy in your genital area, you can help it absorb into the body by doing gentle massage to the area after the Orgasmic Upward Draw. Use your fingertips to rub in gentle circles along your outer labia and inner labia to help the energy absorb.

It is important when you first begin to practice the Orgasmic Upward Draw that you take it slowly and feel how your body responds. Heather, who has been doing the practices for a year, commented, "I needed to take it slow. I've had trouble getting overheated before. It was important for me to take the time to notice the effects of one session of practice before I did another so that I could get to know the changes." If you feel energized and content, the practice is working well. If, however, you are irritable, can't sleep, have headaches, or have unusual sensations of chi (pain, tingling, or burning) in your body, please contact a Universal Tao instructor for assistance. Usually these symptoms can be relieved by changing the way you do the practice or stopping the practice for some period of time. Remember that the body can intrinsically balance itself when given the chance. Unfortunately, most Western doctors will not be able to help you with these symptoms. A practitioner of Traditional Chinese Medicine (acupuncture, herbal, or energetic therapy), on the other hand, can be helpful, as they understand the movement of chi within the body.

SOUL MATING: EXCHANGING ENERGY WITH YOUR PARTNER

It's important to learn to circulate your sexual energy within your own body during partnered lovemaking so that no matter what position or frame of mind you're in, you can use your sexual energy to vitalize your body. You can do this, literally, at any time and in any position simply by using your mind (and any movements that might be helpful) to move your sexual energy through the Microcosmic Orbit.

The practice is bound to be awkward at first, especially if your partner is not doing it. When she first learned the practice, Gabriella, a 32-year-old accountant, said, "I noticed when I was trying to do the PC muscle exercises and the Orgasmic Upward Draw, it felt like I wasn't paying attention to my husband. Usually it's like, 'okay, cool, there's this rhythm,' but now I'm trying to do something else, and I almost feel like there's this disconnect between us because he has no idea what the hell I'm doing. He's like, okay, well whatever you need to do, just do it." As the practice becomes more natural for you, it will become easier to integrate it into lovemaking. Be sure to explain to your partner what you are trying to do during lovemaking so that he or she can be your ally in the process. Reassure him or her that you don't think there's anything wrong with him or her, or with your current way of making love. Explain that you want to share a way to have even greater pleasure and intimacy together.

You should also let him or her know that you will need to pause or slow down from time to time during lovemaking. Gently guiding his or her hands, tongue, or genitals when you need to pause while continuing to touch each other can maintain your intimacy. Gazing into your partner's eyes can add tremendously to your connection, as well. Lily had recently learned the Orgasmic Upward Draw in one of my classes. She described what it was like to integrate these practices into lovemaking with her partner. "Greg and I were making love, and we had to stop, circulate the energy, and then make love some more and then stop again, because it was too much to keep it going fluidly into lovemaking and circulate the energy. What happened in that interlude was so intimate and so sweet when we were looking at each other and going, 'Wow, this is cool, look at what we're doing together!'" Pausing during your arousal to circulate the energy and then resuming touch has the added bonus of heightening your sexual sensation. It allows you to collect the sexual energy and amplify it so that when you do orgasm, you've reached a much higher level of sexual energy and therefore, pleasure. With practice, you may not need to pause during lovemaking and will be able to simply visualize the energy moving from your genitals through the Microcosmic Orbit during your arousal and orgasm.

Some partners, male and female, may be somewhat skeptical and perhaps even annoyed when you first introduce the practice. As your partner experiences your pleasure and excitement, however, he or she is likely to want to join in. (Reading *The Multi-Orgasmic Man* will be very helpful for a male partner.) If your partner does not want to do the practice, it is fine to do the practice on your own. Remember to pause and reconnect with your partner through eye contact and touch during lovemaking. It is nice to place your hand over your partner's heart center and for him or her to place their hand over your heart center to connect with your loving attention and compassionate energy for each other. These practices are meant to enhance your sexual experience and your intimate relationships, not detract from them. Be gentle with yourself and with your partner. Simply being sexually intimate, in any loving way, is a boon to your health and happiness. Have intentions without creating expectations.

If your partner is also doing the Taoist practice, however, it can be intimate and erotic to pause and breathe together while you circulate your energies. Once you have learned to circulate sexual energy within your own body, you can learn to share your sexual energy consciously with your partner at the level of your soul. We exchange with our partners by fusing our Microcosmic Orbits at the areas where the most intense energy is exchanged—our genitals and our mouths. Through our concentration and the touching of tongues, we send our chi into our partner and down his or her Front Channel. The chi then travels back to us through our sexual organs and up our Back Channels and around to our tongues. When you receive your partner's energy, let it warm and open your heart center before traveling down to your genitals. This creates a refined and potent combination of sexual energy and compassion that can be healing for you both. This intimate exchange of chi can be a profound experience. Heather recalls doing the Soul Mating practice with her partner. "There were a couple of times that I felt soul closeness and that in each of us was this vast universe."

Soul Mating

Soul Mating transports you beyond just pleasure and into the realm of the spirit. Oriana is a 40-year-old woman who had done extensive exploration of sexuality and extended orgasm with her partner before encountering the Taoist practice. She confided to me that despite their extensive experience, "when we started doing Soul Mating, it exponentially increased our level of intimacy." In addition to exchanging chi through their tongues, she and her partner have experienced spontaneous energy exchange through their third eyes and heart centers as well. When the energy is strong, you can exchange chi through any or all parts of your body, as Chi Kung healers do. This spiritual orgasmic energy is particularly healing to the organs and senses. When you feel the energy coursing through you,

EXERCISE 19

SOUL MATING

1. Pause in your lovemaking after both of you are highly aroused. It is usually easiest to do this exercise in the sitting position, but it can also be done lying down. Make sure that you are facing each other and that your bodies are relatively aligned (head to head, genitals to genitals, etc.). If your partner is male, it is ideal if his penis remains inside of your vagina or against your vagina so that your energy can exchange. If your partner is female, find a position where your genitals (often the clitoris or pubic bone area) are touching.

2. Pump the sexual energy from your genital area to your sacrum by contracting your PC muscle and using the sacral pump. Let the energy rise from your sacrum to your head.

3. Spiral the energy in your head.

4. Touch tongues and let the energy descend from your head down and out your tongue to your partner. It helps to imagine sending energy to your partner on the out-breath and drawing your partner's energy into your own body and down your Front Channel with your in-breath.

5. Let your partner's energy cascade down to your heart center. Feel your heart warm and open.

6. Smile and bring the energy down to your abdomen and then to your genitals.

7. Circulate the energy from your genitals to your partner's genitals and around the energetic circle in a figure eight.

8. After circulating the energy three or more times, imagine that this refined, orgasmic, sexual-spiritual energy is emanating from your crown center and forming your soul body about 2 feet over your head. Visualize your soul body joining above your head with the soul body of your partner.

you can direct it with your hands to your partner's body. Soul Mating gives you an opportunity to heal each other.

After circulating the energy three or more times, imagine that this refined, orgasmic, sexual-spiritual energy is joining above your head with the energy of your partner. You can picture this energy emanating from your crown center, as if the energetic images of each of you are in sexual union above your heads. This allows your souls to unite. When women practice Soul Mating with their partners for years, they develop such a strong spiritual connection that even when separated by distance, they can meditate simultaneously and let their soul spirits join in union above them. Collette confirms, "With the Healing Love practice, my energy goes out of my body to meet my lover at another level when he's traveling."

Learning to channel your chi through the Microcosmic Orbit and the Orgasmic Upward Draw allows you to access and influence your vital energy in a profound way. You can also use these techniques to multiply and expand your orgasmic pleasure. In the next chapter, I will teach you how to multiply your orgasms and expand your pleasure so that it nourishes your body, heart, and soul.

CHAPTER 7

MULTIPLE ORGASMS AND BEYOND

We've already discussed that orgasm is quite variable for every woman; the same is true for multiple orgasms. In this chapter, you will explore the full range of your orgasmic possibility. When you learn how to direct your sexual energy, pleasure and orgasm can unfold in any way that you like. The pattern of pleasure can be so unique in its unfolding that it is really even more than multiple orgasms, it is *beyond* orgasm. We begin by learning how to have multiple orgasms whenever you would like.

BECOMING MULTI-ORGASMIC

Any woman can become multi-orgasmic. I have known many women who could orgasm only once during lovemaking, but with patient persistence were able to retrain their bodies, and their minds, to orgasm many times. When a woman orgasms only once during lovemaking or a self-cultivation session, she is probably having what I referred to in chapter 4 as a terminal orgasm. Her sexual energy builds up prior to orgasm and drops precipitously afterwards. Marisa, a 42-year-old counselor, described her experience like this: "I find that generally, pretty much every time, I just feel really relieved after a full orgasm, and I don't have the desire to try to keep building. I just feel done." There is certainly nothing wrong with "being done," if that is what you wish, but it is possible to hold onto your sexual energy after orgasm and have as many additional orgasms as you would like. The intention here is not to raise expectations but to offer you new possibilities. There are tired nights when one orgasm is just what the doctor ordered, and there will be more leisurely evenings when multiple orgasms is what you really crave. To make sure that you can satisfy this craving, let's discuss several important techniques to help you experience multiple orgasms.

USING THE ORGASMIC UPWARD DRAW

The most important tool that I have found to help women move from being singly orgasmic to multi-orgasmic is the Orgasmic Upward Draw that you learned in the previous chapter. The Orgasmic Upward Draw allows you to harness all of your orgasmic energy back into your body, so that your sexual energy remains high after orgasm. If your energy is high, it is much easier to climb the next peak of pleasure and enjoy as many orgasms as you would like.

As your arousal increases, pause to channel your sexual energy in the Orgasmic Upward Draw. Then as you crest over into orgasm, remember to contract your PC muscle (it will naturally be contracting with orgasm) and to visualize all of that lovely orgasmic energy pulsing from your genital area into your sacrum. After you orgasm (or at the same time, if it feels natural to you), send the energy up your spine and through the Microcosmic Orbit. Circulate your sexual energy back down to your sexual organs to stoke your orgasmic fire. Within 30 seconds after orgasm, restart genital or nipple stimulation and let your sexual energy send you over the crest into another orgasm.

If you need to pause in self-cultivation or lovemaking to channel your sexual energy in the Orgasmic Upward Draw, you might experience a momentary drop in sexual tension. Do not be concerned, because you are storing up your sexual energy at a deeper level, which will then allow you to access it in order to experience multiple orgasms.

Remember that once you can direct your sexual energy, you can have a variety of sexual experiences. Sometimes it will feel like many

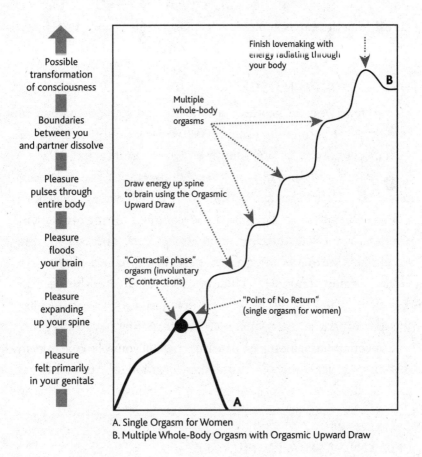

Possible
transformation
of consciousness

Boundaries
between you
and partner dissolve

Pleasure
pulses through
entire body

Pleasure
floods
your brain

Pleasure
expanding
up your spine

Pleasure
felt primarily
in your genitals

Finish lovemaking with
energy radiating through
your body

B

Multiple
whole-body
orgasms

Draw energy up spine
to brain using the Orgasmic
Upward Draw

"Contractile phase"
orgasm (involuntary
PC contractions)

"Point of No Return"
(single orgasm for women)

A

A. Single Orgasm for Women
B. Multiple Whole-Body Orgasm with Orgasmic Upward Draw

discrete orgasms; sometimes you may reach an orgasmic plateau
where the pleasure undulates continuously, without discrete phases.
This is also known as "valley orgasm." When you are able to harness
and direct your sexual energy, it is possible to have orgasms not just
in your genitals but throughout your body. Julie, who has been practicing Healing Love for 8 years, described how her body feels doing
the Orgasmic Upward Draw: "After Taoist lovemaking, my entire
body feels as if it is pulsing with gentle energy. I'm deeply relaxed
but also have an increased awareness and connection to my partner
and the universe." The increased chi throughout your body can be
experienced in a variety of ways: tingling, pulsing, or just sheer plea-

sure. Using the strength of your PC muscle allows you to build and harness that sexual energy for greater pleasure.

USING THE PC MUSCLE

In chapter 5 you learned how to identify and strengthen your PC muscle. Now is the time to make that muscle fulfill its reputation as the sex muscle. As your desire builds, try contracting your PC muscle in the rhythm of your sexual stimulation. This will bring blood flow to the area and activate your sexual energy. Remember that the PC muscle is the muscle that contracts during orgasm and contracting it can both bring on orgasm and make orgasm stronger and longer. In one of my classes, I taught Carmen, a 48-year-old college administrator, PC techniques. One week later she gleefully reported, "The PC muscle, which I practiced a lot, seemed to just increase my sexual energy in every way, including stronger orgasms and more orgasms. And contracting the PC muscle consciously during an orgasm did seem to make it last longer." Certainly not

---

EXERCISE 20
FLEXING YOUR PC MUSCLE

These exercises are designed to be performed during vaginal penetration.

1. Contract rhythmically around the head of the penis (or dildo or fingers) just as it enters you to stimulate the entrance to the vagina and the G-spot area. This can also exert pleasurable pressure on the sensitive head of the penis.

2. Contract and draw in your PC muscle rhythmically as you are slowly penetrated, as if you were sucking in your partner.

3. During in and out thrusting, squeeze your PC muscle while your partner withdraws and relax during penetration. This creates suction against the walls of the vagina as the penis/dildo is withdrawn and is pleasurable for both partners.

4. While your partner's penis or dildo is deep inside you, contract steadily against it while your partner remains still. Play with different rhythms, contracting short and then long to keep him guessing and wanting more.

everyone has such immediate results, but try it out for yourself this week and see if it enhances your sexual strength and sensitivity.

In the Flexing Your PC Muscle exercise are some PC skills to enhance your pleasure, and, if you have a male partner, *dramatically* enhance his as well. If your PC muscle is strong, you may be able to make your male partner orgasm simply from contracting it rhythmically around his penis. So careful, girls, you've got a concealed weapon in your pants (as if you didn't already know it).

TEASING

One of the best ways to retrain your body and mind is the basic, but beautiful, technique of teasing. In the simplest sense, teasing means building your arousal, backing off, and then building it again to a higher peak. The concept is simple, but to tease yourself, or your partner, in a manner that is fluid and sexy, and not abrupt and irritating, takes some practice. For example, if you (or your partner) are stroking your clitoris and building towards orgasm, you are likely using a rhythmic pattern of caresses to get you there. Teasing would mean that you would intentionally hold back one of the strokes that is expected in the rhythm and let your arousal drop a fraction. Then resume the pattern and allow the pleasure to build to an even higher peak, yet still short of orgasm, and interrupt the pattern again. Teasing is all about "I know what you want, and I'm gonna give it to you, but not . . . just . . . yet." It harnesses the energy of anticipation and magnifies desire. Our bodies and their nerve endings get accustomed to regular patterned touch and become increasingly desensitized. Teasing allows you to keep your nerves constantly guessing, constantly wanting, and therefore constantly sensitive.

In order for your partner to play the instrument of your body with finesse, you need to communicate to him or her just what it is that you enjoy. If you love what they're doing, tell them—with words or sounds. As they gauge your desire and the pace of your arousal, they will know when to give you what you want, and when to hold

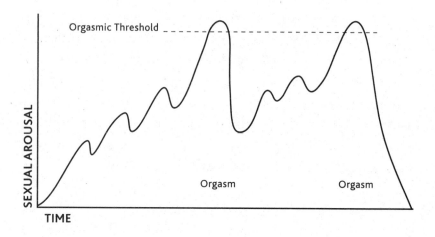

back, just for a second, and let you stew in your juices. The line be-tween holding back just enough to get you going when they renew their caresses and pausing so long that you lose your momentum is subtle. It takes practice, connection, and communication to be able to play upon one another's desires like a virtuoso. But the rewards of teasing are well worth the efforts.

Teasing "instructs" the body that after each peak of sensation, another one is coming. This is very helpful when you want your body to orgasm and then reach for more sensation, rather than losing all of your desire. Because your body expects another peak to come after each lull of teasing, it is more likely to expect another wave of sensation, even after orgasm. Fulfill this promise by begin-ning to stimulate yourself or have your partner stimulate you shortly after the orgasmic wave. When one has a terminal orgasm, all of the sexual energy is spent in orgasm and returns to baseline. After teasing and your first orgasm, begin stimulation within 30 seconds to your clitoris, breasts, vagina, or wherever feels best, in order to keep your sexual energy high. You will then be able to more easily build your energy up to a second orgasmic peak.

Once you have learned how to multiply your pleasure from one orgasm to two, increasing to three or more simply uses the same techniques. As your body gets used to higher levels of pleasure, you will stop counting, or caring!

TAKING YOUR TIME

In one of my workshops, we discussed the pressure some of us feel to "hurry up and have an orgasm" so that we don't impinge on our partner's goodwill. It's all fine and dandy to have goodwill toward one's partner, but if you want to learn to be multi-orgasmic, it is vital to be able to *ask for the time you need*. Because this is difficult for many women, I often suggest that you schedule a sexual date with your partner that is specifically focused on cultivating your multi-orgasmic pleasure. If you are worried about your partner, it will be difficult to focus on your own sensations and to do the Taoist practice. It is also awkward, at first, to combine the Taoist practice (and all of the steps to becoming multi-orgasmic) in partnered love-making. "Wait, hold on honey while I consult step number three!"

If you don't want to have a sexual session purely focused on stimulating you, try agreeing to make love with your partner for a certain amount of time, regardless of whether he or she has already had an orgasm. It's important to negotiate with your partner to get the time you need. My 44-year-old student Lily described her struggle with taking the time that she needs: "For me this is about finding that space where we're not in a rush and saying, 'Can we do this for half an hour? Can we relax, and if I have an orgasm, can we continue to make love and play around and maybe have another orgasm for me?' Because if my partner is saying, 'And how many now?' then I think, 'Have I reached my quota? I've had four, so that's it?' I'd like to change how we think about it so that I can fully explore my pleasure." We all need to find that space for ourselves where we can play in our pleasure and push against our known limits so that we can find the bubbling fountains of sexual energy and ecstasy that exists in each of us. The next exercise summarizes these steps for quick reference.

BEYOND ORGASM

A number of sexual experts over the past several decades have taught women and men how to reach prolonged pleasure states that supersede the momentary bliss of singular orgasm. Various authors and researchers have described this state as continuous multiple orgasm, blended orgasm, or extended or expanded sexual orgasm.[1] The heart of the Taoist sexual practice is to channel your sexual energy in order to reach an "expanded" state of full body pleasure and heightened spiritual consciousness. The possibilities to "expand" your experience of orgasm are as endless as your imagination. I'll discuss a few of these practices here.

EXTENDING ORGASM

It is possible to extend your usual orgasmic time from around 8 seconds to more than 60 seconds. This may not sound like a long time, but when you are in the intense throes of orgasm, a minute feels as if it goes on forever. In order to extend the time of your own orgasm, several techniques are helpful. Contracting your PC muscle during orgasm and moving the orgasmic energy into the Microcosmic Orbit will help to keep your arousal high. You can then extend the orgasmic time by continuing to contract your PC muscle, *even when you would have normally ceased having an orgasm.* You are consciously continuing and encouraging the pulsations, and as you train your body, you will find that you can keep the pleasurable waves coming.

The other essential ingredient is the use of your breath. As you begin to orgasm, slowly breathe out, and if you are at all able, make noise. The Taoists believe that the throat and the vagina are con-

---

1. For research on continuous multiple orgasm, see William Hartman and Marilyn Fithian's *Any Man Can: The Multiple Orgasmic Technique for Every Loving Man* (New York: St. Martin's Press, 1984). See also Alan and Donna Brauer's groundbreaking book *ESO* and, more recently, Steve and Vera Bodansky's *Extended Massive Orgasm.* In a similar vein, see Patricia Taylor's *Expanded Orgasm.*

EXERCISE 21

BECOMING A MULTI-ORGASMIC WOMAN

1. Set your intention not to hold back on your pleasure.

2. Awaken your sexual energy. Prepare yourself and your location with whatever erotic qualities support your desire, relax you, and turn you on—candles, oils, pillows, massage. Explore sexual fantasy or erotica if you enjoy it. Play sensual music, dance, caress your body with oil, or partake of any other pleasures that kindle your sexual desire. Remember that the hotter your pot of desire is simmering, the easier it will be to boil over into multiple orgasms.

3. Using the Inner Smile, smile down to your heart and feel it soften and open. Smile down to your uterus and ovaries, to your clitoris, lips, and vagina, feeling them warm with chi. Massage your breasts and nipples and send their awakened sexual energy down to your sexual organs through the Front Channel.

4. Caress your pleasure anatomy. Remember to stroke your entire body, neck and arms, breasts and legs. When you are aroused and ready, begin stimulating your clitoris with your hands, vibrator, or your partner's tongue. Use any strokes that worked for you in the Body Exploration from chapter 5. If your pleasure wanes, change the area that you are stimulating or the quality of your touch (smooth or vibrating, gentle or rough).

5. Use the teasing technique to prolong and intensify your pleasure. Build up your pleasure and then hold back your stroking for just a moment, then continue.

6. Contract your PC muscle to send your sexual energy into your spine as your arousal climbs. Pause, circulate the energy briefly, then continue.

7. Surrender to orgasm with clitoral stimulation. Pump your PC muscle to send the orgasmic energy into your spine as you orgasm and just after.

8. Circulate the energy through the Microcosmic Orbit and back down to your genitals, feeling them fill with warm, orgasmic energy.

9. Start slow, gentle stimulation of your clitoris again within 30 seconds after the first orgasm. Find a stroke you like and stick with it, using the teasing technique again.

10. Stimulate your clitoris and vagina together. Move to penetration and stimulate sensitive vaginal spots. Squeeze your PC muscle rhythmically to gather the energy in the vaginal area. Let your pleasure climb and surrender to the bliss of orgasm again.

11. After your orgasmic pleasure, hold both hands over your navel, smile down to your belly, and spiral and collect the energy in your abdomen.

nected, which is perhaps why it is easier to extend your orgasm if you are expressing your pleasure through your voice. As long as you can extend your exhalation and continue to make sound and contract your PC muscle, you can extend your orgasm.[2] It is a great incentive to practicing meditative breath control! Ultimately, as your control of your sexual energy matures, you will be able to extend your orgasm through one long out-breath, a quick intake of breath, and then another one or two breaths. Your throat is open to sound and your genitals are open to pleasure, which allows the orgasmic wave to continue to flow through you. So soundproof your room if you need to, use the power of your sex muscle, and ride your pulsations into extended orgasm.

EXPANDING ORGASM

Other sexual experts consider expanded or extended sexual orgasm to be a state of heightened sexual energy, connection, and even a spiritual state of expansion. In this state, one experiences extraordinary pleasure, total relaxation, and increased awareness. People sometimes reach a state of expanded orgasm and wonder, "How did I get here?" I'm going to discuss several methods to reach an expanded orgasmic state so that you can travel the path there whenever you like.

DEEP PELVIC ORGASM

Alan and Donna Brauer first described a method for reaching a state of expanded sexual orgasm that involves an alternative orgasmic response. In early arousal, the outer vagina (near the opening) swells and narrows, the deep vagina elongates and balloons out, and the uterus elevates. Typically, the onset of orgasm is marked by a short burst of pleasurable "squeeze contractions" of the PC muscle. In high states of arousal, women are also capable of having orgasms that are marked by deeper "push-out contractions" of the deep pelvic mus-

---

2. This idea is discussed in Charles and Caroline Muir's *Tantra: The Art of Conscious Loving.*

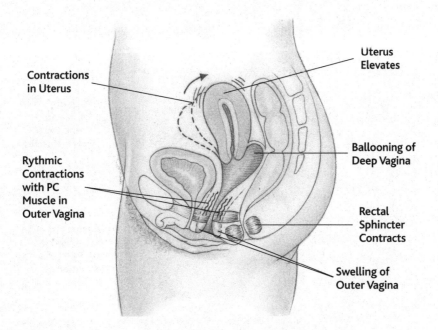

Contractions
in Uterus

Uterus
Elevates

Rythmic
Contractions
with PC
Muscle in
Outer Vagina

Ballooning of
Deep Vagina

Rectal
Sphincter
Contracts

Swelling of
Outer Vagina

Physical Changes with Clitoral Orgasm

cles of the uterus and back of the vagina. These orgasms are what some women think of as "vaginal orgasms" and likely originate in the pelvic nerve that innervates the vagina and uterus. Instead of the rhythmic contractions of the PC muscle, the PC muscle is actually *relaxed* during push-out contractions and the *deep* vagina tightens. (Similar physiologic responses occur with G-spot stimulation.) Although some women have these orgasms spontaneously, most women need to be taught how to access their potential for deep pelvic orgasm.

In typical orgasms, heart rate increases and muscular tension is high, but expanded orgasm is a state of total relaxation, with near normal heart rate and full surrender. The pleasure feels deep, full, and more diffuse. It is experienced more by *releasing* and less by *grasping*.

Generally, clitoral stimulation results in what we call a "typical orgasm" with squeeze contractions of the PC muscle. In order to experience expanded orgasm with push-out contractions, most women need vaginal stimulation, either of the G-spot, the AFE zone,

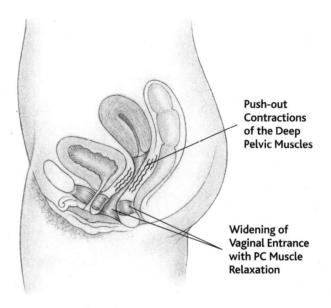

Push-out
Contractions
of the Deep
Pelvic Muscles

Widening of
Vaginal Entrance
with PC Muscle
Relaxation

Physical changes with deep pelvic orgasm

or any other sensitive vaginal spots (refer back to chapter 5 for exploration of these areas). Begin with clitoral stimulation and move on to simultaneous stimulation of clitoral and vaginal spots. The easiest way to do this is with a dildo or your partner's tongue, fingers, or both. The key to having an expanded orgasm is to be very relaxed and to let go of any mental resistances that you may have to fully experiencing your pleasure. Many of us are afraid to "push out" with our pelvic musculature because of early training that these muscles must be held tightly to prevent "accidents" with urine or feces. To experience expanded orgasm, however, we need *relax* our PC muscle and try pushing out and *reaching* for our pleasure. Emptying your bowels or bladder before lovemaking can help with fears about having "accidents." If this is difficult for you, practice the Relaxing the PC Muscle exercise on page 111 to help you learn to relax and push out.

TAOIST EXPANDED ORGASM

It is possible to reach a similar state of expanded orgasm using Taoist sexual techniques, whether you are alone or with a partner. Using the Orgasmic Upward Draw and spreading your orgasmic energy through the Microcosmic Orbit and your whole body leads to a similar state of deep relaxation, surrender, and well-being. You can combine the Taoist practice with any of the techniques that I've discussed to intensify and deepen your pleasure. The Jade Egg exercises in chapter 8 are extremely helpful in awakening vaginal pleasure spots and paving the way for deep pelvic orgasm. They will help you develop conscious control over your sexual energy in your vagina and allow you to spread the sexual energy of deep pelvic orgasm throughout your body.

The Brauers recorded electrical brain patterns of people in a state of extended sexual orgasm, which show the same activity that's present in states of deep meditation. Use of the Microcosmic Orbit to circulate and amplify one's sexual energy has had very similar results. In 1996 at the Institute for Applied Biocybernetics Feedback Research, the brain activity of Mantak Chia was evaluated during states of Taoist meditation, including the Inner Smile, Microcosmic Orbit, and the Orgasmic Upward Draw. The levels of brain potentials, or electrical currents, that are correlated to clarity, health, and concentration rose higher in Mantak Chia during these meditations than in any other human measured at the Viennese center. And, unlike other persons measured who used mantras or chanting, Mantak Chia's high levels of these brain potentials continued to rise for 20 minutes *after* he finished his meditation, *and remained high for the next 15 hours!* All of the sensors indicated that although his energy continued to rise *throughout* his body, his muscles remained relaxed and his heartbeat calm.[3]

This suggests that simple Taoist meditative and sexual practices

3. This study was conducted on October 25, 1996, at the Institute fur Angewandte Biokypernetik und Feedbackforschung (Institute for Applied Biocybernetics Feedback Research) in Vienna, Austria. Ultralente (ULP) brain potentials in the left and right brains were measured using a PCE-Scanner and other vital bodily functions were monitored (data unpublished).

are capable of accessing a state of expanded consciousness and pleasure that truly allows us to access what is most precious in our human potential. It is important to note that Master Chia achieves this state of profound pleasure and relaxation by opening his heart and feeling profound love through the Inner Smile and then continuing to remain open, calm, and peaceful in his heart center while circulating his orgasmic energy. If you wish to feel the high energetic state of expanded orgasm, begin with the Inner Smile and remember throughout lovemaking to continue to move the sexual and orgasmic energy into your heart center, keeping it warm and open, and focusing your attention on love for yourself and/or for your partner. In Taoist wisdom, the heart is not just the love center, but the center of joy and spirit as well.

It is the combined power of desire and spirit, passion and compassion, that opens us to our greatest potential. Many people have described feeling closest to God, Goddess, their higher power, the universe, or the Tao (however you name the universal power that is greater than yourself), while making love with a beloved partner. When we open our hearts and surrender to our passions, we are capable not just of orgasm within our bodies, but of fusing with the pulsations of joy and life throughout the universe.

FEMALE EJACULATION

Female ejaculation was documented in the West by sexual researchers as early as the 1950s, but only recently has female ejaculation been accepted as an actual phenomenon in the lay press. Although it may seem new to our culture, the ability to ejaculate has been with women for millennia. Several thousand years ago, Su Nu, the female sexual advisor to the Yellow Emperor, discussed the importance of the "three waters" of women and described the "copious emissions" of a woman's inner heart (synonymous with an area of her vagina) during high sexual arousal. Tantric sexual practices from ancient India described female ejaculate, amrita, as a life-giving ambrosia to be sought and savored.

WHAT IS FEMALE EJACULATION?

Female ejaculation is now documented in many clinical trials, in countless videos, and in the personal stories of thousands of women. When Alice Ladas, Beverly Whipple, and John Perry published the first popular book on the G-spot and female ejaculation in 1982, an entire nation of nervous women concerned about "wetting the bed" heaved a sigh of relief. Do all women ejaculate? No, but surprisingly more women ejaculate than you might imagine. An anonymous questionnaire of 1,183 professional women in the United States and Canada in 1990 revealed that 40 percent of them reported releasing a fluid at the moment of orgasm.

Female ejaculate can vary from just a few drops to enough to soak the sheets. Some women ejaculate in a forceful stream while others (likely the majority) seep fluid that is more often identified as "the wet spot." You may *already* ejaculate and not even know it. Heather describes the first time that she noticed ejaculation: "I was masturbating and all of a sudden a bunch of fluid came out into my hand and I thought, 'This is what a man does.' It has since happened during lovemaking that sometimes I have a flood of fluid and my partner notices it."

Before recent decades, many women ejaculators were quite concerned that they might be urinating with intercourse. Unfortunately, some of them even had surgical correction for what was misconceived by their doctors as urinary incontinence. The content of female ejaculate has been analyzed by Ladas, Perry, and Whipple, as well as several other research teams, all of which have determined that the content of female ejaculate is quite different from that of urine. In fact, female ejaculate actually contains chemicals identical to those produced by the male prostate and present in male ejaculate, which are known as prostatic-specific antigen (PSA) and prostatic acid phosphatase (PAP). Female ejaculate also has a much higher sugar content than urine. It also has a much *lower* concentration of the waste products that make urine smell, well, like urine—urea and creatinine. If you are wondering whether you are, indeed, ejaculating, smell the secretions. Urine has a distinctive odor that is different from female ejaculate. I suspect that as science pays more attention to female ejaculation, we will find that it is not unusual at all, but simply varies in intensity.[4]

Most sex educators believe that female ejaculation emanates from the G-spot when it is stimulated. In fact, the G-spot is really a collection of glandular tissue that surrounds the urethra and can be felt through the walls of the vagina. It is analogous to the prostate gland in men (meaning that it originates from the same embryonic tissue). Stimulation of the G-spot is thought to cause a release of fluid from this "female prostate" into the urethra and out of the body, often with the contractions of orgasm. Taoists, however, believe that this is only one of the sources of ejaculation in women.

Most people familiar with the Taoist system (and the theory that male ejaculation can be depleting to a man's energy) ask, "Isn't female ejaculation depleting as well?" Female ejaculate is different from male ejaculate in that it does not contain the sexual cells (sperm) and therefore, less sexual energy is lost. As long as a woman is well (not ill or exhausted), ejaculation is usually experienced as energy-*giving* rather than depleting. This is because women are naturally yin and watery and connected to the earth. When a woman ejaculates, the earth energy returns to her and revitalizes her. Yet, if your energy is low and you do feel depleted by "terminal orgasm" or female ejaculation, doing the orgasmic upward draw and circulating your energy will help you to contain more of your sexual energy.

Like many sex educators, I am concerned that female ejaculation will become the next sexual standard for women and that non-ejaculatory

---

4. Interestingly, in the study by F. Cabello Santamaria and R. Nesters, they tested women's urine (and ejaculate, if they had any) before and after orgasm. They found that not only did the female ejaculate have high levels of PSA, the post-orgasmic urine samples in the non-ejaculatory women also contained PSA (though at lower levels). This suggests that even women who do not ejaculate visibly may be "ejaculating" into their urethra but not expelling it or "retrograde" ejaculating up the urethra and into the bladder.

women will now feel inadequate. There is certainly no reason that any woman *needs* to ejaculate. Women who do ejaculate identify a feeling of release and sometimes an intensification of orgasm with ejaculation. But ejaculation is not necessary for sexual satisfaction or fulfillment. I am often asked, "Can every woman ejaculate?" We cannot be certain, but I think that it is likely that almost every woman has the capacity to ejaculate, whether she does so or not. Consider ejaculation to be a fun aspect of your physiology that you get to explore if you wish. If you want to learn to ejaculate, or to intensify your ejaculation, I give suggestions to experiment with below.

THE THREE WATERS

As I mentioned, the ancient Taoists referred to the three waters of women, which were to arise from the three gates. With all of the research into female ejaculation, it is now possible to link the three gates referred to by the Taoists with the Western anatomical structures of the clitoris, the G-spot, and the cervix.

THE FIRST GATE

The first gate of a woman is the clitoris, which stimulates the release of the first water, or the first female ejaculate. The first water is thin and light. It will vary in taste throughout a woman's cycle, but it can be very sweet or somewhat tart. We know that some women ejaculate, even copiously, from clitoral stimulation alone. This ejaculate may arise from Skene's glands, which are on either side of the urethral opening. With clitoral stimulation, other women may ejaculate through the urethra from their G-spot areas, as I mentioned earlier.[5]

To encourage the release of the first water from the clitoris, you must be very relaxed and in a high state of arousal. Ejaculation can be achieved alone or with a partner, though several ejaculators with whom

---

5. This may sound anatomically implausible, but the clitoral matrix is connected to the G-spot through the clitoral bulbs. (See the illustration on page 119.)

I spoke said they found it much easier to ejaculate with a partner. If you are with a partner, it is essential that you feel a sense of trust and relaxation. It can take anywhere from 30 seconds to 30 minutes to open the first gate, so patient, loving attention is a must. Use any of the clitoral stroking techniques from chapter 5 that work for you.

The clitoris is extremely sensitive, and the key to letting your waters flow is to allow your pleasure to build up to a point where it almost feels like too much. Instead of backing off of the stimulation, breathe deeply and then circulate your sexual energy from your clitoris into the Microcosmic Orbit to expand your capacity for pleasure. Let your pleasure guide you to the next level and keep your PC muscle open and relaxed. Some women feel that a slight bearing down of the PC muscle releases their water. The waters are most often released with orgasm, but not always. Simply a high state of arousal can also allow your waters to flow. Monique, a 36-year-old student, describes her experience: "I have ejaculated with my boyfriend, and it was so unbelievable to me. For me it really gets wet all over. I can ejaculate by myself, too. It has a lot to do with bearing down, and it's easier sitting up. The orgasm is different. I have the clitoral orgasm first, and I do circles on and around the clitoris. I then circulate and concentrate on my breathing, and I ejaculate. It feels more like letting go and being relaxed. It helps to have something in the vagina. I feel very relaxed afterwards. I use the feelings to feed my organs and enjoy the sensation of letting go."

THE SECOND GATE

The second gate is the G-spot and is the most common way that women ejaculate. To open the second gate, it is helpful, although not necessary, to have opened the first gate. When arousal is already high and the heart is open, it is much easier to open the second gate. For most women, as one moves from the first to the third gates, the level of surrender and emotional intimacy necessary for the opening increases. If you do not experience clitoral ejaculation, it is still much easier to open the second gate if you have already had a clitoral orgasm. If you are stimulating yourself, use your fingers to curl into your vagina and apply firm, consistent, and fairly strong pressure to the area of the G-spot on the anterior vagina. (Refer back to the description in chapter 5.) Many women find it most comfortable to use a dildo or vibrator that is curved for G-spot stimulation. You might try reclining or even squatting to help you get at the correct angle. If you are with a partner, have your partner use his or her fingers in a "come hither" motion, palm up and fingers curved, to create a pulling motion over the G-spot area. Have him or her move his or her fingers back and forth, kneading and pulling forward on the spongy area of the G-spot.[6] Lying on your back with a pillow underneath your bottom, or approaching from the back while you are "doggie-style" with your head down, will also make the approach to the G-spot easier.

As your G-spot is stimulated, you will likely feel as if you are going to pee. Breathe deeply and relax, knowing that you won't urinate if you emptied your bladder beforehand. If you try to hold in what feels like urine, you will not be able to ejaculate. Healing Tao instructor Saida Desilets, who has also trained in the Tantric Arts, counsels women that "G-spot massage is deeply sacred and can induce feelings of vulnerability and even anger. With awareness and warm, loving, heart energy, deep healing can occur as a side effect of the (second gate) activation. The more open and soft the woman's heart is, the more she will relax. Both partners can start to breathe more deeply and encourage sounds to come from deep within the body. Using your voice to activate your throat center also helps to open this gate. In the Tantric traditions, like in the Taoist tradition, the throat chakra and sex chakra are intricately linked and affect each other. Activating your voice will help further activate your sex chakra and release the waters."[7]

6. This technique is adapted from Tristan Taormino's *Pucker Up*, pages 115–120.

7. My sincere thanks to Saida Desilets for her wisdom and contribution to this topic. Her article, "Female Ejaculation: The Ancient Art of Ambrosia," (2003) is available online at www.universal-tao.com.

THE THIRD GATE

The third water arises from the stimulation of the cervix and the area just around it. We discussed the AFE zone in detail in chapter 5, which is located on the deep vaginal wall just on the anterior, or belly, side of the cervix. Stimulation of this area, and in some women, of the cervix itself, causes a further opening to deep pleasure and release. The third waters are thought to come from the glands inside the cervix, which regularly secrete mucous. Cervical ejaculation is the least frequently observed of the three waters, and our information is therefore anecdotal. Women who have experienced it report that the ejaculation is lesser in volume and is a thicker, viscous fluid.

In order to activate the third gate yourself, use a dildo or vibrator to apply pressure and stroking to the AFE zone and all of the areas around the cervix. Some women enjoy rhythmic pressure on the cervix or gentle to firm rubbing. If you are with a partner, he or she can use fingers (if they are long enough) or a penis or dildo to stimulate these areas. Refer back to chapter 5 for positions that are ideal for stimulation of the AFE zone and cervix. In Taoism, the cervix is associated with the heart, as discussed in the Jade Egg practice in the next chapter (see also the illustration on page 219). Saida comments, "I have found that direct stimulation of the cervix can often result in an intense opening of the heart—feelings of love and vulnerability are commonly felt. The more a woman can allow herself to fall deeper into her own mysterious ocean, trusting herself to guide her partner to her full release, the more likely the third gate will open. The sensation of this opening is very, very deep and releases the third water. The cervix may feel like it is opening and closing or sucking as it contracts in orgasmic release."

OPENING THE THREE GATES

Opening the three gates is an act of love and surrender and will bring you into a high state of expanded orgasm. The more regularly you are able to open your gates, the easier it will be to access this ability within yourself. With the opening of each gate, pause and circulate the bubbling chi through the Microcosmic Orbit. With the full opening of the sexual organs and the heart center, and the flow of a woman's natural, watery yin essence, the plentiful chi is refined into spiritual essence, or *shen*. Opening the three gates with a partner is a sacred experience. Doing the Soul Mating exercise on page 175 will allow you to share your essence with one another and blend your souls.

In this chapter, you learned how to magnify our sexual energy into multiple and expanded orgasms. It is, however, difficult to access our highest potential within if we are challenged from without by the demands and hormonal shifts that can accompany different life stages. In the next chapter, I will take you through the developmental gifts, and sometimes challenging physical shifts, of each stage in a woman's life. As with our sexual pleasure, Taoist practice has much to teach us about remaining healthy and whole throughout our life cycle.

CHAPTER 8

CULTIVATING SEXUAL HEALTH THROUGHOUT YOUR LIFE

O ne of the many gifts of the Taoist practice is that it teaches us how to tune our bodies and maintain our vibrancy throughout our lives. By far our strongest healing force is our body's ability to heal itself. When you strengthen your chi force and your ability to direct it, you can send that healing chi and the love from your heart center to wherever you need healing. This "holistic" healing takes place at physical, emotional, and spiritual levels. My experience as a physician has led me to believe that although many of my patients are ill physically, many more are ill emotionally and spiritually. Our society spends tremendous resources trying to keep people physically healthy using drugs and technology, but more and more research is showing that people who are resistant to disease and live long lives have social, emotional, and spiritual health that keep them *physically* healthy. Because chi, or life force, pervades every level of our being and our connections to others, profound healing is possible when we sense and direct the power of our chi with the compassion of our hearts. The secret of the Inner Smile is the engendering of *real* love and compassion within us, in order to bless and heal ourselves.

Monique, a graceful young woman, worked as an erotic dancer for years in order to support herself. She had significant premenstrual symptoms for which she took medication. When going through an emotionally difficult time in her life, she encountered the

Healing Love practice. "I went to a workshop where I learned to connect my uterus with my heart," Monique said. "I was so deeply depressed. I saw that my uterus was my jewel. I became more protective of my energy. I didn't want to play games anymore." Monique stopped her work as an erotic dancer and embarked on a path of Taoist exploration. With the Taoist practices, her PMS eased and her depression dissolved. Monique made many changes in her relationships, as well, and now inspires other women to honor their bodies. "I would hope that every woman should love her body, and I don't mean decorating it. You need to make yourself feel good from the inside out—whatever makes us juicy. I want to help other women to be in their sexual power."

I have witnessed and been the recipient of stories of seemingly "miraculous" cures, from a Western viewpoint, from people who have used the power of chi to cure their bodies of any number of diseases, from terminal cancer to spinal misalignment to the restoration of vision. In each of these cases, the person suffering focused on their intention to heal and channeled healing chi to the area in question, or had another practitioner skilled in the art of channeling chi (called medical Chi Kung in the West) direct the chi for them.

Such hands-on healing has been a subject of debate and derision within Western medicine for decades, but such healings *can* and *do* occur, despite the inability of science to explain them. As a scientific community, we have not even begun to scratch the surface of what the human body is capable of, and almost every physician has stories of patients who have unexpectedly undergone "spontaneous" healing.

Sarina Stone, a Healing Tao instructor from St. Paul, Minnesota, relates that in her experience of teaching the Healing Tao practice, "On a physical level, it is a joy to see personal issues and reproductive issues clear themselves up as the negative environments transform to more balanced states. There is also an undeniable 'youthening' that occurs for advanced practitioners." When the

Taoist practice brings your body into a state of balance, you will feel more vital and be ill less often. Although I am cautious about the current anti-aging movement, as I think aging is a normal and natural process, I must admit that all of the Taoist instructors that I have met are remarkably vital and appear younger than their chronological ages. The Taoists did not resist getting older; they resisted the decay that so often accompanies aging. The Taoists sought the fountain of youth in their own bodies and sought to emulate the vitality of children.

You can use the power of your own chi to heal you and help keep you well. Sexual energy, when combined with the love and joy of your heart center, is a particularly potent force for health and healing. But you do not need to take my word for it. Experiment within your own body using the exercises in this chapter—including Breast Massage, Ovarian Breathing, and the Jade Egg practice—and see what happens within you. Or, the next time that you have a headache or sore back, try channeling sexual energy and love from your heart center to that area. Let the pain drain down your body and into the earth and allow the joyous energy of love and passion to fill that area. You may be surprised at how much power you already possess to heal yourself.

CULTIVATING BREAST HEALTH

Breasts have been a symbol of women and female nurturing for millennia. They are associated with the heart charka and hold the energies of love and joy. The current societal obsession with breasts as sexual symbols for men, however, leaves most women feeling ambivalent about their breasts. Add to this the rising rate of breast cancer, and you'll find that *most* women have some fear and insecurity about their breasts. Breasts, like bodies, come in a wonderful variety of shapes, sizes, and colors. Unfortunately, plastic surgeons are making a fortune from the societal prejudice that all breasts should be large, like a fully grown or nursing mother's, and pert, like a teenager's—an obviously impossible ideal. Of course, breast size and shape have *nothing* to do with the pleasure that a woman feels from having her breasts caressed or with her ability to breastfeed her children.

Very few women are fully satisfied with their breasts as they are. Women with small breasts feel less sexy. Women with gracefully drooping breasts feel old. Women with large breasts resent the unwanted attention their breasts (rather than their eyes or their minds) attract. And some women with large breasts have such pain in their necks and backs that they need to undergo surgical reduction procedures.

Women who have nursed babies know that there are few pleasures in life as satisfying as providing the ideal nourishment for their precious children. But we spend the great majority of our lives with breasts that are not nursing. I want to encourage you to think of your breasts *primarily* as the symbol for *nurturing yourself*. For many women, this may seem counterintuitive since we often think of our breasts in relationship to *providing for others* (our baby's or our partner's pleasure). But particularly in this time of increasing breast cancer, we need to focus on cultivating the nourishing energy *within* our breasts for ourselves.

This does not mean that we shouldn't enjoy our partner's appreciation for our breasts. On the contrary, if you can take in this appreciation as love and pleasure, all the better. However, I want you to start experiencing your breasts *from the inside out* rather than from the outside in. I want you to treasure your breasts for what they do *for you*. Do they feel good *to you*? Do *you* enjoy touching or having someone else touch them?

None of us can judge another woman for her decisions, because we all deal with complex motivations and needs, but I am concerned about the increasing rate of breast implantation surgery, particularly because of how it short-circuits a woman's own pleasure. This surgery can impede the neural and energetic pathways to the breast,

The Kidney Meridian Travels through the Breast and Sexual Organs

decreasing a woman's sensual pleasure. It can also run the risk of reducing her ability to breastfeed, should she wish. Here is a procedure that can decrease a woman's pleasure from her breasts in order
to *increase* her partner's (or other's) pleasure. This is a classic example of a woman decreasing her own vital energy by giving it up to
another person. I do have a number of women in my practice who
have chosen to have breast implants for their own satisfaction or
for cosmetic purposes after breast cancer surgery. Certainly if your

intention is to affirm yourself, the energetic effect of breast implantation is more benign. Regardless of what decisions you have made
about your own breasts, it is vital to continue to engender compassion and healing energy for your breasts. If you have had breast
surgery, it is even more important to practice breast clearing and
breast massage to clear negative energy from your breasts and rein-
vigorate their chi. If your breasts are not very sensitive, doing breast
massage will help to awaken their chi and will still give all of the
benefits of breast massage.

From the Taoist viewpoint, breast stimulation or massage is important to a woman's overall health. The breasts are glands that can
secrete milk and promote the secretion of hormones. When the
breasts are stimulated, the hormones oxytocin and prolactin are released from the pituitary gland. These hormones influence lactation
in nursing women, but in all of us, they produce feelings of relaxation, calm, and connection to others. In Taoist thought, stimulation
of the breasts is also thought to stimulate the functioning of the
pineal and thymus glands, as well as the pituitary gland. Breast massage is a lovely way to start becoming aware of the feelings that you
have within your breasts and to start the process of self-nurturing.

BREAST MASSAGE

Breast Massage is a simple practice that increases the flow of chi to
your breasts and your entire glandular system. I recommend doing
breast massage prior to almost any other Taoist practice, but especially before doing Ovarian Breathing and the Jade Egg practice,
which we will learn later in the chapter. Breast massage is also a
lovely way to get your sexual energy moving and active before practicing the Orgasmic Upward Draw. The kidney meridian, which provides chi and vitality to the sexual organs, passes through the breasts
and is stimulated with breast massage. This is one of the reasons that
breast, and particularly nipple, massage often stimulates sexual energy in the clitoris and vaginal area.

EXERCISE 22

BREAST CLEARING

1. Remove restrictive bras or clothing from your breasts.

2. Stand in horsewoman position. (See the illustration on page 226.)

3. Bring your loving attention to your breasts and notice any negative experiences or feelings that may come to you.

4. Bring your fingertips together with your palms face down in front of your forehead (as in the Venting exercise on page 159).

5. Take a deep breath into your belly and with your exhale make the sound "heee" while moving your palms down your body and feeling the negative energies flowing from your breasts with the lowering of your hands. Feel these negative energies moving down through your feet and into the earth.

6. Do this as many times as you need until you feel that your breasts are clear.

7. Focus on your third eye and feel a golden light coming from above you through your third eye and flowing down to your breasts to fill them with light and love. Let the negative energies continue to flow out and be replaced with golden light.

8. End your practice by sending gratitude to your breasts.

Not everyone feels comfortable touching her own breasts. Most of us were taught that this is somehow naughty, and it can be difficult to shed old patterns. Also, some women have had negative experiences with breast touch from partners, and these feelings can reawaken when they touch their own breasts. As with every exercise in this book, do not do breast massage if it feels wrong in *your* body. It is possible to move the chi and get some of the benefits of breast massage by moving your fingertips in the air over your breasts and visualizing the chi moving with them. Doing the Breast Clearing exercise may help some women drain some of the negative energies from their breasts.[1] You can do breast clearing at any time that you

---

1. This exercise is based on the Venting exercise on page 159, but its direct use for clearing breast energy was inspired by one of Mantak Chia's students, Maitreyi Piontek, who has written about the women's sexual practice in her excellent book, *Exploring the Hidden Power of Female Sexuality*, pages 107–109.

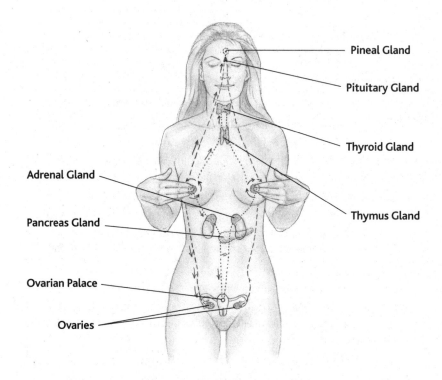

Pineal Gland

Pituitary Gland

Thyroid Gland

Adrenal Gland

Thymus Gland

Pancreas Gland

Ovarian Palace

Ovaries

Breast Massage with Stimulation of All the Glands

feel the need. It is helpful to do it prior to beginning breast massage. If touching your breasts seems daunting, start slowly by cupping or gently running your fingers over the skin of your breasts. Stop if you start to feel bad or uncomfortable. Some women feel nauseous with nipple stimulation. If this is the case for you, simply do your massage without touching your nipples.

Breast massage can be performed "dry" by rubbing a silk or taffeta cloth over your breasts. You can also use a natural oil (almond, olive, grape seed, or sesame are all nice) to lubricate the breasts for the massage. Using essential oils in your oil can add an additional healing touch to breast massage. Geranium, lemongrass, lavender, and rose essential oils all balance breast energy. I would recommend using 30 drops of any mixture of essential oils per 2 tablespoons of a "carrier" oil, such almond, olive, grape seed, or sesame. Never apply an essential oil directly to your skin unless you are familiar with its properties because many essential oils, even when diluted, can cause irritation to sensitive skin. If you're concerned, apply a drop of the essential oil in a small amount of carrier oil, apply it to the inside of your wrist or elbow, and don't wash it off; if you don't have itching or redness, it's safe for you to use the oil. Essential oils should *never* be applied to the vulvar area, however, or taken orally.

Breast massage is a wonderful way to love and appreciate your breasts and to benefit from their energy. When she first learned the practice, Desiree, who is now a grandmother, said, "It was so comforting. I realized that sometimes when I'm upset I spontaneously touch my chest over my breasts. It's like—this is the place of comfort. And so to do that for myself felt so good, really healing and nurturing and calming." Carmen commented, "Because I've been losing weight and, at 48, moving into perimenopause, my breasts have suddenly changed. I've never in my life worn a bra, and I've always had pretty perky breasts. Now they're starting to fall and soften, and I

EXERCISE 23

BREAST MASSAGE

1. Find a comfortable position and take three deep belly breaths. Relax.

2. Rub your hands together until you create heat and then rest them over your breasts. Send your breasts loving chi from your hands.

3. Using breast oil or a piece of material, gently rub your fingertips in circles around your breasts, about an inch and a half from your nipples. Begin by circling from the inside of your breasts up and around to the outsides. Do this at least nine times. This will stimulate the kidney meridian on the inside of the breasts as well as the liver, pericardium (heart muscle), and spleen meridians.

4. Now massage your entire breast by gently pressing the tissue against the chest wall and rubbing in circles. Pay attention to what feels good to you and vary your strokes from feather-light caresses to stronger touches. Caressing your nipples will increase the hormonal release and sexual energy that you generate.

haven't been liking them. I've been looking in the mirror sideways and asking, 'Oh man, where'd you go?' And it was really important to fall back in love with my breasts, and the breast massage helped me to do that."

Begin breast massage as you would any of the other practices by finding a quiet and private place. Take off any bras or restrictive clothing and let your breasts "breathe." It is fine to keep a loose-fitting shirt or dress on if you wish.

PREGNANCY, BIRTH, AND SEXUALITY

Pregnancy is a miraculous experience and, for most women, includes the most dramatic physical and hormonal shifts that they will ever undergo. The experience of pregnancy, emotionally and physically, is different for every woman. I have had patients who suffered from perpetual nausea, vomiting, and migraines throughout the pregnancy and patients who said they had never felt stronger or more energetic than when they were pregnant. Most women are somewhere in between. Combine all of the changes of pregnancy with the hope and fear that surround pregnancy and birth, and you have a profoundly life-altering experience. It will come as no surprise that your sexual life is altered as well.

For normal pregnancies, it is perfectly safe to remain sexually active throughout the pregnancy. Intercourse and orgasm will cause gentle uterine contractions, which do not harm the baby unless there is a risk for premature labor. Women who have premature labor are usually put on "pelvic rest." On the other hand, if you are looking for ways to bring on labor at the uncomfortable end of pregnancy, intercourse with orgasm is a great way to do it!

Physical discomforts, such as nausea and fatigue in the beginning of pregnancy or heartburn and backaches near the end, can put a damper on desire. If you are not feeling well, cuddling and massage remain important ways to connect with your partner physically. Remember that it is still possible to do Taoist massage and even the Soul Mating practice without having sex, by simply touching and circulating your energy. On the other hand, because of the hormonal changes during pregnancy, many women actually have *increased* desire. If this is the case for you, take advantage of the time you have for lovemaking and bonding before the baby is born.

After the birth, you will need to take a break from sexual activity to allow your body to heal. And finding a time and place for lovemaking while caring for an infant can sometimes be very challenging. Remember to continue to touch each other, whether or not you have sex. This keeps those bonding hormones flowing between you. If you breastfeed your child, your prolactin and oxytocin levels will remain high, increasing mother-infant bonding and delaying the onset of your menstruation. Unfortunately, these "baby bonding" hormones also have a profound affect on libido, decreasing it significantly in most women. Have heart: When you decrease and eventually stop breastfeeding, your desire will generally return to normal. Most nursing moms find that when they do have sex, they enjoy it just as much and their orgasms are just as strong. It may make sense to plan lovemaking, even if you're not "in the mood," knowing that afterward you will be glad you did.

Many women do not realize that the hormones of breastfeeding also affect the vaginal lining, causing thinning and decreased lubrication. These changes are similar to those that occur after menopause and can make penetration extremely uncomfortable. Keep this in mind the first time that you attempt penetration after delivery and go very slowly with lots of lubrication. All some nursing moms need is additional lubricant, but others, especially mothers nursing multiple children, will still have pain. Consult your physician to determine the exact cause, but if it is vaginal thinning, applying a topical estrogen cream will increase vaginal elasticity and lubrication and reverse the process.

Some women feel there is a conflict between their upcoming motherhood and their sexual selves. This is understandable since our society itself generally portrays women as *either* mothers *or* sexual beings, but not both. It is important to acknowledge and discuss your feelings with your mate. In the families that I have worked with, however, when the romantic and sexual bond between partners gets completely subsumed by childrearing, it endangers the marriage bond. It is actually important for a child's sense of security to know that her parents love each other and want to spend time together. It is normal for the frequency of sex to decrease when you are caring for small children, but it is well worth the advance planning necessary to set aside some couple time for loving connection and lovemaking. Keeping an active, if discreet, sex life nourishes you as a couple, but it also provides the loving foundation of your family life. The love of the parents for one another nourishes children, just as the love they receive directly does. It also models healthy, loving relationships for them in their own lives.

Many of the Taoist practices are ideal during pregnancy and early motherhood. The Inner Smile, the Microcosmic Orbit, and the Orgasmic Upward Draw are all helpful in toning and increasing one's chi. One of the practitioners with whom I spoke did the Inner Smile and Microcosmic Orbit during pregnancy to soften and open her heart, and then send the loving energy through her uterus to her unborn child, feeling it move in his or her orbit. Breast Massage can be helpful with painful and engorged breasts. The Healing Sounds are vital to balancing your chi and calming emotional swings. Tai Chi and Chi Kung are moving meditation practices that are low impact and facilitate calm focus (of which there is usually little during early childhood!) and the free movement of chi.

Because of the nature of Ovarian Breathing, which we will explore next, it is best not to do the practice when trying to get pregnant or during pregnancy itself. Ovarian Breathing draws chi from the developing egg in the ovaries and "harvests" it to nourish your body. When you are trying to get pregnant or are pregnant, you want to charge the egg or embryo with as much good chi as you can. Doing the Orgasmic Upward Draw or Breast Massage and sending the chi to the ovaries is a wonderful way to do this. But for the majority of your life, when you are not pregnant or trying to get pregnant, you can use the extraordinary power and energy in your ovaries to strengthen and vitalize yourself.

HARNESSING OVARIAN POWER

The Taoists believe that women's most powerful chi, our principal chi energy, is located in our eggs and ovaries. This is the chi that we are born with and that I referred to in chapter 2 as being our backup generator. This chi has so much creative yang fire that it is able to create life. If we do not become pregnant during a cycle, the egg, and its chi, passes out of our bodies during menstruation. The practice of Ovarian Breathing is intended to "harvest" the principal chi of our eggs before they leave in menstruation and transform that chi in our bodies to improve our overall vitality. (If you want to get pregnant, of course, you should not try to draw chi from the egg.)

Many menstruating women who do Ovarian Breathing on a regular basis notice that their menses are less heavy and less painful. Inga is a Swiss woman who has been practicing Ovarian Breathing for 14 years. She says, "My menstrual cycle changed from 23 days 15 years ago with many premenstrual symptoms to a 28-day cycle with no side effects and short menses. When I practice more intensely, I will drop two or three cycles." Most women who do the practice continue to menstruate, but their menses are lighter, and they have higher levels of energy and libido. Some women also note that symptoms of premenstrual irritation or depression are eased, as they were for Collette from Canada. She notes, "Ovarian Breathing helped me diminish my pain, blood loss, tiredness, and sadness with menstruation." Advanced practitioners can have, from a Western scientific point of view, miraculous control over their cycles. When I spoke with Tamara, a 39-year-old Universal Tao instructor, about her Ovarian Breathing practice, she confided to me, "I have been able to control how many eggs I release per year. I did not choose to stop menstruating. I *did* choose to menstruate every 45 days instead of 28. I also only menstruate for 1 day instead of 5." This degree of integration with one's physiology is truly incredible.

Heather, a 28-year-old single mom of two young children, confided to me, "I recently started doing Ovarian Breathing, which has worked well for sexual frustration," she says. "I was so 'hot' one day and felt that I had to have sex, so I did the Ovarian Breathing and was able to change the energy from hot to cool. I felt calm afterwards."

Women of all ages, whether menstruating or menopausal, can do this practice. The ovaries, even after menopause, still have principal energy that can be accessed by the practice. In fact, many menopausal women who do the practice regularly report that they have almost no menopausal symptoms and they retain their sexual energy and vaginal lubrication throughout menopause. A week after I taught Carmen, one of my menopausal patients, the Ovarian Breathing practice, she reported, "I never meditated until I joined this class, and I'm feeling that the enormous hot flashes I've been having are subsiding. I've slept better in the last three nights, and my libido's very high." Not everyone receives such immediate benefits, but I have been astounded at the number of women who practice Ovarian Breathing and have little or no menopausal symptoms. As a female physician who treats many menopausal patients, I find that almost miraculous. I'll discuss more about holistic approaches to menopause starting on page 234, but I would strongly recommend to any menopausal woman that she try the regular practice of Ovarian Breathing, as it is completely safe and seems to accomplish what drugs and herbs cannot—an almost symptom-free menopausal transition with normal libido and vaginal lubrication.

If you have had your uterus or ovaries, or both, surgically removed, you still can benefit from this practice. The organs themselves may be gone, but the energetic field of the organs still remains and can be balanced by the practice. Several women who had lost their pelvic organs reported that this practice helped them to resolve ambivalent feelings that they held after their surgery. It also helped improve the chi in their pelvic areas and their sexual energy.

HOW DO I BREATHE WITH MY OVARIES?

Breathing, or respiration, is simply the exchange of energy between the air and our blood. This is accomplished within our lungs. Taoists often discuss the "breathing" of our other organs. In actual fact, every cell in our body "breathes," exchanging waste products for nutrients and oxygen. From a Taoist perspective, our organs breathe when they take in fresh chi from their environment and release waste (which may be congested chi, negative emotions, or heat). Ovarian Breathing is the exchange of energy (or chi) between the ovary and the rest of the body.

If you are no longer menstruating, you can do the practice at any time. If you are pregnant, it is best not to do this practice, as you don't want to draw any energy away from the fetus. If you are still menstruating, it is ideal to do Ovarian Breathing between the end of the menstrual cycle and ovulation (when the egg is growing and developing). (I discuss the timing of ovulation on page 264.) At this time the principal chi of the egg is yang and hot. This energy is good for creative action and revitalization. For most women, this is a good time to take action in their lives. It is an ideal time to plan activities, large projects, and all good work in the outer world.

After ovulation, the energy of the egg changes to become more cool and yin. Women can benefit from focusing on healing and inner exploration during this "premenstrual" phase. I have observed in many of my patients that their PMS symptoms, both emotional and physical, are exacerbated by their busy schedules and multiple external demands. When they lighten their schedules during this time and concentrate on accessing the richness of this yin, dark phase, their irritability and depression ease. It can be difficult to do this in our busy modern world, but to whatever extent you can give yourself personal time to reflect during the week before and the first several days of your menses, the rewards can be great. Many female artists do their best creative work during this reflective time. Just as the earth needs fall and winter to shed and regenerate, our bodies need rest and inner focus to nourish and align ourselves.

PRACTICING OVARIAN BREATHING

Begin this practice like any other by arranging for uninterrupted time and finding a warm, comfortable position. Ovarian Breathing is an adaptation of the Microcosmic Orbit and can be performed in a seated position (as described for the Microcosmic Orbit) or standing in the horsewoman stance. (See the illustration on page 226.) Begin the practice with Breast Massage, which will help awaken the energy of your ovaries. After Breast Massage, send the awakened chi of the breasts directly down to your ovaries. If you have trouble feeling your sexual energy, it may be helpful to sit with a hard ball, rolled towel, or one heel against your vagina and clitoris to awaken your energy. You can also do this practice while lying comfortably on your right side with a pillow under your head, your left leg bent, and your right hand supporting your head and keeping your ear slightly open. Keeping the ears open helps to balance this powerful energy when it gets to your head. It is also helpful to do the Inner Smile prior to Ovarian Breathing to open up the channels for energy flow.

Smile down to your uterus and ovaries. To find the location of your uterus, also called your Ovarian Palace, and ovaries, place your hands on your abdomen with your thumbs touching over your navel, as you did on page 149. Let your first fingers rest against each other creating a triangle and your remaining fingers fan out over your belly. Your first fingers should be resting over the approximate location of your uterus. Your little fingers will be approximately over your ovaries. As we have discussed previously, every woman has her uterus and ovaries in slightly different locations, but an approximation will do for this exercise, as it is our mental focus on the ovaries and uterus that matters, not an exact anatomical location.

Smile down to the ovaries and rub them with your fingers, visualizing them getting warmer. Simultaneously, lightly squeeze the PC muscle and open and close your vagina as delicately as the petals of a flower. Focus on your ovaries and feel the energy stir within them. You may feel warmth, tightness, tingling, etc. If you feel nothing, simply concentrate on the ovaries and visualize the energy gathering in them.

Breathe in one long gentle inhalation through your nose, and with your mind bring the energy from the ovaries into the Ovarian Palace (located near the center of the uterus). Some women find it easier to move the ovarian chi by taking short "sips" of air during one inhalation, as we do to bring the chi up the spine, letting the chi move with each short inhalation. Relax and let the energy gather during your exhalation. Continue to lightly squeeze your PC muscle so that the gathering energy does not leak out through your perineum. The contraction of the PC muscle is very gentle; any less of a squeeze would be nothing.

Now bring the energy from the uterus down through the vagina to your perineum. The energy may go directly to the perineum or may move along your labia to your clitoris and then back to your perineum. (See the illustration on page 216.) Let the energy now gather at the perineum. Rest and feel the easy flow of the energy from the ovaries to the perineum while you continue to breathe. Resting is important, as sometimes the energy flows more easily when we relax and don't block it, but keep your PC muscle gently contracted so the energy doesn't flow out completely. Feel the energy gather at the perineum. If it helps you to touch the perineum, feel free to do so.

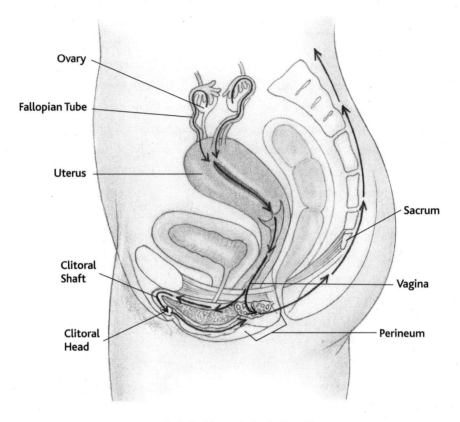

Ovary

Fallopian Tube

Uterus

Sacrum

Clitoral Shaft

Vagina

Clitoral Head

Perineum

The Path of Energy in Ovarian Breathing

Use the sacral pump to move the ovarian energy from the perineum into the sacrum. Squeeze your PC muscle and anus and rock your hips, pumping the energy into the lower spine. Many women experience ovarian energy as denser than chi. It may move more slowly, like honey, and require more active use of the sacral pump to move it up the spine.

Using sipping breaths, as if you were drawing the chi up through a straw, and the sacral and cranial pumps, move the ovarian energy up the spine and circulate it in your head. Spiral the energy outward from the center of the brain, and then move inward again, as you learned in the Microcosmic Orbit. Imagine it nourishing your brain and glands. Now bring the energy down your Front Channel by

EXERCISE 24

OVARIAN BREATHING

1. Sit in meditation position, stand in horsewoman's stance, or recline in the position discussed in the text.

2. Do Breast Massage as described on page 207 and feel the chi awakening in your sexual organs.

3. Do the Inner Smile to your uterus and ovaries, sending the chi activated by Breast Massage to your ovaries.

4. Massage the skin over your ovaries with your fingertips and feel them warm. Simultaneously, very gently squeeze your PC muscle and open and close your vagina.

5. Inhale gently and with your concentration bring the ovarian chi to the Ovarian Palace.

6. Now focus on bringing the energy from your uterus down through your vagina to your perineum on the inhalation. Keep the PC muscle lightly contracted so that the energy does not leak out at the perineum.

7. Use the sacral pump to move the energy from the perineum into the sacrum and then up the spine to the crown center.

8. Spiral the ovarian energy in your head, inward and then outward, to nourish your brain and glands.

9. Touch your tongue to your palate and bring the energy down the Front Channel, as in the Microcosmic Orbit.

10. Spiral the energy at your heart center, inward and outward, feeling it soften and open.

11. Bring the energy to your navel center and spiral it there as well, so that it absorbs into your abdominal center and organs.

touching your tongue to your palate as you learned in the Microcosmic Orbit. You can circulate the energy at your heart center to nourish your loving and joyful self. Feel your heart softening and opening. Bring the energy down to your abdomen and circulate it around your navel so that it absorbs into your abdominal center and your organs.

As with all the practices, when you first begin, it takes time to feel the energy activate and move. With practice it will flow more easily. Do the practice as many times as you would like. Start with one time. With practice and skill you can do Ovarian Breathing nine times in each sitting. The breathing and movements help you to focus on the chi, but once your focus is trained, you can use your mind alone.

As with the Microcosmic Orbit and the Orgasmic Upward Draw, it is possible for the ovarian chi, which is yang and hot, to feel "stuck" in the brain. Use the recommendations in chapter 6 for drawing the energy back down to the abdomen—Bringing the Energy Down on page 158 and Venting on page 159—as needed, to clear the energy from your head.

Ovarian Breathing can be helpful throughout your life to tone your reproductive hormones and increase your energy. It can be even more powerful when done in concert with the Jade Egg practice, which you will learn next.

THE JADE EGG PRACTICE

In ancient China, the jade egg practice was used exclusively by the women of the Royal Palace to strengthen the vagina and reproductive organs. By inserting a jade egg into the vagina, these women were able to tone and strengthen the PC and pelvic muscles. This was thought to improve health, both physically and spiritually, since these exercises provide more power to the PC muscle (and the sacral pump) to lift the sexual energy inward and upward where it will be transformed into higher spiritual energy. With the jade egg in the vagina, it is easier to feel and exercise the PC muscle and to develop more conscious control over your sexual energy. The techniques for using the jade egg are simple, and you will notice results (in increased strength and sensitivity) within weeks. If you have a male partner, you will be able to use your new-found skills to give him extraordinary pleasure during intercourse.

Most women who use the egg note an increase in their sexual energy, particularly in the vaginal area. This is helpful for women who are developing their vaginal sensitivity, trying to experience deep pelvic or expanded orgasm, or to open the Three Gates. For women who are already "hot" and have high sexual energy, the egg exercises may be too stimulating for your sexual energy. Universal Tao instructor Raven Cohan says, "I feel the egg exercise is good for students who need to tonify their sexual energy. If one is already very hot in nature, it can bring excess." Alternatively, other women with "hot" energy find that the egg exercises help them absorb and balance their energy. Experiment yourself and see how they work for you.

Many women find that not only does the egg practice increase their sexual energy, it is very healing as well. This is likely because, as

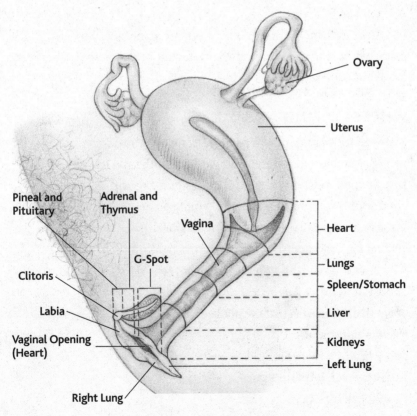

Acupressure points of the genitals

mentioned earlier, the vagina contains acupressure points that relate to all of the vital organs of the body. Many people are familiar with acupressure foot massage techniques. In Traditional Chinese Medicine, the entire body—with every major body part or organ system— is represented by acupressure points along the feet. The same is true for the vagina and the penis. Stimulating all of these areas during sexual play and penetration can promote the balancing of one's chi.

Massaging and stimulating these points can have a healing effect on your entire being. One 72-year-old practitioner described a quite amazing side effect of the practice, "When I use my egg, my gray hair goes away, and I feel juicy. When I don't use my egg, the gray hair comes back." While I cannot recommend the exercises generally to improve your hair color, it is true that they will help balance and vitalize you.

Although the Jade Egg exercises are generally very safe, it is probably best to avoid doing them during pregnancy or when you have an active vaginal or bladder infection.

WHERE TO FIND AN EGG

Many gem and mineral shops have stone eggs. Just as we are all varying heights and weights, our vaginal widths and lengths vary tremendously. You should choose an egg that is comfortable for you. In general, if you have never had a baby vaginally, you may want to choose a smaller egg. Women who are larger in size or who have given birth vaginally may want to choose a slightly larger egg. The average size of the eggs that are made for this purpose are 1 inch in diameter and 1½ inches long. They vary, however, from the size of a quail's egg to the size of a jumbo-sized chicken egg.

Stone eggs are made from various substances: jade, obsidian, rose quartz, and others. You can use any of these that appeal to you for the exercises. The most frequently used eggs for beginners are the jade eggs, as they gently calm and harmonize the uterus. (In ancient China, the vulva and vagina were referred to as the Jade Gate.) Some women are interested in the energetic or healing qualities of other stones. If this is the case for you, you may want to choose your stone after doing a little research. I highly recommend that you let your intuition be your guide in selecting a stone as you (and your body) know what will be most healing for you better than any expert on stone qualities.[2]

You can purchase stone eggs directly from the Healing Tao center by using the contact information in appendix 2. These eggs are the "average" size. They are also drilled vertically so that you can thread a string through them, which allows you to easily remove the egg.

I want to emphasize that you should only do these practices *if they feel good in your body*. Many women have experienced rape, incest, or even aggressive or uncomfortable consensual sex. These memories stay not just in our brains, but in our sensitive genital areas as well. This can make any kind of penetration emotionally difficult. If this is the case for you, please go very slowly with these exercises. Listen to the needs of your body and *never force the egg into your vagina*. Your body needs to be receptive and ready before the egg is inserted.

It is ideal to do this exercise after your sexual energy has already been awakened and your sexual secretions have already begun to flow. You can do this by stimulating yourself or by doing Breast Massage. If you are naturally dry, you can use a water-soluble lubricant before inserting the egg. Saliva also works well for this purpose.

---

2. Maitreyi Piontek is a teacher of Taoist sexual healing for women who originally trained with Master Chia. She has a Web site with information regarding different types of eggs, www.tao-of-sexuality.com.

After you can comfortably move the egg as described in the exercises, you can insert the egg during any of the other exercises (Inner Smile, Microcosmic Orbit, Healing Sounds, or Ovarian Breathing), which will enhance and intensify the flow of sexual energy.

EGG CARE

It is important that your egg (and anything else!) be clean before inserting it into your vagina. Before starting the practice, put the egg in water and bring it just to the boiling point. Then remove it and allow it to cool. This is only necessary before using the egg the first time. Subsequently, it is sufficient to rinse the egg with warm water after removing it from the vagina. If you have a vaginal infection, it would be wise to boil the egg again after the infection has cleared.

If your egg is drilled, check to see that all of your vaginal secretions have cleared from the drilled hole. If they have not, the easiest way to clear them is to blow into one end of the egg. It also works to soak the egg overnight in a 50-50 solution of water and vinegar, which will dissolve the secretions. If secretions are still stuck inside, you can use a pipe cleaner or other thin, elongated object to push them out.

It's a good idea from time to time or when you have some blood or other thick secretions, to wash the egg with soap and water. Remember that the vaginal tissue is *very* sensitive to fragrances and soaps and can easily become irritated. Use a mild, non-fragranced soap and, most important, rinse well.

Some women are concerned about the egg getting "lost" in the vagina. The egg can usually be easily expelled by squatting, coughing, or bearing down, as if you are going to have a bowel movement. Until you have good control of the movement of your egg, it is helpful to insert a string into the drilled hole so that the egg can be easily withdrawn. Thread a length of string into the narrow end of the egg and knot it on the outside of the wide end. Or fold a 2-foot length of floss in half, then insert the folded end though the drilled hole in the egg.

Now insert the strings of the free end of dental floss through the loop that you just created at the other end and pull tight. If it is difficult to thread your egg, you can also use a large-bore needle to insert the dental floss or string and then loop the floss around the outside and tie it to itself. Having a string in place will also help you to attach weights to the egg, if you wish, for further vaginal strengthening.

THE EGG PRACTICE

As with all practices, you will need to have time and privacy, as well as a loving atmosphere. It also really helps to have a healthy sense of humor, because your first several attempts at this practice are bound to be awkward! Once you've got the practicalities down, the practice itself is really quite simple.

I suggest that you begin your practice by getting to know your egg. And no, I'm not suggesting that you have a conversation with it, although you certainly may, if you wish. I want you to feel very comfortable with your egg because for this practice, as for life in general, nothing (or no one) should get to be inside your body without your permission. I want you to use the utmost gentleness with yourself when doing this practice. It should enrich and enliven you, not cause you discomfort or pain. If at any time you feel anxiety or discomfort, please stop the practice. It is more important that you love and respect your feelings than that you do the practice "correctly."

Begin by lying on the floor and placing your egg on your pelvic belly, just below your belly button. You can hold or roll your egg on your belly both to allow your body to get used to it and to bring it to body temperature. If you have ever had a pelvic exam with a cold speculum, you know how difficult it is to relax and invite that thing in when it feels like the arctic invasion. I take the time to warm speculums in my medical clinic, and I strongly encourage you to take the time to warm your egg before inserting it in your vagina.

Take several deep belly breaths through your nose and into your abdomen and relax. Do the Inner Smile. Smile down to your heart and feel it warm and open like a rose. Then smile down to your sexual organs (your uterus, ovaries, vagina, and clitoris), feeling them fill with the golden light of love and begin to warm.

It is ideal to do Breast Massage to further warm the body and the sexual organs. As we discussed, stroke your breasts in a circular fashion, using varied pressures to awaken the chi that naturally connects your breasts with your genitals. You want to massage your breasts and awaken their chi so that they will in turn allow your Jade Gate (the vulva) to swell and lubricate in preparation for the Jade Egg practice.

You can insert the egg at any time, but it's ideal if your Jade Gate is lubricated and ready beforehand. To further awaken your sexual chi, you may want to self-cultivate by stroking your clitoris or vagina. When the egg is warm, move the wide end to just in front of your vaginal opening and get used to the feel of it. Begin to slowly contract your PC muscle around the egg. You may need to keep your hand on the egg in order to do this. When you feel comfortable, exert slight pressure on the egg and continue to contract your PC muscle to draw it into your body. If you are not lubricated, use a water-soluble lubricant or natural oil on the egg to ease its entry.

You may notice that the "tightest" part of the vagina is the PC muscle itself and that after the egg passes the muscle, it easily slides in. Depending on the size of your egg and the size of your vagina, it may feel that you are being stretched or that you can't feel anything at all (did anything really go in there?). Both of these experiences are entirely normal. If you have trouble feeling the egg at all, strengthening the PC muscle with the exercises from chapter 5 and doing the Jade Egg practice will greatly improve your sensitivity. It is common not to feel the egg after it has gone past the PC muscle (in the same way that you don't really notice a tampon when it is in).

If you have attached string to your egg, pull it out slightly while contracting your PC muscle. You should feel a slight tug or resistance. If you do not, you may want to further strengthen your PC muscle, or you may need a larger egg. If you have birthed children vaginally, and particularly if your perineum was torn or cut during birth, it can be difficult to retain the egg in the vagina at all. If this is the case for you, I suggest that you continue the practice while lying flat or slightly propped up.

If you are comfortable, move to a standing position. The traditional position for this practice is that of the horsewoman. (See the illustration on page 226.) It is a very strong posture and is the basic posture for most Chi Kung practices. Chi Kung is the practice of moving chi through the body while doing basic movements that facilitate the chi moving along the meridians. The egg practice is like a Chi Kung practice for your reproductive organs. Stand with your feet shoulders-width apart and firmly grounded, ankles and knees bent and relaxed, pelvis tucked under so that your sacrum points toward the earth, spine and neck aligned, head slightly bent so that the crown of your head reaches up and your chin is tucked in, and hands in gentle fists resting at the top of your thighs, where they meet your hips, with your palms facing up, elbows slightly bent.

In order to hold your egg inside, you may need to lightly squeeze your PC muscle. It helps to wear underwear because those slippery eggs are likely to fall out frequently when you begin the practice, and if they hit the floor, they may break. Alternatively, you can practice naked over a towel or rug. Now gently squeeze your vagina around the egg and see if you can sense it there. (See the illustration on page 227.) Squeeze and release up to nine times or until you are tired. At no point during these exercises should you feel pain. If you do, please stop and reposition or remove the egg. It is common to feel a warmth and/or soreness from using muscles that have not been used a lot.

Now try to move the egg in an up and down direction (an in and out direction if you are lying down) by squeezing and releasing your PC muscle. The egg should move up toward your cervix and then down just short of your PC muscle. If the egg moves down (or out)

Horsewoman Stance

beyond your PC muscle, it will probably fall out (or fly out, depending on the strength of your muscles!). Visualizing the egg
moving in the direction you wish will facilitate its doing so.

If you want to check whether the egg is moving or not, you can
feel the string between your fingers to see whether it is moving up
or down. Alternatively, you can attach a piece of material or a small
ring or other object to the string and watch to see how it moves. This

is easiest if you are standing in front of a mirror. You can also put a finger inside your vagina and feel whether the egg is moving away from your finger and toward it again. The up and down motion happens between the PC muscle and the cervix.

If your egg is not moving, it may be too far up in your vagina. Try pushing the egg down (or pulling it down with the string) and repositioning it just above the PC muscle. It may help to squeeze the PC muscle and pull up with your out-breath. Push down as if you are having a bowel movement in order to move the egg down (or out). If you want to expel the egg, push down in this way while holding your breath. These movements are difficult in the beginning because we are not used to using our pelvic and PC muscles. With practice, they will become much easier.

Once you are able to move the egg up and down, try moving it

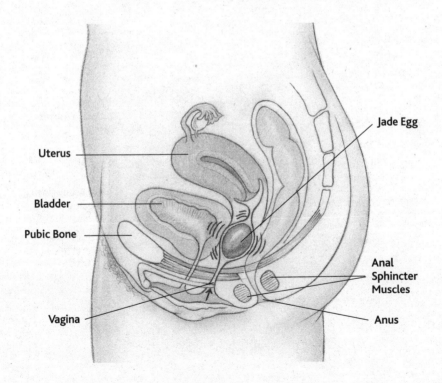

Squeezing the Jade Egg

left and right. This is a little more difficult and requires the use of some pelvic and abdominal muscles as well. To move the egg left, contract the left side of your PC muscle and the pelvic abdominal muscles on the left. By contracting, or shortening, these muscles, the egg will move to the left. There is another muscle, the transverse perineal muscle, which can be strengthened and trained to assist with this movement. It is activated by the same mechanisms. Contract the same muscles on the right to move the egg to the right. Again, feel the movement of the egg with your fingers or watch the movement of an attached object in the mirror. The object may swing back and forth like a pendulum as you do this. Try to keep your hips steady and still cause the object to swing.

Now combine your movements, moving up and down and then side to side. When your muscles are tired or you are out of breath,

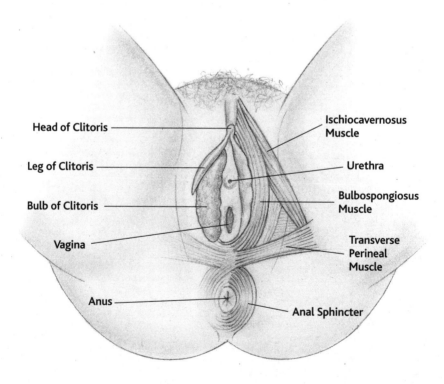

The Transverse Perineal Muscle

rest. A lot of chi is produced by these practices, and you want your sexual organs to have time to absorb it.

This exercise can be integrated into many of the other practices you've learned. To do the Jade Egg practice with Ovarian Breathing, prepare yourself with Breast Massage, then insert the egg. Move the egg up and down and side to side. The egg can help multiply the sexual energy in the vagina and enhance the practice of Ovarian Breathing. Proceed with Ovarian Breathing, using the presence of the egg to increase your focus on the chi and to collect and transfer the chi to the perineum, and then through the Microcosmic Orbit. Ovarian Breathing and the Jade Egg practice are a dynamic duo that will cultivate the health and strength of your reproductive organs and your sexual fire throughout your life. They will also increase the strength—and sensitivity—of your vagina as you grow older.

The Jade Egg practice can also be integrated into the Healing Sounds. I first learned this innovative practice from Universal Tao instructor Saida Desilets and have found it extremely useful for cleansing the genital area of negative experiences or emotions that each of us holds there.

COMBINING THE JADE EGG PRACTICE WITH THE HEALING SOUNDS

Because the vagina has each of the major organ systems represented within it, as shown in the illustration on page 219, it is possible to do the Healing Sound for each organ while the jade egg is in the correlated position in the vagina. For this exercise, I suggest that you have the "Summary Sheet" of the Healing Sounds (see page 84) in front of you. Prepare for the Jade Egg practice as above and insert your egg; you may also want to do some of the basic movements to awaken your vaginal chi. You are going to contract around the egg at each of the major organ points as you do the Healing Sound for that organ.

You may notice on the illustration that the heart area is at both the entrance to the vagina and at the cervix. This is because the uterus has its own acupressure system, starting with the heart at the cervix and the lungs around the cervix. The ancient Taoists taught that you had to open a woman's heart before entering her vagina because the heart area is also at the entrance to the vagina. If your own heart is loving and open toward yourself, your PC muscle at the entrance to the vagina will relax, and this exercise will be much more pleasurable. If you are feeling tense or uncomfortable, doing the Inner Smile to your heart and your sexual organs will help you relax and open to the practice.

Begin by lying comfortably, either flat or propped at an angle. Place your egg between your inner lips, which symbolize your lungs. Smile down to your inner lips and breathe in deeply. Exhale, releasing any sadness that is associated with your sexual organs and make the sound SSSSSSS. Release any sadness that you may have experienced, and stored, in your genitals. Some women find it helpful to visualize releasing their "negative emotions" into the egg itself. Breathe in the white light of courage and feel it fill your vagina. Repeat this two more times, relaxing in between sounds. As is true with the Healing Sounds, you can choose any emotion associated with that organ that resonates with you.

Now place the egg just inside the vagina in the kidney region, where you can squeeze around it with your PC muscle. As in the PC Pullups exercise, relax the PC muscle as you breathe in and contract as you breathe out. Breathe in deeply and then exhale, squeezing your PC muscle around the egg and making the sound CHEWWWW. Exhale releasing any feelings of fear that you hold in your vagina into the ground or into your egg. There is no need to hold on to your fears from the past. Relax and let them flow out of you. As you relax and inhale, breathe in the blue light of gentleness. As with all of the sounds, repeat two more times.

Now move your egg into the Liver region, just past the PC muscle. As you did before, exhale and squeeze your egg, breathing out SHHHHHH. Release any anger that you hold in your vagina. As you relax and inhale, fill your vagina with the bright green light of kindness.

Move your egg further into your vagina to the Spleen and Stomach area in the mid-vagina. Exhale and squeeze your egg, breathing out HOOOOOO. Release any guilt or worry that you hold in your genitals. Relax and inhale, filling your vagina with the golden yellow light of compassion.

Finally, move your egg as far in as it will go so that it is in contact with your cervix. Simply push your egg with your fingers toward the back of your vagina, and it will likely be next to your cervix. Don't worry—the egg will not get "lost," as the vagina is a closed space. Exhale and squeeze around the egg, pushing the cervix and the egg together, and breathing out HAAAAAW. Release any impatience that you may have had with your sexuality into the ground or into your egg. Breathe in, filling your vagina and your cervix with the red light of joy and spirit. Remember that softening and releasing the cervix will help you to open the third gate of your waters.

Let all of the colors and positive emotions mix within your vagina, now shining with chi. Rest for a few minutes and allow the energy to absorb. Then gently remove your egg. If you have visualized the negative emotions flowing into your egg, you will want to purify it. Running it under water for a few minutes or letting it sit in water overnight will allow the negative energies to flow harmlessly out and back to the earth.

The Jade Egg exercises can help all women to keep their sexual organs toned and energized. This is particularly important when entering the later years of life, when vaginal tone and lubrication can decrease. The Jade Egg is one of the practices that can help each of us become "juicy crones."

BEYOND MENOPAUSE: BECOMING A JUICY CRONE

"The most creative force in the world is the
post-menopausal woman with zest."
—Margaret Mead

Once ignored or medicalized, menopause is finally being taken seriously as the profound, and sometimes rocky, transition that it is. A woman's experience of menopause varies dramatically depending on her particular physiology and her life circumstances. I have witnessed women sail through menopause with few symptoms and a certain amount of joy at being done with menstruation and passing into the next phase of their lives. I have witnessed other intelligent, balanced women crash and burn emotionally and physically, feeling as if their normal lives had been overtaken by a tornado. It does not help that perimenopause and menopause often occur in the phase of life when children are sometimes in their difficult teen years and parents' health and independence are often failing. It can be difficult to sort out what are menopausal symptoms due to menopausal changes and what may be emotional factors due to numerous stressors.

Menopause begins on the day when your menstrual cycle has stopped for 1 year. However, the changes leading to menopause, such as declining estrogen and progesterone levels, begin up to a decade before menopause. This often results in irregular menses, which can be lighter or significantly heavier. Sexual desire can fluctuate with shifts in the levels of hormones. During the menopausal transition, up to 85 percent of women in the United States experience hot flashes, according to the North American Menopause Society. Other symptoms are common, but by no means universal, including memory loss, poor concentration, and vaginal discomfort. Once a woman's body has completed the menopausal transition, most symptoms, with the exception of vaginal dryness, disappear. Reproduction of children may no longer be possible, but a birthing of a new creative self certainly is.

Most of the Taoist practitioners that I have interviewed have had very few menopausal symptoms and have finished menopause with their vitality and their sexual selves intact. Given how disturbing the symptoms of menopause can be for some women, I have been impressed at the relative ease with which Taoist practitioners have gone through the menopausal transition. I was fortunate to meet Andrea, a vibrant 60-year-old Healing Tao instructor, who shared with me that she had no menopausal symptoms and her menses simply stopped, with no hot flashes, emotional changes, or vaginal discomfort. She continues to have abundant sexual energy and a satisfying sex life.

HELP FOR MENOPAUSAL SYMPTOMS

Treating menopausal symptoms is important to a woman's sexual fulfillment because many of the symptoms—insomnia, mood swings, irritability—will dramatically affect sex drive. The symptoms of menopause vary widely between women and between cultures. As I mentioned, up to 85 percent of women in the United States experience hot flashes while in Japan only 15 percent do. These differences may be genetic, cultural, or dietary. It's hypothesized that it might be due to the much larger amounts of soy products in the Asian diet. Some women easily move through menopause "naturally" while others are sorely afflicted by emotional, intellectual, and physical symptoms. (See "Symptoms of Menopause.")

SYMPTOMS OF MENOPAUSE

• Hot flashes	• Vaginal dryness
• Insomnia	• Tiredness
• Headaches	• Anxiety
• Joint pain	• Irritability

The treatment of menopausal symptoms could fill an entire book, but I will comment briefly on holistic treatments that can be helpful. Once viewed as the "cure-all" for any menopausal distress, hormone therapy with estrogen, and sometimes progesterone, has now been shown to increase the risk, albeit slightly, of breast cancer, heart disease, stroke, blood clots, and dementia. Because of this, it is essential that women maximize the use of non-hormonal strategies and use hormonal therapy only when absolutely necessary for relief of symptoms and for as little time as possible.

TAOIST MEDITATIVE PRACTICES

Many menopausal symptoms are amenable to non-hormonal treatment. Taoist practitioners seem to experience fewer and less severe hot flashes when doing the Ovarian Breathing and Microcosmic Orbit practices. Rayna, a Healing Tao instructor, describes her experience, "For myself, when I went into menopause and started having hot flashes at age 45, Ovarian Breathing moved me quickly through any discomfort. I could disburse a hot flash in 3 to 5 minutes. I have had no symptoms now at all for about 6 years as I approach 58." If you are having perimenopausal or menopausal symptoms, experiment with doing Ovarian Breathing on a daily basis for a month and see if it helps.

Several recent studies have suggested that any meditative practice can decrease hot flashes by as much as 50 percent. And exercise—in addition to decreasing heart disease, building bone mass, and improving sleep—also decreases menopausal symptoms. Obesity and cigarette smoking both worsen hot flashes, so weight loss and smoking cessation will help with menopausal symptoms and also reduce the risk of heart disease and osteoporosis. Avoiding hot flash "triggers" is also helpful. (See "Hot Flash Triggers".) Many of my patients have benefited from working with a practitioner of Traditional Chinese Medicine, using herbs and acupuncture to treat their symptoms.

HOT FLASH TRIGGERS

- Alcohol
- Caffeine
- Hot or spicy foods
- Stress
- Hot drinks
- Warm environment

BLACK COHOSH

Black cohosh is an herb that appears to decrease hot flashes and other menopausal symptoms. It is well tolerated by most women, though a few may experience nausea, sweating, or visual changes. I recommend getting herbal supplements from reputable distributors, as the content of supplements are not monitored by the FDA and often vary widely. Often, asking an herbal expert at your local health food store or herb store will help you determine which brands in your area are reliable. Most studies have been performed using the brand Remifemin, which is a standardized extract. Dosages range from 20 milligrams to 1,000 milligrams, 2 to 3 times a day. As with all medications, use only as much as you need for the desired effect. Taking it with food will decrease nausea.

PHYTOESTROGENS

Currently, about half of the many clinical studies performed support the effectiveness of phytoestrogens in relieving hot flashes, and about half do not. This is clearly not an overwhelming reason to run out and buy a phytoestrogen supplement, but increasing the amount of natural-phytoestrogen foods in your diet may be a good idea, as they have many health benefits—and may also decrease your hot flashes. Phytoestrogens are estrogen-like compounds found in plants; they are much less potent than estrogen itself. In some tissues they act like estrogen, and in others they may oppose estrogen's action.

There are three categories of phytoestrogens—isoflavones, lignans, and coumestans. (See the table on page 236.) Isoflavones, especially those in soy, are the most potent phytoestrogens and by far the most extensively studied and most widely available. Soy isoflavones are present in fresh or boiled soybeans (edamame), tofu, soy milk, and other soy products. Soy has a number of other beneficial health effects, such as decreasing cholesterol and heart disease risk and stimulating immune function.

Although countries with the highest amount of phytoestrogens in the diet appear to have a *lower* incidence of breast cancer, some concern exists regarding the effects of phytoestrogens on breast cells. Some studies have shown that phytoestrogens can increase the growth of normal human breast tissue in the laboratory, making us question whether they could increase the risk of breast cancer. Dietary phytoestrogens appear to be safe for everyone, but many experts would caution women with breast cancer or a strong family history of breast cancer against taking a concentrated phytoestrogen supplement. (Also, be cautious if you are taking the blood thinner warfarin (Coumadin), as soy can alter its effects.)

In addition to increasing the amount of soy and other legumes in the diet, adding flaxseed to your diet can be beneficial for a number of reasons. Two tablespoons of flaxseed daily may decrease hot flashes. Flaxseed also contains extremely beneficial omega-3 fatty acids, which improve cholesterol, decrease heart disease risk, and have a general anti-inflammatory effect that can be useful for eczema, arthritis, and other inflammatory conditions. You can ingest flaxseed oil if it is kept cold and not heated before use (for example, used on salads, not in cooking). I generally encourage women to use flaxseeds, which have the advantage of also being a great fiber sup-

PHYTOESTROGEN CLASS	FOOD SOURCE
Isoflavones	Legumes (soy, chickpeas or garbanzo beans, red clover, lentils)
Lignans	Flaxseed, lesser amounts in lentils, whole grains, beans, fruits, vegetables
Coumestans	Red clover, sunflower seeds, sprouts

plement, but they need to be ground in a spare or otherwise unused coffee grinder just before use to release their oils. Then sprinkle the powder on cereals or salads or put it into smoothies.

NUTRITIONAL SUPPLEMENTS

It can be difficult to get all of the nutrients you need from your diet. I recommend a good multivitamin that contains more than the standard RDA of B complex to all of my patients, but especially to menopausal women. The B vitamins can help with breast symptoms and also contribute to the prevention of heart disease. Vitamin E at 200 to 300 IU may have a beneficial effect on menopausal symptoms, as well. Taking calcium in any form, 500 milligrams twice daily with 200 to 400 IU of vitamin D, is important to prevent osteoporosis. I sometimes recommend that my patients make a nutritional "menopause" smoothie in the morning with a powdered or liquid calcium supplement, a powdered or liquid multivitamin, 2 tablespoons of ground flaxseed, silken tofu or soy milk, sweetener (I prefer stevia, which is available at natural food stores), and your favorite frozen fruit (berries add antioxidants). This power shake gives you a nutritional boost as you start your day and may decrease menopausal symptoms.

HORMONE THERAPY

After trying all of the above recommendations, some of my patients continue to have debilitating hot flashes, emotional swings, insomnia, or difficulty with memory or concentration. In these cases I do prescribe hormones, in as low a dose as is effective and only for as long as is necessary. I generally try to wean women off estrogen around the age that the menopausal process naturally ends—55 on average. We now have evidence that continuing on estrogen for more than 5 years after the age of menopause increases the risk of breast cancer, so I encourage my patients to stop estrogen prior to this time, if possible.

The reliable studies that we have available on hormone replacement therapy use a synthetic estrogen, Premarin, that differs from the estrogens that our body naturally produces. We have no studies indicating that "bio-identical estrogens," that is, ones that are identical to those produced in your body, are any safer when used in menopause. When I prescribe hormones, however, it makes sense to me to use estrogens and progesterones that the body is already used to seeing. Estradiol, estriol, and estrone are bio-identical estrogens that are available in tablets, patches, and creams. These estrogens can be compounded into creams, capsules, or troches (flavored packets that dissolve in your mouth) by a compounding pharmacist. Prescription tablets and patches are also available with estradiol.

If you are still the proud owner of your uterus, you will need to take progesterone along with the estrogen in order to prevent uterine cancer. Progesterone keeps the uterine lining from "proliferating," or getting so thick that cancerous cells are more likely to grow. "Natural progesterone" (sold under the brand name Prometrium) is available in capsules for this purpose. Some of my patients who want to avoid estrogen have tried natural progesterone capsules or creams without estrogen for the treatment of hot flashes with good success.[3]

SEX AND MENOPAUSE

One of the major complaints that I hear from my perimenopausal and menopausal patients is that their sex drives have decreased. Physiologically, sex drive is driven primarily by testosterone, which also decreases with menopause. It's important to note, though, that these women do not experience a decrease in sexual *satisfaction*. Because sex and pleasure have many benefits—increased sex hormones, intimacy, and overall well-being—I encourage my patients

---

3. Natural progesterone creams will need to be made by a compounding pharmacist. A number of wild yam progesterone creams are available over the counter, but research has not shown them to be effective.

to plan for time to be sexually intimate, whether or not they feel the same burning sexual desire they did when they were 30. As one of my 52-year-old patients said, "Now my mind has to do the work my body used to do." Most of my menopausal patients are able to orgasm with the same intensity as previously, and once they have chosen to make love are glad that they did! When I spoke with my patient Danya about her experiences with desire after menopause, she said, "Literally across the board with myself and my closest friends—and we're all self-described 'hotties' in the past—the desire just left. We all felt that, okay husbands, you just have to work for it here; you have to get us interested. But once we're interested, it's as good as, if not better than, before."

Interestingly, the post-menopausal women who are Taoist practitioners seem to continue to have a full and active libido. Since they cultivate their sexual energy in their daily practice, it makes sense that their sexual energy, or jing chi, remains high. In fact, the "use it or lose it" phenomenon also has a physiologic basis. When you have sex and orgasm, many hormones are released, including testosterone, estrogen, and DHEA, which all help your body to want to be sexual another time. Although this positive feedback loop (sex increases desire, which leads to more sex) happens throughout life, it is particularly important during older life, when sexual hormones are naturally lower.

A number of herbs and supplements are formulated to purportedly increase libido. However, no good studies currently exist in the United States that demonstrate their effectiveness. And although taking supplemental estrogen clearly assists with vaginal lubrication, estrogen does not necessarily increase sex drive. Supplementing with testosterone, on the other hand, has been shown in many studies to increase sexual interest. What you may *not* know is that testosterone also acts as an antidepressant in both sexes. Unfortunately, other signs of active testosterone include thinning of the hair on our heads and hair growth in traditionally male places—chin, upper lip, breasts, and belly—and, in high levels, a deepening of the voice. Interestingly, testosterone is increased by sexual activity or thoughts, by exercise, and by winning competitions or arguments. It is higher than average in career women, but it is *vital* to the well-being of post-menopausal women. Testosterone levels do decrease after menopause, but proportionally, estrogen levels actually decrease *more*, so that your body may respond to a *relatively higher* level of testosterone and manifest *more* effects of testosterone. This may be the reason that a few women have *increased* libido (as well as more chin hair) after the menopausal hormonal shifts are complete.

Women who have their ovaries removed lose a source of post-menopausal testosterone (and estrogen as well). After having her uterus and ovaries removed at age 50 and going on estrogen replacement, Danya notes, "My libido really dropped. I was really sad about it. It wasn't gone, but I was really hot before that. It was like, what happened here?" In these women, many physicians recommend replacing estrogen and testosterone until what would have been the natural age of menopause. Unfortunately, we don't have any long-term studies on testosterone use in post-menopausal women. We do know, however, that testosterone worsens a woman's cholesterol profile and cardiac risk when taken orally. I prescribe testosterone in the form of a cream that can be applied to the skin or vulva. Using a cream prevents the negative effect that oral testosterone can have on one's cholesterol. Since testosterone can potentially stimulate reproductive organs, there is also some concern as to whether testosterone use will increase rates of breast, ovarian, or uterine cancer. Some of my patients, however feel such a profound loss of sexual drive that they want to pursue supplementing testosterone. This is perhaps even more appropriate in women who have had their ovaries removed, as their levels of testosterone are naturally lower. In women who have their ovaries removed well before the age of menopause, we usually prescribe estrogen, progesterone, *and* testosterone.

Another common sexual complaint during and after menopause is that vaginal tissues can become thinner and less elastic due to lower amounts of estrogen. The more delicate vaginal tissue also secretes less lubrication, making penetration sometimes uncomfortable. If you continue to be sexually active—especially if it involves penetration—your vaginal tissues will retain more elasticity and will be more resistant to injury and infection. The Jade Egg practice is an excellent way to maintain the strength and flexibility of your vaginal tissues after menopause. Some sexually active women, however, will still experience pain with penetration. Using a lubricant during sex is helpful. (See the list in on page 262.) Other lubricants are designed to be used more regularly to relieve ongoing symptoms of vaginal dryness—whether or not you are having sex. These "vaginal moisturizers" contain carbopols, which stick to the vaginal cells for several days. Replens is a common brand and is typically used two to three times a week with more added as needed for sex. Some studies show that eating more phytoestrogens can also decrease vaginal dryness.

If sex continues to be uncomfortable, I usually prescribe a vaginal estrogen cream, ring, or tablet to increase the thickness and elasticity of the vagina. Estrogen creams can be placed in the vagina daily for 2 weeks and then once or twice weekly to improve lubrication and comfort. Estrogen tablets are used with the same frequency as the cream, but they are a little less messy. Because of the very small amounts of estrogen that are absorbed from the vagina into the circulation with these low dose treatments, they are not thought to increase the risk of breast or uterine cancer or blood clots. However, we do not yet have any studies of long-term use. Any woman who has had breast cancer should likely avoid any kind of estrogen treatment, including vaginal estrogen.

Because of the changes in vaginal elasticity, post-menopausal women who are not regularly sexually active can have a narrowing of the vaginal opening, making future sex and even pelvic exams painful.

Reinitiating sexual activity requires a gentle touch and lots of lubrication. For these women I usually recommend a vaginal estrogen. If this still does not work, I recommend the use of graduated dilators, tubes of increasing size, that can slowly stretch open the vagina over the course of a few weeks until penetration is comfortable.

Penetration and intercourse are, of course, optional parts of sexuality. Many women find oral sex and manual stimulation to be even more satisfying than intercourse. And many older men have a challenging time with erection. So don't forget that there are many choices available for couples in the smorgasbord of sexual touch. If penetration doesn't work for you, try other options. Danya, for example, recently started a relationship with an ex-lover who is 79. She says, "He can't sustain an erection yet, and I don't care at all. He keeps thanking me for my patience and there is no need to. What women usually don't get enough of is all the other stuff (kissing, touching, oral sex). I have Viagra in my possession, and he's willing to take it, but I haven't wanted to give it to him. I am enjoying all this other stuff." Many older couples find that instead of vaginal thinning and erectile difficulty limiting their sexual possibilities, it opens up a broader and even more fulfilling range of sexual possibilities.

Taking good care of yourself—eating right, exercising, doing Taoist meditative practices, and having an active and heartful sex life—will help you become the vital, juicy, and wise older woman that Margaret Mead described as the most creative force in the world. This reflects the experience of Saskia, a Universal Tao instructor from the Netherlands, who told me, "In my case the combination of eating natural food and no meat, dairy, sugar, or alcohol and the Ovarian Breathing has helped me to have no hot flashes at all, and suddenly at about age 48 my menstruation has stopped completely." Every woman's menopausal experience is different, but I have been privileged to witness a large number of my friends and patients reach the other side of menopause and come into their full power as wise women and as sensual beings. Ending one's reproductive years can allow for the rebirthing of oneself, with new approaches to spiritu-ality, creativity, and sexuality. My patient Danya, who is now 63, has entered the most dynamic, creative, and sexually fulfilling time of her life. She told me, "More than at any time in my life, I am able at this age to be who I fully am sexually, and I still feel like there's a ways to go. In a way, I want to know how far I can go and if there is an end. I'm not sure there *is* an end!" When I asked Danya what con-tributed to her feeling more sensual and free now than at any other time in her life, she answered, "I only have me, for the first time in my *whole* life, to focus on. I don't have to take care of anybody. I'm in my own rhythm." I hope for all of you who are transitioning into "juicy crones"—or already are one—that you will take the time to focus on yourself, to find your own rhythm, and to fully explore the limits of your sexual self. You may also find that there is no end.

The Taoist practice offers many paths to cultivating our health and, in particular, our sexual health, throughout our lifespan. But no matter how experienced you are in the Taoist practice, there will likely still be times that you are confronted with physical issues—genital infections and pain—that can prevent you from feeling your full sexual pleasure. In the next chapter, we will discuss a compre-hensive, holistic approach to genital health so that when it is neces-sary, you will have the power to heal yourself.

CHAPTER 9

SEXUAL HEALTH
AND HEALING

I f you regularly practice the Taoist exercises in this book, or any spiritual practice that focuses on compassion and self-love, you will improve your health and strengthen your immune system. We all have incredible power within our bodies, and if we practice regularly and fill ourselves with good chi, we will get sick less often. This does not mean you will never get sick. As a doctor, I know that sometimes illness just happens to patients. We all have bodies that become injured and times that our resistance to illness is lowered due to physical and emotional stressors. And most of us have particular body patterns that show our vulnerabilities at times of stress. Low back pain, neck pain, headaches, sore throats, respiratory illness, and stomach pain are common ones, as are genital infections and genital pain in women.

Women are somewhat vulnerable to pain and frequent infections of our genital areas because of the sensitivity of our tissues and the internal nature of our reproductive organs. Although the vagina and vulva have amazing powers to heal, even after significant trauma such as childbirth, many women will suffer from vaginal pain or infections at one time or another. And it is often not just physically distressing, but also emotionally distressing, to have pain or discomfort in our genitals, as they are strongly linked to our sexual and female identity. Because of societal taboos around women's bodies, it is difficult to discuss something as normal as menstruation, let alone those new bumps on your vulva or that funny-smelling vaginal discharge. But it is darn near impossible to have a playful, erotic sex life if things aren't going well "down there." And nearly every single woman will have an issue with her genital health at one time or another.

COMMON GENITAL INFECTIONS

Almost every woman will, at some time in her life, have a vaginal or urinary tract infection. I'll discuss in detail the simple preventative measures that you can take to prevent these irritating and outright painful episodes. Some women may have recurrent issues with genital pain or infection that significantly affect their sexual lives. I give guidelines for holistic treatment of persistent infections to keep your health, and your sex life, in balance.

URINARY TRACT INFECTIONS

Because of our anatomy, women are particularly vulnerable to genital and urinary infections, especially when sexually active. The distance between our external urethra and our bladders is short, making the trip a lot easier for invading bacteria. Urinary tract infections (UTIs) were often nick-named "honeymoon cystitis" because the ins and outs of intercourse help drive bacteria into the female urethra, where they then "climb up" into the bladder, causing a "bladder infection." ("Urinary tract" infections refer to infections of the urethra, bladder, ureter, or kidney. The most common of these is the bladder infection.) This occurs most often in new couples because your bacteria are "still getting to know one another." For reasons we still do not fully understand, long-term couples are less vulnerable to this phenomenon, theoretically because you build up immune defenses against your partner's now-familiar bacteria and are less vulnerable.

Regardless of whether you are currently in a relationship, it pays to follow two simple rules to prevent urinary tract infections. *Drink plenty of water* so that your frequent urinating flushes out any potential bacteria. *Always pee after any sexual activity.* If any bacteria have been propelled into your urethra by sex, you want to flush them out.

If, despite these measures, you begin to have symptoms of a UTI (see "Signs and Symptoms of a UTI"), but do *not* have a fever or back pain, immediately begin drinking large amounts of water—at least 2 to 3 liters a day. If you drink enough, in some cases you can flush the bacteria out faster than they can multiply. Drinking 8 ounces (1 cup) of cranberry or blueberry juice (ideally, unsweetened) or taking cranberry concentrate tablets (often easier because you get the helpful cranberry without the sugar that is in common cranberry juice preparations) will help. Cranberry tablet preparations differ, but generally, taking the equivalent of 1,200 milligrams once or twice daily will suffice. Cranberries and blueberries contain a natural substance that prevents bacteria from climbing up the urethra and into the bladder. Abstain from intercourse or penetration of any sort until your symptoms have resolved. It may be necessary to continue with extra fluids and cranberry juice or tablets for 3 to 5 days.

If your symptoms worsen, continue for more than 3 days, or are associated with a fever or flu-like symptoms, please seek medical attention. Once the infection is established, it can be difficult to treat it with natural means. A short course of antibiotics (3 days) will usu-

---

SIGNS AND SYMPTOMS OF A UTI
- Burning with urination
- Feeling the need to urinate more frequently, even when very little urine comes out
- A dull ache or cramping just above your pubic bone
- Dark, bloody, or cloudy urine
- Any of the above symptoms combined with fever, back pain, and flu-like symptoms (which might indicate a kidney infection)

ally cure a simple bladder infection, but see your doctor if you continue to have symptoms. If left untreated, a bladder infection can progress up the urinary tract and cause a kidney infection (also called pyelonephritis), which is evidenced by UTI symptoms along with fever, back pain, and flu-like symptoms. A kidney infection, as any woman who has had one will attest, is a *serious* infection and needs to be treated with a longer course of strong antibiotics. Untreated kidney infections can progress to blood infections, or sepsis, which can be deadly. Many women can be treated at home for kidney infections, but some are serious enough that hospitalization is required. If you are ever unsure as to the treatment of your symptoms, please seek your health care provider's advice. Sometimes urinary tract infections can be confused with other illnesses and further laboratory tests are needed.

If you continue to get urinary tract infections despite drinking large amounts of water and peeing after sex, drink 8 ounces of cranberry juice or take three cranberry concentrate tablets on a daily basis. If you're using a diaphragm, cervical cap, or spermicide, try a different birth control method, as these can increase UTIs. Also avoid condoms that are coated with spermicide. Avoid regular, firm stimulation of the G-spot area as it can cause inflammation and irritation of the urethra. Acupuncture can be helpful in treating recurrent UTIs. Some holistic practitioners believe that oral acidophilus supplements are helpful in replacing the "friendly" normal bacteria in the colon, vagina, and vulva that are disrupted by antibiotics, spermicides, and some lubricants. The growth of friendly bacteria keeps the numbers of unfriendly bacteria that infect the urinary tract at a lower level. In the Taoist system, the kidneys are related to the bladder and all of the sexual organs, so use the Inner Smile and Healing Sounds to send chi to your kidneys.

Finally, if you continue to get UTIs, taking a "narrow spectrum" antibiotic tablet just prior to sexual activity can prevent the development of further infections. A narrow spectrum antibiotic is *spe-*

cific to the infecting bacteria in question and less likely to wipe out *all* of your friendly bacteria. Typically, a woman would need to continue taking the tablet prior to sex for 6 months. This allows the chronic irritation of the urinary tract from repeated infections to heal. I have occasionally had women who needed to continue with preventative antibiotics for years, but this is rare. If you are taking an antibiotic on a regular basis, it would be wise to also take a "probiotic" supplement, one that replaces the friendly bacteria killed by the antibiotic, so as to avoid other infections, such as yeast infections. I'll discuss probiotics in detail in the next section.

VAGINAL YEAST INFECTIONS

The vagina is a warm, wet, friendly environment for organisms. When all is well, your vagina hosts a number of friendly bacteria, especially lactobacilli, that compete with yeast and other non-friendly bacteria and keep them in check. The lactobacilli secrete substances that impair the growth of other bacteria and maintain the vagina in a healthy, acidic state. A yeast infection occurs when this balance is disrupted, and the yeast grow to large numbers. The yeast produce irritating substances that cause most of the symptoms of yeast infections: vulvar pain, burning, and itching. Most of the time women have symptoms associated with yeast infections (see "Signs and Symptoms of Vaginal Yeast Infections"), but not always. Unlike UTI's, untreated vaginal yeast infections are unlikely to be dangerous to your health. If you have symptoms, however, they are *deadly* for your comfort and sex life. The pain and itching can be quite intense.

SIGNS AND SYMPTOMS OF VAGINAL YEAST INFECTIONS
- Itching, pain, or burning of the vaginal and vulvar areas
- Thick, white vaginal discharge
- Pain with penetrative sex, especially at the entrance to the vagina
- Pain with urination because of the urine hitting the inflamed vulva

---

Perhaps the most common cause of vaginal yeast infections is antibiotics. Antibiotics kill the friendly bacteria in the vagina that compete with the yeast for resources and allow the yeast to flourish. This is why it is important to take probiotic supplements during and after any course of antibiotics.

Yeast infections are more common in women who have male sexual partners. Some of this may be due to the fact that your sweetie's semen will change the acidity and perhaps the good bacteria in your vagina. If you are getting yeast infections and have a male partner, you may want to ask him to not ejaculate inside of you, to use a condom, or, preferably, to become multi-orgasmic so that he can enjoy his pleasure but not mess up your vaginal acidity. Some men may be resistant to this, but explain that a yeast infection is going to keep him out of the pleasures of your jade chamber *completely*, so it is in his own best interests to find other outlets, so to speak. As is the case with most vaginal infections, having multiple or new partners seems to be more likely to cause problems than having one long-term partner. Over time, a monogamous couple likely "balances" their mutual bacteria and immune responses (sounds romantic, doesn't it?). Although yeast infections are sexually *associated*, they are not usually sexually transmitted; that is, you don't typically infect your partner who then infects you back. If you are sexually active with a woman and have any kind of vaginal infection, it is important not to share any sex toys and to avoid vulva to vulva contact until you are treated. In rare instances, women with chronic yeast infections may be getting reinfected by male partners. Yeast can live under the foreskin of an uncircumcised penis and in the seminal vesicles, which produce some of the semen when a man ejaculates. Your doctor can culture his ejaculate, if this is a concern.

Any increase in estrogen will also increase the risk of yeast infections. This includes taking birth control pills, using birth control patches or rings, and using post-menopausal hormones. Not surprisingly, the higher levels of estrogen and progesterone during pregnancy (as well as higher sugar levels in the vagina) *also* increase the rate of yeast infections. Interestingly, IUDs increase the risk of yeast infections, not because they change estrogen levels, but likely because of the effect the "strings" of the IUD have on the vaginal ability to clear organisms.

Some women get vaginal yeast infections only during or after their menses, either from the hormonal fluctuation or because blood makes the vagina less acidic *and* wetter. For my patients who suffer from this problem, I recommend that they use the acidifying boric acid treatment, discussed on page 254, one to three times during their menses. This can often prevent the menstrual yeast infection.

Women with diabetes are also much more prone to vaginal yeast infections. This may be because the increased sugar levels in the vaginal secretions provide a favorite food source for the yeast. It is also likely that the impaired immune defenses due to diabetes are a factor. Some evidence exists that suggests that consumption of large amounts of sugar or dairy products in the diet may encourage yeast infections. Eating a normal, well-balanced diet with limited sweets and dairy is a good idea for your overall health, in any case, but if recurring yeast infections are a problem for you, experiment with eating less concentrated and refined sugar and dairy products. There is also growing evidence that some women with recurring yeast infections may have poor vaginal immune responses to yeast because of a genetic predisposition.

There are simple measures that you can take to prevent vaginal yeast infections. Keep your vulva and vagina relatively "dry," meaning that normal lubrication is present on the small lips and vagina, but not excess moisture (from sweat, water, etc.). Yeast like to live in a warm, wet place. I know that we have been talking about how to *make* you warm and wet throughout the rest of the book, but we want to reserve that hot, juicy vulva for lovemaking. When not engaged in sexual pleasure, you can keep your vagina happy by not staying in wet clothes (such as a bathing suit or work-out clothes) for long periods of time. Wear cotton underwear (as opposed to synthetics), which are less likely to hold in moisture and therefore allow your vagina to "breathe." This is especially important if you live in a hot, humid climate. Loose pants and skirts are less likely to hold in moisture and irritate your vulva than tight pants and shorts. Panty hose are doubly irritating in that they are both tight and synthetic and can retain yeast organisms. If you need to wear panty hose for work, consider thigh highs or the old-fashioned but always sexy garter belt. During your menses, if you are prone to yeast infections, change pads and tampons more frequently or consider using a menstrual soft cup, which collects the menstrual fluid at the cervix (it's available at most pharmacies). Using panty liners on a regular basis (not just during menses) can also increase vaginal moisture—because they hold in your natural sweat—and itching. And finally, some women find it helpful to use a hair dryer (on a low, not-too-hot setting) on their vulva after bathing to keep the area dry. It also feels really nice!

If you develop the symptoms of a yeast infection and it is your first occurrence, it is worth consulting your physician as other infections, most commonly bacterial vaginosis (which we'll talk about next), can be confused with a yeast infection. If you have had prior yeast infections and are fairly certain that you have another one, it is fine to attempt to treat it yourself using an over-the-counter antifungal cream or suppository or any of the holistic strategies I discuss below, all of which will effectively treat most yeast infections. Relief should ensue within 2 to 3 days, but if your symptoms persist, see

---

FACTORS THAT PREDISPOSE ONE TO VAGINAL YEAST INFECTIONS

• Antibiotics	• IUD
• Birth control pills	• Keeping the vagina in a wet environment
• Hormone therapy	• Diabetes
• Pregnancy	

your health care practitioner for a definitive diagnosis. My clinical experience is that the 1-day formulas do not work as well as the 3- or 7-day ones, and the infection often returns. These treatments are safe and are good strategies for women who only rarely get yeast infections. An oral tablet, fluconazole 150 milligrams, is also available by prescription. One dose will cure a simple yeast infection, but for those women who get infections frequently, I usually recommend combining the fluconazole with an antifungal cream, as well as implementing the preventative measures discussed previously and the holistic options discussed on the following pages. If you have recurrent yeast infections (more than three in one year), or your symptoms are not relieved by the antifungal treatment, please see your doctor, as other infections can mimic yeast infections, and certain rare forms of yeast require different, and longer, antifungal treatments.

If your symptoms are not severe, avoiding things that predispose you to yeast infections (see "Factors that Predispose One to Vaginal Yeast Infections") and taking a probiotic, such as an oral lactobacillus acidophilus supplement with one to two billion live organisms daily, can be helpful for prevention or treatment. In Europe, a lactobacillus identical to the human lactobacilli is available, and theoretically, more effective. This is not yet available in the United States, so I would suggest simply purchasing a good quality lactobacillus supplement. If a yeast infection is active, you can assist in its healing by directly putting some of the probiotic powder inside your vagina. If you are inserting a probiotic into the vagina yourself, you can simply pinch the powder between your thumb and first finger and insert it; if the powder is packaged in capsules, you will need to open the capsule, or, alternatively, you can insert the capsule itself. The only drawback is that the capsule substance will then dissolve and drip from the vagina, which can be irritating if the vulva is already inflamed. If you are purchasing capsules for this purpose, you will need to use the capsules made of actual gelatin, as the vegetarian gel caps will not dissolve in the vagina. Insert one capsule twice a day for two weeks.[1] This is also a good regimen to follow during and after taking antibiotics to restore the natural bacteria.

Restoring the acid balance of the vagina is another good preventative measure and a good treatment, especially when antifungal medications are not working. Boric acid is a white powder that's available at any pharmacy and has been shown to be effective at treating yeast infections. It sounds scary, but boric acid is a very mild acid and is safe for topical use. Insert a pinch of boric acid into the vagina before bedtime when infected or every other day during menses to prevent vaginal yeast infections. Most studies have looked at twice-a-day use with an amount close to 600 milligrams of boric acid. Because the increased vaginal discharge associated with it can be irritating, I suggest starting with once-a-day use at night. You can also pack the powder into gelatin capsules and insert them into the vagina as well, which some women find easier. If you wish, ask your physician to write a prescription for boric acid capsules equivalent to 600 milligrams that can be prepared by a compounding pharmacist and used 1 to 2 times daily for 14 days. Boric acid is effective at treating even yeast infections that do not respond to antifungal treatment when used in a dosage of one to two capsules daily for 2 weeks. For more typical infections, only 1 week is required. *Never* ingest boric acid, as it is poisonous when taken orally. It would also be prudent to use it on an as needed rather than a regular basis to prevent too much systemic absorption.

Because you are putting a dry powder into the vagina, the vagina will "sweat," and you'll notice a watery discharge while using the boric acid. For this reason, it is most convenient to insert it at night. Usually this is not a problem, but when the vulva is very irritated, the discharge can further exacerbate the irritation. In this circum-

---

1. There is now available a prepackaged probiotic supplement designed for oral and vaginal use twice daily for 2 weeks called GyNaTren by the Natren company. This is available through health food stores or online at www.natren.com. It's convenient but expensive, however ($25), and you can probably do it yourself for a more reasonable fee.

stance, I recommend using an ointment on the vulva to protect it from the irritating vaginal and yeast secretions, allowing the vulva to heal more easily. Excuse the comparison, but the strategy is similar to that for preventing diaper rash, using an ointment to separate the skin from the irritating moisture. A simple non-allergenic ointment that does not contain fragrance, herbs, or essential oils (which can be irritating) will do. Some women actually use a diaper rash cream, but keep in mind that the zinc component (which makes it white) can be very drying to the skin. A natural alternative that is soothing and works very well is a formula made from olive oil, beeswax, and royal jelly called Egyptian Magic. It is available at health food stores and over the Internet and also doubles as a handy lubricant if you are not using latex birth control methods. Other physicians have had success with simple petroleum jelly. All of these "ointments" can degrade latex condoms, cervical caps, and diaphragms, so avoid using the ointments just before sex if you're using latex.

BACTERIAL VAGINOSIS

Many of the principles of keeping your vagina healthy and free from yeast infections apply to bacterial vaginosis (BV) as well. BV occurs when the natural balance of the vaginal bacteria is upset and a particular bacteria, gardnerella, or another type of bacteria called anaerobic, grow to large numbers. As the bacteria take over the vaginal population, so to speak, they change the naturally acidic state of the vagina created by the lactobacilli. When the vagina is less acidic, unfriendly bacteria and other organisms, such as trichomonas, thrive. BV is the most common vaginal infection, and it is frequently asymptomatic, meaning that the woman has no idea that she has it. I often find that a woman has BV when it is discovered during a routine Pap test. When BV does cause symptoms (see "Signs and Symptoms of Bacterial Vaginosis" on page 256), they are difficult to distinguish from other vaginal infections.

SIGNS AND SYMPTOMS OF BACTERIAL VAGINOSIS
• Irritation of the vaginal or vulvar areas
• Thin, white to gray, foul or fishy-smelling discharge
• Pain with intercourse (rarely)

BV has always been considered a potentially irritating, but otherwise benign, infection. Most physicians treated it only if it was bothersome. This has changed somewhat in the past decade, as it has become apparent that BV can predispose pregnant women to premature labor. More recent data shows that the presence of BV makes a woman more likely to have abnormal Pap tests. BV causes inflammation of the cervix, which can be confused with the pre-cancerous conditions that the Pap test screens for. In order to differentiate between inflammation caused by BV and actual pre-cancerous changes, further workup, including repeat Pap tests or even biopsies, may be needed. Additionally, BV can, in rare instances, advance from the vaginal cavity into the uterus, causing a more serious infection, Pelvic Inflammatory Disease (PID). It is still true that *most* women with BV will not suffer any serious health problems, but it may be in your best interest to treat it if it is diagnosed. If you have symptoms of BV, see your health practitioner for diagnosis with a pelvic exam, a vaginal pH check, and an examination of your vaginal secretions under the microscope.

Like vaginal yeast infections, BV thrives when the normal bacteria are destroyed by antibiotics or douching. It also likes a less acid environment than the normal vagina and therefore is more apt to grow when substances like menstrual blood or semen decrease the vaginal acidity. Because of this, many of the same strategies for yeast infections will prevent and treat BV as well. Avoid douching in all cases, as it disrupts the normal bacteria. Take probiotics orally and consider inserting vaginally when you're taking antibiotics.

Your physician is likely to prescribe a prescription antibiotic, metronidazole or clindamycin, which is formulated, theoretically, not to kill off the friendly bacteria. Both oral and vaginal prepara- tions are very effective. The difficulty with BV is that it often recurs and will require repeat treatment. In very recalcitrant cases, using boric acid in the same doses as for yeast infections—600 milligrams inserted vaginally once or twice daily—will treat the infection. It is also possible to prevent recurrent infections by inserting a pinch of boric acid once or twice weekly. Sometimes, using a prolonged course of vaginal or oral metronidazole (10 to 14 days) is required for recurrent infections.

SEXUALLY TRANSMITTED INFECTIONS

Although a thorough discussion of sexually transmitted infections (STIs) is beyond the scope of this book, most of us have either had an STI or have had sex with the fear of contracting an STI, so I will dis- cuss them briefly. The most common STIs, human papilloma virus (HPV) and genital herpes, are transmitted from skin-to-skin contact. Unfortunately, this means that although condoms reduce transmis- sion, they cannot prevent it entirely, as lots of skin-to-skin contact hap- pens outside the condom. Genital herpes is painful, but not usually dangerous, and can be well treated by prescription anti-viral medica- tions. Unfortunately, once you have herpes, you have it forever. HPV is the most common STI, sometimes causing genital warts and occa- sionally causing pre-cancerous and cancerous changes in the cervix. The most important measures you can take to protect yourself are to limit the number of sexual partners you have and get yearly pap tests to screen for cervical cancer. Syphilis, crabs, molluscum contagiosum, and pubic lice are less common STIs that can also be transmitted by skin-to-skin contact. Unlike herpes and HPV, however, these infec- tions can be easily treated and usually cured, so if you have any itching, pain, or rash that you cannot explain, please get medical help.

Chlamydia and gonorrhea are common STIs that can be prevented by condom use. It is important for young women to be tested for these after new sexual partners, as they can cause asymptomatic infections of the uterus and ovaries that can impair future fertility. Trichomoniasis is a vaginal infection whose transmission is significantly decreased by condom use. HIV and hepatitis B are serious STIs whose transmission can be significantly decreased by regular condom use. So if you want to expand your sexual play, please play safe. Use condoms with all new partners for intercourse, and condoms or dental dams for oral sex. If you are in a long-term relationship, get tested for STIs before doing away with the condoms. You may save not only your sex life, but your life.

GENITAL PAIN AND ITCHING

So what if you *continue* to have genital pain or itching and your doctor has confirmed that you have no vaginal infection or STI? Unfortunately, you are not alone. Many women suffer from genital pain and pain with sex. Because the skin of the vulva is quite sensitive (a good thing for pleasure), it is also easily irritated (a bad thing for pleasure). If you seem to have a "sensitive vulva or vagina," think of her as a spectacular Italian race car, needing a lot of maintenance, but "Oh, when she's running well, look out!" There are several basic principles to help you keep your genitals in fine running order.

AVOID KNOWN IRRITANTS

If you have vaginal or vulvar irritation, avoid tight-fitting or synthetic clothes. Your vulva needs to "breathe" and not be constricted. Avoid douching. Avoid using soap on your vulva, or if you must, use a non-scented, gentle soap. (Dove, Neutrogena, and Basis are all good.) Try not to use a panty liner on a daily basis. Get out of sweaty or wet clothes quickly. Avoid other potential irritants and allergens that may be irritating your sensitive skin. (See "Potential

Vulva-Irritating Substances" and "Potential Allergens in Products for the Genitals.")[3]

POTENTIAL VULVA-IRRITATING SUBSTANCES

- Scented or harsh soaps
- Bubble bath
- Some lubricants
- Bleach and fabric softener, especially dryer sheets
- Perfumes, shampoo, and hair conditioner

- Nonoxynol-9 and other spermacides
- Scented laundry detergent
- Tea tree oil (topically)
- Deodorant hygiene products
- Scented toilet paper

POTENTIAL ALLERGENS IN PRODUCTS FOR THE GENITALS

- Benzocaine (topical anesthetic)
- Neomycin (topical antibiotic)
- Chlorhexidine in K-Y jelly
- Disinfectants
- Fragrances
- Propylene glycol (found in many lubricants)

- Antifungal creams
- Latex condoms, diaphragms, and cervical caps
- Dyes
- Semen (rare, but it happens!)
- Preservatives (including methyl- and propylparaben)

USE LUBRICATION AND LOCAL HORMONES

Some women simply *need* more lubrication than others, and few things are more irritating to your vulva and vagina than rubbing without lubrication (ouch!). You may need more lubrication at certain times of the month due to hormonal changes, and tampon use will also dry out the vagina. Women who are on birth control pills, are nursing babies, or who are menopausal are hormonally predisposed to have less natural lubrication. Some nursing moms and

---

3. Great thanks to Dr. Elizabeth Stewart for discussing these in detail in her book *The V Book*, page 259.

many menopausal women need additional vaginal estrogen in order to restore the normal thickness, elasticity, and lubrication of the vulva and vagina, as we discussed in the past chapter. Some medications (including allergy meds or antihistamines) can also dry vaginal secretions when taken long-term.

Lubricants can be helpful in any of these situations and may be necessary with prolonged use of sex toys or even condoms (which require more secretions to slide gently across your skin). Many lubricants are available with different properties. If you are using condoms, a diaphragm, or a cervical cap, you will need to use a water-soluble or silicone-based lubricant, as oil-based lubricants will cause the latex to break down.[4] When water-soluble lubricants begin to dry out, simply add more water (or saliva) to "wet" them again. Because they are water-soluble, they easily wash off and out of the vagina. Water-soluble lubricants with glycerin stay wet longer, but some women find that the glycerin can be irritating or contribute to vaginal infections. Non-glycerin lubricants will simply need to be revived (with water) or reapplied more often. Water-soluble lubricants vary from the thin and slippery (which imitate natural vaginal secretions) to thicker and gel-like. Thicker lubes last longer and are helpful for clitoral play and for cushioning anal penetration.

Silicone-based lubricants stay "wetter" longer than other, water-soluble lubricants. Because they are not absorbed by the vaginal tissues, they stay on the surface of the vulva and vagina, making them long-lasting, but preventing them from being washed off with water. Some companies make "wash up" products to use to remove the silicone lubricants after use. Using a gentle soap also works, if it is not irritating to your skin. Silicone lubricants are safe with latex, but can, however, degrade silicone sex toys.

---

4. One exception to this are non-latex condoms (Avanti and the Reality female condom) and gloves made from polyurethane. Apparently, one manufacturer is also beginning to produce a non-latex cervical cap, but it is not widely available. You can buy non-latex safe sex items at the retail and online stores listed in appendix 2.

If your vulva is sensitive, any of the chemicals in artificial lubricants can be irritating and cause burning or itching with application.
Most women have no reaction to lubricants, but ingredients that have
been known to cause sensitivity include propylene glycol, nonoxynol-
9, and the "parabens" (such as methylparaben and propylparaben),
which are used as preservatives. If you have sensitivity, be sure to read
the labels. Women who are prone to vaginal infections should avoid
sugar-like substances in lubricants, including glycerin and sorbitol.
"Natural lubricants" are made from plant-based and sometimes
organic materials. They may or may not contain the allergens listed
above; you have to check the labels. Some will contain other plant ex-
tracts that can also be irritating. The best way to find a good lubricant
for you is to try them out. Many high-quality sex stores (see "Woman-
Friendly Stores for Sexual Products" on page 289) carry sample sizes
of many of the lubricants. Almost all of the sex stores listed include
product ingredients and recommendations for their lubricants on their
Web sites. You can then make informed choices before buying.

Oil-based lubricants include everything from Vaseline and
Crisco to lotions and vegetable oils. All of these will compromise
latex condoms, diaphragms, cervical caps, and dental dams. If you
do not use latex, oils can be safely used. Because they are not water-
soluble, oils will remain in the vagina after sex longer than water-
soluble lubricants. There is conjecture about whether this upsets the
normal vaginal balance, but no research indicates that it does. If you
are sensitive to artificial lubricants, oils may be the best option for
you, and I recommend choosing a natural oil without added fragrance—such as almond or olive—that is less likely to be irritating.
Lotions are poor lubricants in that they dry out quickly and contain
other chemicals and essential oils that may irritate your vagina.

SEE YOUR DOCTOR FOR PELVIC PAIN

Most of the infections and sensitivities that we have discussed can
cause pain or irritation to the vulva and the entrance to the vagina,

RECOMMENDED LUBRICANTS AND THEIR PROPERTIES

WATER-SOLUBLE LUBRICANTS	"NATURAL" WATER-SOLUBLE LUBRICANTS	SILICONE-BASED LUBRICANTS	OILS
Astroglide and Astrogel	Bliss Lube	Eros	Almond
Embrace	Hathor Aphrodisia	ID Millennium	Olive
Eros water formulation	O'My	Wet Platinum	Grape seed oil
ForPlay	Probe	—	(no added fragrances)
Hydra-Smooth	Sensua Organics	—	—
ID Glide	Sylk	—	—
K-Y Liquid	—	—	—
Liquid Silk	—	—	—
Maximus	—	—	—
Pleasure Glide	—	—	—
Slippery Stuff	—	—	—

making penetration painful. Some women, however, have pain, not with initial penetration, but with deep penetration. If this happens to you only occasionally, it may be that your partner is hitting your cervix. This is more likely to happen in positions that allow deep penetration (for example, the missionary position with your legs or knees drawn up, or almost any position from behind). Hitting your cervix with some force will cause a deep, crampy, "get-the-hell-away-from-me" pain that will slowly subside over several minutes.

If you experience pain with deep penetration on a regular basis, and especially if it is typically in the same place or with the same position, it may be due to a number of other medical problems. Common causes would include ovarian cysts (more common around ovulation), endometriosis (a painful condition where the uterine lining implants *outside* the uterus), or pelvic inflammatory disease (PID, infection of the uterus and fallopian tubes). In any case, you should see your doctor for evaluation should you continue to have pain.

SEE A SPECIALIST FOR CONTINUED PAIN

Unfortunately, the training many doctors receive on sexual health is poor at best. Combine this with any personal discomfort with the subject, and it is possible that you will encounter a physician who cannot answer your questions or help you resolve your issues. Ask for a referral to a specialist who is knowledgeable about genital pain. A growing number of women have a condition of chronic genital pain with no known cause called *vulvodynia*. There are effective treatments available for this, but you will need to see a physician who specializes in treating vulvodynia. Many times this will be a gynecologist, but even some gynecologists are ill-informed about these issues. For references and information, see appendix 2. Biofeedback, Traditional Chinese Medicine, and acupuncture can be helpful additions to a treatment plan for vulvodynia.

BIRTH CONTROL, FERTILITY, AND SAFER SEX

For many women, birth control is a double-edged sword. Your birth control method may interfere with the spontaneity or pleasure of your sex life, but the fear of pregnancy *also* interferes with sexual enjoyment. Having reached menopause, Desiree confided, "After I didn't need birth control anymore, sex really got a lot better. Before, I was using a diaphragm and jelly, and there was the interruption but there was also the barrier. I felt it made such a difference not to have that physical barrier. I think it's a psychological thing, too, that fear of getting pregnant when you don't want to. When I didn't have that, it really made a difference." Hanna, a 24-year-old international health worker, complained to me, "I lost all of my desire on the birth control pill, and I didn't even realize it until I went off it. Now I can see why it works so well—you never want to have sex!"

What is a girl to do to prevent pregnancy and still nurture her desire? The birth control options available to women are far from ideal, but I can usually assist my patients in finding an option that will work effectively and not make them crazy. Finding a birth control option that does not decrease your libido or significantly interfere with the flow of your sexual life is important to having your full desire.

To understand your birth control options, you need to understand your reproductive system. In an ideal world, all young women would be lovingly educated about the cycles of their bodies when they start adolescence. But for most of us, this is not the case. I recommend to all my patients of child-bearing age, whether or not they want children and regardless of their sexual orientation, that they learn some of the basics about how their reproductive system functions. The reason for this is that you will understand a lot more about monthly fluctuations in mood, desire, and vaginal discharge so that you can move with your cycles, instead of your cycles controlling you. For instance, if you know that you struggle with patience premenstrually, you can avoid over-scheduling yourself and do more self-nurturing when you are in that phase of your cycle. If you know that you get more emotional during ovulation, you will better be able to understand why you are weeping during the morning news. And if you are using any kind of birth control other than hormonal contraception, knowing your cycle will help you to make your birth control most effective.

UNDERSTANDING YOUR CYCLES (OR NATURAL FAMILY PLANNING AND FERTILITY)

The concept behind natural family planning or trying to boost your fertility is that it is possible to predict ovulation in most women. If you know when you are going to ovulate, then you can avoid intercourse, or make sure to have intercourse if you want to

get pregnant. Most women have menstrual cycles that occur somewhat regularly (ranging from 21 to 40 days). You may also be one
of the women who do not have regular cycles, which is simply another normal variant of how our bodies function. Irregular cycles
are only a problem if you go for more than 3 months without a period, in which case you need to consult your health care provider
to determine the cause. Irregular cycles do make it more challenging to predict ovulation, and I would urge you to use another
method of birth control along with natural family planning for
pregnancy prevention.

For most women, approximately 2 weeks before they begin
menstruating, they will ovulate, releasing an egg from the ovary
that travels through a fallopian tube to the uterus over the next 48
hours. If the egg is met by a friendly sperm, fertilization can take
place, and the zygote (beginning cells of a baby) will attach to the
uterus and begin a pregnancy. If no fertilization takes place, 2
weeks later the egg (about the size of a pin head) and the uterine
lining slough off, causing a menstrual period. Most of this is likely
to be familiar, but many women do not know that their cervix
softens and moves toward their backs when they ovulate. In addition, the cervix begins to secrete a stretchy mucous that resembles
egg whites (though some of my patients describe it as "snot") to facilitate the straight swimming of those sperm to their target. Your
basal body temperature (the temperature of your body at rest)
drops just before ovulation and then rises quickly. All of these signs
are used to predict ovulation. If you'd like to have more detailed instruction regarding predicting ovulation, I've listed many good
sources in appendix 2.

With the exception of hormonal contraception (birth control
pills, patches, and vaginal rings, which we'll discuss coming up),
other birth control methods allow you to continue ovulating, and
knowing *when* you are ovulating can significantly reduce your
chances of getting pregnant while using condoms, a diaphragm, or

a cervical cap. If you are trying to get pregnant, knowing when you ovulate can help you conceive more effectively. Some women feel a surge of desire, and some women feel particularly emotionally sensitive around ovulation because of the hormonal shifts that accompany the release of their eggs. It is not uncommon for a woman to feel the egg bursting out of the follicle in her ovary, usually sensed as a sharp or pinching sensation in the right or left pelvis.

Using natural family planning alone as birth control can be effective for women who are committed to the process, and particularly for women with regular cycles. It is not, as one would suspect, foolproof. When used perfectly, meaning that you regularly check your cervical mucous and basal body temperatures in order to determine your time of peak fertility and that you *never* have sex during your fertile period (5 days out of the month), the pregnancy rate at 1 year is still close to 1 in 10. The average person practicing natural family planning, who slips up now and then, has a yearly pregnancy rate of 1 in 5. If you are truly not ready to become pregnant but are interested in natural family planning, I suggest that you combine it with other methods, such as condoms, diaphragm, cervical cap, or withdrawal. (This means that a male partner withdraws from the vagina before ejaculation. Note, a non-ejaculatory practice is not good enough by itself to prevent pregnancy because some seminal fluid with active sperm may leak from the penis before ejaculation.) If it is truly important to you that you do not get pregnant, choose a more effective method, such as those I discuss next.

PILLS, PATCHES, AND VAGINAL RINGS

"The pill" is the most commonly used birth control method in North America, and it's convenient and reliable. It is composed of synthetic forms of estrogen and of progesterone (of varying types) that override your body's hormonal cycles and "trick" your body into thinking you are pregnant, thereby preventing ovulation. You still will have menstrual periods in the week that you go off the pill (or take the "blank" pills). Often periods are lighter and less painful on the pill, and sometimes I prescribe it for this reason alone. Some pills also have the potential benefit of decreasing acne. The new contraceptive patch (Ortho Evra) and vaginal ring (NuvaRing) work the same way as the pill, but the hormones are constantly being secreted and absorbed in small amounts through the skin, instead of through the digestive system. Some of my patients experience less nausea and emotional side effects with these non-oral methods.

Whether or not you will have side effects on the pill is impossible to predict, as it is different for every woman. And some women will feel great on one brand of pill and feel like the wicked witch on another brand. There is no way to tell which is most compatible with your body without trying them. In general, the lower dose pills have fewer side effects, but they can cause irregular bleeding in some women. For women who have very painful periods or severe premenstrual symptoms (PMS), or for those who simply don't want their periods, it is safe to take the pill continuously for 12 weeks and then to stop and have a regular period. Seasonale is a new contraceptive pill that is formulated to be taken in just this way, though you can use any birth control pill that is not "phasic"—that is, does not vary in content throughout the cycle. I know that this sounds "unnatural," but in truth, the pill is already controlling your cycle in its entirety, and having a period more frequently than every 3 months does not make you any healthier. Some women take the "mini-pill," which is a progesterone-only pill. In general, the side effects are similar to a combined pill (with estrogen and progesterone), except that most women will have irregular menstrual periods or spotting between cycles on the mini-pill. I generally prescribe this pill to women who are nursing (because it is safer for the baby) and women who have side effects to estrogens, such as frequent migraines.

From a sexual standpoint, the pill allows spontaneity and 97 to 99.9 percent effectiveness against pregnancy. (See "Birth Control Methods and Their Effectiveness" on page 270.) Unfortunately, the pill can also suppress sex drive, sometimes significantly. Different brands may have different effects, so don't give up hope if you take the pill and are experiencing decreased libido. It is also true that you may be drier, with less vaginal secretions. Women on the pill also have a higher risk for vaginal yeast infections. And since the pill provides no barrier, it does not protect at all against sexually transmitted diseases. While all of this is true, some women have such a reduction in PMS, painful periods, or heavy bleeding, that the trade off is well worth it, and their sex lives improve as a result. Additionally, for women who take the pill for 6 years or more, their risk of ovarian cancer in decreased by almost *50 percent*, an impressive reduction of a very rare disease. Recent studies have also suggested that long-term use of the birth control pill (greater than 4 years) can reduce the risk of endometrial and cervical cancer as well. In an average woman, the pill does not increase the risk of breast cancer. However, a few studies that have examined women with a strong history of breast cancer in their families (that is, a mother or sister with breast cancer) have suggested that these women might increase their risk for breast cancer with long-term birth control use. The birth control pill also causes a small increase in the risk of blood clots. This risk becomes more of a concern in women over 35 and women who smoke.

CONDOMS, DIAPHRAGMS, AND CERVICAL CAPS

Unlike the pill, these barrier methods do not affect your cycle, and you will continue to ovulate and have periods when using them. Condoms have the great advantage of significantly reducing the transmission of STIs, particularly HIV, chlamydia, gonorrhea, trichomonas, and hepatitis B. Condoms also reduce, but do not eliminate, the transmission of herpes, HPV, and syphilis. For this reason, I strongly encourage all my patients, readers, friends, family, and random people on the street to use condoms with all new partners. Respect yourself and respect your body by playing safe. A female condom is also available, though it is more likely to "slip in" and increase the chance of pregnancy than the male version. If you are allergic to latex, non-latex condoms are available made of various materials (see appendix 2). These condoms, with the exception of those made from animal skin, also protect against STIs. I generally do not recommend using condoms with spermicide, as the spermicide can be irritating to the vaginal tissues and, because of this, can even increase the transmission of STIs (because of vaginal inflammation). Lubricated condoms help with the increased lubrication that you may need with condom use; we talked about condom-compatible lubricants in detail earlier in this chapter.

If you have a regular partner, the diaphragm and cervical cap offer an alternative barrier contraception that works by covering your cervix instead of a man's penis (which is why they do almost nothing to protect against STIs). The diaphragm is a larger, quarter-cup-sized soft latex barrier that fits around the area of your cervix. The cervical cap is a smaller, tablespoon-sized cup that fits with suction on the cervix itself. They both are filled with spermicidal jelly or foam on the inside of the cup to kill those little sperm swimmers before they can enter the cervix. The diaphragm, being bigger, needs to be filled with more spermicide, about 2 tablespoons. The cervical cap requires about a teaspoon of spermicide. This is relevant if you are sensitive to spermicide, which can increase vaginal and urinary tract infections or simply cause an allergic reaction of the vulva. Fortunately, most women are *not* sensitive to spermicide, and many of my patients who want to avoid hormonal contraception are happy with the diaphragm or cervical cap.

Both the cervical cap and the diaphragm need to be inserted before intercourse and left in place for 6 to 8 hours afterward. If you have intercourse again during that time period and are using a diaphragm, you will need to insert another applicator full of spermicide. The cervical cap can be left in place for 48 hours. Both the diaphragm and the cervical cap need to be fitted and prescribed by a health care practitioner.

The major advantage of all the barrier methods is that they do

BIRTH CONTROL METHODS AND THEIR EFFECTIVENESS

BIRTH CONTROL METHOD	FAILURE RATE WITH PERFECT USE	FAILURE RATE WITH TYPICAL USE	POTENTIAL SEXUAL SIDE EFFECTS
Natural family planning	1 to 9%	20%	Inability to have inter-course during fertile period
Combined birth control pill	0.1%	3%	Decreased sex drive, vaginal dryness
Mini-pill (progesterone only)	0.5%	3%	Decreased sex drive, vaginal dryness, irregular bleeding
Male condom	3%	14%	Latex allergy, decreased penis sensation
Female condom	5%	21%	Reduced vaginal sensation, decreased spontaneity
Diaphragm	6%	20%	Latex allergy, bladder infections, vaginal sensitivity to spermicide, decreased spontaneity
Cervical cap	6%	18%	Latex allergy, vaginal sensitivity to spermicide, decreased spontaneity
Withdrawal	4%	19%	Possible frustration for the male
Spermicide alone	6%	26%	Vaginal sensitivity to spermicide, decreased spontaneity
IUD	0.1 to 0.6%	0.1 to 0.8%	Not safe with multiple partners, increased vaginal infections
Depo-Provera	0.3%	0.3%	Decreased sex drive, vaginal dryness, irregular bleeding
Norplant	0.05%	0.05%	Decreased sex drive, vaginal dryness, irregular bleeding
Vasectomy	0.1%	0.15%	None
Tubal sterilization	0.5%	0.5%	None

not affect your hormonal cycle. The major disadvantage is that they are not nearly as effective as other methods. In average users—meaning that it does not always get on or in soon enough, or in the correct way—the pregnancy rate after 1 year of condom use is 15 percent. With the diaphragm or cervical cap it is 20 percent, or 1 in 5. If you use the diaphragm and cervical cap as instructed, the pregnancy rate in 1 year is only 6 percent. With correct condom use, the pregnancy rate drops to 3 percent a year. You can increase the effectiveness of condoms and decrease the 1-year pregnancy rate if you use them with spermicide. This means that the condom goes on and spermicide gets placed inside the vagina before intercourse. In all of my patients using these methods, I recommend that the woman track her cycle and become familiar with when she ovulates, as she is only fertile for 5 days out of the month. Using an additional method of pregnancy prevention during those 5 days can significantly reduce your chance of pregnancy. For example, use a condom with your diaphragm or cervical cap when you are fertile. Or combine withdrawal (pulling out before the man ejaculates) with any of these methods to lessen the chance of pregnancy. If your man is multi-orgasmic and can control ejaculation, any of these methods will obviously be even more effective.

THE INTRAUTERINE DEVICE (IUD)

The IUD is emerging from the controversy that began to surround it in the 1970s, due to serious adverse effects of the Dalkon Shield, an IUD that has been withdrawn from the market. There are now two safe, well-tested IUDs available in the United States (and others in other countries). After sterilization, the IUD is the most common form of birth control in the world, likely because it is the most effective form of birth control other than vasectomy or hormonal injections (which have many side effects). The IUD is a small, T-shaped device that is inserted into the uterus in a doctor's office and remains there for 5 to 10 years, depending on the type of IUD. It works primarily by impairing the ability of sperm to reach the egg in the fallopian tube. When sperm do reach the egg, the IUD prevents a fertilized egg from implanting in the uterine lining. When used in the right setting, the IUD has a very low rate of complications.

Some women will experience heavier and more painful periods with the copper IUD (ParaGard). If this is the case, the Mirena IUD may be the answer. It is formulated so that it slowly releases a small amount of progesterone into the uterine cavity. Because of this, most women with this IUD have lighter menses and occasionally no menses at all. Progesterone in birth control pills can cause side effects, as I discussed, but so far no evidence exists that the small amount secreted into the uterus by the Mirena IUD has any systemic effects.

Because the IUD has strings that hang below the cervix and connect to the IUD in the uterine cavity, it can facilitate the travel of STIs (especially gonorrhea and chlamydia) into the uterus and fallopian tubes, causing a serious infection called Pelvic Inflammatory Disease. This infection can be treated but can cause scarring of the uterus and tubes that can prevent pregnancy. Because of this risk, I put IUDs only in women who are monogamous and have already had at least one child or do not desire any children. This obviously limits its use, but it is a good option for the women who fit this profile, as it provides excellent birth control, full spontaneity, and virtually no hormonal side effects.

HORMONAL IMPLANTS AND INJECTIONS

Both of these methods use a long-acting form of progesterone to provide long-term birth control. The injection (Depo-Provera) gives pregnancy protection for 3 months. The progesterone implants (Norplant) are surgically inserted just under the skin of the inner arm and remain active and effective for 5 years. Both of these methods have extremely low failure rates and allow for sexual spontaneity. In my experience, however, many women have significant emotional and physical side effects to the high levels of synthetic progesterone, including depression, weight gain, acne, decreased sex drive, and irregular menstrual periods. Many women will stop having periods entirely on this form of contraception. If you have used this method before and had no side effects, it is fine to try it again as it has many benefits. For anyone wanting to try one of these methods, however, I usually recommend several months of the mini-pill (progesterone only pills) to simulate the effects before getting a 3-month injection that cannot be reversed and whose side effects (interruption of normal menses) can last for 6 months. Likewise, before having the Norplant inserted, a simple surgical procedure, I counsel women to try the mini-pill or Depo-Provera first.

STERILIZATION

If you are certain that you do not desire future fertility, sterilization is a reliable option that offers spontaneous, synthetic hormone–free sexuality. If a woman is already having a pelvic surgical procedure, such as a Cesarean section, it is possible to "add on" a tubal ligation (cutting and "tying off" the fallopian tubes) without much increased risk to the woman. In any other circumstance, however, vasectomy (the cutting and tying off of the seminal tubules in the male scrotum) is a much safer, and even more reliable, option. It is performed by a physician as an outpatient surgical procedure that is simple and relatively safe. Talking a man into letting someone cut into his scrotum, however, is often far from simple. It is my view that since a woman usually bears the brunt of contraception, pregnancy, childbirth, and most infections and STIs, it is the least he can do. I can also understand, however, his reluctance to have a surgical procedure on the most sensitive part of his body. There are rare reports of men having recurrent pain after routine vasectomies, and although this is the exception, it is certainly a valid concern. The decision will have to be made between you and your partner, weighing all the risks and benefits.

The most important thing to consider when having a sterilization procedure is your certainty that you do not desire further fertility. It is almost impossible to reverse a tubal ligation and only slightly less so to reverse a vasectomy. Be sure that you and your partner, in any circumstance, do not want any more children.

SECRETS OF WOMEN'S SEXUALITY

I hope that this chapter can serve as a resource for you in maintaining your sexual health and spontaneity. Women's bodies are truly remarkable in their ability to recover from imbalance, disease, and trauma and still feel enormous pleasure. Use the information in this chapter to help you recover from any genital discomfort you may experience and to keep your sexual organs vibrant with life-giving chi and pleasure.

It's been my pleasure to share with you some of the life-affirming understandings of women's sexuality that I have been fortunate enough to receive from many great teachers. I hope that these practices have helped you to realize the true value of your passion and sexual energy. These practices, as you have no doubt seen, are about discovering your full desire, pleasure, and vitality; they weren't created just to help you have more orgasmic pulsations. These practices certainly can and indeed are the most effective techniques that I have encountered to increase orgasmic pleasure, but this is just the beginning of the benefits that they offer. These practices can help you manifest a whole new level of energy, health, and well-being.

For thousands of years, these practices were closely guarded secrets taught from one initiate to another. Mantak Chia and I believe that in this day and age, women around the world need to have access to these powerful and profound teachings. Our world needs women who are in touch with their strength, their vitality, and their intuition. Do not value these practices any less because you did not need to apprentice for years to learn them. They are a gift for you and for any one you choose to share them with. As you truly love yourself and claim your birthright as a fully sexual and spiritual being, you will be all the more able to give your gifts to your loved ones and to the world. And our world needs the gifts that you have to give. Blessings on your path.

SELECTED NOTES
ON THE TEXT

CHAPTER 1

Page 16: Lilka Woodward Areton. "Factors in the Sexual Satisfaction of Obese Women in Relationships," *Electronic Journal of Human Sexuality*, vol. 5 (Jan. 15, 2002).

CHAPTER 2

Page 49: Sachman and Ramamurthy, in *Behavioral Medicine in Primary Care: A Practical Guide*, edited by Mitchell D. Feldman and John F. Christensen. (New York: Appleton and Lange, 1997).

Page 55: Sandra Blakeslee. "Complex and Hidden Brain in the Gut Makes Stomachaches and Butterflies," *New York Times,* January 23, 1996.

CHAPTER 5

Page 118: Natalie Angier. *Woman: An Intimate Geography* (Boston: Houghton Mifflin Company, 1999), 58.

CHAPTER 7

Page 191: C. A. Darling, J. K. Davidson Sr., and C. Conway-Welch. "Female ejaculation: Perceived Origins, The Grafenberg Spot/Area and Sexual Responsiveness," *Archives of Sexual Behavior* 1990, 19(6): 607–11.

Page 191: Alice Kahn Ladas, Beverly Whipple, and John D. Perry. *The G-spot and Recent Discoveries about Human Sexuality* (New York: Henry Holt and Company, 2005).

F. Cabello Santamaria and R. Nesters. "Female Ejaculation: Myths and Reality." Paper given at the 13th congress of Sexology, Barcelona, Spain, August 29, 1997, and quoted in Chalker, *The Clitoral Truth.*

Josephine Lowndes Sevely. *Eve's Secrets: A New Theory of Female Sexuality* (New York: Random House, 1987), 47–48.

Page 193: Dr. Desmond Heath. "An Investigation in to the Origins of a Copious Vaginal Discharge During Intercourse: Enough to Wet the Bed-That Is Not Urine," *Journal of Sex Research* 20:2 (May 1984): 197.

CHAPTER 8

Page 233: M. G. Glazier and M. A. Bowman. "A review of the evidence for the use of phytoestrogens as a replacement for traditional estrogen replacement therapy," *Archives of Internal Medicine* 2001;161:1161–72.

Page 235: D. H. Upmalis, R. Lobo, L. Bradley, et al. "Vasomotor symptom relief by soy isoflavone extract tablets in postmenopausal women: A multicenter, double-blind, randomized, placebo-controlled study," *Menopause* 2000;7:236–42.

G. L. Burke, C. Legault, M. Anthony, et al. "Soy protein and isoflavone effects on vasomotor symptoms in peri- and postmenopausal women: the Soy Estrogen Alternative Study," *Menopause* 2003;10:147–53.

E. E. Krebs, K. E. Ensrud, R. MacDonald, and T. J. Wilt. "Phytoestrogens for treatment of menopausal symptoms: a systematic review," *Obstetrics and Gynecology* 2004;104:824–836.

CHAPTER 9

Page 249: A. E. Sobota. "Inhibition of bacterial adherence by cranberry juice: potential use for the treatment of urinary tract infections," *Journal of Urology*, 1984; 131:1013.

Page 252: Elizabeth Stewart. *The V Book: A Doctor's Guide to Complete Vulvovaginal Health* (New York: Bantam Books, 2002), 205–6.

APPENDIX 1: COMMON ILLNESSES AND MEDICATIONS THAT MAY AFFECT SEXUAL PLEASURE

COMMON MEDICAL CONDITIONS THAT CAN DECREASE LIBIDO OR ORGASMIC FUNCTION

Addison's disease

Alcoholism

Anxiety

Asthma (severe)[1]

Cancer of any kind

Chronic fatigue

Chronic infections

Chronic obstructive
pulmonary disease

Chronic pain

Cigarette smoking

Depression

Diabetes mellitus

Drug addiction of any kind

Eating disorders

Fibromyalgia

Heart disease

Hypercholesterolemia

Hypertension

Hypothyroidism
(low thyroid)

Kidney failure

Multiple sclerosis

Obsessive-compulsive
disorder

Panic disorder

Parkinson's disease

Schizophrenia

Seizure disorder

Sleep deprivation

Stroke

Systemic lupus

Temporal lobe epilepsy

Vascular disease

COMMON HORMONAL STATES THAT CAN DECREASE LIBIDO OR ORGASMIC FUNCTION

Breastfeeding

Menopause

Surgical removal of the ovaries

---

1. Asthma itself does not decrease libido, but people with severe asthma can have exacerbations from sexual activity that limits their ability to enjoy sex. Optimizing preventative asthma treatment is important for full enjoyment of sexual activities.

COMMON SURGERIES AND INJURIES THAT MAY DECREASE LIBIDO OR ORGASMIC FUNCTION

Extensive bicycle riding[2]
Pelvic fractures or trauma
Pelvic surgery of any kind (including hysterectomy)[3]
Spinal cord injuries
Straddle injuries (falling onto a pole or beam with legs spread and injuring one's pubic area)

RECREATIONAL DRUGS THAT MAY DECREASE LIBIDO

Cocaine (chronic use)
Heroin, methadone, opiates, "downers"
Marijuana

COMMON DRUGS THAT MAY DECREASE LIBIDO

Acebutolol (Sectral)
Acetazolamide (Diamox)
Amiodarone (Cordarone, Pacerone)
Amitriptyine (Elavil, Vanatrip)
Atenolol (Tenormin)
Barbiturates, such as butalbital (Fiorinal)
Betaxolol (Kerlone)
Birth control pills
Bisoprolol (Zebeta)
Carbamazepine (Atretol, Carbatrol, Epitol, Tegretol)
Carteolol (Cartrol)
Carvedilol (Coreg)
Chlordiazepoxide (Librium)
Chlorpromazine (Thorazine)
Chlorthalidone (Thalitone)
Cimetidine (Tagamet)
Clomipramine (Anafranil)
Clonidine (Catapres)
Clorazepate (Tranxene)
Desipramine (Norpramin)

Digoxin (Digitek, Lanoxin)
Doxepin (Sinequan, Zonalon)
Esmolol (Brevibloc)
Estazolam (ProSom)
Ethosuximide (Zarontin)
Famotidine (Pepcid)
Fenfluramine (Pondimin)
Flurazepam (Dalmane)
Gemfibrozil (Lopid)
Hydrochlorothiazide (Dyazide, HCTZ, Microzide, Oretic)
Imipramine (Tofranil)
Interferon
Isocarboxazid (Marplan)
Ketoconazole (Nizoral)
Labetolol (Normodyne, Trandate)
Lithium
Maprotiline (Ludiomil)
Medroxyprogesterone acetate (Amen, Curretab, Cycrin, Depo-Provera, Provera)

2. Constant pressure of the traditional bicycle seat can injure the nerves and blood flow to the clitoris, impairing sensation.
3. Pelvic surgery can injure the nerve or blood supply to the vagina and clitoris, resulting in a loss of sensation or lack of arousal or lubrication. Injuries do not, by any means, always occur. Hysterectomy sometimes affects sexual arousal and sometimes does not. For further details see chapter 5.

Megestrol (Megace)
Methadone
Methyldopa (Aldomet)
Metoclopramide (Reglan)
Metoprolol (Lopressor)
Nadolol (Corgard)
Nizatidine (Axid)
Norethindrone (Aygestin,
    Norlutate)
Nortriptyline (Aventyl, Pamelor)
Penbutolol (Levatol)
Phenobarbital (Luminal)
Phenytoin (Dilantin)

Pindolol (Visken)
Primidone (Mysoline)
Prochlorperazine (Compazine)
Progesterone (Prometrium)
Propranolol (Inderal)
Protriptyline (Vivactil)
Ranitidine (Zantac)
Reserpine (Serpasil)
Risperidone (Risperdal)
Spironolactone (Aldactone)
Timolol (Blocadren)
Tranylcypromine (Parnate)
Trimipramine (Surmontil)

RECREATIONAL DRUGS THAT MAY INHIBIT ORGASM

Alcohol (more than 12 ounces beer, 4 ounces wine, or 1 shot hard liquor a day)
Cigarettes
Ecstasy
Heroin, methadone, opiates, "downers"

COMMON DRUGS THAT MAY INHIBIT ORGASM

Acebutolol (Sectral)
Alcohol
Amitriptyine (Elavil, Vanatrip)
Atenolol (Tenormin)
Betaxolol (Kerlone)
Bisoprolol (Zebeta)
Carbamazepine (Atretol,
    Carbatrol, Epitol, Tegretol)
Carteolol (Cartrol)
Carvedilol (Coreg)
Chlorazepate (Tranxene)
Chlordiazepoxide (Librium)
Chlorothiazide (Diuril)
Chlorpromazine (Thorazine)
Chlorprothixene (Taractan)
Citalopram (Celexa)
Clomipramine (Anafranil)
Clonidine (Catapres)
Clorazepate (Tranxene)
Codeine (Tylenol with codeine)
Desipramine (Norpramin)

Dexmethylphenidate (Focalin)
Dextroamphetamine (Adderall,
    Dexedrine, Dextrostat)
Diltiazem (Cardizem, Cartia, Dilacor,
    Diltia, Diltiazem, Taztia, Tiazac)
Disulfiram (Antabuse)
Doxepin (Sinequan, Zonalon)
Escitalopram (Lexapro)
Esmolol (Brevibloc)
Estazolam (ProSom)
Ethosuximide (Zarontin)
Fenfluramine (Pondimin)
Fentanyl (Actiq, Duragesic patches)
Fluoxetine (Prozac)
Fluphenazine (Prolixin)
Fluvoxamine (Luvox)
Hydrocodone (Lorcet, Lortab, Maxi-
    done, Vicodin)
Hydromorphone (Dilaudid)
Imipramine (Tofranil)
Ketoconazole (Nizoral)

Labetolol (Normodyne, Trandate)
Loxapine (Loxitane)
Maprotiline (Ludiomil)
Meperidine (Demerol)
Mesoridazine (Serentil)
Methadone
Methotrexate (Rheumatrex, Trexall)
Methyldopa (Aldomet)
Methylphenidate (Concerta, Metadate, Methylin, Ritalin)
Metoprolol (Lopressor)
Modafinil (Provigil, Alertec)
Morphine (Avinza, Kadian, M-eslon, MS Contin, Oramorph, Roxanol, Statex)
Nadolol (Corgard)
Nifedipine (Adalat, Procardia)
Nortriptyline (Aventyl, Pamelor)
Oxazepam (Serax)
Oxycodone (Endocodone, OxyContin, OxyFAST, OxyIR, Percocet, Percodan, Percolone, Roxicet, Roxicodone, Supeudol, Tylox)
Oxymorphone (Numorphan)

Paroxetine (Paxil)
Penbutolol (Levatol)
Perphenazine (Trilafon)
Phenobarbital (Luminal)
Phentermine (Adipex-P, Ionamin, OBY-trim, Phentercot, Phentride, Pro-Fast, Teramine)
Pimozide (Orap)
Pindolol (Visken)
Primidone (Mysoline)
Prochlorperazine (Compazine)
Propoxyphene (Darvocet, Darvon, Wygesic)
Propranolol (Inderal)
Protriptyline (Vivactil)
Risperidone (Risperdal)
Sertraline (Zoloft)
Sibutramine (Meridia)
Thioridazine (Mellaril)
Thiothixene (Navane)
Timolol (Blocadren)
Trifluoperazine (Stelazine)
Trimipramine (Surmontil)
Venlafaxine (Effexor)
Verapamil (Calan, Chronovera, Covera, Isoptin, Verelan)

APPENDIX 2:
RESOURCES FOR SEXUAL
HEALTH AND HEALING

OTHER *MULTI-ORGASMIC* BOOKS

The Multi-Orgasmic Man: Sexual Secrets Every Man Should Know by Mantak Chia and Douglas Abrams. San Francisco: HarperSanFrancisco, 1997.

The Multi-Orgasmic Couple: Sexual Secrets Every Couple Should Know by Mantak Chia, Maneewan Chia, Douglas Abrams, and Rachel Carlton Abrams, M.D. San Francisco: HarperSanFrancisco, 2002.

For more information and to order an audio CD that will guide you through the exercises in this book, go to www.multiorgasmicwoman.com.

UNIVERSAL TAO BOOKS

Healing Love Through the Tao: Cultivating Sexual Female Sexual Energy by Mantak Chia and Maneewan Chia. Huntington, NY: Healing Tao Books, 1991.

Taoist Secrets of Love: Cultivating Male Sexual Energy by Mantak Chia and Michael Winn. Sante Fe, NM: Aurora Press, 1984.

Taoist Ways to Transform Stress into Vitality: The Inner Smile Six Healing Sounds by Mantak Chia. Huntington, NY: Healing Tao Books, 1985.

Awaken Healing Light of the Tao by Mantak Chia and Maneewan Chia. Huntington, NY: Tuttle Publishing, 1993.

Awaken Healing Energy Through the Tao by Mantak Chia. Santa Fe, NM: Aurora Books, 1983.

Tao Yin: Exercises for Revitalization, Health and Longevity by Mantak Chia. Lodi, NJ: IHT Publications, 1999.

The Inner Structure of Tai Chi: Tai Chi Chi Kung I by Mantak Chia and Juan Li, Huntington, NY: Tuttle Publishing, 1996.

Bone Marrow Nei Kung: Taoist Ways to Improve Your Health by Rejuvenating Your Bone Marrow and Blood by Mantak Chia and Maneewan Chia. Huntington, NY: Tuttle Publishing, 1991.

Chi Nei Tsang: Internal Organ Chi Massage by Mantak Chia and Manweewan Chia. Huntington, NY: Healing Tao Books, 1991.

Chi Nei Tsang II: Internal Organ Chi Massage, Chasing the Winds by Mantak Chia and Maneewan Chia. Huntington, NY: Healing Tao Books, 2000.

Chi Self-Massage: The Taoist Way of Rejuvenation by Mantak Chia. Huntington, NY: Healing Tao Books, 1986.

Fusion of the Five Elements I: Basic and Advanced Meditations for Transforming Negative Emotions by Mantak Chia and Maneewan Chia. Huntington, NY: Healing Tao Books, 1989.

Iron Shirt Chi Kung I: Once a Martial Art, Now the Practice That Strengthens the Internal Organs, Roots Oneself Solidly, and Unifies Physical, Mental and Spiritual Health by Mantak Chia. New York: Healing Tao Books, 1991.

Sexual Reflexology: Activating the Taoist Points of Love by Mantak Chia and William U. Wei. Rochester, VT: Destiny Books, 2003.

Golden Elixir Chi Kung by Mantak Chia. Rochester, VT: Destiny Books, 2004.

Tan Tien Chi Kung: Foundational Exercises for Empty Force and Perineum Power by Mantak Chia. Rochester, VT: Destiny Books, 2004.

Taoist Cosmic Healing: Chi Kung Color Healing Principles for Detoxification and Rejuvenation by Mantak Chia. Rochester, VT: Destiny Books, 2003.

To order Universal Tao books, audiocassettes, CDs, posters, or videotapes, you can write, call, fax, or e-mail the Universal Tao Center, 274 Moo 7, Laung Nua, Doi Saket, Chiang Mai 50220, Thailand. Phone 66-53-495-596 or 66-53-865-035. Fax from Asia 66-53-495-852.

E-mail universaltao@universal-tao.com or visit the Web sites www.multi-orgasmic.com and www.universal-tao.com.

UNIVERSAL TAO INSTRUCTORS AND CLASSES

There are more than 1,200 Universal Tao instructors throughout the world who teach classes and workshops in various practices, from Healing Love to Tai Chi to Chi Kung and Inner Alchemy. For more information about instruction and workshops in your area, contact the Universal Tao Center. You can also visit the Web site at www.universal-tao.com or locate an instructor at www.taoinstructors.org.

Many thanks to the excellent instructors who contributed their time and energy to this book. You can find one of them or an instructor in your area by contacting the Universal Tao Web site.

Fransje Bannenberg
Amsterdam, Holland
"BODY and TAO"
Healing Tao and Healing Ways
31-20-624-8104
youknow@xs4all.nl

Raven Cohan
314 Oak Street
Hollywood, FL 33019
954-927-2836
Nevarco@aol.com

Saumya Comer
503-226-6822
taoisthealing@yahoo.com

Saida Desilets
Jade Goddess
Pelham, NY
212-696-9479
info@jadegoddess.com
www.jadegoddess.com

Minke de Vos
Silent Ground Retreats
1601 Comox Street, #12
Vancouver, British Columbia,
    Canada V6G 1P4
www.SilentGround.com
(604) 505-4613

Lee Holden
Pacific Healing Arts
Santa Cruz, CA
888-767-3648
lee@pacifichealingarts.com

Jutta Kellenberger
Tao Garden
274 Moo 7, Luang Nua, Doi Saket
Chaing Mai, Thailand

Marcia Wexler Kerwit, MPH, PhD
Bay Area Healing Tao
PO Box 10824
Oakland, CA 94610
510-834-1934
bahealingtao@yahoo.com

Janette Nutis
janutistao@hotmail.com

Dena Saxer
Universal Tao of Los Angeles
Topanga, CA
310-455-1936
DenaSaxer@universaltaola.com

Sarina Stone
1023 Central Avenue West
Saint Paul, MN 55104
651-645-5714
taolady@hotmail.com

Nicole Tremblay
338 Chemin St-Louis
Quebec, Canada G1S 1B5
418-688-1711
psyacutao@videotron.ca

Angela Wu
Wu's Healing Center
1014 Clement Street
San Francisco, CA 94118
415-752-0170
wushealingctr@aol.com

PROFESSIONAL ORGANIZATIONS

GENERAL WOMEN'S HEALTH

American Academy of Family Physicians, PO Box 11210, Shawnee Mission, KS 66207-1210, 800-274-2237, www.aafp.org. This national organization of family practice physicians provides a wide variety of educational materials in women's health.

American College of Obstetricians and Gynecologists (ACOG), 409 12th Street, SW, PO Box 96920, Washington, DC 20090-6920, 800-410-ACOG, www.acog.org. This is a national Organization of Obstetricians and Gynecologists that provides a wide variety of educational materials on genital health, STDs, menopause, breast health, and pregnancy.

Family Violence Prevention Fund, 383 Rhode Island Street, Suite 304, San Francisco, CA 94103-5133, 415-252-8900, www.fvpf.org. This Web resource works to prevent violence within the home and in the community.

National Women's Health Information Center, 8550 Arlington Boulevard, Suite

300, Fairfax, VA 22031, 800-994-WOMAN, www.4woman.gov. This Web site and toll-free call center were created to provide free, reliable health information for women everywhere.

National Women's Health Network, 514 10th Street, NW, Suite 400, Washington, DC 20004, 202-347-1140, www.womenshealthnetwork.org. This is an excellent independent organization that provides accurate, unbiased information to women. They recently published a book on menopause called *The Truth About Hormone Replacement Therapy.*

National Vulvodynia Association, PO Box 4491, Silver Spring, MD 20914, 301-299-0775, www.nva.org. The National Vulvodynia Association (NVA) is a nonprofit organization created in 1994 to improve the lives of individuals affected by vulvodynia, a spectrum of chronic vulvar pain disorders.

North American Menopause Society (NAMS), PO Box 94527, Cleveland, OH 44101, 800-774-5342, www.menopause.org. NAMS is an excellent resource for up-to-date information and research on menopause.

SEXUAL HEALTH

American Association of Sex Educators, Counselors, and Therapists (AASECT), PO Box 1960, Ashland, VA 23005-1960, 804-644-3288, www.aasect.org. This organization assists in locating resources for sex therapy in your area.

American Social Health Association (ASHA), PO Box 13827,

Research Triangle Park, NC 27709, 919-361-8400, www.ashastd.org. ASHA is a nonprofit organization dedicated to STD prevention. ASHA's special site for teens is www.iwannaknow.org.

Planned Parenthood, 434 West 33rd Street, New York, NY 10001, 212-541-7800, www.plannedparenthood.org. This site covers resources including abortion, birth control, pregnancy, and parenting. It includes current news and articles on reproductive rights, FAQs, and an extensive database on these issues.

Sexuality Information and Education Council of the United States (SIECUS), 130 West 42nd Street, Suite 350, New York, NY 10036-7802, 212-819-9770, www.siecus.org. The council publishes a journal, bibliographies, brochures, and pamphlets related to sexuality research, education, and legislation.

The Sexual Health Network, 3 Mayflower Lane, Shelton, CT 06484, 203-924-4623, www.sexualhealth.com. This group provides information, educational materials, referrals to sexual health professionals, and knowledge about disabilities and chronic diseases.

MENTAL HEALTH

American Association for Marriage and Family Therapy, 112 South Alfred Street, Alexandria, VA 22314-3061, 703-838-9808, www.aamft.org. The AAMFT is the professional association for the field of marriage and family therapy that provides resources, referrals, and a wide array of information.

American Psychological Association (APA), 750 First Street, NE, Washington,

DC 20002-4242, 800-374-2721, www.apa.org. This Web resource including search engines, professional associations, and testimonials on emotional problems.

BOOKS AND VIDEOS

ORGASM

Becoming Orgasmic: A Sexual and Personal Growth Program for Women by Julia Heiman and Joseph LoPiccolo. New York: Fireside Books, 1992.

Celebrating Orgasm (Video) by Betty Dodson, Ph.D. Pacific Media Entertainment, 2000.

ESO: How You and Your Lover Can Give Each Other Hours of Extended Sexual Orgasm by Alan P. Brauer and Donna J. Brauer. New York: Random House, 1983.

Expanded Orgasm: Soar to Ecstasy at Your Lover's Every Touch by Patricia Taylor. Naperville, IL: Sourcebooks Casablanca, 2002.

The Big O: Orgasms: How To Have Them, Give Them, and Keep Them Coming by Lou Paget. New York: Broadway Books, 2001.

Selfloving (Video) by Betty Dobson, Ph.D. Pacific Media Entertainment, 2000.

Sex for One: The Joys of Selfloving by Betty Dobson, Ph.D. New York: Crown Publishing Group, 1991.

Extended Massive Orgasm: How You Can Give and Receive Intense Sexual Pleasure by Steve Bodansky and Vera Bodansky. Alameda, CA: Hunter House, 2000.

The Illustrated Guide to Extended Massive Orgasm by Steve Bodansky and Vera Bodansky. Alameda, CA: Hunter House, 2002.

GENERAL FEMALE SEXUALITY

Clitoral Truth: The Secret World at Your Fingertips by Rebecca Chalker. New York: Seven Stories Press, 2000.

Femalia: Lovely Selections of Tasteful and Artistic Photographs of Women's Genitals edited by Joani Blank. San Francisco, CA: Down There Press, 1993.

For Women Only: A Revolutionary Guide to Overcoming Sexual Dysfunction and Reclaiming Your Sex Life by Jennifer Berman and Laura Berman. New York: Henry Holt and Company, 2001.

For Yourself: The Fulfillment of Female Sexuality, revised edition by Lonnie Barbach. New York: Signet, 2000.

Good Vibrations: The Complete Guide to Vibrators by Joani Blank. San Francisco, CA: Down There Press, 1989.

How to Give Her Absolute Pleasure: Totally Explicit Techniques Every Woman Wants Her Man to Know by Lou Paget. New York: Broadway Books, 2000.

Pucker Up: A Hands-on Guide to Ecstatic Sex by Tristan Taormino. New York: ReganBooks, 2000.

Guide to Getting It On!: The Universe's Coolest and Most Informative Book About Sex for Adults of All Ages by Paul Joannides. Chicago, IL: Goofy Foot Press, 2000.

The Multi-Orgasmic Couple: Sexual Secrets Every Couple Should Know by Mantak Chia, Maneewan Chia, Douglas Abrams, and Rachel Carlton Abrams, MD. New York: HarperSanFrancisco, 2002.

The New Good Vibrations Guide to Sex: Tips and Techniques from America's Favorite Sex Toy Store by Cathy Winks and Anne Semans. San Francisco, CA: Cleis Press, 1997.

The Ultimate Guide to Anal Sex for Women by Tristan Taormino. San Francisco, CA: Cleis Press, 1997.

Cunt: A Declaration of Independence by Inga Muscio and Betty Dodson. New York: Seal Press, 1998.

G-SPOT AND FEMALE EJACULATION

The G Spot: And Other Discoveries About Human Sexuality, 2nd edition, by Alice Kahn Ladas, Beverly Whipple, and John D. Perry. New York: Holt, Rinehart, and Winston, 2005.

Tao of Bliss: The Art of Female Ejaculation, part 1 (Video) by Saida Desilets, Tao of Tantra Productions 2004. (This can be purchased at www.taooftantra.com or ordered at 212-696-9479.)

How to Female Ejaculate: Find Your G-Spot (Video) by Fannie Fatale, 1992.

The Amazing G-Spot and Female Ejaculation: The G-Spot Revealed (Sex Education Video) Access Instructional Media, 2000.

SEXUALITY AFTER 40

The Time of Our Lives: Women Write on Sex After 40 edited by Dena Taylor and Amber Sumrall. Freedom, CA: Crossing Press, 1993.

Sex After 50: A Guide to Lifelong Sexual Pleasure (Video) narrated by Lonnie Barbach. Focus International, 1991.

Still Doing It: Women and Men Over Sixty Write About Their Sexuality edited by Joani Blank. San Francisco, CA: Down There Press, 2000.

The New Ourselves, Growing Older: A Book for Women Over Forty by Paula B. Doress-Worters and Diane Laskin Siegal. Revised and updated edition. New York: Simon & Schuster/Touchstone, 1994.

The Pause: Positive Approaches to Perimenopause and Menopause by Lonnie Barbach. New York: Penguin/Signet, 1994.

The Truth About Hormone Replacement Therapy: How to Break Free from the Medical Myths of Menopause by National Women's Health Network. Roseville, CA: Prima Publishing, 2002.

WOMEN'S HEALTH

The V Book: A Doctor's Guide to Complete Vulvovaginal Health by Elizabeth G. Stewart, MD, and Paula Spencer. New York: Bantam Press, 2002.

A New View of a Woman's Body by Federation of Feminist's Women's Health Centers. New York: Feminist Health Press, 1991.

Taking Charge of Your Fertility: The Definitive Guide to Natural Birth Control and Pregnancy Achievement by Toni Weschler. New York: HarperCollins, 1995.

The New Our Bodies, Ourselves by Boston Women's Health Book Collective Staff. New York: Simon and Schuster, 1998.

TANTRIC SEX/TAOIST SEX

Fire in the Valley: An Intimate Guide to Female Genital Massage (Video) directed by Joseph Kramer and Annie Sprinkle. EroSpirit Research Institute, 1999.

Fire on a Mountain: An Intimate Guide to Male Genital Massage (Video) directed by Joseph Kramer. EroSpirit Research Institute, 1993.

Tao of Amrita: A Woman's Guide to Deeper Intimacy and Passion (Sex Education Video) by Saida Desilets, 2004. (This can be purchased at www.jadegoddess.com or ordered at 212-696-9479.)

Tao of Bliss: The Art of Sensual Intimacy, part 2 (Video) by Saida Desilets, Tao of Tantra Productions 2005. (This can be purchased at www.jadegoddess.com or ordered at 212-696-9479.)

The Tao of Sexual Massage: A Step-by-Step Guide to Exciting, Enduring, Loving Pleasure by Stephen Russell. New York: Fireside Books, 1992.

Tantra: The Art of Conscious Loving by Charles Muir and Caroline Muir. San Francisco, CA: Mercury House, 1990.

The Art of Sexual Ecstasy: The Path of Sacred Sexuality for Western Lovers by Margo Anand. New York: Putnam, 1991.

The Art of Sexual Magic: Cultivating Sexual Energy to Transform Your Life by Margo Anand. New York: Putnam, 1995.

Exploring the Hidden Power of Female Sexuality: A Workbook for Women by Maitreyi Piontek. York Beach, Maine: Weiser Books, 2001.

EROTICA

The Best American Erotica edited by Susie Bright. New York: Touchstone Books, 2005.

Best Black Woman's Erotica edited by Blanche Richardson. San Francisco, CA: Cleis Press, 2001.

Best Lesbian Erotica 2005 edited by Tristan Taormino. San Francisco, CA: Cleis Press, 2005.

Best Women's Erotica edited by Marcy Sheiner. San Francisco, CA: Cleis Press, 1996.

Delta of Venus: Erotica by Anais Nin. New York: Harcourt, 1977.

Erotique Noire: Black Erotica edited by Miriam DeCosta Willis, Reginald Martin, and Rose Ann Bell. New York: Doubleday/Anchor, 1992.

Herotica 2: A Collection of Women's Erotic Fiction edited by Susie Bright and Joani Blank. New York: Plume Books, 1992.

Herotica 3: A Collection of Women's Erotic Fiction edited by Susie Bright. San Francisco, CA: Plume Books, 1994.

Herotica 4, 5, 6, and 7: A Collection of Women's Erotic' Fiction edited by Marcy Sheiner. San Francisco, CA: Plume Books, 1996/1998/1999/2001.

Herotica: A Collection of Women's Erotic Fiction edited by Susie Bright. San Francisco, CA: Down There Press, 1998.

Little Birds: Erotica by Anais Nin. New York: Simon & Schuster/Pocket Books, 1996.

On a Bed of Rice: An Asian American Erotic edited by Geraldine Kudaka. New York: Anchor, 1995.

Pleasures: Women Write Erotica edited by Lonnie Barbach. New York: Harper and Row, 1984.

The Erotic Edge: 22 Erotic Stories for Couples edited by Lonnie Garfield Barbach. New York: Plume, 1996.

Under the Pomegranate Tree: The Best New Latino Erotica edited by Ray Gonzalez. New York: Washington Square Press, 1996.

BODY IMAGE

Big, Big Love: A Sourcebook on Sex for People of Size and Those Who Love Them by Hanne Blank. Berkeley, CA: Greenery Press, 2000.

The Don't Diet, Live It! Workbook: Healing Food, Weight and Body Issues by Andrea Lobue and Marsea Marcus. Carlsbad, CA: Glirze Books, 1999.

Fat? So!: Because You Don't Have to Apologize for Your Size by Marilyn Wann. Berkeley, CA: Ten Speed Press, 1999.

Intuitive Eating: A Recovery Book for the Chronic Dieter; Rediscover the Pleasures of Eating and Rebuild Your Body Image by Evelyn Tribble and Elyse Resch. New York: St. Martin's Paperbacks, 1996.

LESBIAN

Best Lesbian Erotica 2005 edited by Tristan Taormino. San Francisco, CA: Cleis Press, 2005.

Susie Sexpert's Lesbian Sex World by Susie Bright. San Francisco, CA: Cleis Press, 1990.

The Lesbian Love Companion: How to Survive Everything From Heartthrob to Heartache by Marny Hall. San Francisco, CA: HarperSanFrancisco, 1998.

SEXUAL ABUSE AND VIOLENCE AGAINST WOMEN

Battered Wives: Inside the Heart of Marital Violence by Del Martin. New York: Simon & Schuster/Pocket Books, 1990.

Sexual Healing Journey: A Guide for Survivors of Sexual Abuse by Wendy Matlz. New York: HarperCollins, 1992.

Sexual Violence: Our War Against Rape by Linda Fairstein. New York: Berkley Publishing, 1995.

The Courage to Heal: A Guide for Women Survivors of Child Sexual Abuse by Ellen Bass and Laura Davis. New York: Harper/Perennial, 1994.

Trauma and Recovery: The Aftermath of Violence, From Domestic Abuse to Political Terror by Judith Herman, MD. New York: Basic Books, 1992.

Violence Against Women and the Ongoing Challenge to Racism by Angela Davis. New York: Kitchen Table Women of Color Press, 1997.

The Survivor's Guide to Sex: How to Have a Great Sex Life After Child Sexual Abuse by Staci Haines. San Francisco, CA: Cleis Press, 2000.

WOMAN-FRIENDLY STORES FOR SEXUAL PRODUCTS

A Woman's Touch, 600 Williamson Street, Madison, WI 53703, 608-250-1928, www.a-womans-touch.com. Woman-owned and -run retail store of quality sex toys, sensual playthings, woman-friendly adult videos and DVDs, safer sex supplies, and information about sexuality and sexual health. Offers irritant-free product ingredients.

Blowfish, PO Box 411290, San Francisco, CA, 94141, 415-252-4340, 800-325-2569, www.blowfish.com. Mail-order catalog of toys, books, and videos. Offers irritant-free product ingredients.

Come As You Are, 701 Queen Street West, Toronto, Ontario, Canada M6J 1E6, 877-858-3160, www.comeasyouare.com. Canada's premiere cooperatively-owned sex toy, book, and video store also offers classes, workshops, and irritant-free product ingredients.

Eve's Garden, 119 West 57th Street, Suite 1201, New York, NY 10019-2383, 800-848-3837, www.evesgarden.com. Established in 1974, this woman-owned and -run feminist store and catalog offers an array of toys, books, videos, and lingerie. Also offers irritant-free product ingredients

Good For Her, 175 Harbord Street, Toronto, Ontario, Canada M5S 1H3, 877-588-0900, www.goodforher.com. Toronto's cozy, comfortable place is where women and their admirers can find a variety of high-quality books, sex toys, videos, and sensual art. This woman-owned and -run retail store also offers classes and workshops, as well as irritant-free product ingredients.

Good Vibrations, 938 Howard Street, Suite 101, San Francisco, CA 94103, 800-289-8423, 415-974-8990, www.goodvibes.com. This worker- and women-owned cooperative retail store and mail-order catalog offers erotic and informative books, sex toys, and adult videos; also offers classes, workshops, and irritant-free product ingredients.

Grand Opening! Sexuality Boutique, 308A Harvard Street, Suite 32, Brookline, MA 02446, 617-731-2626 and also at 8442 Santa Monica Blvd., West Hollywood, CA 90069, 323-848-6970, www.grandopening.com. Woman-owned and -run retail store and mail-order catalog of books, sex toys, safer sex products, and videos; also offers human sexuality classes, workshops, and events.

Toys in Babeland, 707 E. Pike Street, Seattle, WA 98122, 206-328-2914 (store), 800-658-9119 (mail order) and also at 94 Rivington Street, New York, NY 10002, 212-375-1701, www.babeland.com. Woman-owned and -run retail store and mail-order catalog whose mission it is to promote and celebrate sexual vitality. Offers books, sex toys, and videos, as well as classes, workshops, and events.

Men and women have different sexual energies—and too often this leads to discontent in the bedroom, preventing us from fully exploring our sexual potential. *The Multi-Orgasmic Couple* shows you and your partner how to create sexual harmony, passion, and intimacy.

"This book does what *The Joy of Sex* did for millions of readers: it shines a clear light into foggy areas of sex that have been shrouded, overly mystified, or misunderstood."
—Rebecca Taylor, Amazon.com

"A life-changing book! If you only read one book on sexuality, this should be it. This book will allow you to deepen your relationship with your lover and give you both a new source of energy that can be channeled into all aspects of your life. Buy it!
—A reader from Champaign, Illinois

"An excellent, informative book! This book was a worthwhile purchase. It not only imparts important information, but does so in a way that is unassuming and even fun! I enjoyed the book, as did my husband, and we have explored new sexual horizons through its use."
—A reader from Norman, Oklahoma

The original book for men who want to be multi-orgasmic and their partners who want to help them. It also provides a chapter on common male sexual problems (like impotence and premature ejaculation) as well as a chapter for gay men. *The Multi-Orgasmic Man* offers men (and their partners) a healthier and more pleasurable experience of male sexuality.

"Our laboratory research found multiply orgasmic men were not only able to maintain an erection in intercourse longer but had more orgasms of greater intensity than singly orgasmic men. This book teaches you everything you need to know to become multiply orgasmic."
—William E. Hartman, Ph.D., and Marilyn A. Fithian, Ph.D., codirectors of the Center for Marital and Sexual Studies

"This book is the best available for teaching men to have multiple orgasms."
—Bernie Zilbergeld, Ph.D., *San Francisco Chronicle*

"No man should have sex until he reads this book!!! This book absolutely changed my life . . . surprisingly easy to learn and use. My only regret is that I wasn't exposed to this book a long time ago!"
—A reader from Rolla, Missouri

"You'll be begging for more. This book expands the realm of possibility. . . . Run, don't walk . . . buy this book for yourself, and then make your significant other read it as well."
—A reader from San Francisco, California

INDEX

Underscored page references indicate boxed text.
Boldface references indicate illustrations.

Plus:

Plus: Insights, Interviews, and More

An Interview with Rachel Carlton Abrams

1. Why do so many women complain that they can't have an orgasm? What is the biggest obstacle, in your opinion?

About 25 percent of women have never had an orgasm and fully two-thirds of women cannot orgasm when they want to, so this is really a majority of the population! There are two major obstacles to having an orgasm. The first is that many women do not have the detailed information they need about their pleasure anatomy in order to unlock their orgasmic potential. The second is that they are either inhibited about exploring their own bodies or are not able to fully trust and surrender to a partner in order to allow an orgasm to unfold.

2. Your book is very graphic and teaches women to know their bodies. Do you believe women are still shy about their bodies? What should women know about their bodies that would greatly improve their sex lives?

I think that women are still quite shy about the sexual aspect of their bodies, whether or not they are not shy about revealing their bodies to another person. Our culture still holds the mistaken belief that our sexual pleasure is the responsibility of another person—our sexual partner, boyfriend, husband—I even see this dynamic in lesbian couples. We are all responsible for our own orgasm, literally. We need to understand what we need for pleasure and be able to communicate that effectively to our partners in order for them to please us. Most partners really do want us to enjoy ourselves, but don't always know how to go about helping us. Exploring one's own pleasure zones and kindly communicating what you need to a partner can go a long way toward creating a mutually exciting and evolving sexual relationship. This does mean, of course, that you need to choose partners who want to please you sexually—why, really would you want to gift them with your body if they don't? In terms of specific anatomical advice about finding sexual pleasure, *The Multi-Orgasmic Woman* goes into great detail about the wonders of the female body and how you can happily own your own pleasure.

3. Some therapists say having an orgasm isn't so important if the woman is enjoying sex anyways. Do you agree?

I certainly agree that orgasm is not the point of sex—the point of sex is connection and pleasure. Some of the advice that I give to women who don't have orgasms, is to stop thinking about trying to have an orgasm and to follow their pleasure. Orgasm is really just an expanded form of pleasure and can take many forms—some of which don't seem like "an orgasm." Orgasm for women can be long and undulating or simply a prolonged plateau of pleasure. Many women who don't think they orgasm but really enjoy sex actually DO orgasm—they just don't realize that their experience is a form of orgasm, because it doesn't look like the typical male pattern of explosive, singular orgasm. When sex is happening in an organic and creative way, no one is thinking about orgasm!

4. What are some of the physical and psychological benefits of having orgasms frequently and having a healthy sex life?

According to medical research, people who are sexually active live longer, are sick less often, and are less depressed than similar people who are not sexually active. There are many reasons for this. We are communal beings and are made, physiologically, to benefit from physical touch. Levels of oxytocin, which helps with feelings of calm and contentment and decreases stress, go up when one is touched (or is touching) someone they love. With sex and orgasm, DHEA, estrogen, and testosterone peak. These hormones act as anti-depressants and help with clear thinking. Sex releases endorphins which reduce levels of pain. A vigorous bout of sex burns 200 calories—what a way to lose weight! Sex is one of the peak human experiences for which we are created and when it is in the context of caring and love, is extraordinarily healing for our minds and bodies.

5. Do women have a sexual peak? Can they maintain the same level of pleasure (or increase it) throughout their lives?

I have, literally, seen women reach their "peak" at 30, then again at 40 and even at 75! Sex, thank God, is a human expression that we get to grow with throughout our lives. Sex as we age may not look like the cartoon versions of "hot sex" that we see in the movies (which are VERY unlikely to be satisfying for the woman, as they are too quick!), but sexual life can unfold and transform into affection, warmth, pleasure, and spiritual connection that is just as exciting at 75 as it is at 35. It is very important not to hang on to rigid expectations of what sex has to look like to be "good."

6. You mention a few exercises that can help improve sex. Which ones are the best and which ones can be recommended for all women?

All women can benefit from learning about and exploring their pleasure anatomy. I also think that strengthening, relaxing, and even becoming aware of the PC (pubococcygeus) muscle is important to sexual pleasure as it makes orgasm and multiple orgasm much more likely.

About the Author

Rachel Carlton Abrams, MD, MHS is also the co-author of *The Multi-Orgasmic Couple* and teaches classes and workshops throughout the nation on holistic health and sexuality. She is the medical director of Santa Cruz Integrative Medicine & Chi Center, where she and her colleagues fuse the profound wisdom and ancient practices of the East with the cutting edge medical advances of the West to offer a dynamic and effective approach to healthcare. You can learn about upcoming workshops or contact Dr. Abrams at www.santacruzintegrativemedicine.net or www.multiorgasmicwoman.com.